Game
of
Spies

Game of Spies

PAMELA MINGLE

Entangled Publishing, LLC
2614 South Timberline Road
Suite 105, PMB 159
Fort Collins, CO 80525
rights@entangledpublishing.com

Amara is an imprint of Entangled Publishing, LLC.

Edited by Erin Molta
Cover design by Liz Pelletier
Cover photography by Period Images
FairytaleDesign/Deposit Photos

Manufactured in the United States of America

First Edition June 2019

In memory of my beloved friend
Caroline Stutson
I still miss her

Chapter One

October 1570

In the coolness of an autumn dusk, Gavin Cade picked his way along a street littered with garbage, trash, and broken bits of glass. He was in Berwick, an English garrison town so far north it might as well be in Scotland. Outside the ramparts, the town ran to squalor. Without the protection of the garrison, it had deteriorated until the only prosperous citizens left were criminals.

Gavin was heading toward one of the few reputable alehouses in the area. It was clean, and he'd be able to get a meat pie for his supper and a decent bed for the night. And sleep without a hand on his knife. The evening air smelled like rotting fish, with an overlay of human waste and boiled onion. The huge bastion, Meg's Mount, completely blocked the sun, and he was grateful for the comforting warmth of his plaid.

The Cade family supplied the garrison and had done so for years. Gavin and his crew had finished unloading too late to depart for home. He refused to risk making camp along the road at night. With so much unrest between the English and Scots, the chance of an attack was too great. He'd told his men to find lodging in town. They would leave at first light.

Entering the tavern, the Queen's Ramparts, Gavin glanced around for a table. Hungry men hoisted tankards and ate greedily, while others played cards or diced. Gavin was interested only in food and drink. It was noisy, but not raucous. Nell, the proprietress, didn't put up with drunken troublemakers. He stopped at the bar to greet her. "Nell, lass, 'tis good to see you again. Have ye a bed for me tonight?"

Nell's kindhearted face crinkled up into a smile, and her eyes danced with mischief. "Mayhap I do, if ye don't mind sleepin' with me, love."

"I wouldn't be getting much sleep then, would I? And I must be up at dawn." They stared at each other, until Nell could no longer hold in her laughter. She released it in loud bursts, and Gavin joined her. This was a familiar ritual for them. Their conversation went much the same way each time Gavin brought his custom to Nell.

"Always a room in my establishment for ye, Gavin. Ale and a pie, love?"

"Aye." He tipped his head toward the window. "I'll be over there."

A strange voice, behind and to Gavin's left, said, "Pray bring Master Cade's repast to my table, mistress. We have something to discuss."

Gavin jerked around for a quick look. "Who the bloody hell are ye?"

"Name is Nicholas Ryder. If you'll join me, I'll explain."

Gavin had never seen him before, of that he was certain. He didn't care for strangers who sneaked up on him wanting to "talk." Especially English strangers. In truth, they usually wanted something more tangible—money, a job, a favor. He wasn't interested.

"I prefer to eat alone, and I've nothing to discuss with ye." He made to push past the man, but Ryder, nearly as tall as Gavin, held up a staying hand. He did not touch Gavin, which was a good thing.

"Just hear me out. That's all I ask."

Gavin studied the man. He was clean and well dressed, with a neatly trimmed beard. There was nothing menacing about him. With a sigh, he nodded to Nell and followed Ryder to his table, back in the far corner. "What is it then?"

"I'm on the queen's business. We have need of a man who can be both Scots and English. A man who can use his brain, but one who is also strong enough to hold his own in a fight."

"And what makes you believe I am that man? You do not know me, sir." A tavern wench plunked tankards of ale down on the scratched oak table, and Gavin took a long pull on his.

"I know enough. My father has had men watching you."

At that Gavin got to his feet and thrust back the bench he'd been sitting on. "You've no right to spy on me. You can take your business and stuff it up your arse. Get out of here and let me eat in peace."

"Pray be seated, Master Cade. I am not here to force you into this."

After a moment, Gavin grudgingly resumed his seat, and Nell soon appeared with their meat pies. Sensing the tension between them, she said, "Everything all right here, gentlemen?"

Gavin nodded. "Thank ye, Nell. All is well." After she left them, Gavin asked, "Why would I be interested in working for you…for the queen?"

Ryder leaned closer. "You appear ready for a new challenge."

Gavin cut into the steaming pie with his knife and scooped out a hunk of meat. Ah. Beef tonight rather than the mutton he hated. He'd have to give Nell a little extra for that. The truth was, Ryder had the right of it. He *was* bored, and restless, too. Since his wife Anna's death, and his subsequent discovery of her betrayal, he'd simply been going through the motions. Attending to his work in a trancelike state. Taking no pleasure from anything.

Ryder did not speak again, but began eating. He was a patient man.

Gavin was torn. But he couldn't decide without knowing more. "Tell me what you have in mind."

Ryder quaffed his ale, looking at Gavin over the rim of his tankard. If he felt victorious, he hid it well. "Until you make a commitment, I cannot reveal much. Should you agree, you would travel to the middle of England, to…a location where a person of interest to the queen is currently residing. Your mission would be to ferret out information and report to me. Of necessity, you'd need to make yourself popular with a certain group of women."

Gavin raised a brow. "I'm not known for whoring."

"I am glad of that. It would interfere with your mission. But you may find that the women involved will want you to bed them. Your job will be to let them think you might, while your true mission will be to uncover the information we seek."

"Why me? For all you know, I'm a loyal Scot and hate the English. I am wearing a plaid, in case that escaped your notice."

Ryder set down his tankard. "What I notice is that you talk like a Scot around the people from hereabout, but in speaking with me, you sound like a well-educated Englishman. Your mother is Scottish, and you wear her clan's tartan. But your father is English. He saw to your education—tutors for all his children, including the females. You keep the books for your family's business. French comes naturally to you, among other languages. You are Presbyterian—but you have not attended services since the death of your wife."

Merciful God, the man knows about everything. Even

Anna. Exactly how long had they been watching him?

Gavin lifted his hands. "Enough. There are many other men who possess these same qualities."

"None who fit so well as you into both worlds. Your knowledge, your talents—they're wasted in the work you are doing."

Gavin rubbed the back of his neck and tried to sort through his warring thoughts. On the one hand, this could be good for him. A challenge, a way to get his mind off Anna and the newborn son who had died with her. On the other hand, the location was some distance away, and Gavin had a very affectionate family. He'd not have survived these last months without their love and the endless small kindnesses they'd shown him while he'd grieved. His mother would miss him fiercely.

"Think on it tonight. You can give me your decision in the morning."

Gavin nodded. "I'll meet you outside the garrison at daybreak. My men expect to be leaving then."

"And I must return home as well. I live near Carlisle. It is a long journey for me."

They said their farewells and Gavin signaled Nell for another ale. He swallowed long drafts while he mulled over Ryder's offer. He had no doubt that this affair concerned Mary Stewart, the Scots queen. It was common knowledge that she was in England as the queen's guest. Or prisoner—nobody knew for sure. God's nails, he never thought he'd be in this position. He hated deceit and trickery. But he also had an ingrained distrust of Mary Stewart. She was more French than Scot, having been raised there. In her young life, she'd had three husbands, and rumor was that she and the third one, the Earl of Bothwell, had conspired to murder the second, Lord Darnley. The father of the infant king, James VI.

No, he did not trust her at all. When he finally made his way upstairs, he knew what answer he would give.

. . .

Isabel Tait's stepfather breathed his last at ten o'clock on a cold autumn night, and she was glad of it. For the past few months, she had devoted both her morning and evening prayers to beseech the Almighty for that very outcome, and now it appeared her fervent pleas had been answered. Possibly, Isabel should fear eternal damnation, but that could not be worse than what she'd endured at the hands of Nathaniel Hammond.

Her mother, composed and serene as always, said, "I shall send word to your brothers in the morning. Pray, summon the midwife to prepare the body."

Gladly.

The following week passed in a flurry of activity and preparation. Isabel's half brothers, Thomas and Andrew, arrived home from university for the funeral. Afterward, they summoned her to the study. "You must marry, Isabel," Thomas, the older of the brothers, said. "The sooner, the better. You're approaching the age of spinsterhood."

Isabel was twenty-five. Being a spinster did not seem such a dreadful state to her, but others saw it differently—the worst fate to befall a woman. She'd known this would come up, but hadn't anticipated it so hastily. "Why the rush? I had planned to remain here with Mother. She is alone now, after all."

"She has plans to remarry and does not want to see you hurt once again. Mother believes it would be better for everybody if you were no longer a part of the household. It was difficult for you when she married Father."

"She already has someone in mind? But how could that be? And who is he?"

"Peter Fleming, Father's solicitor. They were thrown together a good deal during the years of Father's illness and became close. They now wish to marry."

Isabel was too dumbfounded to speak. Thomas was reviewing candidates for her hand, but she was still reeling from the news about her mother. She gave her head a shake and said, "May I not choose my own husband? I can draw up a list of prospects, and you or Andrew could arrange introductions. We could jointly weigh their suitability."

"'Tis reasonable, brother," Andrew said. "I will not force Isabel to marry where she does not have an interest." Tears blurred her vision. Andrew, her favorite brother, had always stood up for her.

"I wonder why Mother has mentioned nothing of this to me," Isabel said.

Her brothers looked uncomfortable. "She didn't wish to worry you," Andrew said.

Isabel nodded, but a weight pressed on her heart. It was as she'd always suspected. Her mother cared nothing for her, and now couldn't wait to see her gone. It was hard to bear, but she'd withstood worse. "Thank you for informing me. I'll get started on preparing my catalog of potential husbands." She winked at Andrew as she left the room, and he ducked his head to hide a smile.

During the sennight following the funeral, Isabel had ample time to think matters over. She had no intention of making a list of prospective husbands, since marriage was the furthest thing from her mind. Although Isabel had no doubt her mother could make life unpleasant for her, she could not have her forcibly removed from her home. Could she?

Biding her time, Isabel kept to her chamber, pretending

to work on the list of likely bridegrooms. Instead, she was reading a new edition of Montaigne's *Essays* Andrew had brought her. And rereading Homer and the Greek plays she loved. All the while, she was hoping Thomas would not ask to see her list. When a knock sounded at her door one afternoon, she guiltily shoved her books under her pillow.

It was one of the servants, Sarah. "Mistress Hammond asks for you."

Her mother had kept to her chamber since the funeral, emerging only for meals, which had been quiet, depressing affairs. No doubt Thomas had informed her of the delay in obtaining a husband for Isabel. She was certain to be displeased and would perhaps issue an ultimatum.

As Isabel approached the withdrawing room, she heard voices, both female. A caller. That was unexpected, especially one who required Isabel's presence. She lingered in the doorway, waiting for her mother to notice her.

"Isabel, come. We have a guest who wishes to meet you."

Considering the visitor, Isabel ventured forward. In her youth, the lady would have had an arresting face. Her long nose pointed toward her upper lip, which was narrow and bowed. Dark red hair, streaked with gray, framed a narrow face, one Isabel did not recognize. She judged the woman to be in her forties. By her dress, she would be of the upper classes, possibly nobility.

Before Elizabeth Hammond could make the introductions, the woman said, "I am Lady Shrewsbury. I need a moment of your time, mistress."

Isabel curtsied. Her mother appeared flustered, glancing from her ladyship and back to Isabel. Lady Shrewsbury then said, "In private," and looked pointedly at Isabel's parent.

"Of course." Thus was Isabel left alone with this pompous stranger.

"Be seated," she said. Isabel obeyed.

"I shall get to the point, so as not to waste my time or yours. I need a young lady with impeccable credentials to become one of Mary Stewart's ladies-in-waiting. I have good reports of you. My sons are acquainted with your brothers, who say you are highly intelligent, speak French, and love reading. What have you to say?" She looked down her long nose at Isabel, who was reminded of an anteater. She'd once seen that creature pictured in a book.

Isabel found herself fumbling for a response. "I-I—Mary Stewart? Do you refer to the Scots queen?"

Lady Shrewsbury clucked her tongue. "Aye, of course. Who else? One of her oldest friends, who has been with her since childhood, has had to leave. Temporarily. We need a young lady to take her place."

Isabel knew only that Mary was currently in England and had resided at Carlisle Castle for a time. "Where is she at present?"

"Tutbury Castle, in Staffordshire, not far from us here in Derbyshire."

"What would be my duties as Queen Mary's lady-in-waiting?"

Lady Shrewsbury sighed, indicating she'd hoped to get this interview over with more quickly. "Converse with her. Eat with her. Entertain her. She is very sociable and enjoys dances, cards, games, needlework, playing with her dogs. She likes having someone about who will read to her."

"I see." Isabel began to appreciate the appeal of this offer. Was this her chance to escape a marriage she did not want? Or life with her mother and new stepfather, who did not want her? Before assenting, she thought it fair that Lady Shrewsbury know the truth about her. "Did my mother inform you of the sheltered life I have led? I've been nowhere outside of this part of England. I've never been permitted to go out in Society, so I've no experience with dancing or games. I possess the scholarly assets you speak of, but lack the social graces one acquires through experience."

"You speak your mind and are truthful. In my view, that will suffice. The 'social graces,' as you call them, will come with practice. Now, what say you?"

"I would be honored," Isabel said. She hoped that was an appropriate response. Excitement was swelling in her bosom, because this rare piece of luck, which seemed to have dropped from the heavens, provided the opportunity she longed for to leave home on her own terms. *My mother will be pleased.*

Lady Shrewsbury smiled for the first time. "Excellent. Summon your lady mother, and we shall work out what needs to be done to prepare you. I wish to leave early next week."

Isabel opened the door and found her mother loitering just outside. For the next hour, the two older women discussed Isabel's wardrobe, shoes, jewelry, and other accoutrements. Did she have a lady's maid she wished to bring? She could not wear mourning; that would not do for one of Mary's companions. That was fine with Isabel, since she was in no way mourning the loss of a loved one.

Lady Shrewsbury circled around Isabel, eyeing her from stem to stern. "You will need to have your hair cut and arranged differently. I've never seen such dark hair—it's nearly black. But those unruly curls need taming." Isabel's cheeks flamed, but she merely nodded.

At last, the interview was over. Lady Shrewsbury would arrive in her coach on Monday next, promptly at nine of the clock, and she and Isabel would travel to Tutbury together.

Isabel did not know whether to laugh or cry.

Chapter Two

True to her word, Lady Shrewsbury arrived on schedule. Isabel's trunk, containing her meager stock of personal belongings, was loaded, and, after an indifferent parting from her mother, Isabel set off for Tutbury Castle. The day was gray, with a lowering sky, and she hoped the rain would hold off until they reached their destination. A vision of the coach mired in a quagmire was all too vivid in her mind.

The vehicle was comfortable. Luxurious, even. The earl's coat of arms was painted on the side, and it was decorated with crimson silk hangings and boasted padded seats. Never having traveled in a coach, Isabel wondered if all of them were so well appointed. Should she speak to Lady Shrewsbury, who was bent over a piece of needlework? Isabel determined to wait and see if the lady spoke to her. She should have brought a book to read. Instead, she watched the landscape pass by and tried to imagine what her new life would be like.

Finally, Lady Shrewsbury broke the silence. "Did you bring your work, mistress? Mary is quite fond of her embroidery."

Isabel gulped. She had never learned to embroider because all her time had been spent with her studies. "No. I never acquired the skill, madam."

Lady Shrewsbury's eyebrows shot up. "Your mother never taught you to sew? But that is shocking! We must remedy that posthaste. Mary and I spend hours every day sewing—it is her chief pleasure."

Isabel's heart sank. What could be more tedious? "My stepfather thought my education should take precedence over everything else," she said by way of explanation.

"*Hmph*. That man had some strange notions, if you ask me. All of Mary's ladies sew, and you will simply have to learn. There are ample supplies you may avail yourself of."

"Yes, madam."

Lady Shrewsbury returned to her work, and Isabel resumed gazing out the window. After a time, the motion made her stomach roil. Perhaps watching the landscape speed by was not wise. She stared down at her hands, because the only other choice was to look directly at her companion, and that would not do. When the coach slowed and the coachman's voice boomed out a command to the horses, Isabel clenched her jaw and held her breath.

"We're crossing a stream, Isabel. No need to worry," Lady Shrewsbury said, not unkindly. "You have never traveled in a conveyance of this sort?"

"No, ma'am."

I've never traveled in a conveyance of any sort.

"Do you ride?"

Isabel shook her head, prompting a long sigh from her companion. "You have much to learn."

"Aye."

"I wish to caution you on one matter, Isabel. If you should overhear, or unwittingly become a party to, any conversations or acts that seem…questionable…you must inform me or the earl immediately."

"I am not sure of your meaning, madam."

"I mean improper. Odd. Suspicious." She was eyeing Isabel down her long nose. "After you've been in residence for a time, you will understand."

"Very well, my lady. I shall do my best." Isabel doubted she could make such judgments, but she held her tongue. Was she not simply a companion to Mary, as she'd been told? This sounded very much like spying. And did the lady refer only to the queen, or to all the members of her circle?

After a time, it began to rain. Lady Shrewsbury looked up and said, "It won't be long now. I am glad the rain held off until the end. Here is the River Dove."

By now the rain was pounding down, creating a cacophony inside the coach. As they rattled their way over the bridge, Isabel could feel her gorge rising and hoped she would not vomit inside the coach. The contents of her stomach pushed up higher and higher with every jolt, every bump. Folding her arms, she held them tightly against her middle and tried to think of something else. But everything she thought of made her stomach even queasier. Meeting a queen. Dancing. Socializing. Embroidering. These activities were customary for most young ladies, but not for her. She closed her eyes tightly and prayed for strength.

The coach turned and she dared to glance out the window, glimpsing nothing but mist, fog, and more rain. Finally, the vehicle jolted to a stop, and Lady Shrewsbury said tersely, "Follow me." At some point, the woman had laced pattens onto her shoes, and she popped out of the carriage and walked briskly to... Isabel did not know where. Fresh air blew in, and she drew in long breaths. Grasping the sides of the door, she pulled herself up. She looked down into a sea of mud, dung, and very wet dogs.

She couldn't hold it any longer. Feeling as though she were disgorging her entire stomach along with its contents, she retched in hard, wrenching gasps, until there was nothing left inside her.

And then she looked up into the face of the most beautiful man she'd ever seen.

. . .

God's wounds. Who was this woman who'd just puked all over Gavin's boots? Not that it made any difference, since they were already covered in mud. Whoever she was, she needed his help. She swayed, and he reached out a hand to steady her.

"I am Gavin Cade. Allow me to assist you, mistress." Her face was as pale as alabaster, and he feared she might collapse. Gavin had thought to lift her down and set her on the ground, but she wore no pattens. Her flimsy slippers would fill up with water and mud in no time, ruining both shoes and stockings. It would not do. He lifted her into his arms and followed Lady Shrewsbury toward the building that housed Mary Stewart and her ladies. So slight was the young lady, it was like carrying one of Mary's tiny, yipping dogs. She burrowed into his shoulder, and for a moment, he wanted to rest his cheek against that small head. It felt comforting to hold a woman, one making no demands, against him.

They entered the queen's lodging. Before setting her down, Gavin asked, "Do you think you can stand up?"

"Of course I can stand. I'm not a weakling."

Gavin chuckled. Feisty, she was. "I thought since you had just puked your guts up, you might be feeling a bit faint." Gently, he set her onto the flagged floor.

"Where is Lady Shrewsbury?" she asked, now sounding timid.

"She's probably gone up to Queen Mary's rooms." He extracted a handkerchief from his pocket and handed it to her. "Wipe your face. And there, on your bodice, there is some—"

A rosiness suffused her cheeks. "Aye. Thank you." She brushed at the evidence of her illness. "Is there any water about?"

"There is." He stepped to one side where a ewer and cup rested on a table and poured her a small measure. After she drank, he said, "Come, I'll show you the way. It's up these stairs." He motioned for her to go ahead of him. He wanted to make sure he could catch her if she fell. On the way up, he enjoyed the drape of her petticoats over swaying hips.

At the top, Gavin heard an undercurrent of chatter from Mary's ladies. But Lady Shrewsbury held sway. From the tone of her voice, he could tell that she was lecturing them about making the new addition feel welcome. They would pay it no mind, because most of them were pampered, selfish creatures who cared for nobody save themselves. Instinctively, Gavin grasped the young lady's elbow as they entered the presence chamber.

"There you are," Lady Shrewsbury said. "Ladies, may I introduce you to Isabel Tait? She is to take the place of Mary Fleming. She will need your help in learning how things are done here."

Dead silence prevailed. Isabel Tait bobbed a hesitant curtsy, and Lady Shrewsbury immediately corrected her while the ladies snickered behind their hands. "No need to curtsy, except to Queen Mary. She is currently abed with a stomach ailment, but you will meet her later."

"Yes, madam."

"Frances, will you show Isabel to her chamber?"

"Of course. Come, Isabel. You are to share with me."

Before she left the room, Isabel glanced quickly in Gavin's direction. She looked lost. Lost and frightened. He touched her shoulder and said, "You'll be fine." And then she was gone, following Frances Barber. As the kindest of Mary's circle, she was a good choice to bunk with Isabel. Lady

Shrewsbury disappeared into the queen's privy chamber.

The remaining ladies surrounded Gavin, greeting him effusively with seductive words. It had been thus since he'd accepted Nicholas Ryder's commission. Ryder had been correct—most of them were interested in bed sport with him, and they were not shy in letting him know. In the month he'd been here, he had not succumbed, although he flirted like a man for whom pleasures of the flesh were paramount.

"You were carrying her," Dorothy Vere said. "You've never held one of us in your arms."

Oh, hell, they must have been watching out the windows. "Mistress Tait was"—he almost said ill, but thought better of it—"not wearing pattens. Her feet would have gotten wet and her shoes ruined."

"How very chivalric of you," Alice Alymer said. "She's an odd-looking creature, is she not?" The others laughed.

"How so?" Gavin asked.

Cecily Blake joined the chat. "Her clothing—not in the first stare of fashion, is it? And her hair is...unfortunate. Perhaps Frances can help her with it."

"Her manner," Dorothy said, "was so timid. Like a little mouse. I'm shocked that Bess chose her, given her many flaws."

They were sharpening their claws, and Gavin feared Isabel would be no match for them. He thought it prudent to make no response to their snide comments, even though his instinct was to defend her. "I must return to my duties, ladies. Farewell for now."

Gavin's official title was Equerry to the Earl of Shrewsbury. He liked the work and spent part of each day performing his duties. In addition to him, the earl employed an experienced Master of the Horse. When Gavin had arrived and first met with Shrewsbury, he had suggested, given his background, that he act as a quartermaster. The man in charge of supplies—principally food and wine, but including candles, tools, wood, coal, and the like. However, his chief purpose was something else again.

Gavin had a suite in the South Tower, which suited him. His office was adjacent to his personal chamber and was a suitable distance from the private suite belonging to the earl and his wife. Holding his woolen cloak closed, he made his way to his office, walking as swiftly as possible through the rain, dodging puddles and the worst of the mud. Since the castle sat on a promontory, the water would drain quickly, provided it ever stopped raining. He sat down at the table that served as his desk and glanced at the correspondence of Queen Mary he'd been studying for the past week.

Lately, she had been writing to Thomas Howard, the Duke of Norfolk, who had been released from the Tower in August of this year. The missives had been decoded—almost too easily, in Gavin's opinion—and seemed innocuous, but Gavin suspected there was more to them than met the eye. Mary expressed her continuing devotion and affection for the man. She seemed resigned to the fact that her French and Spanish allies had little interest in her, and stated that she still wished for a match with Norfolk. The duke had never replied, unless a missive had been smuggled in to Mary unbeknownst to himself and Shrewsbury. She made no mention of any grand scheme to usurp the English throne and restore Catholicism. Her main concern seemed to be her freedom.

Was there some hidden meaning they were missing? A union with Norfolk could be a real danger to Elizabeth. The only duke in all of England matched with the Scots queen, who had a legitimate claim to the throne. Elizabeth would never permit it. A secret plan between Mary and Norfolk to wed was what had landed him in the Tower to begin with. From the little they'd gotten from the current letters, and the lack of response from Norfolk, there was nothing to worry about at present. Expressing a desire for something was a far cry from taking steps to make it happen.

Ryder had asked Gavin to find out whatever he could about an Italian banker named Roberto Ridolfi. William Cecil, Queen Elizabeth's chief councilor, suspected him of masterminding an elaborate plot to overthrow Elizabeth, with Mary at its heart.

But thus far, he'd found nothing to support that.

• • •

Lady Shrewsbury had ordered a bath for Isabel. When she and Frances entered the chamber, it was in the wake of servants carrying in hot water. A lady's maid, who Frances introduced as Ann, began helping her disrobe. "I'll leave you to your bath, Isabel. May I call you that?" Frances asked.

Isabel, who wanted only to be left alone, nodded.

"Come back to the presence chamber when you're ready. Do you mind if I look at your apparel?" She didn't wait for an answer, but began sorting through Isabel's clothes. "*Hmm.* Wear the gown tonight. There's to be dancing after our meal."

"Very well."

At the door, Frances paused and turned her head. "And Isabel, do not let the others frighten you. They will test you, and may seem cruel. 'Tis best to laugh along with them or ignore them." Then, without another word, she left.

The maid departed as well. Isabel removed her smock and lowered herself into the tub. The hot water enveloped her body like a warm coverlet. If only she did not have to spend her evening in the company of the ladies she had just met, she would feel relaxed and happy. They had eyed her from head to toe, assessing her travel costume, no doubt noticing the stains left by her illness. Her hair had been askew, her face ashen. Not a good first impression.

Unbidden, Gavin Cade's fine-looking countenance floated into her mind. A chestnut-haired man who possessed the beauty and strength of Achilles, he hadn't seemed disturbed by her looks or behavior. Even though she'd cast up her morning meal all over his boots. He had carried her across the bailey to Mary's lodgings without even breathing hard, and she had felt warm and safe in his arms. And something beyond that. A sensual awareness of her body where it bumped against his. After he'd set her down, he'd kept a firm grip on her elbow, steadying her and sending her a silent expression of support. Isabel had appreciated that.

As she and Frances had walked down the passage, Isabel had heard the others cooing and purring Gavin's name, and then quizzing him about her, sounding jealous. Well, they had nothing to worry about. Someone like Gavin Cade would want nothing to do with the likes of Isabel. Compared to the other women, she was too dowdy, too shy, too…everything. And nothing. He was a gentleman, and that explained his kindness to her, even though she'd soiled his boots.

Isabel splashed water on her face, then washed with the linen cloth she'd been given. She tried not to dwell on her fears, her isolation, her inferiority. Mary's ladies had all been wearing gowns or petticoats slashed in the front to reveal their kirtles. Tightly corseted bodices had displayed their breasts to great effect, and French hoods had adorned their heads. It looked to Isabel like court dress, or what she imagined court dress would be like. Perhaps Queen Mary insisted on it.

Frances had been friendly, and Isabel appreciated her advice. Although she was not at all sure she could behave as suggested. To a person, Mary's ladies were all quite lovely. Alice's flaxen hair, Frances's fine complexion, Dorothy's richly colored ruby petticoats. Lady Shrewsbury had approved Isabel's wardrobe, but Isabel could not compete with their clothing, looks, or decorum. She would have to do the best she could. If Lady Shrewsbury decided to send her home, perhaps she would be compiling that list of eligible men after all.

Ann entered the chamber and, after helping her out of the copper tub, handed her a drying cloth. When Isabel dressed, with the maid's assistance, the young girl said, "Would you like me to arrange your hair, mistress?"

"Oh, aye. After the journey and the rain, it looks like a raven's nest."

Ann giggled and brushed Isabel's hair until it crackled. Then she braided thick strands on each side of Isabel's head, pinning them at the back, and letting the remainder of the hair flow down her back. "That looks very pretty, if I say so myself," Ann said.

Isabel studied herself in the glass. "Thank you, Ann. It's lovely." She thought of the elaborate dress and hair arrangements of Mary and her ladies. "Do you wait upon all the women, Ann?" Surely not.

"Nay. There is also Aimee. She is the queen's maid, but sometimes helps the others." One final stroke of the brush and smoothing of Isabel's hair. "You have beautiful locks, mistress. Thick and wavy. Easy to work with."

Isabel nodded, pleased at the compliment. Maybe Ann would be someone on whom she could rely. "Where is everybody?"

"In the presence chamber, mistress. They'll be there until the evening meal."

"Thank you." Isabel inhaled a deep breath and uttered a quick prayer. Then she bobbed her head, once. She was ready to face whatever would come.

They're only a bunch of spiteful women. I've borne a good deal worse.

And then she walked down the hall to see what awaited her.

Chapter Three

Gavin lounged against the wall in Mary Stewart's presence chamber. He thought it one of her stranger quirks that she insisted on the terms "privy chamber" and "presence chamber." But the woman had little to brighten her life, so he could tolerate it. Besides himself, two other men were present. That toad, John Lesley, Mary's envoy to Elizabeth, was there. So was Philip Blake, the brother of Cecily, one of Mary's ladies. While he'd become a friend to Blake, he thought Cecily the haughtiest of women.

Alice Alymer approached him—sidled up to him—and said, "You're looking devilishly handsome tonight, Gavin Cade." Could she be any less subtle? He'd changed from his plaid to a fine lawn shirt, slashed doublet, trunk hose, and canions. Apparently, Lady Alice approved. He nodded, not trusting himself to remain polite. "Oh, do look," she said. "Here is our little mouse!"

Isabel Tait stepped into the room, not looking the least bit mouse-like. Her gown, a deep aubergine, paired well with her glossy, near-black hair. She did not bedeck herself with anything like farthingales, stomachers, or ruffs, all of which he despised. They hid a woman's natural beauty. She was the unlikeliest of ladies for Mary's entourage, and yet she possessed a quiet dignity, clear to him, even if others could not see it. Nobody greeted Mistress Tait.

Suddenly, Mary herself took notice. Carrying her spaniel, she rose from her cushioned settee and approached Isabel. "*Bonsoir*, mistress. *Tu es* Isabel, *n'est-ce pas*?"

"*Oui, madame*." She curtsied deeply, wobbling a bit. But at least she realized this was the queen. Gavin chuckled to himself. This one would be entertaining, if she could survive the cats.

"*Alors*!" Mary said, "pray sit beside me, Isabel. *Isa-belle*. You are a beauty. I believe, friends, we must shorten her name to 'Bel'." The other ladies looked unenthused.

Alice quickly lost interest and droned on in a low voice. A mumbled "eh" or "aye" every so often was all the encouragement she needed from Gavin. In truth, he was straining to hear Mary and Isabel's conversation. Evidently, Isabel loved dogs. Mary thrust the little spaniel into her arms, and judging by the way she caressed the pup and kissed its nose, she was delighted. They spoke English, and Gavin suspected Isabel knew only a few phrases in French. Their conversation was of mundane matters, until Mary started in on her favorite subject: her unjust detention by Queen Elizabeth.

"*Mon dieu*, I do not comprehend why my cousin forces me to stay here at Tutbury. It is a cold, damp residence, not fit for a queen. My health suffers. You will see. But I believe in her heart, Elizabeth loves me. She writes to me kind letters asking about my well-being." Isabel made polite responses.

"I have not been permitted to see my son," Mary continued. "It is a great sadness to me. Last spring it was arranged but did not happen. Some men made an impetuous plan to rescue me, and when the plot was discovered, James's protectors took him back to Scotland." Mary cast her eyes down.

"How sad for you, madam. You must miss your son terribly."

"I bear it the best I can." A servant appeared at the door and Mary said, "It is time for dinner, *mes amis*. Let us proceed to the dining chamber." She reclaimed her pup from Isabel and put him on the settee.

John Lesley offered his arm to Mary, and they led the way. Alice clung to one of Gavin's arms, Dorothy Vere grasped the other. Blake's sister, Cecily, latched on to his arm and urged him forward before he might offer his other to Isabel. This would not do. "Alice, join Blake and Cecily, pray. We must not leave Isabel without an escort to supper." She looked unhappy, but did as he requested.

"Mistress Isabel?" Gavin crooked his elbow at her, and she curled her fingers around his arm. She had turned quite pale, and her eyes were suspiciously bright. Mary insisted Isabel sit beside her at the dining table, and Gavin made sure to sit on her other side.

. . .

Isabel, mortified, laid her toothpick case on the table. If it hadn't been for Gavin Cade, she would have been forced to walk alone to the dining chamber. Cecily Blake, to whom she'd not yet been introduced, had deliberately tried to humiliate her. Why? Mary, with her lovely auburn hair and doe eyes, had welcomed Isabel with warmth and kindness. Why wouldn't her ladies have followed her example?

Isabel had to get through this dinner somehow, and the dancing afterward. If Lady Shrewsbury had been present, Isabel would have felt more at ease, but neither she nor her husband, the earl, were there. The older gentleman who had escorted Mary to supper prayed before the meal, and afterward general conversation broke out.

Mary was chatting to the man on her right. Isabel turned to Gavin and said, "Pardon me, sir, but where are the earl and his wife?"

"I believe they have retired to their castle at Sheffield for a few days' respite."

"I see." She did not see. Lady Shrewsbury had dropped her into this situation and left her there without even a by-your-leave? Isabel had depended on having her guidance for the first several days. She sighed, ducking her head.

She felt a reassuring, masculine hand grasp her arm. "Mistress, do not distress yourself. It is obvious Mary was quite taken with you. Her ladies will be forced to accept you, and you may count on me for help."

Isabel had barely uttered a thank-you before the lady on Gavin's other side demanded his attention. In the meantime, the first course was served, a beef broth, and Isabel waited until Mary had begun supping before she drank hers. A small loaf of manchet sat between her and Gavin. When he'd finished his soup, he broke off a piece and offered it to her.

"Thank you," Isabel said, smiling. "It was not our custom at home to eat such fine bread as this."

"Oh, there is nothing but the finest for Queen Mary," he said, eyes alight with amusement. His eyes were an icy blue color, an interesting contrast to his chestnut hair, and rather mesmerizing.

"Where is your home, mistress?"

"Near Derby."

"And you live there with your parents? Husband and children?"

That drew a laugh from her, and she quickly covered her mouth. "My mother and half brothers. My stepfather recently died."

"You have my sympathy."

"That is kind of you, but not necessary. I hated him." Isabel felt her cheeks flush. What possessed her to reveal something so personal? Something that made her sound crass.

His brows drew together. "There is a story there, I'd wager. Perhaps you will share it with me one day."

Her cheeks warmed. "'Tis not a very agreeable one, I fear."

"Nevertheless, if you ever wish to unburden yourself...I am a good listener."

She nodded her thanks, but she could never tell Gavin about the abuse she'd suffered at the hands of her stepfather. It would be humiliating.

Isabel turned her attention back to the meal. Fish was served next, pike, with buttered peas and salads. The plate was silver. No expense was spared for this queen, it seemed. The room was hung with tapestries, and a chandelier with at least one hundred candles illuminated not only the table, but all those seated around it.

"What news to share, Bishop?" Queen Mary asked her dinner companion. Her voice was of sufficient volume that Isabel assumed this discussion was meant for the table.

"Elizabeth, with her ceaseless raids, continues to punish the Scots who sheltered the rebels. I can't think anyone yet remains who hasn't felt the sting of her wrath over the rebellion. At this point, innocent citizens are paying the price."

"They should never have attempted such a foolhardy mission," Mary said.

Gavin snorted, hiding it with a cough.

Isabel knew about the rising. A few of the northern earls, Northumberland and Westmoreland, had attempted to overthrow the queen and restore Catholicism to the realm. It had been a haphazard effort, at best. From what Isabel had heard of it, the rebels themselves had not even been sure of their objectives. Freedom for Mary may or may not have been on the table. Some extremists may have wished to put her on the English throne. The earls and many of their cohorts had escaped over the border, although it was said Northumberland would be sold back to the English.

"On another matter, I understand that Cecil and Walsingham are negotiating with the French for a marriage between Elizabeth and the Duke of Anjou."

All conversation ceased, and Isabel noticed the other women staring at Mary. She neither looked up nor commented, but she'd gone exceedingly pale. Isabel didn't understand what was occurring; perhaps Gavin would explain it to her later.

"We are to have dancing tonight, *oui*?" Mary asked, and the awkward moment passed. A third course was served of roasted venison, duck, and lamb, and, last, marchpane and other sweets.

"Do you dance, Mistress Isabel?" Alice asked.

Isabel's stomach muscles tightened, but she smiled. "I do not."

Alice laughed, a high, tinkling sound. "Pray, why not?"

"I never had the opportunity to learn. I did not go into Society, so I suppose my mother felt it was not necessary to teach me."

Tittering ensued, with no attempt to hide it. One of the women said, in French, "She must have lived in a nunnery," and the others laughed. They did not expect her to understand, and she didn't correct them.

"What *did* you do, mistress?" This from Cecily Blake.

"I studied alongside my brothers. Latin, Greek, history, philosophy, mathematics. I-I enjoyed it." Andrew used to say Isabel had a powerful thirst for knowledge. The methods her stepfather employed had often been cruel and unjust, but she had loved learning about the past. And studying the classics. The *Iliad* and the *Aeneid*. Jason and the Golden Fleece. Romance and adventure had transported her to another world and time, which had been exactly what she needed. Philosophy and mathematics had been a greater challenge for her, but she'd always put forth the effort to understand.

"How very odd for a young lady," Dorothy Vere said.

"I think it admirable you have so much learning," Master Blake said. "Not many women could rival you in such an accomplishment." Master Blake was a handsome man, with a deep cleft in his chin.

Isabel smiled gratefully. *A gallant defender.*

"Well, I do hope you enjoy sewing. That occupies much of our time here," Alice said.

Bel had been dreading this. "I never learned to embroider. I'm afraid you will have to instruct me. Lady Shrewsbury said—"

"You are of an advanced age to possess so few graces. Mayhap you can help in the kitchens or tend the herb garden while we are at our work," Dorothy Vere said snidely, prompting more laughter.

Isabel felt the fragile hold on her temper loosening. "I am knowledgeable about herbs and would be happy to take charge of the herbery."

"Ladies, our duty is to make Bel feel welcome. We will instruct her in whatever way is required," Mary said severely. "Now, if we have finished our meal, let us exit the room so it may be readied for dancing." A servant circled the table with a bowl of water, and after washing their hands, everyone rose.

Gavin pulled Bel's chair out for her. He offered his arm and she accepted. As they started to walk away, Mary stopped them. "I wish to have a word with Bel, Gavin."

"Of course, madam." He bowed and left them.

While the servants commenced clearing the plates,

tankards, and wineglasses, Mary looped her arm through Isabel's and steered her off to one side. "*Ma chere* Bel, my ladies can be malicious at times. Over the years, they have grown competitive with one another and with any new arrival. In time, they will become accustomed to your presence here."

"How do you suggest I should respond, Your Majesty?"

"Do not allow them to intimidate you, and never let them sense that you are weak."

It was the second warning in less than a few hours, and from the queen herself. *This was not what I agreed to.* Not part of her bargain with Lady Shrewsbury.

"*Oui, madame.* I will do my best to…to thwart their efforts." Isabel was not at all sure she could bring this to pass. Or even how to begin.

And now she must dance.

• • •

Gavin made small talk with Blake while waiting for the dancing to begin.

"The new lady—Isabel—is a different sort from the usual women surrounding Mary," Blake observed.

Gavin chuckled. "I suppose she is. She's certainly better educated."

Blake's brow furrowed. "'Tis puzzling why her parents kept her so sheltered. And why Bess chose her. I fear the others will make her life a living hell unless she learns to stand up to them."

Too true. "And your sister will lead the way. Can you speak to her about it? There's no need for her to be so vindictive."

"It is Cecily's way, as you know. I have little influence over her. Isabel would be better served by developing a thicker skin." Blake's attention was diverted by the tuning of instruments. "I must do my duty, if you'll excuse me," he said.

"You're not going to dance?"

Blake played the lute, and his talents were in demand on these evenings.

"I said I would play for the first few dances. Then I'll give over to somebody else."

"The ladies will be disappointed," Gavin said, laughing, as Blake strode off toward the musicians.

Gavin's eyes scanned the room. Isabel was standing off to the side, alone, with a blank stare on her face. The other ladies huddled together, chattering behind their fans. Mary was speaking to John Lesley, but after only a moment, she left. If he were to learn anything useful to Ryder, Gavin needed to listen in on some of the conversations between those two. A couple of the men who guarded the castle's perimeter entered the room, invited for the dancing, no doubt. Strictly speaking, they should not leave their posts, but there were never enough men for these entertainments, and Shrewsbury allowed it.

Without intending to, Gavin moved toward Isabel. He would ask her to dance. He would instruct her. But before he'd walked five steps, Alice waylaid him. "Sir, won't you partner me for the first dance?" To refuse would be churlish, so he said, "It would be my pleasure," and they took their place in the line of other dancers. All the ladies, save Isabel, were among them.

The first set was a galliard, a rather energetic dance, and Gavin deemed it fortunate that Isabel was sitting this one out. It wanted practice before attempting. Mercifully, there was not much opportunity for conversing. He'd spent enough time this evening listening to Alice. As soon as the dance finished, he escorted her back to her friends and moved toward Isabel.

"May I have the next dance, Mistress Isabel?"

She resembled a deer just before the hunter let fly an

arrow. Desperate to escape, but knowing it was too late. "But, sir, I do not dance. I have never learned."

Gavin held out his hand. "And that is why I will teach you. This is a simple country dance. You'll have no trouble following my lead." Just when he feared she intended to refuse him, she placed her hand in his.

"If it pleases you, then yes."

• • •

Isabel's heart thumped so hard, she thought Gavin might hear it. Or see it pulsing against her bosom. "Look at me," he commanded. He grasped her other hand and squeezed, forcing her to look directly at him. "First, I bow and you curtsy, like so." That was easy enough, and she did as he instructed. He dropped her hands and they moved apart.

He spoke a little louder now, because of the greater distance between them. "When I step toward you, you do the same." Gavin was light on his feet, and she tried to imitate him. Isabel may never have danced, but she'd observed others dancing, had even tried out some of the steps in the privacy of her chamber at home. He held out his hands and she grasped them. "Now, move in a circle." He smiled at her, his face alight. Isabel hadn't thought he could be any more handsome than he already was, but his smile changed that. She suddenly felt warm, in some very odd places. "That's right, well done," Gavin said.

After a time, it grew easier to simply mimic whatever he was doing, and Gavin had a gentle way of correcting her if she erred. Bel lost herself in the music and the unfamiliar, quite pleasant feeling of standing so close to another person. *To him.* She liked it more than she should. All too soon, the dance ended and he led her toward a few of the other women.

"Pray, I would prefer to stand over here, Master Cade."

Eyebrows raised, he said, "By yourself? That is not a good way to become acquainted with the others." They had paused in the middle of the room. "Frances is among them. She is a good person to have as a friend."

Bel sighed. It was not Frances who worried her—it was Cecily Blake, who was at her side. "As you say, then."

"Thank you for the dance, mistress." Gavin bowed, and then he was gone.

"There, Bel, you are not so bad at dancing," Frances said.

Cecily snickered, and Bel thought it was time to embolden herself. "We have not been properly introduced, mistress. I am Isabel Tait, from near Derby."

As though suddenly remembering her manners, the other woman replied. "And I am Cecily Blake, from Edinburgh and Paris." Just then, the young man Isabel knew to be Cecily's brother joined them. "And this is my brother. Philip, Mistress Isabel Tait."

Philip Blake smiled and bowed. Up close, he was an exceptional specimen of manhood. Wide-set brown eyes, wavy dark hair, and a sensuous mouth. "Welcome to Tutbury, Mistress Isabel," he said.

"Thank you. You were playing the lute, were you not?"

"Aye. But I cannot miss out on all the merriment. Would you dance with me, mistress?"

Isabel, shocked and pleased, was on the verge of accepting when the older man who had escorted Mary to dinner suddenly appeared at her side and said, "I've come to claim a dance. Blake, you'll have to wait."

Blake's face was impassive. "Of course, Bishop."

Isabel had no choice but to accept. He held out a hand and she let him lead her to the line of dancers. Philip Blake chose Frances, and Gavin claimed Cecily as a partner. Dorothy and Alice partnered with two other men, the ones who had joined the group after supper. Where was the queen? For the first time, Isabel realized she hadn't seen her since they'd spoken after supper.

Isabel and the bishop lined up across from each other. His long nose and scraggly beard seemed to point directly at her. When the dance began and they drew closer together, he introduced himself. "I am John Lesley, Bishop of Ross and Queen Mary's envoy to Elizabeth. I travel a good deal between here and London."

They separated, and when they came back together to join hands, Lesley said, "And you are?"

His hands were dry and leathery. "Isabel Tait, sir. From near Derby."

"How came you to be here, Mistress Isabel?"

The man was full of self-importance, his questions sounding more like demands than polite inquiries. "Lady Shrewsbury knows my family, and she invited me, sir."

"Did she? Well. Who are your people?"

"Nobody you have ever heard of, I assure you." She hoped that would put a stop to this interrogation. Asking a question of her own might distract him. "Where is Queen Mary? I thought she would join the dancing." Again, they separated, so she had to wait for an answer.

When they came back together, he said, "She retired early. The queen suffers from many complaints. I blame her detention. She does not get sufficient fresh air or exercise."

At last the dance ended. After a curt bow, Lesley hurried away. Isabel was glad to be left alone. But it was not for long. Philip Blake hurried over and asked her to dance. It was a galliard, and she told him he would need to instruct her. Laughing, he said, "Essentially, you stand still while I hop and jump around you. You can do that without too much trouble, I'll wager." In the beginning, that was fine. But Isabel soon became aware that the other women were hopping, leaping, kicking, and jumping along with their partners. Blake did not seem to mind her ineptitude, and nobody was pointing at her and snickering. "We shall have dancing lessons one afternoon. I, for one, would be happy to tutor you," he said, as the dance ended.

Isabel laughed, because it had been fun, even though she hadn't done much more than stand still, hands on her hips, watching while he performed the steps. During the remainder of the evening, she danced with each of the two men who had arrived after supper, learning that they were castle guards. And once more with Blake, but never again with Gavin. He partnered all the other ladies, at least twice each, and Bel couldn't help noticing how he flirted with each of them in turn. They all gazed at him with adoration, laughed at whatever he was whispering in their ears, and touched him as much as possible.

He's probably bedded them all.

She'd no idea what had caused that most unwelcome thought to pop into her mind. Usually, she did not think of such things, although she was not naive. Her brother Thomas had fathered a child with a servant girl. Isabel's family believed she did not know of this, but one of the maids had told her. The same one who had vividly described the act of procreation.

The merriment finally ended, and Isabel followed the others toward the bedchambers. On her way down the passage, she remembered what Lesley had told her about Mary's illnesses. According to him, she had many restrictions placed upon her and was limited in what activities she was permitted. Isabel felt compassion for her predicament.

The passage was ill lit, and the ladies with the candles had gotten far ahead of her. Isabel caught a glimpse of two figures huddled together a bit farther on, close to Mary's rooms. In a moment, she identified them by their voices as the queen and John Lesley. She paused, uncertain whether to continue. And then someone grabbed her from behind, covering her mouth with his hand and dragging her backward into a window embrasure. She could not cry out, and she wasn't strong enough to wrench herself away from him.

Chapter Four

Gavin had frightened her, and he was sorry for it. Her heartbeat thudded against his forearm. But it couldn't be helped. This was his chance to listen in on an exchange between the queen and the bishop. If Isabel had proceeded down the passage, they would have ended their conversation.

He whispered in her ear. "*Shh.* It's Gavin. I mean you no harm. I'll remove my hand if you'll not cry out." When she nodded, he did so. Instantly, she relaxed against him, her posterior touching his privy part, which immediately grew hard. He hated to let her go, because her body felt so damn good against him, but she would feel his throbbing cock and then she might indeed scream. Slowly, he removed his arm from across her body, his hand brushing the underside of her breasts.

He again signaled Isabel to be silent and whispered, "Don't move." Then, surreptitiously, he took a few cautious steps toward Lesley and Mary. When he could go no farther without being seen, he stopped, listening closely.

"Why did you not tell me of my cousin's intention to wed the Duke of Anjou? You should not simply have announced it at supper."

"May we not go inside, madam?" Lesley asked, "where we might have privacy?"

"*Non.* There are ladies in the presence chamber, and there is no one about here. Pray answer my question."

"The answer is simple. I thought you already knew."

"How could I? Do you think my cousin keeps me informed of her marriage negotiations? This does not bode well for me—I will lose the support of the French if she forms an alliance with them."

"Aye, I fear that is true."

Queen Elizabeth was continually negotiating with one country or another for a marriage. Her councilors wanted her to marry and have children, to ensure the succession. But she resisted. Always, she resisted. Gavin couldn't imagine this time would be different.

"Do not despair, madam. We still have allies."

"Norfolk? He cannot be relied upon. I have thrown myself at his feet, offered myself to him. He moves like a tortoise."

"I will have a word with him. But we must look to Spain for help also, and to the Pope. And there is someone else we may soon rely on in that quarter."

"Ah. Who might that be?"

"An Italian. A banker named Ridolfi. He has an interest and…connections."

Booted footsteps on the flagstone floor warned Gavin that the nighttime sentries were approaching. Silently, he backed up into the alcove.

"I must retire now," he heard Mary say.

"Sleep well, Your Majesty." Mary's door closed, and Lesley disappeared into the darkness of the passage.

Gavin turned and looked at Isabel. Her eyes were wide. And accusing. "What are you up to?"

"I'll explain later," he said. The sentries were close, and

there was only one solution. He grabbed Isabel and said, "Play along." And then he drew her close and kissed her. Startled, she emitted a little gasp. It was a chaste affair—the kiss of a woman who had never had the pleasure, but sweet and arousing nonetheless. Her lips were soft and supple, and she opened them slightly. Gavin coaxed them open farther, but resisted the urge to deepen the kiss. He sensed the moment she began to enjoy it, because she relaxed into him, as she had before, and slowly, her arms slid up and around his neck.

"Well, what have we here?" The two sentries, who sounded well into their cups, chortled.

Gavin, who had nearly forgotten the reason for the kiss, pulled away from Bel. "Good night, mistress," he said. As Isabel emerged from the window embrasure, he gave her a playful slap on the arse. Had to be convincing, did he not?

The sentries carried candles, and Gavin could clearly see annoyance written all over Isabel's face as she walked away, glancing at him over her shoulder. He would need to invent a reason he was spying on Mary and Lesley, and it had better be believable. He had the feeling Isabel would recognize a lie when she heard it.

"Good night, lads," Gavin said as he sauntered off.

But it had been a good night's work. For the first time, he'd heard the name Ridolfi spoken by one of Mary's closest associates. And Lesley had confirmed there was something afoot. Now he would need to find out exactly what that might be.

· · ·

Isabel crept into her chamber, believing Frances would already be abed. To her surprise, the other lady was not in her bed, or even in the room. Ann entered and helped Bel disrobe to her smock. Before the girl left, Bel asked her if she should leave a candle burning for Frances.

A smile flashed across Ann's face. "Nay, mistress. She'll bring one with her when she retires."

Where is she? Perhaps talking with the queen and the other ladies, but, given Ann's smile, Bel guessed Frances was with a man. Perhaps they all partnered with someone every night. It was their business. Isabel did not care, provided nobody expected her to do the same.

After washing, Bel climbed into bed. She said her prayers and then lay still, trying to quiet her mind. But the events of the evening, both the good and the bad, sang like a Greek chorus, demanding her attention. She had half a mind to inform Lady Shrewsbury that she wished to return home. Other than Frances, the queen's ladies had neither welcomed her nor eased her way, even after Mary had bid them to do so. She could expect no different from them in the coming days. Why must she accept their scorn and mistreatment?

But the alternative was to scurry back to her mother, who feared Isabel would get in the way of her happiness with a new husband. The question of Bel's own marriage would be revisited, and she would no doubt end up with one of the men her brother had put forward.

No, she would have to remain here and endure it as best she could. In time, she would find an opportunity to prove herself to the queen and her entourage. Isabel only hoped it would come sooner rather than later.

Tonight, she would rather fall asleep remembering her dances with Philip Blake and Gavin. A pair of virile and handsome men. And they both seemed to like her, although Gavin had danced with her only once. But that kiss. Oh, she was well aware of why he'd done it: to distract the sentries and prevent them from asking why she and Gavin were lurking in the passage. But his kiss had seemed more than that. It had been sweet and tender. He must have realized she was inexperienced, and it had been considerate of him to respect that. That slap on her bottom had been unnecessary, though. The scoundrel.

Why had he been listening in on the queen's conversation with John Lesley? From her place in the window embrasure, Isabel had made out only a few words. Philip. Spain. The Pope. And a foreign sounding name she didn't recognize. Surely Mary had many supporters among Catholic Europe.

Isabel had no idea what tomorrow would bring. At present, her only alternative was to carry on.

In the morning, a rank odor pulled Isabel from the depths of sleep. It reeked like sewage, and she certainly hadn't smelled it the night before. While Ann was helping her dress, Bel asked her about it.

"'Tis foul today. It depends on which way the wind is blowing. The fumes result from inadequate drainage."

"Cannot some laborers fix the problem?"

Ann laughed. "The stench has existed since the queen has been in residence, and nobody has done a thing about it."

Frances had not stirred. She must have retired late. Isabel was afraid of waking her, but Ann said there was no danger of that—Frances could sleep through anything.

"You may break your fast in the dining chamber, mistress," Ann said.

Isabel, having assumed she'd be dining alone, was surprised to see the queen already seated at the table. She curtsied and said, "Good morrow, Your Majesty." One of Mary's gentlemen attendants began to steer Isabel toward a smaller, separate table, but Mary stopped him by simply lifting her hand.

"*Mais non.* Bel will join me. George, help her, *s'il vous plait.*"

Obligingly, he pointed out the food offerings. Isabel selected cheese, bread, frittered apples, and fresh pears. George carried it all to the table and helped Bel with her chair.

"And did you sleep well, *ma chere*?" Mary asked. "I trust Frances to be a kind and helpful friend to you."

Isabel thought it best not to reveal she hadn't seen Frances since last evening's entertainment, except for making out her form under the covers this morning.

Bel simply nodded. "Will Lady Shrewsbury be returning soon, madam?"

Mary patted Bel's hand. "Ah, you feel her absence. Tomorrow, I believe. I trusted her to find another lady to serve me, and she made a good choice in you."

"Thank you. I hope you are feeling better this morning, Your Majesty," Isabel said, after eating a slice of pear. "The bishop told me you were not well."

"I suffer from many complaints. It is the rank air, the lack of exercise. You have noticed the odor this morning. Or should I say, the malodor?" Sighing, Mary leaned back in her chair. "Shrewsbury says I have 'grief of the spleen.' Perhaps. I also experience pain in my joints. Rheumatism."

Isabel wished to be sympathetic, but thought it best not to encourage Mary to wallow in self-pity. Ultimately, that would not serve her well. "What shall we do today to lift your spirits, Your Majesty?"

"Ha! I like you, Bel. You will be a tonic for me. My health will improve with your arrival." She began slicing a frittered apple and eating small pieces of it. "We do have something amusing planned today. There is to be a tennis match between Master Cade and Philip Blake." She paused to slide a piece of apple from knife to mouth. "The men have cleared out a ruined section of this monstrosity of a castle and transformed it into a court. This will be the first use of it as such." Mary bent her head toward Isabel. "I have given my favor to Philip."

When Isabel raised her brows and smiled, Mary said, "It means nothing. I shall give one to Gavin the next time. Or another handsome man." She laughed, a tinkling sound. "Now, *ma chere*, if you have finished your repast, will you not rouse the other ladies? The tennis is scheduled for later this morning, and they must rise and dress."

When the queen got to her feet, Isabel did likewise. "Come to my rooms at eleven of the clock. We shall proceed from there." She squeezed Isabel's shoulder before hurrying away.

Isabel had no enthusiasm for the task she'd been given. What if some of the ladies had gentlemen in their beds? Bel entered her own chamber first, hoping Ann might be there dressing Frances. But, to her dismay, the lady was still asleep. Isabel gently shook her by the shoulder until she opened her eyes and said a groggy, "What is it?"

"The queen wishes us to attend her at a tennis match at eleven o'clock. You must get up. I'm going to rouse the others."

As she exited, Frances said, "Send Ann to me, pray."

"I will, if I can find her."

Knocking lightly on the chamber door adjacent to hers, Bel slowly cracked it open. Dorothy and Alice lay sleeping. "Ladies," Isabel said. "You must get up. The queen wants you to attend her by eleven." They shifted and groaned, and Isabel was satisfied they were awake.

Growing rather impatient with women who couldn't wake up on their own and prepare for the day, she rapped on the next door and, without pause, pushed it open. A sight she'd never thought to see greeted her. The Bishop of Ross, John Lesley, was sitting up in bed between Cecily Blake and the elusive Ann. His chest was bare, but the two women, thank the Virgin, were wearing their chemises. They were not engaged in any carnal activity at present, but it was obvious they had been. Isabel's jaw dropped, and she was perfectly incapable of speech. Ducking her head, she half-covered her eyes. A hot flush started at her neck and worked its way up. Her expression prompted much laughter among the three in the bed.

"Care to join us, mistress?" Cecily asked.

At last Isabel found her voice. "The queen wishes you to attend her at eleven of the clock. And Frances needs you now, Ann."

Among the three, Lesley was the only one who appeared to be embarrassed. When Isabel left, he'd been tugging his shirt on. Where could she go, what could she do until eleven? She didn't wish to engage with any of them. The castle had a bell tower, and during the daylight hours, someone rang it on the hour and half hour. She could safely exit and keep track of the time.

Bel hurried down the stairs to the door, but a guard stopped her. "Where are you going, mistress?"

"I need a breath of fresh air, sir. Where may I walk?"

"Why, in the queen's garden, ma'am." He opened the door and pointed. "'Tis just there."

She thanked the man and hurried on her way. The day was fine, the air crisp but comfortable. High, scudding clouds floated above. In these late days of autumn, no flowers were blooming, but the foliage had turned deep red, orange, and yellow. Isabel inhaled deeply and began to calm down and consider what she'd seen.

A man and two ladies. It repulsed her, yet at the same time, fascinated her. She had enough difficulty imagining the sex act between one man and one woman, let alone among three people. And John Lesley! He was an old man, at least forty. Oh, the ways of the world puzzled her exceedingly. She strolled about the garden until she heard the bell ring the half hour, and then reluctantly made her way back inside. As soon as word spread, the ladies would tease her unmercifully.

Chapter Five

By the time everyone had gathered in Mary's hall, there was
no opportunity to mock Isabel. Although, when she'd entered
the room, snickers, sly looks, and whispers proliferated.
Frances approached her and said, "Walk with me, Bel." She
didn't wait for an answer, but looped Bel's arm through hers
and let go only to descend the stairs.

Once outside, they lagged behind the others. Mary was
on the arm of one of her male attendants, and the other ladies
clustered about her. Frances didn't say anything at first, but
when everybody had moved beyond hearing range, finally
spoke. "You mustn't be too shocked by our behavior, Bel. It is
lonely here, and we are bored much of the time. We do what
we can to amuse ourselves. You will too, eventually."

Isabel almost laughed. *I will never be in the same bed as
John Lesley...* "I understand. But perhaps all of you might
consider my feelings. All my life I have been sheltered and
protected. I will not judge you or the others and would hope
to receive the same consideration."

"Fair enough," Frances said. "'Tis best to take these
things in your stride. Of necessity, we are close and wary
of outsiders. As I said last night, it will take time to gain

acceptance from everybody." She drew Isabel closer. "Trust that you already have mine."

As Mary had described, the tennis court was a large space that may have served as a banquet hall in ancient times. There was no roof, but all four walls were at least partially intact, forming a rectangular space. A few chairs and benches had been set off to one side. The queen arranged herself, then looked about until she spotted Isabel. She gestured. Isabel looked at Frances for guidance.

"You have been summoned to sit beside her." She gave Bel a little shove. "Go."

Isabel curtsied, then lowered herself beside the queen. They were the only two who had chairs. The others sat on benches, pulling their skirts close to make room for each other.

"Ah," Mary gestured, "here are the competitors."

Isabel glanced up and, for the second time that day, was rendered speechless by what she saw. Both Gavin and Philip were wearing shifts which they'd knotted at their sides. Trunk hose and tight canions emphasized their muscular thighs and…other parts of their anatomy—parts that were normally concealed by doublets. Isabel had to force herself not to stare. Both men approached the queen.

"Your Majesty, you will honor me with your favor?" Blake asked.

She cooed like a lovesick young lass. "*Oui*, Philip," Mary said, gracing him with her handkerchief. He bowed and stepped back.

Gavin moved forward and bowed to the queen. "Your Majesty." Then, unexpectedly, he turned to Bel. "Mistress Isabel, would you honor me with a favor?"

She was stunned, and worse yet, she'd forgotten a handkerchief. An embarrassing silence reigned, although Isabel heard giggling from some of the ladies. She had only one personal item with her, and it was a ridiculous thing to give a man who would be involved in vigorous exercise. But it was all she had, so she pulled it from a pocket in her petticoats and held it out.

"A book," Gavin said, a smile tugging at his mouth. "Christine de Pizan."

Raucous laughter broke out among the other ladies, and Isabel spoke hastily to cover up her embarrassment. "It is my most valued possession, but perhaps not suitable as an honor."

Gavin raised his voice, which quelled the mirth. "On the contrary, I'm certain it will bring me luck. Thank you, mistress."

Both men bowed and walked off, taking their places on the court. Isabel could not see what Gavin had done with the book, but she was certain he had it somewhere on his person. And then she did not think of it again, so absorbed was she in the match.

The queen whispered to her. "One man serves and one receives, at the opposite end. Philip is serving first."

The game was played with long-handled rackets and an odd-looking ball. The action was lightning fast, the two players vigorously smacking the ball back and forth over the net. Isabel's head moved to one side of the court and then the other. *Whap! Bam!* Several times, the ball flew over their heads and struck the wall behind them. Every so often, a man standing off to one side called out the score, and the ladies would clap and cheer. At first Philip seemed to be the superior player, but he tired faster than Gavin, who quickly gained the upper hand.

Isabel was mesmerized by the agility and strength of their bodies. By Gavin's body, because he was the one she watched. Every time he swung his racket, his shoulder and back muscles flexed. And all the running, leaping, and diving showed off his tight buttocks, thighs, and calves. He was sweating, running his sleeve across his forehead. Even that seemed titillating. Isabel clapped when she heard the others clapping, cheered when appropriate, but it was secondary to the spectacle before her eyes. So when the heavy tennis ball smacked her square in the forehead, she never saw it coming, never even had a chance to duck.

They told her that Gavin had carried her back to the lodgings after she'd been struck by the ball. That the queen had been very solicitous of her well-being. They'd summoned a physician, who pronounced her concussed, but said she would recover with a few days' rest. Isabel remembered none of this. She woke up periodically, with either Ann, Frances, or Dorothy standing by with doses of strong herbal tea for the pain. When she regained full consciousness at last, an entire day had passed, and she suffered a raging headache. Ironically, there was no one about. She lay back down and tried not to dwell on the pain.

She could not recall what, precisely, had happened. What she did remember was the tennis match and her excitement at watching the men at their sport. Then, darkness. If she'd been paying attention to the match rather than masculine attributes, perhaps this would not have happened. She groaned. The door opened and Frances entered.

"You're awake! The queen—all of us—have been so worried."

Isabel thought it was more likely that her latest faux pas had only intensified their poor opinion of her, but she kept that to herself. "My head. May I have more of that remedy?"

"The willow bark tea? Of course, I'll see to it. And your bandage needs to be changed. We've been applying oil of clove to the wound."

"No wonder I smell like an apple tart."

Frances laughed. "I'll see to the tea and send Ann in to change the bandage." She paused on the threshold. "Gavin has been waiting to see you. He's most concerned, because it was he who struck the ball that hit you."

Isabel's heart beat a little faster. "Of course. Later, after I've drunk the tea and Ann has changed the bandage. And I'd like to wash."

"I'll tell him," Frances said, smiling.

• • •

Gavin waited outside the chamber Isabel shared with Frances, pacing back and forth. He still could not believe his ball had struck Isabel so hard she'd been knocked unconscious. By the Virgin, he hoped there were no lasting effects. At length, the door opened and Frances gestured to him to come in.

"Don't tire the patient, Master Cade," she admonished, slipping out and closing the door.

Momentarily, Gavin paused on the threshold, studying Isabel. She was sitting up in her bed, propped against some pillows. Her long, dark hair lay in billowy waves about her shoulders. A woolen shawl covered her chemise, and a white linen bandage was wrapped about her head. Suddenly, she turned her head toward him. He felt like a school boy caught out by the master.

"Gavin?" she said. "You may come in."

He gave his head a shake and strode toward her. A heavy oak chair rested at her bedside, but he ignored it and lowered himself to the bed. Taking hold of her hands, he said, "Isabel. I am so terribly sorry. What a cods-head I am."

That drew a smile from her. "You didn't mean to do it, sir." She drew back and squinted at him. "Did you?"

Now it was Gavin's turn to laugh. "Had it been anyone but you, I may have." She was truly quite extraordinary when she smiled. "Tell me, how do you fare? Is it painful?"

"As a matter of fact, it is. But the tea helps, and so does the salve they've applied to the wound. The physician visited me and said he thought after a few days' rest, I would be fine."

"May I see it?"

"I don't know if that's a good idea—"

He cut her off. "Nonsense. I've dealt with all sorts of injuries." Very gently, he slid the bandage up and away from the wound, and when he glimpsed the damage he'd done, he gasped. "God's breath, Isabel, I'm surprised I didn't kill you." He re-covered the wound and said, "Is there anything I can do for you? Anything you need?"

Her brandy-colored eyes sparkled. "Aye. You can get me out of this bed and walk about with me. I feel as if I've been lying here for days."

He cocked his head at her. "Is that wise? You were unconscious for some time."

"I will tell you if I feel weak or dizzy, I swear. Pray, let me. They are treating me as if I'm on my death bed."

"Very well, but you must do as I say. Agreed?"

Isabel nodded. Gavin stood and turned back her covers. When she made as though to climb out of bed, he tutted like his grandmother. "I'll carry you to the passage, and then we shall see."

He set her down in the passage, which was deserted, and pulled her arm through the crook of his elbow. He was impressed. She made it all the way to the stairs.

"Pray, let's go outside."

Hands on hips, Gavin glowered at her. "Out of the question. The queen would have my head. Not to mention Frances and the others."

"They don't need to know. Please, Gavin. The fresh air

will do me good."

He gave her his most intimidating look for another few seconds, and she returned it in kind. Trying to dissuade her was hopeless; she would not change her mind, so he may as well give in. "As you wish." Before she could protest, he picked her up and carried her down the stairs, alerting the guard to their destination. "Queen's Garden."

Luxuriating in her scent, he was loath to let go of her. Her hair brushed his cheek, and her arm rested on his back. Isabel's mere touch shot a bolt of desire through him. He hadn't had a woman since his wife had died, and that had been long ago. He'd like nothing better than to lose himself in her, but that would be a major distraction, ultimately bringing him nothing but trouble.

"Gavin. You may put me down now."

He set her down, but held on to her arms. "Are you sure about this, mistress?"

"Aye."

"And you remember your vow?"

Her brow wrinkled. "Vow?"

"That you will tell me if you—"

"Ah. If I feel dizzy, and the rest. I will, but what if it's too late? I may simply die right here, and you would be forced to carry my lifeless form to the burial ground."

"Not funny." He let go of her, and she looped an arm through his. They set off, moving slowly. "Did you enjoy the tennis match?"

God's teeth, why had he asked such a thing? *Fool.* But if she thought him callous, she hid it, answering the question with no reference to her injury.

"I loved it." She smiled to herself, and he wondered what she was thinking.

"Tell me more."

She glanced up at him. "It was exhilarating. The fast

pace, the energy and excitement, from the players and the audience." Her generous mouth was enticing, and Gavin thought he could look at it all day. "Do females play?"

"What? Nay, none that I've ever heard of. Ladies would be hindered by their clothing. I'm afraid it would be judged unladylike in the extreme."

Real disappointment flickered in her eyes, surprising him. But then, she surprised him in many ways. "For someone who was flattened by a tennis ball, you are most eager to subject yourself to further injury."

"But the players were not injured, neither you nor Philip. We females are left out of all the fun."

Gavin knew he should not offer, but he couldn't stop himself. "When you are fully recovered, I will teach you. We'll need to find you some appropriate attire."

She halted abruptly. "Honestly? Oh, thank you, Gavin. I shall look forward to it!"

He chuckled and patted her hand. "Not until you are feeling back to normal." He paused a moment, then said, "How are you faring with the ladies?"

Isabel shrugged. "I can only imagine their amusement over what happened at the match. They will think I was to blame, and perhaps I was."

"You are too hard on yourself. Any of them could have been struck."

"To answer your question, since my injury, I've only seen Frances and Dorothy, and they've been kind."

"Good. Stand your ground with them, Bel. But don't lose your temper. That is what they want, because they hope you will look a fool before Queen Mary."

"How does that benefit them?"

He scrubbed a hand across his face, thinking. "They are thrown so much together. A rivalry has taken root among them. I've only been here a month, but even I see it. And they're jealous because Mary has shown a preference for you."

"She's simply being kind to make me feel welcome." Isabel sighed, and he regretted being so forthcoming. "What do you do here, Gavin?"

There, she'd surprised him again. "I am equerry to Shrewsbury and do whatever he requires, especially in regard to supplying the castle. Mary and her entourage require an inordinate amount of food and drink."

"I detect a slight Scots accent in your speech," she said innocently. "Are you English or Scottish?"

"Some of each. My mother is Scots to the bone, and my father is English and just as loyal."

"I thought it was against the law to marry a Scot. And vice versa."

"Supposedly, it is. But there are countless marriages among Scots and English at the border. How could we expect anything else?"

"May I ask why you were eavesdropping on the queen's conversation with the bishop?"

Gavin should have anticipated this question, but given Isabel's injury, he'd hoped she'd forgotten about it. Expedient to be honest, as much as possible. "The earl asked me to. They fear Mary may involve herself in an escape plot."

"So it's true—she is a prisoner rather than a guest of Queen Elizabeth?"

"I don't believe anybody is certain of her status." They had been walking for several minutes, and Gavin thought it was time to return her to the castle. She protested, but feebly, and he interpreted that as an admission to feeling tired. At the castle entry, he picked her up and carried her to her chamber. Outside the door, he fished in his pocket for something. "Here is your book, Isabel. Thank you for honoring me with it. I believe it brought me luck. I won, if you didn't know."

"I did not. Well done, Master Cade." Her smile was beguiling.

He glanced down at the book, written in French, as he handed it to Bel. "Christine de Pizan. She was quite an accomplished woman. An illuminator and writer."

"You're familiar with her work? Most people have never heard of her."

"I am an admirer of hers. You read, write, and speak French, do you not? Yet you haven't revealed that."

Isabel looked embarrassed. "I am waiting for the right moment."

"I won't give you away." He glanced up and down the passage to see if they were alone before saying one last thing. "Have a care around John Lesley. It is rumored he has fathered more than one bastard, and he's as cunning as the slipperiest of eels."

Isabel's face blanched. Had he shocked her? "You must get some rest." Brushing a lock of hair back from her face, he said, "Until later, Bel."

Chapter Six

A fortnight passed, and November was full upon them. The days grew short, and the hours of daylight fewer. Lady Shrewsbury returned from her respite at Sheffield, drew Isabel aside, and asked how she fared. Isabel was honest with her but, sadly, the lady did not offer any suggestions that were helpful. Only the same advice the queen and Frances had already given her regarding Mary's ladies-in-waiting. The vixens-in-waiting, as Isabel had come to think of them.

Don't let them intimidate you. Ignore them. Laugh along with them.

Meanwhile, Lady Shrewsbury and the queen spent their days in each other's company embroidering. They seemed consumed by it. The two women reclined on fine upholstered chairs, chattering about designs and stitches, while everybody else, Isabel included, sat on footstools. After several attempts by various ladies, including the queen, to teach Isabel the art of embroidering, Mary decided they would all be better served if Bel read to them while they sewed. Humiliated by her clumsiness with the needle, she was much relieved.

Mary, like Isabel, was an early riser, and on most mornings, they ate breakfast together. In truth, Isabel ate while Mary regaled her with stories of her youth. Isabel did not mind—the queen's life was full of adventure, romance, and, regrettably, lost hopes.

Mary told Bel of her first husband, Francois, the dauphin, later king, of France. How they had been devoted to each other from childhood and married when they were only in their teens. He died suddenly a few years later. "Love inevitably leads to heartbreak, Bel. Never let anyone say otherwise." She sighed. "*Mon dieu*, I wish you could have seen my wedding—it was at Notre Dame Cathedral! My dress, so elegant! White, with a sweeping train, and embroidered with jewels. All the dignitaries in Paris were in attendance—from the monarchy, the church, the ruling class. Oh, how I long for those days!" Mary lapsed into a reverie.

That was the beginning of Isabel's compassion and sympathy for Queen Mary.

The ladies-in-waiting frequently conversed in French among themselves, assuming Isabel had no idea what they were saying. While they talked, she played with the queen's spaniel, whose name was Bisou. She was growing exceedingly fond of him.

Sometimes the women talked about Isabel. She didn't mind the jokes about her incompetence with the needle, or her rudimentary dancing skills, but she hated it when they made fun of her looks or her background. Her hair was a great source of amusement for them, although between Frances and Ann, Isabel thought the style greatly improved from the day of her arrival. They said she was too studious for a lady, and there was nothing about her that would attract a man. Wasn't it odd, Cecily asked, that Gavin spent an inordinate amount of time watching her?

Isabel had noticed that, too. And wondered. Since Gavin's visit after her injury, he'd kept his distance. He danced with her, but not as often as he did with the other ladies. He flirted outrageously with them, but never with her. Yet she often looked up and found him gazing at her. Once she'd caught his eye and held it. When he'd smiled, she'd ducked her head.

"It's simple," Alice said. "He wants to bed her. Have a little taste of something different. But he doesn't want to waste his time wooing her or even flirting." Isabel felt the sting of tears and quietly departed the room with Bisou before anyone suspected. She sat in one of the window embrasures in the passage to gather her emotions. At least Frances was kind to her. She'd been teaching Isabel how to play primero and sometimes, with Philip Blake's assistance, instructing her in dancing when the others weren't around.

The ladies spoke often of French fashions, hair styles, and life at court. Isabel usually paid scant attention, but one afternoon when she heard the phrase *membre viril*, she sat up and took notice. The ladies were discussing the size of a certain male part, even arguing over who possessed the most formidable attributes. In this way, the fact that Gavin hadn't bedded any of them was revealed. They could only speculate as to his...part. Did it resemble a pickle, a sausage, or was it shaped more like an artichoke, as the bishop's was?

An artichoke? At that point, Isabel grabbed Bisou and hurried outside. As soon as she reached the garden, she whooped with laughter while the little dog jumped about her feet, yipping, as though he wanted in on the joke. She recalled a time she'd seen her brothers swimming naked, coming upon them by accident one day when they'd been in their teens. Several other boys had been there too, and nobody's breeding organ had resembled an artichoke.

"It is good to see you laughing, Isabel." Gavin appeared out of nowhere.

"*Bonjour*, Gavin." She couldn't contain herself, because the very sight of him reminded her of the subject at hand. So she kept right on howling with mirth. He waited patiently, and at last, her laughter petered out. She felt like a simpleton. "Forgive me. I do not usually lose control of myself."

"Would you care to let me in on the joke?"

She shook her head vehemently. "Nay. I couldn't."

"I won't press you. Come, let's sit on the bench. There won't be many more days as fine as this."

When they were seated, Isabel lifted Bisou onto her lap. "You have made a friend, I think," Gavin said.

"Aye, a worthy one. He has such sad eyes, but I've decided this is a characteristic of the breed. What would he have to be sad about—he is so pampered by the queen."

Gavin chuckled. "And you." He scratched the dog's ears, then said, "I have wondered since your arrival at Tutbury, Bel. Why did Lady Shrewsbury choose you to be part of Mary's circle?"

Isabel had pondered this herself, and still couldn't decide if she was glad or sorry Lady Shrewsbury had appeared at her door that day. "In truth, I'm not certain. Her sons knew my brothers, and she said they had given good reports of me. She seemed in a great hurry to choose someone and was impatient when I asked questions about my role here."

"And the matter was settled forthwith?"

"Aye, on that very day." Why was Gavin so curious about this? What was it to him? Perhaps he thought her completely unsuited to the position. "Is there a reason you are asking me about this? Do you think Lady Shrewsbury made a poor decision?"

He turned and grasped her by the arms. His big, warm hands sent shivers through her. "Nay. She was very wise in choosing you. But it has been hard on you, Bel." His blue eyes studied her, and for a moment she thought he was going to kiss her. Then, suddenly, he dropped his hands and a sheepish look stole over his face. "Are the other women treating you kindlier?"

"Nay. But they are more circumspect about their jibes. Mary, and sometimes Lady Shrewsbury, admonish them to cease. Or glower at them. Usually, they speak French and assume I don't understand."

"You're still keeping that a secret?"

"*Oui!* It is the one thing that makes me feel...powerful. Although sometimes they say things about me I would prefer not to hear. Other times, they make me laugh excessively. Like today."

"Still won't share what was so funny?"

Isabel thought about it. What harm could it do to tell him? A modified version, anyway. "They were discussing the...appearance of male...organs. Comparing them."

"By the Virgin, they did not mention my, ah, organ, did they?" Gavin asked.

She couldn't resist having a little fun with him. "Well..."

He leaped to his feet and paced away from her, then swiveled back, looking furious. "Those scheming little liars. I've not bedded any of them!"

"And they are not so happy about that. They were speculating..."

"God's teeth. You knew the truth. Now you've embarrassed me, and I do not embarrass easily."

Isabel giggled. "You asked."

He rose and looked askance at her. "My mistake. You must be shocked by their boldness."

"No longer. The second day I was here—the day of the tennis match—Mary asked me to rouse the ladies. I knocked on one of the chamber doors, looked in, and found John Lesley in bed with two of them."

Gavin let out a loud bark of laughter. "What did you do?"

Bel grimaced at the memory. "I covered my eyes, delivered the message, and backed out of the room. But not before they asked if I wanted to join them."

Gavin's eyes sparked with amusement. "I suppose you would not share the names of the—"

"No, I would not. I'll say only one thing. Frances was not one of them. I trust you will be discreet about this?"

He laid a hand over his heart. "I vow I'll tell no living soul. Other than Blake and the earl."

"Gavin! You wouldn't."

He grinned, the scoundrel. "Of course not. I'm teasing you. But do let me know if you wish to engage in such bed sport. I'm sure I can arrange something."

Isabel sprang to her feet. "I should not have told you. Now you will mock me like the others." She began walking back toward the castle, but Gavin stopped her, grasping her wrist.

"Pray don't go, Bel. Forgive me. I won't mention it again. I would never mock you."

His expression was so earnest, she believed him. They remained in the garden a while longer, until the air began to cool, and Isabel realized she'd been absent a long time. Gavin drew her arm through his and accompanied her back inside.

• • •

Walking at a leisurely pace toward his suite, Gavin thought about Isabel. He'd been wise to hold her at arm's length. Every time he allowed himself to talk to her, spend time in her company, he regretted it. Because he was undeniably attracted to her. Not just to her body, although his cock stiffened whenever he thought of unwrapping the layers of clothing hiding her curves. After spending time with her, he felt more alive. She was a beacon of light in this desolate place.

Perhaps Lady Shrewsbury had also seen something special in Isabel. In truth, she was not suited to the demands of a lady-in-waiting, which must have been clear to Bess.

She was a perceptive woman and would have seen that Bel was unsophisticated in the extreme. And yet she chose her. Mayhap it was simply expedient.

To get his mind off Isabel, Gavin badly needed to bed someone. Perhaps he could ride to Derby, spend a night there. Otherwise, he might be in danger of succumbing to one of the ladies-in-waiting, or worse yet, allowing himself to become involved with Isabel. Women were not to be trusted, and therefore, giving his heart to Bel was out of the question.

After his wife, Anna, had died in childbirth, Gavin found a letter she'd left for him in a coffer secreted in her wardrobe. In it, she revealed he wasn't the father of the babe she had born, a son, who had died shortly after his birth. Around the time of the child's conception, Gavin had been away a good deal for the family business, once for an entire month. So it was certainly possible, even likely. Anna had named the swine who'd cuckolded him, one William Samuelson. Gavin found out what he could about the man, who was in the employ of the Earl of Westmoreland, and had considered seeking him out. But he'd quickly discarded the idea. Had the child survived, he'd have felt an obligation. But under the circumstances, it would have served no purpose.

A hand at his elbow wrenched him from his memories. "A word, Cade," a voice said. It was John Lesley.

Gavin jerked his arm away but did not break his stride. "You have my attention, Bishop. What do you want?"

"You have some influence with Shrewsbury. Can't you convince him to grant the queen more time out of doors? She suffers from lack of fresh air and exercise."

Gavin had heard that the queen was an avid rider and once had loved hunting and hawking. She did seem to be suffering from ill health, often taking to her bed for one complaint or another. Her continual confinement would be hard to bear.

Lesley spoke again. "Her humors are out of balance, Cade. She is melancholic, signifying an excess of black bile. Some days it is difficult for her to rise from her bed." The man's voice had morphed into a whine.

"I'll speak to the earl. But it is entirely his decision," Gavin said.

"Understood. I believe you have more sway with him than anybody else."

"Indeed?" Gavin drawled.

Lesley looked at Gavin with narrowed eyes. "Aye. You know you do. You are an astute observer of both people and events, and I have wondered what your true purpose here is."

"I am equerry to the earl. My purpose is to serve him in whatever way he requires. Most of the time that means ensuring the castle runs as smoothly as possible, so that nothing distracts him from his work for the queen."

"Ah. You refer to the other queen. Elizabeth."

"Aye. That one." Gavin glowered down at Lesley, who was not a tall man. "I've work to do and must see to it. I will speak to Shrewsbury."

"I thank you. I travel to London tomorrow, returning in a sennight."

"Safe journey," Gavin said, and strode away.

After a cursory glance at the papers on his desk, Gavin concluded there was nothing worth his interest. Perhaps he'd see if Shrewsbury was available. He made his way to the earl's office and rapped on the door.

"Come."

Gavin entered and studied the man while he dipped his quill and completed the sentence he'd been composing. George Talbot, the Earl of Shrewsbury, and his wife Bess had been Mary's keepers for a year, having been appointed to the position by Queen Elizabeth. Gavin had only met him a little over a month ago, but Shrewsbury made no secret of the fact he considered the job a great burden. He kept a beautifully bound copy of Morison's *Exhortation* on his desk, perhaps as a reminder that Englishmen should always rally round their monarch.

"Good evening, Cade. Is anything amiss?"

"Not at all, my lord. I merely wish to pass on a request from the good bishop."

Shrewsbury shared Gavin's opinion of Lesley. He snorted and his brows shot up, traveling halfway up his high forehead. He claimed he was losing his hair because of Mary. "What is it now?" Dropping his quill, he leaned back in his chair and focused his attention on Gavin.

"He believes Mary is deprived of fresh air and exercise and is melancholic because of it."

"I have heard that before." He gestured to the other chair. "Be seated, Gavin."

When Gavin was settled, he said, "He has a point, sir. I hate to agree with anything he says, but Mary does suffer from many complaints. An outing a few times a week would do her good and may thwart any escape plots."

The earl ran a hand through the hair he still possessed. "I suppose you have a point. But she would need to be closely guarded."

"Her guards would accompany her, of course. Blake and I as well. She won't like that, but if she wishes to take the air, that is the way it must be."

Shrewsbury rose and went to the mullioned window. Looking out at the wooded slopes, he said, "Do you have something in mind?"

Gavin shrugged. "While the fine weather holds, Mary and her ladies might enjoy an excursion to the river. We could take hampers of food and eat along the banks."

"God's teeth, let's not make this an all-day affair!"

"No, no, a couple of hours should suffice." Gavin paused. He didn't want to press his luck but forged ahead anyway. "In my opinion, sir, we should allow Mary access to nature regularly."

The earl heaved a sigh. "That woman is going to be the death of me. The money it takes to maintain her extravagant way of life! Crystal glassware. Gold plate. Tapestries, chandeliers, her four-course meals. And Elizabeth grants me the paltriest stipend—the rest comes from my own pocket."

"At least you reduced the size of her retinue when you moved her to Tutbury," Gavin said, trying to forestall more complaining. "That has helped to some degree."

Shrewsbury swiveled around and resumed his seat. Voice lowered, he said, "It seems we're making little progress in the Ridolfi matter. I assume you've learned nothing new since Lesley's mention of him in the conversation you overheard."

"If something is afoot, it's moving slowly. But Lesley did tell Mary that Ridolfi was someone they would be able to rely on—a man with connections. Since Lesley is traveling to London, his purpose may be to set things in motion."

"A meeting with our dear friend, the Duke of Norfolk, perhaps? It's possible."

"He'll be back in a sennight and then, with any luck, we'll find out more." Gavin got to his feet, having achieved his ends. "I'll inform the ladies and the cook of the outing. I'd like to do it in the next few days, before the bishop returns from London. And while the weather remains fine."

The earl was squeezing and releasing his folded hands, but looked up. "Do your worst."

Chapter Seven

One morning, when Mary was suffering from a gastric ailment, she summoned Isabel to her private chamber. It was as sumptuous as the outer hall, boasting a tester bed hung with crimson silk, and tapestries on three walls. Isabel recognized what must have been some of the queen's own embroidery on display.

Mary was seated at a dressing table, her maid Aimee arranging her hair. "*Mon petit* Bisou needs you, Bel," Mary said, thrusting the pup into Isabel's arms. "Will you take him out for a bit? Then come back here, to me, *s'il vous plait*."

Isabel donned her cloak and did as Her Majesty requested. When she returned with the dog, Mary lay on her bed propped up with pillows. Dorothy was hovering about her. She always seemed to be the one who looked after Mary when she was struck down by one of her complaints, but now the queen shooed her away. "I wish to talk privately with Bel."

"Yes, madam," Dorothy said. She glared at Isabel on her way to the door.

Mary sighed. "I am so glad you are here, Bel. The others bore me. We have been too much together." She held her hand out to Bel, who initially thought Mary simply wanted to clasp hands. But then Isabel saw that she was in fact handing her a very small item. It was a miniature portrait of an infant.

Isabel studied it, the light dawning. "This must be your son. The little king." She smiled at Mary, who looked pensive and sad. "How old is he?"

"*Oui*. James. He is four, and I have seen him only once in the last two years. They will not allow it, Bel. That is cruel, *non*?"

Returning the portrait to the queen, Isabel said, "Most cruel. May I ask whose decision that was?"

"The Earl of Lennox, his paternal grandfather, is the regent at present, appointed by my cousin, Elizabeth. I imagine they decided jointly. Lennox despises me, for he believes I conspired in the murder of his son. My second husband, Henry, Lord Darnley."

Isabel did not know what to say. She'd not known of this and couldn't imagine Mary conspiring to murder anyone.

"Do not look so shocked, Bel. Have you not heard the rumors?"

"No, Your Majesty. But I have led a very sheltered life and never learned much of the world outside my village."

Mary smiled, though her eyes still looked sad. "It is a long and complicated story, and much of it is best kept private. The crux of it is…Henry's body was found in the garden after a powerful explosion destroyed the house where he'd been staying in Edinburgh. I was at Holyrood with my son at the time."

Isabel wondered why husband and wife had not been together. "The explosion killed him?" Isabel could not interpret Mary's expression, but it seemed guarded. Something flashed in her eyes and vanished. "Why would anyone accuse you, if you were not even there?"

Mary seemed to consider her words. "You will condemn

me when I tell you the rest. After Darnley's death, I was convinced—forced, in truth—by my advisors to wed the Earl of Bothwell." She glanced quickly at Isabel, as though to gauge her thoughts on the matter, then went on. "It was a mere three months after I'd lost Darnley. I-I found out later that the earl truly *was* complicit in Darnley's death. It was assumed, then, that I, too, bore responsibility." Tears trailed down Mary's face, and she brushed them away. "Perhaps I did. Had I obeyed the dictates of my own heart instead of listening to others, I would still be in Scotland with my son."

"Or you and your son may also have been killed by the explosion. It is fortunate you were not there, even if your heart tells you otherwise."

Mary held out her arms, and Isabel went to her. The queen sobbed for some time while Isabel patted her and made soothing sounds. At length, she pulled away. "A handkerchief, please, Bel. In the drawer."

In the sudden silence, excited voices, male and female, drifted into Mary's chamber. She dabbed at her eyes, then said, "We must see what the fuss is about, Bel. Thank you, my dear, for listening to my pathetic chatter."

Isabel, in whom the queen had induced profound feelings of tenderness and warmth, said, "I am honored to have your trust, Your Majesty. Believe me, I will never betray it." Aimee appeared and helped Mary, who looked rather pale and weak, out of bed. The queen's mood seemed improved. Mayhap she had simply needed to unburden herself. She grasped Isabel's arm and they entered the outer chamber together.

"What is all this excitement about, *mes amis*?" Mary asked.

Gavin and Philip Blake stood in the middle of a circle of women, whose excited chattering ceased when they heard the queen's voice. "Your Majesty," Alice said. "Gavin has just informed us we have the earl's permission for an outing!

We're to ride out tomorrow and enjoy an entertainment by the river. Isn't that good news?"

Mary stood there watching the others, stroking Bisou's head. Finally, she said, "Why? Why is this allowed now, when all my previous requests to take the air have been denied? What has changed?"

Voices quieted, and Gavin stepped forward. Sometimes it hurt Isabel just to gaze upon such masculine beauty. It caused stirrings within her that would be best left dormant.

"It's no mystery, Your Majesty. The bishop had a word with me, and I had a word with the earl. It was he who had a change of heart, and you must ask him, if you wish to know why."

Mary looked skeptical and stared at Gavin for so long, Isabel wondered if she would refuse the opportunity. He must have wondered too, because he said, "Madam, have you never heard the expression, 'Don't look a gift horse in the mouth'?"

"Ah, the given horse, *n'est-ce pas*? I should simply be grateful. And I am. Convey my thanks to Shrewsbury." She turned her gaze on the others. "We shall be merry, eat our fill, and enjoy the dying days of autumn."

"Oh, I do hope the day will be fine!" Alice said.

"It shall be," Mary said. "I decree it!"

An evening of cards and a rare early bedtime revealed how eagerly they were all awaiting the day to come.

It rained in the morning, and Isabel assumed their outing would be postponed. But by ten o'clock, the shower had passed and the sun shone strong and bright. An air of anticipation prevailed, and along with it, high spirits. Isabel dressed carefully, after consulting with both Frances and

Ann, in petticoats with a slashed skirt, and an emerald green bodice embroidered with gold threads. She walked with the queen and her entourage to the stables, where they were to meet the men.

"Are we walking to the river?" Isabel asked.

"*Non, ma cherie*, we shall ride." Mary smiled. "We could walk, but then we would have less time to enjoy ourselves."

Isabel sighed. "I do not ride, Your Majesty. I shall go on foot and meet you by the river." This was the cause of much laughter among the other ladies.

With ridicule dripping from her voice, Cecily said, "Aye, we shall see you approaching as we are leaving. That is how long it will take you to walk."

"Do not be ridiculous, Bel. You shall ride with one of the men," Mary said.

Isabel felt her face growing hot, but nodded. She hoped it would be Gavin, but he was intent upon the queen as they approached. He helped Mary to mount, then directed guards to position themselves so there were two at the head of her horse and two at the rear. Gavin and Philip Blake climbed onto their mounts and moved to either side, at a slight remove from the others.

Gavin paid Isabel absolutely no attention. She may as well have been a tree. Or a rock.

The other ladies mounted with the assistance of grooms, while Isabel waited for somebody to notice her. Lady Shrewsbury clucked her disapproval. "We must see to riding instruction for you, Isabel," she said in an annoyed tone. "How your parents could have been so neglectful of your education in womanly pastimes I cannot fathom."

"Mistress," a small voice said, and Bel turned to see who it was. A young, ginger-haired boy, no more than thirteen or fourteen years old, stood there holding the reins of an ancient-looking horse. Isabel could hear the others sniggering, and she wanted more than anything to simply turn around and walk back to the lodging. But that would make her seem an even bigger fool.

"Is this horse for me?" she said to the boy.

"Aye, mistress. I'll help you up."

The animal was so short, Isabel feared her feet would touch the ground. Once she was seated, the boy told her to hook her right knee over the pommel. It felt awkward, but she did it. Then he adjusted the stirrup for her left foot. "I'll lead the horse for you, mistress. Her name's Birdy. She's a sweet lass." At that, the women burst into full-fledged laughter. The men were talking to Mary, and to each other, possibly planning a strategy for protecting the queen if it should come to that, and Isabel didn't think they were paying her any mind.

She looked at the boy. "Very good. Excellent. And what is your name, if I may ask?"

"Arthur, ma'am."

"I'm ready, Arthur."

Lady Shrewsbury signaled, and they set off. In addition to the men surrounding Mary, there were guards at the front and rear of their party. Isabel wasn't sure what they feared, but they certainly seemed prepared for the worst. Some of the guards carried lances. All the men wore rapiers, and no doubt had daggers concealed somewhere on their person.

The ladies soon lost interest in Bel, and although she still clung tightly to the pommel, she began to relax and appreciate her surroundings. Trailing after Arthur, Birdy proved sweet and docile. Heading north, they kept to a trail that led downhill in a meandering fashion, and before too long, Isabel heard the water gurgling in the river. Soon they crossed a stone bridge, the horses' hooves clattering loud enough to scare pheasant and grouse from their hiding places.

"Why are we crossing to the other side of the river?" Isabel asked.

"You'll see," Arthur said. And indeed, she did. On the Tutbury side, the riverbanks were steep, but on the opposite side, the terrain sloped gently downward. There was a wider expanse of grass, which meant more room for them to spread out. And for their horses to graze. Arthur helped Isabel dismount. The ground seemed to sway beneath her at first, but after a few steps, she felt steadier.

Servants were spreading coverlets out on the grass and unloading food and drink. The ladies stood in a circle chattering, but Isabel didn't bother to join them. Instead, she began walking south, following the flow of the river, breathing in the fresh, crisp air. Guards were posted on both sides of the river. They moved back and forth, turning in slow circles, surveying the landscape. Before long, she heard someone calling her name and swiveled around. Arthur was running toward her.

"Mistress, they want you to come back. There's going to be games and such."

Oh, perfect. Another means of humiliation.

"I'll be there in a moment, Arthur, thank you."

"Bel!" Mary said as Isabel approached. "The men are running foot races. You don't want to miss the competition, do you?" Bel sighed in relief—nothing would be required of her except to watch.

Sure enough, some of the men were marking starting and finishing lines with fallen branches, while the others waited. Gavin and Blake walked along the course, picking up and tossing aside anything that might trip up one of the runners. When they finished, they walked over to the ladies. "We need prizes for the winners," Philip said.

"What do you suggest?" Mary asked.

"A kiss from the lady of your choice, Your Majesty," Gavin said. The women tittered. Isabel rolled her eyes.

"What do you think, ladies? Shall we allow this?"

They all squealed in delight, except for Isabel. Really, she would much prefer exploring her surroundings than standing around watching overgrown boys display their physical prowess. The men began shedding their doublets, and she revised her opinion. Perhaps this would be more enjoyable than a walk after all. Isabel followed the other women, who were gathering along the course.

Arthur served as the starter. In the first race, several of the guards and sentries and Philip Blake competed. Isabel was surprised to see that being fleet of foot wasn't the only skill needed. The men shoved, tripped, and grabbed each other—anything to gain an advantage—and the women laughed and cheered them on. Philip eked out a win despite all the trickery. As was to be expected, he requested a kiss from Mary, and she obliged him with a chaste peck on the cheek. He smiled, bowed, and walked back to the men.

The next group lined up, Gavin among them. Isabel couldn't take her eyes off him, and she cheered loudly. Embarrassed, she checked herself. She did not want to be subjected to more teasing. Halfway down the course, one of the other men tripped Gavin, and he fell, sprawling headlong. In the blink of an eye, he picked himself up and flew toward the finish line, passing several other runners. When Gavin drew close to the one who had tripped him, he grabbed the man's shirt and yanked. It was enough for Gavin to win.

Isabel watched as Gavin made himself presentable for his kiss. He smoothed his shirt, wiped his brow, and ran a hand through his hair. Then he walked toward them. He was looking right at Isabel and seemed to be heading directly for her. She could barely breathe. Would he kiss her in front of all these people? Oh, how she wished he would!

At the last moment, he veered off toward Cecily, and Isabel's heart plunged.

"Mistress, a kiss, pray." But in contrast to the innocent

kiss Philip had bestowed upon the queen, Gavin pulled Cecily toward him, wrapped his arms around her, and kissed her on the lips. Her friends laughed and applauded, as did the men who were watching.

Isabel was crushed.

In truth, there was no justification for feeling hurt. Gavin never flirted with her, as he did with the others. He kept her at arm's length during their evening entertainments. It was only when they were alone that he seemed to open up to her. But the way he'd kissed Cecily, her nemesis, wounded her nonetheless. So ardently, as though he savored it. Well. Most likely, he did. When he'd kissed Isabel, it had only been to distract the sentries.

The races continued, and when Philip won a second time, he claimed his prize from Isabel. He leaned in and kissed her cheek, then whispered, "I've been waiting to do that." She was taken aback. A little thrill raced through her. He was a handsome, dashing man, and he'd been hoping to kiss her, Isabel Tait. That made her smile, even though she wished it had been Gavin doing the kissing.

Finally, Mary called a halt. "Enough! It is time to eat. Come, let us sit, and enjoy our repast."

Isabel watched Gavin disappear down the riverbank. In the middle of filling a plate for Mary, she heard the others jeering and whistling. Bel looked up to see Gavin wading into the water. He'd removed his boots and rolled up his hose. Stooping down, he splashed water on his face and under his shirt, which was now soaking wet and clinging to his body like a second skin. Whistles, taunts, and gibes rang out from the men and some of the women, but he ignored them. He disappeared again, finally emerging at the top of the bank, fully dressed and grinning.

"Quite a show, Cade," Philip shouted.

"At least I won't stink, like the rest of you," Gavin said,

shrugging. The others laughed good-naturedly.

Isabel, mesmerized, was still staring at Gavin, clutching the plate she'd been preparing for the queen. He came to her and said, "May I join you, mistress?"

She nearly dropped the plate. "This is, erm, for the queen," she said, tripping over her words.

"I'll fill plates for us both, then," he said.

"Aye. I'll just give this one to Her Majesty." She hurried over to the queen, worried she might ask Isabel to sit with her. But she was engrossed in conversation with Philip and accepted the plate without comment.

Gavin waved, and Isabel sat down beside him on one of the coverlets. He'd chosen a spot away from the others, for which she was grateful. He quickly sliced pieces of fowl and devoured them, then made short work of cheese and bread. "Your pardon," he said around munching. "Running made me ravenous."

Isabel laughed. "I imagine it would. Whereas I've done nothing more strenuous than stand and cheer." She chewed on a slice of fowl, then tore off a piece of bread.

"You bestowed a few kisses, I noticed."

"Aye, but not as energetically as you."

"Ha. I probably should not have done that. Which was precisely why I did."

Isabel gave her head a shake, not understanding.

"Never mind," he said. Using a fork, Gavin dug into a salad of lettuces and citrus. He devoured his food with such gusto, she could satisfy her own appetite by merely watching.

He set aside his plate and knife. "I'm going to refill my tankard. May I get you more ale, Bel?"

"Nay, I'm not yet finished with mine." She watched him walk away, thinking once again how much pleasure she took in his body. If that made her no better than a doxy, so be it.

Chapter Eight

Before refilling his tankard, Gavin visually checked the guard positions. The first sentries had been relieved, and the replacements were all in position. More than once, locals had tried to capture Mary. One time near Carlisle. He wished now he'd asked Ryder about that. He and his father must have had a part in thwarting it.

He thought better of consuming more ale and instead made his way back to Isabel. When he reached her, he stretched out a hand. "Come. Let's walk." He wanted to make sure everything was as it should be. He had an uneasy feeling, based on nothing specific.

She grabbed hold of his hand and got to her feet. They set off walking along the river, and Gavin let his eyes roam the wooded slopes on either side. They would provide excellent cover for a band of determined men.

Isabel, picking up on his uneasiness, said, "Are you worried, Gavin?"

"It's probably nothing. There have been several attempts to rescue Mary by local families of the old religion, so we must be watchful."

"*Hmm*. Has the queen been involved with any of the

perpetrators?"

He snorted. "Mary? No. She seeks help only from other monarchs."

"You say that so scornfully," Isabel said.

He glanced down at Bel, with her innocent eyes. "I'm only speaking the truth. A band of locals who have no clout with anyone would not benefit her. They might get her home to Scotland, but what good would that do? The factions there are warring with each other. If she fell into the wrong hands, it could be disastrous. They held her prisoner before, you know. George helped her escape and make her way to England."

"George? The man who serves her here?"

"The very same."

"And Elizabeth imprisoned her when she set foot on English soil." Isabel began to say more, but hesitated.

"Go on," Gavin said. "I'm listening." Indeed, he very much would like to hear what lies Mary had been filling Isabel's head with.

"Mary misses her son. I think she wants nothing more than to be reunited with him."

"Is that so?"

Isabel did not register the sarcasm. "She showed me a miniature of him. She has not seen him for so long."

She brought that on herself.

How could he draw Isabel out? In her short time here, she'd become Mary's confidant and may have valuable information. Not that she would recognize it as such. He needed to appear sympathetic. "I can understand why she dislikes living here, separated from her son, and from her people as well."

"She hasn't mentioned that specifically."

"Ah." *Because she doesn't give a damn about the Scottish people.*

"Mary seems a bit obsessed with her health, as you know,"

she continued. "She blames her complaints on the foul air." Isabel chuckled. "It does smell disgusting around the castle grounds at times, but in my opinion, her ill health is due more to her imprisonment than anything else. Even though she's surrounded by people, she's lonely. And melancholy."

Gavin was taken aback that Isabel understood this, since she'd had so little time to assess Mary's situation. She made the same point as Lesley. Nevertheless, most of Mary's troubles were self-inflicted. As the Scots queen, she had dived helter-skelter into one crazy scheme after another. From one man's bed to the next. Usually without weighing the consequences to herself or her son.

He gazed down at Isabel, who was speaking again and tugging on his sleeve. "Are you listening, Gavin?"

"Of course." He captured her hand and looped it through his arm.

"She told me about her marriages, how she'd been widowed twice. The tragedy with Lord Darnley. You must admit, her life has been quite sad."

"What did she say of Darnley?"

"That he was killed in an explosion. She loved him, Gavin. She wanted to be there with him, but her advisors forbade it, thank heaven."

Probably because he had the pox. They did not want to risk him passing it to her. Gavin believed Mary hadn't wanted to be anywhere near Darnley at that point because she'd been conspiring to murder him.

But he couldn't say that to Isabel. "Did she tell you about Bothwell?"

"A bit. She said she was forced into a marriage with him very soon after Darnley died."

He would not fill in the missing pieces of the puzzle, because it was not likely Isabel would believe him. That Darnley hadn't been killed in the explosion, but had been strangled. That Mary had been heavy with Bothwell's child—rumored twins—at the time of her marriage to him. If he mentioned the queen's failings, Bel would defend Mary and likely become Gavin's adversary. He did not want that, for any number of reasons. Not the least of which was how much he enjoyed her company. He steered them into a stand of oak and ash. He wanted to caution Isabel not to believe everything Mary said, but he needed to be tactful about it.

He stopped walking and gently turned her to face him. Isabel gazed at him, her look suspicious. "I am glad you have found a friend in Mary, and she in you. Only, based on her history, be aware she's known to play fast and loose with the truth at times."

"About what?"

"Her husbands, for one."

"Are you saying—"

"I am not saying anything in particular. It is a caution, that is all. I don't want to see you hurt."

She studied him, her unusual amber eyes intent upon him, and her gaze softened. He cupped one side of her face with his hand. It fit perfectly into his palm. Her skin was silken. Soft and lush. "Has a man kissed you, Isabel? Before me?"

He could feel her trembling slightly. "Never, sir."

"Then let's try it again. This time not as a ruse."

Her sweetly feminine scent was intoxicating, her mouth lush and inviting. Slowly, Gavin lowered his head and gently brushed her lips with his own. He'd barely gotten started when he heard a disturbance. Shouts. Horses. Screams. *Jesu*, and here he was, attempting to steal a kiss from Isabel, and about as far as he could be from the queen.

He grabbed Isabel's hand and they ran. "Gavin!" She halted abruptly, panting. "I can't keep up with you. Go without me."

"Stay back from the fighting. Do not place yourself in

danger." She nodded, and he left her.

He assessed the situation as he ran. About ten men on horseback, riding wildly through the area where they'd been eating. As they'd rehearsed, several of the guards had encircled Mary and her ladies, while Blake and the remaining guards fought off the band of attacking men. If the invaders felled the guards, they could easily get to Mary. A circle of men around her would be nothing compared to men mounted on large, strong animals. They had multiple advantages: height, speed, and strength. And plenty of weapons, it seemed.

The Tutbury men needed to unseat some of them and then go in for the kill. Gavin, still moving fast, unsheathed his rapier and dashed into the melee. He went after the first man he came to, who made the mistake of leaning down just a tad too far. Dodging the man's weapon, Gavin grabbed his forearm and yanked him off his horse. The fellow hit his head on a rock when he fell, and Gavin didn't wait around to find out if he was dead or merely stunned.

Blake looked as if he was getting the best of his opponent, so Gavin moved on. He spun around when Arthur called to him. The boy was leading Gavin's horse. "Good lad," he said mounting. "Bring horses for the others." Soon most of the Tutbury men were mounted and on a more equal footing with their assailants. They fought tooth and nail with their rapiers, attacking, parrying. In the end, several men dismounted and engaged their opponents in hand-to-hand combat. Eventually, the assailants retreated, many with injuries. Their mission had failed.

In the end, it came down to one horseman. The man who seemed to be the leader. He was riding fast along the riverbank, and to Gavin's horror, Isabel was directly in his path. By God's light, what the hell was she doing? He'd warned her to stay back. She stood her ground, either frozen with fear or too panicked to think. *Get out of the way,*

Bel! Run! Too late, she started toward the riverbank. The horseman slowed enough to bend down and scoop her up. She put up a fight, flailing her arms about, trying to hit him or unseat him, but the man was too strong for her. Meanwhile, Gavin was gaining on them.

The attacker turned and guided his mount down the riverbank and into the water. Gavin followed, finally reaching them. "Let her go, coward," he shouted. Did the man believe Isabel was the queen? "You have the wrong woman."

"Get back or I'll kill her. She's nothing to me." He'd drawn a dagger from his boot.

"You would kill a defenseless woman? She's no part of this," Gavin said. *Whatever "this" is.*

"There's a price on her pretty head." The villain wrapped his fingers in Bel's hair and yanked, and she screamed in pain.

"This lady is not the queen," Gavin said. "See how black her hair is? Queen Mary is known for her red hair."

A look of doubt crossed his face. "I have heard she wears wigs."

Gavin could not believe he was having this discussion. "You pulled her hair hard enough for any wig to be torn off, fool!" How could he stop this man from killing Isabel? Slowly, he edged closer. He heard his men gathering on the riverbank, poised to help. He hoped they had the sense to restrain themselves. Isabel's fate hung in the balance, and he didn't want it tipped in the wrong direction.

The other man's horse became restive, and he dropped his hold on Isabel's hair to seize the reins. "Stay back, or I'll cut her throat," he said. Gavin glanced at Bel, whose eyes were wide with terror. She lay awkwardly in front of the horseman, somehow holding her head and shoulders upright and staring mutely at him. She was blocking any access Gavin had to the man's upper body.

Then, just when Gavin feared the situation was hopeless,

Isabel jerked free and launched herself into the river. At once, the horseman turned his mount and rode through the water toward the opposite bank. Gavin signaled the Tutbury guards to go after him while he saw to Isabel. God's breath, she might have killed herself. Quickly, he dismounted and sloshed his way to her.

"Isabel!" Blood was seeping from a wound on her head. He tried to lift her—goddamn it, with her heavy, sodden clothes, he could barely manage—until she began to wriggle and protest. He chuckled. She was all right, then.

"Cease, Gavin. I'm not hurt. Only soaked."

He set her down gently and he guided her out of the water to the shingle. "Your head is bleeding, sweetheart."

"Aye, I asked the fellow to cut me. I'm frightfully pale, and the blood will brighten me up." Gavin cocked his head at her. "This is no time for joking, Bel."

"'Tis nothing. Only a small cut."

"And you're sure you are not injured anywhere else?"

"My dignity may be a b-bit b-bruised, but that is the extent of the damage. The w-worst is—I'm f-freezing."

Indeed, her teeth were chattering. "We must get you out of this wet clothing posthaste." When he made as though to unfasten her bodice, she protested.

"Just the p-petticoats, Gavin. The ladies will h-help with the rest. I may need to borrow a d-doublet, if any of the men are willing to part with theirs."

"Of course. I'll give you mine." She looked pale and frightened, and Gavin cursed the bastard who'd treated her life so cavalierly.

It was then that they looked up and saw their entire party gazing down on them, the ladies tittering, the men a bit more interested than Gavin liked. "Get back, all of you. Isabel will need help removing the rest of her attire," he said, glaring at the women.

But it was the men who nodded and smiled. "Be glad to help Mistress Isabel remove her clothing," Blake said, smirking.

• • •

"*Putain stupide*," Alice Alymer said as Isabel and Gavin reached the top. Some of the other ladies laughed. Isabel heard it clearly, and she also heard both Mary and Lady Shrewsbury remonstrate with Alice.

From the stricken look on his face, Gavin had heard, too. What had she done to merit being called a whore? Her wet clothes were clinging to her legs, but she couldn't help that. Gavin grasped her elbow and propelled her forward until they located Frances. "Will you help Bel with her apparel?" When Frances nodded, Gavin removed his doublet and handed it to Isabel.

"When you are ready, I'll take you back to the castle." She nodded, just wanting this ordeal to be over with. He went off to speak to the men about their casualties.

While Frances unfastened her bodice, Isabel said, "Is the queen well? They did not hurt her?"

"She is fine. We are all fine. What happened? Why were you standing there, a prime target for that villain?"

A fair question. "I was with Gavin. When we heard the attackers, we ran. I couldn't keep up, so I told him to go ahead." She paused to get straight in her mind exactly what happened next. "I kept to the trees, but couldn't see what was happening. In the end, I risked coming out because everything had quieted. And there he was. That man."

Frances tugged Isabel's bodice off. "I thought he would kill you. Right before our eyes. Weren't you afraid?"

"I was terrified. But I had faith that Gavin would kill the rogue."

"You saved yourself by jumping into the river."

Isabel's shift was drying quickly, and she put Gavin's doublet on over it. She liked it—the feel of something of his on her body. "I never would have summoned the courage to try if he hadn't been there."

"Well, I think you were most brave," Frances said. "And I'm very glad it turned out well."

Gavin rode up beside them. Isabel thanked Frances, then put one foot on top of Gavin's and pushed with the other. He did most of the work, drawing her up to sit in front of him. Without her customary attire, she felt light. He wrapped an arm around her, and she relaxed against him.

After they'd gone a short distance, Isabel said, "Who were those men, Gavin?"

"I don't know, but I intend to find out. Their intent was clear enough."

"To take Mary?"

"Aye. They were local men, not Scots. Tied to the Catholic church and possibly the Scottish lairds, somehow."

"Do you think the queen was involved? Mary, I mean."

"Doubtful, but it will come clear." Tightening his arm resting under her breasts, he said, "Rest, now, Bel. You suffered a great shock."

She had no problem with that suggestion. Between Gavin's warmth and the gentle movement of the horse, Isabel grew sleepy. She dozed the rest of the way back to the castle, waking only when the motion stopped. Gavin helped her down, and Frances walked her to their chamber, where she turned Isabel over to Ann's ministrations. After washing and donning a clean shift, Isabel climbed into bed and slept until supper.

• • •

As soon as Gavin was persuaded Isabel would be well looked after, he headed for Shrewsbury's office. He was not looking forward to informing the earl of what had just transpired, but it had to be done. He rapped on the door and entered.

Shrewsbury had a stack of parchment before him, but looked up immediately. "How was it?" Then he scrunched up his nose. "You smell like the river, Cade."

"We were set upon by a group of men. One of them captured Isabel, and I went into the river after her."

He sprang to his feet. "God's wounds! I knew this was a poor idea. I should never have allowed it! What of Mary?"

"She's fine. Obviously, they were after her, but they came nowhere near her."

"How did this happen? Didn't you have guards posted?"

Gavin, tired to the bone, pointed to the chair. "May I sit before I fall?"

"Pardon, man. Be seated. Tell me everything."

Shrewsbury poured them both a glass of sack, which he kept on a sideboard and had never before offered to Gavin. It went down well. "We had a surfeit of guards. The attackers seemed to come out of nowhere. After we ate, I asked Isabel to accompany me while I surveyed the area. I had a feeling… but nothing I can be specific about." Gavin shifted in his chair. "As we walked, I checked every guard to make sure they were in position. All was as it should have been." He braced himself for the uncomfortable questions he knew would follow.

"Which direction did they come from?"

"I don't know—I couldn't see from where I was. Somewhere behind me. I was slightly to the west of the others. By the time I got to them, the fighting was well underway. Everyone will need to be questioned about what they observed."

"And why were you so far from Mary?"

"As I said, I was checking on the guards. And attempting to quell my uneasy feeling that something was wrong."

"Dallying with Mistress Tait, were you?" The earl was studying him over the rim of his glass and looking none too friendly.

"No!" Gavin said, perhaps rather too vehemently. "As soon as we heard the shouts, we rushed back."

"Did we lose any men?"

"I've not yet made a thorough assessment, but I don't believe so. A few guards were injured. We did our share of damage to the attackers, but they all bolted. We had a narrow escape involving Mistress Tait." Gavin described what had occurred to the earl, leaving out that he'd felt heartsick throughout, sure he was going to lose her.

"Good God, man! Lucky you were there."

"She launched herself off that horse. I don't know how she had the strength for it. I did not save her."

"Nonsense. Without you providing a distraction, she could never have done it."

Gavin shrugged. "Perhaps. When I leave you, I'll gather all the men together and question them. The ladies, including Mary, will need to be questioned as well. I'll write up a report for you after I've learned all I can."

"Any idea who the bastards were?"

"They weren't wearing livery or any identifying badges, but I'd wager they were local." One thought had been preying on Gavin's mind. Something that had occurred to him while he'd ridden home with Isabel resting against him. How had the assailants known they would be on an outing by the river? They would have needed details: exactly when Mary's party would be there, plus their location. Many agreeable sites were located along the Dove where the Tutbury group might have gone for their entertainment.

Someone in Mary's inner circle was an informant.

Gavin left Shrewsbury without mentioning his suspicions. He wanted to question everybody who had been at the river and analyze all the facts before he reached a conclusion. He was more than a little surprised the earl hadn't voiced any suspicions, but he'd caught the man by surprise. Given time, no doubt he would be thinking along the same lines.

Right now, Gavin badly needed to bathe and change. Then he'd begin the work of questioning the guards and sentries and all the members of Mary's entourage. He would need to interrogate her staff as well. Those who hadn't been with them: the cooks, tailors, grooms, and secretaries, among others. He'd need to enlist someone he trusted unequivocally to help. Blake would do. Their priority would be to question everybody who'd been on the outing. Separately.

Servants brought hot water for him, and he eased himself into the copper tub. He felt his weary muscles begin to relax, and his mind, which had been running in all directions, did likewise. For the first time since the incident at the river, he allowed himself to think about Isabel. The lovely, enticing Isabel. The way she'd looked with her wet skirts clinging to her legs. He wished he could have stripped her naked. He wished she were right here in the tub with him. His breeding organ, as Isabel called it, was now standing at attention. God's teeth, how he'd like to bed her.

For the first time since Anna's death, Gavin felt a genuine and powerful attraction to a woman. But Bel was not an experienced female one could dally with. That was for the best, because his wife's actions had hurt him deeply. Loving her had hurt him deeply. After he lost Anna and the babe, he'd merely gone through the motions of living. He hadn't slept, hadn't eaten for days. And then he'd found the letter and the truth. Since then, he'd become an embittered and cynical man.

Had he met the woman who could transform him? Help

him to revert to his better self? The man he used to be?

The timing was abominable. God's breath, he was working for Ryder on the queen's business. Bel was a diversion he couldn't afford. And she was sympathetic to Mary. He would simply have to put her out of his mind. It had been easy enough not to flirt or dance with her, although he'd been sorely tempted. But the times they did meet, just the two of them, were killing him.

No, he would simply have to train himself to view her as he did the other ladies surrounding Mary. Dangerous, and to be avoided at all costs.

Now, he'd best finish bathing and see to the task at hand.

As soon as he was dressed, Gavin sought out Blake and explained what they must do. Over tankards of ale, the two men made a list of essential questions they would pose: Did you speak to anyone outside the castle about today's plans? Has anybody at Tutbury or elsewhere spoken to you about a plot to kidnap the queen? When did you first see the assailants? From what direction did they come? Did you recognize any of them?

"Depending on their answers, other questions may come to mind," Gavin said.

"Aye. Where do you want to do this?"

"Use my office. I'll remain in the presence chamber if Her Majesty allows it."

"We'll not finish today," Blake said. "Nor even tomorrow."

As the equerry to Shrewsbury, Gavin kept a list of every person employed at the castle, and they worked from that. Initially, Gavin would interview Mary, Cecily, Alice, and Lady Shrewsbury. Blake would question Isabel, Dorothy, and Frances, and the lady's maids, Ann and Aimee. Tomorrow,

Gavin would question the guards and sentries, while Blake interviewed the staff.

Before the evening meal, Gavin and Blake headed for the queen's presence chamber, where everyone would be gathered. Pausing on the threshold, he glanced about for Isabel. She wasn't there. She'd been done in after her ordeal at the river. Perhaps she was still resting. There was a buzz of conversation in the room, which Gavin interrupted. "Hear ye, friends!" He had their attention immediately. "I have a charge from the Earl of Shrewsbury to question all of you about today's events. We will commence now, before supper."

"Surely you can't think we had anything to do with it," Cecily said.

Gavin avoided a direct answer. "There are certain facts we must gather from each of you." He turned to Mary. "Your Majesty, if it pleases you, I will interview you here while Cecily, Alice, and Lady Shrewsbury wait in the passage."

"*Mais oui*, Gavin."

"The passage? Why there?" Alice asked. "Where will we sit?"

"Alice, do as Gavin asks. Now." When Mary used that tone, it was to great effect. There were no further questions.

"Dorothy, Frances, come with me, if you please," Blake said. "And we need to collect Ann and Aimee on the way."

The women uttered a fair number of complaints *sotto voce*, but eventually did as they were asked.

After everyone had left, Gavin waited for Mary to arrange herself. Her little spaniel jumped up and nestled against her side. "I knew nothing of this, Gavin," Mary began. "My worst fear is to be kidnaped by a passel of ruffians who won't have any idea of what to do with me."

"I know that, Your Majesty. We believe these were local men whose only interest is the Catholic church—and perhaps restoring you to the Scottish monarchy. Did you speak of the outing to anybody who comes and goes from Tutbury regularly?"

"*Non*. Only among my ladies. There was much excitement about it."

"And you were not aware of any plot to steal you away from here?"

One brow raised, she said, "Had I known of such a thing, I would have informed the earl immediately."

"I suspected as much, but I had to ask." An attempt to smooth ruffled feathers. "When did you first see the assailants, and do you recall from what direction they approached?"

"It was after we'd finished eating. The servants were clearing plates and packing things away." Mary's lips quivered. "I do not mean to embarrass you, but the ladies were speculating about you and Isabel. If you might be feeling *amour* for each other. You were walking together, you see, as you have at other times."

Gavin chose to ignore this, and when he remained silent, Mary continued. "They rode in from the trees behind us. I believe you and Bel were out of sight by then, if that helps pinpoint the time."

"What specifically do you recall?"

Mary rubbed a hand across her forehead. "The guards shouting. That is the first thing that alerted me. Someone yanked me to my feet, and immediately the ladies and I were surrounded by guards. And Philip."

"Nobody thought to mount?"

"It was too late. They were upon us in seconds. Eventually, the Tutbury guards fought them off, you came running and joined in, and that was that. And then the frightening incident with Bel occurred."

"Thank you, Your Majesty. You've been a great help. One last thing. Did you recognize any of the attackers?"

Something flickered in her eyes briefly, but she quickly

recovered and said, "*Non*. No one."

For now, Gavin let it go. Was one of the assailants known to Queen Mary? And if so, why was she lying about it?

"Thank you, Your Majesty. With your permission, I'll question the others here."

"*Mais oui*. I shall be in the privy chamber. We will postpone supper until all of you have returned."

Gavin summoned Cecily, Alice, and Lady Shrewsbury from the passage one at a time. Essentially, they all gave similar responses to Mary's. Lady Shrewsbury spent most of the interview fussing about Isabel and how she'd been foolish enough to land herself in the middle of the fight. Cecily was bored, examining her fingernails throughout. Alice, sarcastic: "Of course I recognized them. They were all my former lovers."

To which Gavin could not resist responding: "Ah. That explains why one of them was shouting, 'Where's that poxy whore?'"

At that, she rose from her chair and exited the room.

To the devil with her. She'd called Isabel a whore, hadn't she? Apparently, she misliked being called one herself.

Chapter Nine

Ann shook Isabel awake. Groggy, she was not immediately aware of her surroundings or the time of day. "We must dress you for dinner, mistress," Ann said. "I've just returned from being questioned by Master Blake."

"What do you mean?"

"About what happened today. Blake and Master Cade are questioning everybody, even the queen."

"I see." The day's events came roaring back. The outing, the walk with Gavin, and the near kiss. Recalling that, she smiled to herself while Ann fastened her gown in the back and then arranged her hair. While seated in front of the mirror, Isabel's run-in with the attacker played in her mind. She'd been terrified. She had tried to keep her eyes focused on Gavin because she'd known his steady, calm gaze would comfort her.

He had called her "sweetheart." That was the best memory of the day, the one she would hold close and save for herself alone. She knew what was coming tonight. The other women would have a field day at her expense, laughing about her falling into the river.

But that precious memory would sustain her. The sound

of Gavin's deep voice when he'd said it. *Sweetheart.*

Sure enough, when she entered the queen's presence chamber, the titters began. And the taunts. "We thought we would have to go to supper without you, Bel," Cecily said. "Have you recovered from your dunking?" She looked at her acolytes, and they all laughed. Then, in French, they began discussing the incident, calling Isabel stupid, clumsy, and unladylike.

"Perhaps she can entertain us tonight with her one talent. How to plant oneself in *la riviere*," Alice said.

Isabel scanned the room. Both the Shrewsburys were present. Gavin stood near the far wall, talking with Philip, but he briefly glanced at her. To her surprise, John Lesley was back from London and seated next to Mary. Was this the moment she'd been waiting for?

The decision was made for her when Gavin said, "Isabel. Isn't there something you would like to say to the queen's ladies?" The room went silent. Isabel felt her heart thumping, so hard she thought perhaps it would knock her over. The women looked uneasily at each other.

"*Absolument.*" Trying to remain composed, she inhaled a deep, steadying breath. In flawless French she unloaded weeks of pent-up anger and disgust. "You see, vixens, I am not so *stupide* as you believe. I have studied French for many years, and therefore heard and understood every insult you uttered about me. Know that I have had many opportunities to observe all of you. Since you thought me dull enough not to understand anything you said or did, you made free with your speech and actions." She paused to draw a deep breath. "Cecily, you are *quelqu'un qui aime manger*. In fact, I have noticed your habit of secreting food in your handkerchief. Especially sweetmeats."

Nervous laughter broke out, and Dorothy said, "I thought you were getting rather portly, Cece!"

"Shut up, Dorothy," Cecily said.

"And Dorothy," Isabel continued. "For you, it is the drink. You have a habit of over imbibing, which is why you are no good at cards. You tend to nod off when you should be paying attention to which suits are being played."

Dorothy glared at Isabel. "You said you did not play cards."

"I don't. But I know how." Isabel had to fight to keep from looking smug.

Alice laughed hardest. "I suspected you of cheating, Dorothy. Every time your head bobbed, I thought you were concealing something in your lap!"

Isabel had saved Alice for last. "You, *mademoiselle*, referred to me earlier today as a *putain stupide*. I've no idea why you would say that of me. Since I have been in residence here, I've observed that you meet a certain guard every day behind the dovecote."

Alice looked like she'd swallowed a toad.

"And I believe I can safely say he is not alone in receiving your attentions, *n'est-ce pas?*"

Alice began to whine. "I am not the only lady—"

But now all the ladies were shouting over each other. Hurling insults that made Isabel blush. She feared it might end in a brawl. Glancing across the room at Gavin, she found him looking back at her with a distinct warmth in his gaze. She smiled, then, and something visceral took flight inside her and rose slowly upward.

Sweetheart. I am your sweetheart.

Mary clapped her hands to stop the commotion. "Ladies, ladies, Isabel has put you in your places, as you so richly deserved. From now on, you shall show her respect, and we will be done with this foolishness. *Oui?*"

Grudgingly, each of the culprits looked to Isabel and muttered apologies. She harbored no illusion that they would treat her any differently unless Mary was present. Even though they would probably try to get back at her for humiliating them, she couldn't help feeling victorious. Now, perhaps she would have a place here. She'd proved she could stand her ground with them. She could be of some help to Mary. And impress Lady Shrewsbury, thus avoiding an unceremonious homecoming.

And she could bask in the warmth of Gavin's smiles. The ones that were just for her.

As the evening wore on, however, Isabel's ebullience faded. The other women were avoiding her, except for Frances, who was nowhere to be seen. Mary and John Lesley had made themselves scarce as well. The overall mood was subdued, probably because of the scare at the river. Gavin, despite looking at her with what she had earlier deemed affection, had ignored her all evening.

A lutenist and flautist entertained them, but nobody suggested dancing. Gavin made the rounds, spending time with each of the ladies before taking his leave early. Isabel wished to do the same, but Philip had cornered her and said he needed to speak to her about the incident at the river. He suggested they talk in the passage, and she agreed.

They settled on a bench set into a window embrasure. "Shrewsbury charged Gavin with getting to the bottom of the assault, and he asked me to help. We are interviewing everybody who was present."

"I see. Ask your questions, Master Blake, but I doubt I will be of any help."

Although he tried to persuade Isabel otherwise, she'd been correct. She had nothing to add to what they already knew. "If you were to see your assailant again, would you recognize him?" Philip asked.

"Aye, I would. I had a good look at him."

"Well, that's something."

After their interview, Isabel bade him good night and retired to her chamber. Frances was not there, but there was nothing unusual about that. Who was her preferred gentleman? Gavin, perhaps. But Frances had disappeared immediately after supper, whereas Gavin had remained with the others until a short time ago.

Ann helped her undress, teasing her when she could not stifle her yawns. "You slept three hours this afternoon, mistress. How can you be drowsy?"

"My day was quite eventful. That is my only excuse."

Once in bed, Isabel allowed the hurt she'd buried to surface. How could Gavin call her "sweetheart" one moment and act as if she were nothing more than a speck of lint on his doublet the next? She must have misread him. He simply thought of her as a friend. A young lady who needed his guidance and protection.

But he'd said he wanted to kiss her. He would have kissed her, had the attack not interrupted them. Isabel knew she would have allowed it, because she was in no doubt about her attraction to him. If she did not wish to make a fool of herself, she'd best put him out of her mind. Especially since she had finally managed to gain the grudging respect of the others.

All things considered, she would much prefer the ladies hating her than losing Gavin's regard. But she did not seem to have a choice.

• • •

By the time Gavin made his way outside, darkness had fallen. Instead of retiring, he opted to take the night air by traversing the entire perimeter of the inner bailey. He walked briskly and soon approached the receiver's lodging near the gate. Currently, the building was used to house guests and had stood vacant since Gavin had been at Tutbury. Candlelight glowed in one of the windows, which puzzled him. As far as he knew, there were no visitors at the castle at present. The stables were adjacent, and he stuck his head inside to see if an unfamiliar horse was housed there. Secured within one of the stalls was a magnificent-looking stallion munching on oats, a horse that did not belong to anyone at Tutbury. Gavin called for the stable boy, who eventually appeared, rubbing sleep from his eyes.

"Whose horse is this, Tobias?"

"Don't know, Master Cade. The bishop brought him in."

"But it's not his mount?"

"Nay, sir, he fetched his own horse in first."

"Very well, Tobias." He ruffled the lad's hair. "Return to your bed."

Most likely, there was nothing amiss. But after the scare they'd had today, Gavin wasn't taking any chances. Obviously, Lesley knew whose horse he'd led into the stables. Had he informed Shrewsbury? Why had this guest not been invited to dine with the rest of them? He stole softly to the receiver's lodging and pushed the door open. All seemed quiet, but after a moment, voices from a chamber at the far end of the hall drifted his way. From this distance, he could not tell if they were male or female.

Gavin glanced around the hall and saw nothing save darkness. Judging it to be safe, he crept toward the voices. The chamber door was partially open, the odor of fresh rush mats scenting the air. He stopped just short of the entry, straining to identify the speakers. One male and one female, and in a moment, he recognized the woman's voice. It belonged to none other than Mary, the Scots queen. But to whom was she speaking?

"Our marriage will go forward?" she asked.

Ah. Now Gavin could put a name to the other person. *The Duke of Norfolk.* Under house arrest in London since his release from the Tower, miraculously, he was here at Tutbury Castle in Staffordshire.

"I am committed to this scheme, although it disturbs my sleep," the duke said. "The risks are great. If we fail, our lives will be forfeit. But if all goes according to plan, we will steal the throne out from under Elizabeth. You will be crowned queen, and I shall become your consort. But we'll petition Parliament to name me king and thus rule jointly."

The duke paused. "I must have your agreement on that."

Mary must have nodded, because Gavin didn't hear a response.

This was no great romance. They were marrying for the same reasons most aristocrats did. To combine property and fortune—but on a far grander scale.

His tone jocular, the duke said, "Are you sure you wish to become my fourth wife? All my previous wives have died young."

Mary responded, her voice too soft for Gavin to hear. Then, "What of Scotland?"

"I fear they will not want you any more than they do at present. Probably less. It matters not. England is the real prize. And you may bring the Scottish lords round your thumb with time."

"How do matters proceed from here?"

"Lesley brought Ridolfi to meet me in London. Twice," Norfolk said. "I have agreed to his plan. Indeed, I signed a verbal agreement witnessed by Lesley and two servants, the details of which…"

Gavin heard no more. He was struck on the back of the head, and darkness, like an eerie, looming presence, engulfed him.

The rippling and gurgling of the river brought him to his senses. He was bound hand and foot, and about his waist was a thick rope, tethering him to...something immovable. Cautiously, he opened his eyes and tried to determine exactly where he was. Moving his head delivered waves of excruciating pain. The echo of voices vibrated in his ears. Mary and Norfolk. Thinking proved too much for him, and for the moment, he surrendered to the agonizing pain. Resting his head on the soft grass, he fell unconscious once more.

Later, he woke again, this time feeling a bit less woozy. The pain had subsided somewhat. Where was he? *Think, man.* He lifted his head, the only part of his body he could move, and studied his surroundings. A half-moon provided enough light for him to quickly determine his location, and what he discovered was not encouraging.

He was staked on the bank of the weir, along the Dove. In the past, the river had filled it, and it was used as a fish pond. But now it was dammed with brush and timber. The water had slowly drained or evaporated. Whoever had placed him there had opened the dam, so that the water level was now rising at an alarming rate. He could already feel its icy touch on his feet and ankles.

Jesu. Someone wants me dead.

Now was not the time to figure out who. It was imperative, if he did not wish to drown, that he think of a way to free himself. If only he could unbind his hands, but they were tied so tightly it would be a waste of time and effort to try. He strained to thrust himself upward with his feet, but, bound together as they were, he couldn't gain any traction.

He needed to get his boots off. That might loosen the bindings sufficiently for him to extricate his feet and ankles. The rope did not seem as tight as the one binding his hands. The cold, merciless water was now rising over his lower legs, complicating his efforts. Squeezing his legs together, he pushed at the heel of one boot with the toe of the other, and felt his heel release from the boot's hold on it. He knocked the boot against the ground, but it was full of water, heavy and unwieldy. The swiftly rising water had now reached his waist, and with it came an entire swarm of eels darting and slithering around him. God's mercy, that was all he needed.

He was running out of time.

While he worked at freeing himself, Isabel's face popped into his head. Her bottomless brown eyes seemed to be urging him on. What a fool he'd been, thinking to simply cut her from his life. His future. If he did not survive, he'd go to his death regretting that on his last night as a mortal being, he had made up his mind to abandon the smartest, loveliest, and bravest woman he had ever known.

· · ·

Isabel could not settle. Earlier, she had feigned sleep when Frances entered the room and quickly left again. After endlessly squirming about, Isabel threw back the covers and pulled on a dressing gown. Cracking open the door, she made certain the passage was empty and then stole into it. With no destination in mind, she walked toward the far end of the corridor, away from the queen's chambers. Isabel had no desire to be questioned by the guards who stood outside Mary's door.

She had not gone more than a few steps when she heard footsteps approaching. Hastily, she ducked into an alcove and behind a pedestal bearing a bust of Caesar. Isabel drew herself in, making her form as small as possible and praying she would not be seen. There were two people talking animatedly. One was Frances; the other, John Lesley. Unfortunately, she could not make out what they were saying—they passed too quickly. Isabel fully expected Frances to enter their chamber, but she did not. She walked on with Lesley, past Mary's rooms. Lesley paused to speak to one of the guards. Isabel thought something changed hands between them, but she couldn't be sure because of the dim light.

Where had Frances and Lesley come from? Isabel had never ventured to the far end of the passage, having always assumed it was off limits. She remained crouched down in her hiding place until she was certain no one was about, then proceeded to investigate. She peeked into three small chambers, all of which appeared to be storage rooms. One held pieces of furniture, another, boxes of candles, extra plate, and table linens. In the third, wardrobes lined up along the walls. Isabel suspected they held pieces of Mary's extensive wardrobe. At the end of the passage, a door led outside. It was not locked, and she opened it easily. A set of stairs marched down the far end of the building. Wasn't it risky for the door to remain unlocked without a guard posted?

Then a thought occurred to her. Perhaps it *was* kept locked, but Lesley had requested that it remain unlocked tonight, knowing he would be out late and would need to get back in. Which, in turn, meant he'd bribed one or more of the guards.

That was what had changed hands. Lesley was passing coin to the guard who'd left the door unlocked!

Isabel stepped back inside and hurried to her chamber. No doubt the guard would need to lock the door, and she didn't want to be caught lurking about. Should she report this to someone? Tomorrow, she would seek counsel from Lady Shrewsbury and do as she advised.

Chapter Ten

The water, chest high now, held Gavin in its thrall as much as the ropes that bound him. Fearing imminent death, he began to pray. First, he asked God to spare his life. Were he a wagering man, he would say the odds in favor of that were nil. Why should He? Gavin was no exemplar of humanity. He wasn't truly worth saving, was he?

Given the amount of water flowing over him, he wasn't worried about being cleansed of his sins, which were legion. His worst, perhaps, was his unforgiving attitude toward Anna, his wife, after he'd discovered her perfidy. He forgave her now. Gavin had always thought she loved him, and it seemed he would go to his death never knowing what he'd done that had caused her to be unfaithful.

Suddenly, his left boot came free and floated away, allowing him a few inches of extra space to work both feet from the bindings. Feeling a glimmer of hope—maybe the Lord thought better of him than he'd guessed—he began the slow, arduous work of pushing himself up the bank. Unfortunately, when he reached the top, he was still tethered to the stake. Hunkering down with his back to it, he was able to grasp it with his bound hands. Whoever masterminded this foul deed had been in a hurry. The stake had not been pounded in very deep and, once he had hold of it, came loose easily.

Cautiously, Gavin got to his feet. Dragging the stake along behind him, he moved away from the weir and made his way to a little-used trail, deeming it safest. His greatest fear was that someone was keeping watch, to make sure their plan to kill him succeeded. But Gavin refused to give in to that fear. Hiding until morning was not an option. He needed to get to the earl as quickly as possible and report the evening's shocking discoveries. After he'd walked for some time, he stopped, frustrated with his slow progress. The heavy stake was continually catching on fallen branches and foliage. But with his hands bound, he couldn't rid himself of it.

As he neared the castle grounds, the first trace of dawn faintly lit the eastern sky. Gavin looked around for sentries. He did not dare enter through the main gate, because it was too close to the receiver's lodging. Chances were good that the Duke of Norfolk and his men were long gone, but Gavin didn't want to risk it. Some sections of the outer precinct were in ruins, and he headed for one of them.

When he reached it, he paused and surveyed his surroundings. A couple of sentries were walking around the perimeter of the inner bailey some distance away, so it was an opportune moment to reenter the castle grounds. He would rather not be forced to explain what had happened to him. The fewer people who knew, the better. He climbed through the ruins toward the old fortification, no longer in use. An opening into the inner bailey existed there, one very few people knew of.

Once in, Gavin moved as swiftly as he could across the expansive area to the earl's residence. He waited until the sentries had reached the farthest point in their rounds before kicking the door. That should buy him some time before they came to investigate the commotion. Just when he feared they'd be upon him before he was safely inside, the earl's man opened the door. "Will, it's Gavin Cade. Pray let me in. 'Tis urgent."

Astonished, the servant stepped aside, Gavin entered, and the door slammed shut in the nick of time.

"Cut these ropes off me." He looked up to see Shrewsbury, clad in a nightshirt and cap, hastening toward him.

"By God's light, man! What has happened to you?"

Safe at last, Gavin began to shiver with cold. "Before we talk, may I trouble you for a hot bath and a change of clothes?"

. . .

Isabel woke up later than usual. A bit bleary from her restless night, she poured water into her basin and, after washing her face, felt better. She called for Ann to help her dress. As usual, Frances did not stir, and Bel wondered when the other woman had come to bed.

The queen was at her usual spot in the dining chamber. Before her rested a tankard of ale and a plate of bread, butter, and dried apples. But she was not eating, only staring toward the far wall at an embroidered hanging she and Lady Shrewsbury had recently completed. It was mystifying to Isabel—two women upon the wheels of fortune, one holding a lance, and the other a cornucopia, with the inscription *Fortinae Comites.* Companions of fortune. Mary did not look at Isabel, but seemed almost hypnotized by the embroidered work.

Finally, Isabel said, "*Bonjour*, Your Majesty."

"*Bonjour*, Bel." Mary gestured to the tapestry. "My cousin, the queen of England, holds my fortune in her hands." Suddenly, she snapped her head toward Isabel. "Why does she keep me here, in this forbidding stronghold, as though I were someone of no consequence? And why will she not see me?"

Unbidden, one of Mary's gentlemen attendants set a plate of bread, cheese, and fruit in front of Bel, and she nodded her thanks. "Perhaps she is afraid of you, madam."

Mary waved an impatient hand through the air. "Bah. It is I who live in fear. Why would she fear me?"

"You are beautiful, younger than she, and have a claim on the throne. Considering all that, she may not only fear you, but be jealous of you, too."

Mary's eyes lit up at Bel's compliments. "*Merci, ma chere Bel*. But I am no threat to her presently. If I succeed her, so what? She will be dead."

Even though it was true, Isabel drew back from the harsh pronouncement. "But the queen cares a great deal about who succeeds her."

"Precisely! By rights, it should be me. Why does she hate that?" The queen sighed deeply. "If it weren't for all the unfair and unjust things that have been done to me, I would be in Scotland, ruling over my people, my three children by my side."

Three children? Isabel thought she had but the one son, the little king, James.

"I have shocked you again, Bel. I was with child when I was taken prisoner in Scotland and sent to Lochleven Castle. I lost the child, which turned out to be not one child, but two. Twins. It is sad, *oui*?"

"I-I didn't know. I am heartily sorry, Your Majesty." She wanted to ask who the father of the babes was, but that would be impertinent.

Mary ignored Isabel's expression of sympathy. "It was not my choice to abdicate. I was forced to sign the paper someone else—my brother, Moray, no doubt—had written. If only I could return to Scotland as monarch, perhaps I could be reunited with my son and find happiness. I would not obsess over my cousin Elizabeth."

From what Bel knew of it, the political situation in Scotland was fraught, the little king's supporters sparring constantly with Mary's. Bel thought Mary's return would be unlikely in the near future. Possibly never. But she held her tongue.

Just then, a man Bel had never seen before approached. A bit stooped, he stiffly bowed to the queen, and she kissed his ring. "May I join you, Your Majesty?"

"Pray, do," Mary said. When he went off to fill a plate, she said, "That is John Morton. He is my priest and confessor."

Isabel, who had just bitten off a piece of bread, choked. A Catholic priest, in residence at Tutbury? Of course, there was the bishop, but his job was envoy to Queen Elizabeth. Nobody thought of him as a priest.

"Do not be alarmed. Shrewsbury has given permission for me to practice my religion."

Upon his return, Mary introduced Isabel to Father Morton. He greeted her politely, but focused all his fawning attention on the queen. Isabel quickly finished eating and excused herself.

She intended to visit Lady Shrewsbury without delay.

...

"Someone tried to kill me."

Robed in a dressing gown belonging to the earl, Gavin sat on a comfortable, upholstered chair, sipping hot spiced wine. He'd had a bath, and Shrewsbury's man had bandaged his head. Right after his arrival at the residence, before his bath, Gavin told the earl that Norfolk had been on the castle grounds. The earl sent guards to the receiver's lodging, but the duke had already departed on his fine stallion. The men guarding Mary said nobody had been in or out all evening, and the queen was still sleeping. Somebody was lying. They would question Mary in the morning, and Gavin wanted to be present to gauge her reaction.

While Gavin had bathed, the earl dressed, although his hair was rumpled and his beard was unkempt. "You're sure?"

Gavin chortled. "I'd been knocked unconscious. When I regained my senses, I was staked to the bank of the old weir. The culprit had opened the dam, and the water had risen all the way to my chin before I worked myself free." He paused for a swallow of wine. "So I think there can be no doubt that whoever did this wanted me dead."

"God's breath. How did it happen? You'd better tell me everything." He tugged at his beard, a habit he engaged in during anxious moments. "Do you know who 'they' are?"

"I could speculate, but it would be guesswork at this juncture."

Gavin related the story of his discovery of Norfolk and Mary. "They discussed marrying, deposing Elizabeth, and ruling together. They had only just mentioned Ridolfi when I was struck on the head. Norfolk said Lesley had brought the man twice to the duke for consultation. Unfortunately, I missed learning the particulars."

"Treason! I'll send a messenger to London immediately. But I am afraid without proof, nothing will be done. Norfolk will have arrived back at his home along the Thames before our man can get to Cecil. He will say he never left, and his minions will affirm it."

Gavin nodded. "I gathered that. But sir, I believe if we are vigilant, we may discover more right here at Tutbury."

"Explain."

"I did not mention my concerns yesterday because I was not yet persuaded. But now I am. First, does it not strike you as odd that the attack at the river occurred on the same day of the duke's visit?"

"Speak plainly, Cade," Shrewsbury said.

Gavin leaned forward. "The attack was a smokescreen. A distraction. No real harm was done. No men lost, or badly injured. But what were we all preoccupied with last night? The attack. And, it's my belief the duke timed his arrival here with the outing, even with the attack, so that he might sneak in without being seen." Gavin paused to collect his thoughts. "In fact, I would not be surprised to discover the attackers were Norfolk's men and had no intention of taking Mary. When I asked her if she recognized any of them, an odd look passed over her face, and I had a strong sense she was lying."

"Which means—"

"She could be passing messages to Norfolk through one of these men."

Shrewsbury's brows zigzagged together. "But we read all her correspondence."

"So we do, all that we're aware of. This was all timed too perfectly for it not to have been prearranged." Gavin's head was beginning to ache. He badly needed sleep, but there was one more argument he wished to present. "Sir. Rather than questioning Mary, I believe we should keep this to ourselves for the time being. They—the architects of all this mischief—have no way of knowing what I heard before I was rendered unconscious. If we interview Mary, of necessity we'll lay bare all we know. Mary, Lesley, and whoever else may be involved will deny everything, and we'll learn nothing more."

"Whereas if we simply go about our business, we may catch them out."

"Precisely."

Shrewsbury chuckled. "When you make an appearance this evening, let us see who turns pale with shock."

"Indeed," Gavin said.

• • •

Isabel was admitted to the Shrewsbury residence by a servant, who said he would inform Lady Shrewsbury of her arrival. He showed Isabel to a small anteroom to wait. The chamber she occupied was adjacent to a withdrawing room, and she heard voices emanating from it. One was the earl's, and the other belonged to Gavin. It was early for him to be here, but then the same could be said of her.

While she waited, Gavin's words about Mary echoed in her mind. That she played fast and loose with the truth. To Isabel, it appeared that she sometimes told partial truths, possibly unaware she was doing so. Previously, Mary had spoken to Isabel about her son, James. But she'd never mentioned the children she'd lost until this morning. And thus far, she had said very little about the Earl of Bothwell, who must be the father of the dead babes. Were lies by omission actual lies?

Lady Shrewsbury swept into the small chamber. "Good morrow, Isabel. Be seated. Why have you come?"

Isabel had assumed they would adjourn to a larger, more comfortable room, but evidently, the lady wanted the interview to be of short duration.

"I could not sleep last night," she began.

"Understandable, after what you endured yesterday at the hands of that villain."

"Aye." Isabel described her chance sighting of Frances and Lesley and her discovery that the door at the end of the hallway was unlocked. Then she waited for a response.

Bess's brow furrowed, and she said nothing for a time. At last she spoke, hesitantly. "Frances and Lesley, as unlikely as it may seem, are…involved, for lack of a better term." Fussing with her skirts, Lady Shrewsbury continued. "I believe Frances is quite smitten and would do whatever he asked to gain his affection."

Isabel was shocked. She'd caught Lesley with Cecily and Ann, but Frances had not been part of the *menage*. Most nights, she was aware that Frances crawled into bed in the small hours of the morning. Was she spending all those nights with John Lesley? Bel could hardly credit it. "I see," she choked out. So it had simply been a romantic liaison she'd come upon, nothing more sinister than that. Recalling it, Bel believed their demeanor suggested conspiracy rather than romance. But if Lady Shrewsbury wished to discount it, who was she to argue?

"Does the unlocked door not disturb you, madam? And the fact that the guards did not stop Lesley and Frances?"

"I imagine Lesley requested it remain unlocked until he alerted the guards he was safely inside the lodging. I'm sure they locked it then." Twisting the wedding ring she wore, she paused a moment. "As for the guards, Isabel, they are probably accustomed to seeing the two together and do not suspect them of any nefarious deeds."

"But the door would have been unlocked for some time." Bel wasn't sure why she was persisting in this, but after what had happened yesterday, weren't unlocked doors simply inviting trouble? Bess herself, on the way to Tutbury, had urged Bel to come forward if anything untoward occurred. Now it was as if she'd never said it.

Ignoring Isabel's last statement, Lady Shrewsbury rose, saying, "If there is nothing else..."

Isabel got to her feet and curtsied. "My lady." The same servant who'd let her in escorted her to the door. She walked out into the bailey, pondering her strange encounter with the earl's wife, and smack into Gavin. Before she could apologize, he'd spun around and knocked her to the ground.

Chapter Eleven

Isabel struggled for breath, for the great lummox had knocked it right out of her. "Gavin! What do you mean by this? Get off me!" He raised up, and she could see right into his penetrating blue eyes.

"Isabel! God's mercy. I beg your pardon." He quickly rolled off her. "Have I injured you?"

"I'm not sure."

"Can you sit up? Allow me to help you."

Chuckling, Isabel said, "I am not sure that is a good idea, Master Cade." She examined his face, still close enough that she noticed he sported a few cuts and bruises. Crouching down, he slid an arm beneath her shoulders and lifted her to a sitting position.

"Stay there until you catch your breath," he said. "Your head—" He ran his fingers over her scalp, and she fought the desire to burrow into his chest. "I don't feel any wounds, and there is no blood."

"I'm fine. The ground was soft. It was only that I couldn't breathe for a moment. And of course, you scared me to death." She inhaled deeply and exhaled a long breath. "Why did you attack me?"

He raised a quizzical brow. "Why did you bump into me?"

"You have me there. I had a meeting with Lady Shrewsbury, and I was mulling over what we discussed. Her reaction to what I'd told her."

Gavin held on to her arms and helped her to stand. "Which was?" Glancing around, he said, "Do you feel well enough to walk?"

"I think so."

"Then let's move on." Wasting no time, he steered her toward the ruins of the old fortification.

"Where are we going? I should return to the lodging."

"Pray come with me for a little longer. We'll be quick about it."

Isabel wondered why they couldn't talk on the way to the lodging, but she wasn't in a mood to argue. Gavin looked a bit worse for wear. Aside from the cuts and bruises, his clothing did not fit well—his shoulders were straining his doublet. They sat down on a set of crumbling steps.

"Why were you meeting with Lady Shrewsbury?" he asked.

"It was nothing of any import. She did not believe so, in any case, and who am I to gainsay her?"

"It was important enough for you to think so hard about, you crashed into me."

"And you tackled me as though you thought me an assassin."

At that he put his head in his hands and did not look up for some time. "Gavin?" Maybe she'd better answer his question. "I couldn't sleep last night. I left my chamber to walk a bit, but no sooner had I taken a few steps than I heard voices. For some reason, I was frightened, so I ducked behind that bust of Caesar."

She had his attention now. "Go on."

"It was Frances and Lesley. They were talking rapidly, as though excited about something. They'd come in through an unlocked door at the far end of the hall. I expected Frances to enter our chamber, but instead, after stopping to speak to one of the guards, they went downstairs together."

"Did you hear anything of their conversation?"

She shook her head. "I am afraid not. Their voices were low and they had passed me within seconds. But Gavin, I think Lesley bribed the guard to keep the door unlocked. Something changed hands between them."

He looked grim. "God's wounds. Do you know which guard it was?"

"Let me think." Isabel pictured the dark passage, but all she could see was Frances and Lesley. She'd heard the guard's voice, but she could not identify it. She did know any of them well enough. "I'm sorry, but no."

After searching her face for a moment, he spoke. "If I share a secret with you, do you swear to tell nobody else? Not Mary, or any of her ladies. Nor any of the men, for that matter. No one. This must remain confidential. My life—and your own—may depend on it."

Taken aback, Isabel agreed at once. He would not ask this of her over something trivial.

"There was an attempt on my life last night."

Thinking she'd misunderstood, Isabel said, "That is not funny, Gavin. I'm in no state for a jest right now."

Gavin laughed bitterly. "Would that it was a jest." A cold breeze whistled through the ruins, and he sprang to his feet. "Hold a moment." Isabel watched as he prowled about, checking every nook and cranny where someone might be hiding.

Returning, he resumed his seat beside her. Worry pinched his brow, and she no longer doubted his sincerity. Laying a hand on his arm, she said, "I do beg your pardon.

Tell me what happened."

Before she could remove her hand, Gavin enfolded it in his own. He told a tale so dastardly, she was thunderstruck. He'd been staked to the bank of the weir and left to drown.

"You nearly died! What if you hadn't been able to...to extricate yourself?" Her voice had risen slightly, and he put a finger to his lips to remind her to speak softly. The thought of Gavin dying, or even simply going away, left an empty place in her heart.

"I would have drowned. There is no question about that."

"Everybody would have known you'd been murdered, and the perpetrators eventually found out."

"Nay, I believe their plan was to return, untie me, and remove the stake. That way it would have seemed like an accident. They would put it about that I was drunk, and that was why I retired early. In my cups, I went walking along the river and fell into the weir."

"So many holes in that story. You're never intoxicated, and even if you were, you would not be stupid enough to venture all the way to the river. And how would the damn miraculously have opened?"

Gavin shrugged. "It is a moot point, since I survived."

Isabel quieted, thinking. "Who would want you dead?"

He did not speak immediately. At length, he said, "John Lesley is at the top of my list."

"The bishop?" She could not keep the skepticism from her voice. "That requires explanation."

Frowning, he said, "It is a complex situation, Bel. Forgive me, but I cannot reveal all the details. It is better that you not know."

She quirked a corner of her mouth. "Someone nearly killed you, and you cannot tell me anything of your chief suspect? Why would it endanger me? I barely speak to anybody."

"You speak to Mary."

"She tells me of her fondest hopes and of her unhappy past. This morning, she expressed her frustration with Elizabeth. That is all. She has no curiosity about me or my life, other than teasing me occasionally." Isabel looked askance at him. "Surely Mary had no part in this deed."

Gavin didn't argue the point. He finally relinquished her hand, and she felt the loss of his touch keenly. Frustrated, Isabel could see he would likely say no more.

"What did Lady Shrewsbury say when you told her about last night?"

"She was oddly calm about it. It seems Frances and Lesley are engaging in a *liaison.*" Bel chuckled. "As unlikely as that seems. I challenged her about the fact that the door at the end of the passage had been unlocked for quite some time, but she did not seem to agree that was worrisome."

"Lady Shrewsbury is close with Mary and loath to believe there may be anything devious occurring. In her mind, an association with Mary glorifies her own reputation. Do you credit that, Bel?" Gavin asked. "A love affair between Frances and Lesley?"

"I confess I do not know what to think. Given what I saw last night, they may have been involved in the attempt to kill you."

"It is indeed suspicious that they were outside at such a late hour. Lovers would have been inside engaged in... something else."

"What will you do now?"

"Watch. Wait. Hope they make a mistake." He rose and, taking hold of her hands, pulled her up beside him. "One more thing before I let you go. Be wary and use discretion in what you say to the queen. She has some involvement, if not in the attempt on my life, then in the incident at the river. You must not confide in her, even if she demands it."

"What? In the attack? I can't accept that. And if she were involved, I cannot believe she is other than an unwilling dupe."

"You underestimate her."

"And you are too willing to pronounce her guilty."

Gavin heaved a sigh and glanced off to one side. He was annoyed with her, that much was obvious. "You must return before your lengthy absence is noted. We'll talk more of this another time." He paused, then said, "We must not be seen together. You leave first."

She nodded. "You will sleep now?"

He laughed softly. "That is all I am fit for at present." He brushed a hand across her cheek. "Take care, dearest Isabel."

• • •

When Gavin entered Mary's presence chamber before dinner, heads swiveled in his direction. To his dismay, he detected no sign of shock or undue surprise in anyone's expression. Someone must have seen him earlier and mentioned it in passing—or reported it to Lesley. If indeed Lesley was the master of this operation. But it was obvious that if Gavin's assailant was among those gathered here, he was already aware that Gavin had not drowned in the weir.

After parting from Isabel, he'd gone to his residence and slept most of the afternoon. His servant had roused him in time to bathe and dress for dinner. He'd not had sufficient time to organize his disparate thoughts about all that had occurred the previous day, and knew only two facts for a certainty: someone wanted him dead, and Mary and Norfolk were conspiring to overthrow the queen. Now the real work of finding evidence to assign guilt would begin. Gavin must sort out, among all the sycophants, hangers-on, ladies-in-waiting, guards, and staff, who could be trusted.

Gavin trusted Isabel implicitly, but she worried him. She was so open, so naive. In truth, it was her advocacy of Mary's innocence that worried him. Bel possessed an unshakeable faith in the woman. He hated the idea of using her; nonetheless, Bel's close connection to the queen would force his hand. Bright and perceptive, Isabel would catch on if he pushed her too far, so he would need to tread lightly. And then there was the matter of his attraction to her. After almost losing his life, he no longer wished to fight it. She was looking particularly lovely tonight, her glorious hair flowing around her shoulders, her creamy skin glowing in the candlelight. How he would love to bare that skin, caress those shoulders.

Another day, man. Focus. He'd been hovering in the entrance for too long. He accepted a glass of wine from a servant before crossing the room.

"Well met, Cade. Glad you could rouse yourself to join us," Philip Blake said.

"I had some inventory lists to check," he lied. "The supplier had to be on his way, so I couldn't put it off."

"Have you learned anything about who attacked us yesterday, Gavin?" Dorothy asked.

"No. We're still investigating." Gavin noticed Shrewsbury in conversation with the queen, which meant Isabel now sat alone. "Pardon me," he said, and made his way to her.

He bowed. "Good even, Isabel."

She rose and curtsied. "Master Cade." Glancing about to ensure nobody was close enough to overhear, she said, "You appear recovered from your ordeal."

"'Sorrow can be alleviated by good sleep, a bath, and a glass of wine,'" he said, raising his glass. "Now I've had all three."

"I have heard that somewhere before," she said, eyeing him.

Gavin laughed. "Indeed, it is not original with me. Thomas Aquinas said it first."

The queen signaled that dinner would soon be served, and Gavin offered Isabel his arm. "May I have the honor?"

Once in the dining chamber, Mary said, "Bel, sit beside me, *s'il vous plaît*!"

Isabel, caught off guard, momentarily looked dismayed, but quickly flashed a smile. "*Bien sûr*, Your Majesty."

God's wounds, couldn't the queen leave Isabel in peace? Gavin pulled out her chair and excused himself. Unfortunately, the only place left at the long table was between Frances and Lesley. He had no heart for conversing with either of them. Come to think of it, though, he might be able to goad Lesley into making a mistake or revealing something unintentionally.

"I understand there was quite a fracas at the river yesterday," Lesley said to Gavin.

Ah, just the opening he needed.

"That's so. I took your suggestion to heart, that Queen Mary needed fresh air and exercise, and mark the result. Shrewsbury will probably not allow it again."

"That would be a pity for Mary."

Gavin shrugged noncommittally. "I've been wondering how the villains knew not only when, but where the outing would take place," he said.

"Perhaps they'd been keeping watch."

Gavin deftly sliced a piece of salmon from its skin and ate it. "Anything is possible, I suppose."

"Who were they? Any idea?"

After a swallow of wine, Gavin said, "I thought perhaps you might have an idea. As Mary's close advisor and friend, you must keep one eye trained on the machinations swirling around her. What say you, sir?"

Next to him, Frances inhaled sharply. From what Gavin

had observed since coming to Tutbury, nobody challenged the bishop.

Lesley's ruddy complexion seemed to pale. "I? I would have no notions of such schemes, Master Cade. Take care who you are accusing."

"'Tis not an accusation, sir, merely a question. You are close to the queen; therefore, you are under some obligation to discover whether any harm is meant her." When Lesley began to sputter and growl, Gavin nearly laughed.

"Protecting Mary is Shrewsbury's—and your—job. Not mine. I am no food-taster, sir, nor common retainer who follows her about checking behind chairs and under beds."

"I never said you were, Bishop." God's light, Gavin had truly rattled the fellow. It was far too much fun. "What you do is far more complicated, is it not?"

"You are rude and acting above your station, Master Cade. I shall have Shrewsbury deal with you."

"You can try," Gavin said. He fixed his gaze on Lesley for long enough to let him know he was under suspicion. Then he smiled, letting his mouth curve up ever so slightly, mocking the man. Lesley turned away and started a conversation with a lady on his other side.

Gavin took up his knife and began eating a salad of greens, herbs, and flowers. His gaze drifted toward Isabel, and their eyes locked. He allowed his to linger on her generous, sensual mouth, then to drift downward. She was wearing the aubergine gown again. The bodice was tightly corseted, her chest pushed high. Even though she wore a partlet for modesty's sake, he could still discern the swell of her breasts. She blushed and resumed eating, but she knew. She knew he burned for her.

Tonight, he would claim that kiss he'd missed out on at the river.

• • •

Isabel didn't understand why Mary had demanded her presence, because she spoke exclusively to Philip Blake throughout the meal. The Earl of Shrewsbury sat on Bel's opposite side, but conversing with him was a chore. He seemed preoccupied, no doubt distracted by yesterday's events. And then Gavin caught her eye, and she felt his sensual awareness of her all the way to her toes. His scrutiny was an invitation, one she would not refuse. That realization was…disquieting. After that, she set down her knife and ate nothing more. A fluttering in her core grew, dipping and rising. A kind of tension she'd never felt before.

Alice was asking the earl a question, and suddenly voices quieted. "Are we safe, my lord? I vow, I had difficulty sleeping last night for fear those villains would murder us in our beds."

"No, no, rest assured, the castle is well guarded. There is no danger of that."

"But what did they want?" Cecily asked. "They came nowhere near Her Majesty."

"Because our men prevented it," Gavin said. "We believe they were locals, taking part in some impetuous action to kidnap the queen."

"And as I told Gavin, I'm grateful their plan failed," Mary said. "I would love nothing better than to return to Scotland, but not in that way. Who knows what would have befallen me?"

"I hope you discover who was responsible." All heads swiveled toward Frances, usually so reserved. "Else they could strike again." In the abstract, Isabel could believe the woman may have been involved in the attempt on Gavin's life, but here, at the dining table, beneath the beeswax candlelight, she seemed the epitome of innocence and sincerity.

Gavin looked directly at Frances. "We will. Do not doubt

it."

Was that a warning? If she was guilty of anything, Frances might interpret it as such. Showing no reaction to Gavin's statement, she simply picked up her knife and de-boned a piece of salmon.

After the meal, Mary retired. Nobody felt like dancing, but several wished to play cards. While they were organizing their foursomes, Gavin approached Isabel.

"Will you walk with me, Bel?" he asked.

"Now?"

Amusement danced in his eyes. "Aye, now. When else?"

"It is dark, sir."

"Cease calling me sir, Isabel. You know my name. Are you afraid of the dark?"

"Of course not. But I thought you might be." When he frowned at her, she added, "With good reason." Chuckling, he winged his arm and she grasped it. If the others noticed, they gave no sign. Gavin informed the guards of their intention, and one of them smirked, as though he knew what they were up to. Isabel felt her cheeks flame.

When they stepped outside, he said, "Will you be all right without your mantle for a short time?" At her nod, he began to lead her around the bailey's perimeter, as though he had a destination in mind.

"Where are we going?"

"You'll see in a moment."

Isabel hoped he had not formed a mistaken impression of her. Unlike Mary's other ladies, she was inexperienced in the…sensual arts. Had she invented that phrase, or heard it somewhere? She was trembling with excitement, or perhaps fear, but she meant to enjoy this encounter with Gavin, whatever it turned out to be. She trusted him. He would not take advantage of her.

"Warm enough?" It was a windy night, but still mild.

"Aye." It was not the cold that was causing her to shiver—but she did not say that. "The moon is lovely. 'Tis waxing, I think."

He steered her toward a building near the main gate. "What is this place?"

"The receiver's lodging," Gavin said. "It's used to house guests, but we rarely have any at Tutbury."

A thought occurred to Isabel. "Are you sure nobody else uses it for, ah, meetings?"

Laughing, Gavin drew her inside and closed the door. "I am not sure. But nobody else has left the queen's lodging, so I believe we are safe for now." And then he pulled her close. So close she could hear him breathing, feel his heart beating. He smelled of mint and clove. She set her palms on his chest and gazed up at him.

"I have been longing for that kiss snatched away from us at the river," he said, and then set his lips on hers. Taken by surprise, it was a moment before Isabel relaxed into Gavin's arms and the sensation of his kiss. His lips were soft and mobile, gently coaxing hers open. When his tongue pushed into her mouth, she let out a little gasp. Gavin raised his head. "Do you want to stop?"

"No," she said.

"Thank Christ. You are passing lovely tonight, Bel." This time his kiss was more commanding. He took her mouth, possessed it, and she reveled in the extraordinary sensations he was arousing in her. His tongue clashed with hers and explored the soft inside of her mouth. She wanted more of him, so when he ran his hands down her sides and grasped her bottom, she did not stop him. He pulled her against him, and she felt his erection press against her belly.

Definitely not the shape of an artichoke.

She wanted to touch his face. Pulling back a little, Bel reached up and placed her palms on either side of it. He stopped, watching her, waiting to see what she would do. What she wanted. Remembering the sensual pleasure of his fingers moving across her scalp, she slipped her hands into his thick hair, pausing briefly to knead, feeling triumphant when he closed his eyes and groaned aloud. And then she slid them down, caressing his forehead, running her thumbs in a line over his cheeks and lips. When she reached his neck, he spoke, his voice like gravel.

"God's mercy, Isabel, you're killing me." He lifted her, then, and carried her to a settle. Setting her on his lap, he pushed her legs apart and to either side. She didn't know what would come next, only that she might scream in frustration if he stopped. He rained kisses on her lips and neck, and after ripping away her partlet, the tops of her breasts. Skirts hiked up, Isabel pressed her core against his hardness. She had a wild urge to rub herself against him. She had never been intoxicated, but undeniably, she was now.

What a fool I am. This couldn't go on, as much as she longed for it.

"Gavin." Her voice was a whisper. "We must stop."

After one last kiss, he lifted her off him and set her down. "I'm not like the other ladies, you know."

He studied her, his blue eyes gleaming in the dark. "Nay, sweetheart. I am not a man who takes liberties. In fact, I took more than I should have. I only intended a kiss." He got to his feet and pulled her up with him. "I've no intention of bedding you."

Isabel's heart plunged. He was not attracted to her in that way. She was mortified.

"Yet."

To that concise, bold statement, she had no answer. Her cheeks grew hot and the place between her legs that had been throbbing a moment ago came back to life. He smiled wickedly at her speechlessness. "I'll see you back to the queen's lodging."

Gavin held up a hand when Isabel made to follow him out the door. "Hold a moment. I need to make sure we're alone." She waited, for longer than expected. At last, the door opened and he motioned to her.

He held on to her arm and hurried her toward the lodging, keeping closely to the buildings. "Do you still wish for tennis instruction?" Gavin asked.

She laughed. Until this moment, tennis had been the last thing on her mind. "Aye. I assumed you had forgotten about your offer. Or decided it was improper."

He chuckled softly. "Not I."

Dismayed, she said, "I don't have suitable clothing."

"Wear your loosest-fitting bodice and skirts. Try to leave off a few of the layers you normally cover yourself with." They'd reached the door, where a guard stood watch. Gavin jerked to a halt. "And Bel." He grabbed hold of her arm and whispered, "No corset."

She scurried inside, his soft laughter echoing in her head.

Chapter Twelve

Philip Blake sat across from Gavin in his office. They were breaking their fast together, as they'd arranged to do the night before. The two men had yet to discuss the questioning of those who had been present during the outing by the river.

Gavin spooned a large portion of a hearty beef and onion pottage into his mouth and washed it down with ale. "I learned nothing of value from Cecily, Alice, or Lady Shrewsbury."

"The same for me with Dorothy and Frances."

"We have yet to complete our interviews with the guards and staff."

"And what about Lesley?"

"I had an interesting conversation with him at dinner last night."

When he did not elaborate, Blake tore off a hunk of bread and offered it to Gavin. "Ann wasn't at the river, and she'd heard nothing suspicious among the other servants. Isabel was the sole witness who thought she could identify anybody. That's not surprising, since she was the only lady who had direct contact with one of them."

Gavin buttered his bread while Blake continued. "There was one thing, though. Ann said the queen mentioned recently she would not be here much longer. Do you know anything about that?"

Surprised, Gavin rocked his chair backward and eyed the other man. "The earl hasn't revealed any plans to move her again, although that's certainly possible. I'll ask him." When Gavin had first arrived at Tutbury, Shrewsbury informed him that Philip Blake was in his employ. Not officially as a spy, but as someone with whom the others may be willing to share secrets, which he would then pass along. He had the eye of Mary and the devotion of the other women. That was understandable, as he was a handsome man with an uncanny ability to charm, even while arbitrating arguments among the ladies.

"Mary lied to me when I interviewed her," Gavin said, his chair bouncing forward and hitting the floor with a bang.

"What? How do you know?"

Gavin shrugged. "Instinct. When I asked if she'd ever seen any of the attackers before, she said no, but her eyes betrayed her. She was lying."

"How could she have recognized any of those men? She has no dealings with locals."

Frowning, Gavin said, "I'm no longer convinced they were locals."

"But—"

Gavin cut him off. "Would you be shocked to hear that the Duke of Norfolk paid a visit to Tutbury that evening after dinner?"

"You jest."

Gavin paused a moment, assessing Blake's trustworthiness. But Shrewsbury trusted the man, and Gavin saw no reason why he should not do likewise. "Before retiring, I walked the perimeter of the bailey. You are familiar with the receiver's lodging, near the gate?"

Blake nodded, and Gavin continued. "There was a light

in the window. I ducked into the stables and found a fine-looking stallion housed within. I roused the stable boy, who said he didn't know whose it was. Lesley had brought it in."

Blake's eyes riveted on him, Gavin finished the tale, relating everything he'd overheard.

"Norfolk himself, here? This is treason! What's been done about it?"

"Shrewsbury sent a message to London, but Norfolk would have been safely ensconced in his home before Cecil received it. It would be his word against ours, and we have absolutely no proof that he was ever here, let alone hatching treasonous plots with Queen Mary."

Blake gave his head a shake. "You must have informed Shrewsbury immediately. Why didn't you arrest him, hold him until Cecil received the missive and sent word of what to do?"

"There was a delay of several hours before I informed the earl." When Blake looked incredulous, Gavin explained. "Even though they failed to kill me, they did achieve their goals in one sense. We can prove nothing against the duke." Rubbing the back of his neck, Gavin said, "And by the way, the attack at the river was a smokescreen, meant to cover up the duke's arrival. Those were his men, which is why Mary recognized one of them."

"Jesu. Who else knows of this?"

Gavin snorted. "Besides the perpetrators? The earl and..." He broke off, hesitating. "Isabel—although I didn't tell her everything. She knows nothing about the duke being here, or the conversation I overheard."

Eyes dancing, Blake was not going to let this go. "Aha! I knew you had an interest there."

Safer not to deny it. "She's trustworthy, and spends much of her time with Mary. The queen seems to have chosen Bel as her latest intimate. I hope she will be willing to share some of Mary's confidences with me."

"And what about you, Cade? Wouldn't you like the lovely Bel to be your intimate? You do know that's what Mary's ladies believe, don't you? They are positively drooling with envy."

Gavin did not care for the leering expression on Blake's face, but he let it go. "Let them believe what they like. That does not mean it is true."

"You prefer to keep your distance, don't you? No bed sport with any of the women here. I admire your restraint, although you are missing out on a deal of pleasure. If you don't intend to bed Isabel, I may pursue her myself."

Gavin put on his most intimidating face. "No. She's not for you."

Blake nodded once, curtly, and took his leave. He'd gotten the message.

God's mercy, what time was it? Gavin glanced at his timepiece and realized he was late for his meeting with Isabel. After locking up important documents, he grabbed the tennis rackets and balls and hurried outside toward the makeshift tennis court.

He hoped his—and Shrewsbury's—assessment of Philip Blake was the correct one.

· · ·

Pacing around the tennis court, Isabel, attired as Gavin had directed, had grown tired of waiting. Mary's ladies did not have an unlimited amount of time to do as they pleased. In Isabel's favor this morning, Mary was not feeling well, and Dorothy was attending her. Isabel felt guilty about being grateful the queen was ill, but such was her giddiness when it came to Gavin. Apparently, he wasn't as keen to see her.

Glancing around the bailey yet again, she finally

glimpsed him striding toward her, carrying two rackets. He waved at her; she ignored him. Even though she was angry, she couldn't help admiring his form as he approached. The shoulders. The thighs. What was a lady to do?

Out of breath, Gavin said, "I can see you're angry with me. I'm unforgivably late and heartily sorry for it."

"*Hmpf.* I was preparing to return to the lodging. One more minute, and I would have."

"I am exceedingly glad you did not." He dropped the rackets and removed his doublet. Isabel watched, mesmerized.

She hated herself for capitulating so quickly.

Handing her a racket, he said, "Let me show you how to begin." He grasped her arms and turned her toward the net. "Hold the racket in your right hand. Good. Now, watch me."

That would be no hardship.

In one fluid movement, Gavin threw the ball in the air, swung the racket in a downward arc, and struck the ball. *Thwonk!* It bounced over the net to the far side of the court. Unfortunately, Isabel hadn't paid one iota of attention to his technique. She was in a giddy state of suspension, eyes riveted on his body.

He hit a second ball, and after retrieving them both, a third. "Would you like to try?" Gavin asked.

She blinked.

He grinned, perfectly aware of what aspect of the game she'd been studying. How mortifying. Gathering herself, she said, "Of course."

"Toss the ball up and hit it. Try to imitate my motion."

Isabel nodded. "Aye. I will." She looked at Gavin and giggled. Then, in a pathetic display of athletic ineptitude, she threw the ball in the air and made a half-hearted attempt at smashing it with the racket. Regrettably, she did not move fast enough and managed only to bat the ball into the ground.

Gavin scratched his head and said, "*Hmm.* Perhaps this

will be more of a challenge than I anticipated."

By all the saints, was she a complete lackwit? *Snap out of it, Isabel.* "Let me try again."

He moved behind her, grabbed hold of her hand, and gently rotated her arm in an arc. "Like that," he said. He was all business, and she tried to ignore the strong pulsing of her heart and the scorching heat spreading through her body. His touch should not excite her to this extent.

"I'm ready," she said. "I can do it now." Closing her eyes briefly, Isabel visualized the motion she would employ to strike the ball, and the technique worked. She whacked it hard. The ball flew into the net, but it was a good shot nonetheless. "I did it!"

Gavin beamed at her. "So you did. Again, Bel."

She hit ball after ball, lobbing most of them over the net. Then, he took up a position on the other side. "Let's try bandying back and forth."

She worked at it diligently, and in the end, got the hang of it. When she returned one of his shots, she was jubilant. "I am getting good at this, eh Gavin?" Isabel wished she'd brought a handkerchief. While he wasn't looking, she mopped her brow with her sleeve, and looked up to see him approaching her, an odd look on his face.

"Oh, hell, Isabel. Let's have done with tennis." He dropped his racket and pried hers from her hand. Then he wrapped an arm about her waist and pulled her close. "I only want to kiss you. Your cheeks are rosy, and so is the rest of you, I'll wager."

Something wild and untamed surged through her when his lips touched hers. It was a powerful force against which she was helpless. Isabel lunged into him, in a fever for his body, desperate to touch as much of him as possible. Not in need of any coaxing on Gavin's part, she opened her mouth and sucked his tongue inside. He groaned deep in his throat, and she took that as a good sign.

Had she always wanted this and never known it? She pressed her hands against his chest, but that was not sufficient. "I want to feel your bare skin, Gavin. Help me."

"Gladly, love." He pulled his lawn shirt up and off, and then his shift. She stared unashamedly at his beautiful chest, dusted lightly with hair, longing to explore every plane and sinew. But before she could do more, he lifted her into his arms and carried her toward a small enclosure at the far end of the court. Inside was a cushioned settle, and he set her on it. Easing down beside her, he said, "I want to touch you, Bel. May I?"

"Where?" she asked, although it would not matter what he answered.

"Everywhere, sweetheart."

And then they were lost in each other. He let her stroke his chest and shoulders, and when that proved not enough, she kissed her way across his torso, stopping to tongue and suck his nipples, because she wanted to taste him. At last he stopped her, grabbing her hands and stilling her frenzied movement. "Let me, now, Isabel."

She nodded, giving her body into his sensitive hands. He unfastened her bodice, and then her skirts. Only her shift remained between her and his naked chest. She shivered, because it was, after all, nearly December, and the air was cool. "You are cold. Come here. I'll warm you."

After a moment, he lowered the straps of her chemise and exposed her breasts. Shy at first, she quickly overcame such feelings. Gavin's look was so rapt, so worshipful. Then he palmed her breasts in his big hands and gently massaged, lightly tweaking her nipples and making her quiver with need.

He kissed her, whispered in her ear. "I want to pleasure you, Bel." Lovingly, he cradled her in his arms, turning her so her back was to his chest. Sliding up the hem of her chemise, he said, "Will you open your legs for me?"

Of course, she would. *Of course.* She was wild for his touch. He must be laughing about her denials that she was not like Mary's other ladies. And then she felt his hand cupping her there, and she melted inside. She was wet, and he separated her folds and spread the wetness over her core with his fingers. And when he lavished his attention on her most sensitive spot, she cried out from the intensity of it. Twisting her body around, she pulled him down for a kiss. So many sensations assailed her at once, she didn't know if she could bear it.

"Gavin, I—"

He murmured in her ear. "*Shh.* Just enjoy, Bel. You are so beautiful. You've no idea, have you? Let yourself go, sweeting."

And she did, her body convulsing in a paroxysm so sweet, she thought the angels had carried her away. Feeling timid now that it was over, she relaxed against him and nearly dozed off. At length, he turned her around so that she was facing him. "What about you, Gavin? I want to bring you pleasure, too. Will you not let me stroke your..." She could not bring herself to say any of the ridiculous words used for the male organ.

"My cock?"

She laughed, flushing. "Aye."

"As much as I would love that, not today. I don't trust myself with you. Besides, don't you need to get back?"

Her hand flew to her mouth. "God's mercy! I've been absent far too long. What will they think?" Hurriedly, Gavin helped Isabel dress, then set himself to rights. When he glanced about with a puzzled expression, she said, "Your shirt. 'Tis on the court, where you pulled it off."

A devilish grin broke over his face. "Where you nearly ripped it off me, you mean."

Isabel laughed. "Your doublet is there, too." After Gavin was dressed, she said, "I'll walk back alone. If anybody asks, I can say I was walking and lost track of the time."

"Somebody may have seen us, you know."

She sighed, hoping he was wrong. "In that case, I shall say you were practicing your sport and offered to show me how the game is played." She walked a few steps away, then, not relishing the idea of leaving him, turned back and kissed him soundly on the lips. "Until later, then."

"Aye, Isabel. Until later."

• • •

Gavin fetched his shirt and doublet and resumed his seat. The small enclosure served as shelter for the queen if the weather turned inclement, but it had never been used. Until today.

Practicing my sport, indeed. He shook his head and chuckled to himself. And then he sobered. What was he doing with Isabel? When he'd thought death was imminent, he'd judged himself a fool for deciding to cut her from his life. A woman such as she was to be treasured, not cast aside. He rose and tugged his shirt on, then fastened his doublet over it.

In no hurry, he began walking toward his suite, still thinking deeply. Instinctively, he knew it was wrong to dally with a woman like Isabel. She was intelligent, sensitive, caring—the opposite of Mary's other ladies. Did he mean to marry her? *Jesu.* He was not ready for that. His wounds were still too deep, the healing yet in its genesis.

Hadn't he believed in Anna's essential goodness? And by the Virgin, look how that had turned out.

For now, he could draw only one conclusion. He must let Isabel go, before matters progressed any further. If he got her with child…then neither of them would have a choice. They would have to wed, because he couldn't allow a child of his to be a bastard. Gavin would take Isabel aside and tell her of all this. His wife, his marriage, and what had happened. She would understand. He would make her understand.

Gavin was so immersed in his thoughts, he barely registered a man emerging from John Lesley's chambers. With a packet clutched under his arm, the fellow was dashing toward the gate. When he passed Gavin, he reached out and grabbed the man's arm.

"Ho, there, sirrah. I believe you need to come with me."

The man, only a youth, tried to escape Gavin's grasp, ineffectually. "Pray let me go, sir. If the bishop sees me with you, he'll have me head. And these messages is important. Must be delivered posthaste, he said."

"We'll see about that," Gavin said. "It will go better for you if I'm not forced to drag you along. Much less conspicuous, eh?" The boy quit trying to free himself, but Gavin kept a firm hold on him, nevertheless, and hustled him along. He too would prefer the bishop not see them.

They entered Gavin's office, and he pointed to the chair. "Set the packet on the desk and be seated." The lad, a scruffy-looking boy, was clothed in soiled hose and a tattered doublet and jerkin. Whatever Lesley was paying him, it wasn't enough. "How much coin did the bishop give you?"

Reluctantly, the lad threw the packet onto the desk and fished a coin from a pocket. A halfpenny. Gavin snorted. *The miserly bastard.* "There's a shilling in it for you every time you bring his missives to me."

The boy's eyes widened. "Gor."

Gavin sat behind the desk. "Where did you come from, lad?"

"Derby."

"On foot?"

"Aye, sir."

"Did you bring missives for the bishop? And who is on

the other end of these transactions?"

"Don't know what ye're askin' me, sir."

Gavin softened his voice and manner. The boy was practically a child, after all. "Where do you take the documents the bishop gives you? Whom do you give them to?"

"I takes 'em to Derby. Don't know the man's name. But he's not from hereabout, I can tell you that. He's a foreigner. And he gives me missives to bring back to the bishop."

It was all Gavin could do not to gloat, not to revel in this triumph. The packet of documents could be the break they'd been waiting for. "What is your name, son?" he asked.

"Simon, sir."

"Well, Simon, where do you think this fellow may hail from?"

"Don't know, sir."

"Can you describe him for me? What was he wearing?"

"Hose, master. A fancy coat over a doublet, and a cap. The cap were tipped, like, to one side."

"He didn't tell you his name?" When Simon shook his head, Gavin asked, "What did he call you?"

Simon scratched his head. "Rag something. I didn't understand him. Told him my name, but he didn't use it."

Ragazzo. Italian for boy. "Can you describe his appearance, Simon?"

When the lad appeared perplexed by this request, Gavin helped him. "Short or tall? Dark hair or light? Fat or thin? Those sorts of things."

"Shorter than you by a mile, but taller than the bishop. Not fat or thin, neither one, only ordinary. Dark hair what curled under, and a beard." The lad fidgeted, eyeing his packet. He wanted to be off.

God's mercy, this could be Ridolfi himself.

Gavin smiled. "You're doing well, Simon. You've a good

head for details. Anything else you can remember about him?"

"His beard were stiff, like he put egg white on it."

"Ah. Mayhap he does. Men do that in some countries."

He scooted off his chair and said, "I'll take that packet now, sir. I'll be late if I don't leave now. Got to walk to Derby."

When Simon made to grab the packet, Gavin snatched it away. "I'm afraid I can't let you do that, lad. I'll need to read these documents first." Even then, the likelihood of allowing the boy to deliver them was slim. Gavin opened the door and summoned the servant who attended him. "Go to the kitchen in the queen's lodging and bring back a meal for this lad. Stay with him and don't allow anybody else access to him. Understood?"

The man nodded. "Aye, Master Cade."

"I'll wait with him until you return."

Gavin turned back to Simon, and only then did he see the tears in the boy's eyes. "Here, now, no need for that. I promised you a shilling, and you'll get it. And you may keep the coin the bishop gave you."

"He'll hurt me if I don't deliver the packet. He said he'd cut off my bollocks and stuff 'em down my throat."

Gavin cringed. What kind of monster threatened a young lad with torture? The boy stepped into a pool of light, and Gavin saw his face clearly for the first time. He had spots, which meant he was older than Gavin had taken him for. But still, not more than sixteen or seventeen.

Gavin was itching to open the packet and examine its contents, but he dared not do so in front of Simon. "Tell me, lad, how you met the man who gave you missives for Lesley— the bishop."

"I were hangin' about town, sweepin' streets and doin' other jobs to earn a halfpenny or two. He saw me and motioned me over. I was suspicious at first—some of them types have a liking for young boys—but my mum allus needs coin. So I talked to him, and he told me what he wanted."

"How long have you been in his—and the bishop's—employ?"

"Not long. A month, but not much more."

"I see. And how often do they seek your help?"

"This is the fourth time I been up here to the castle." He smiled ruefully. "'Tis a long walk."

A rap on the door interrupted them, but Gavin had learned enough. "Simon, this is Barnaby. He'll take you to another chamber where you may eat and rest. I'm afraid you must remain with us for a bit longer."

Simon had suddenly perked up. The scent of roasted fowl and vegetables wafted from a basket Barnaby carried and soon permeated the hallway. After one more longing glance at the packet, Simon followed the servant out the door. Leaving Gavin free, at last, to examine the documents.

It took only moments to bring him back to Earth. The documents all related to Mary's mundane affairs. One was her request for more tapestries and carpets, as the winter months were closing in and the castle would be subject to strong winds and cold temperatures. Another confirmed what Blake had learned in his interview with Ann, the lady's maid. Mary was to be moved to Sheffield Castle for Christmastide. And last, there were several letters penned by Mary herself to her connections in France, requesting such items as embroidery floss, fabrics, and various cures for her ailments.

Hellfire and damnation. Nothing of any use. *Nothing.*

Gavin placed the documents back in the packet. Young Simon could sleep at Tutbury tonight. He would not like it, but it was growing too late to walk the twelve miles back to Derby. Gavin would send him on his way in the morning, on horseback with an escort. The lad would arrive sooner that way, and without suspicion.

Chapter Thirteen

When Isabel returned to Mary's chambers, a few of the ladies glanced up with knowing looks. Had they guessed where she'd been? Did she look like a woman who'd lately been pleasured by an attractive and wickedly sensual man? Mary and Lady Shrewsbury were in their customary places, while everybody else was relegated to the small, extremely uncomfortable footstools. An afternoon seated on one made Isabel's back ache unrelentingly. After locating the volume she'd been reading out loud, the *Odyssey*, she found her place and settled in for a long afternoon. But it seemed the ladies wished to talk.

"I, for one," Cecily said, "am grateful for the move to Sheffield for Christmastide. Lady Shrewsbury, is it a more salubrious lodging?"

Without glancing up from her needlework, the lady said, "I believe you will find it so, and you have me to thank. I informed the earl that if the latrines were not dug out, and the midden cleared away, I was leaving Tutbury for Chatsworth and not returning."

"We are grateful to you, my lady," Dorothy said. "Perhaps when we return, it will be less malodorous here."

Isabel hid her surprise at the news, since everybody else seemed to know. Perhaps Mary had informed them while she'd been with Gavin. "Is it at a distance?" Isabel asked.

"A full day's carriage ride. We will leave at dawn."

"When?"

"Not until December twenty-third, so we have plenty of time to prepare. We'll remain at Sheffield through Twelfth Night—or until the necessary work here at Tutbury has been completed."

Isabel glanced at Mary. She'd been uncharacteristically quiet during this exchange, concentrating on her needlework. In a moment, she glanced up and caught Isabel watching her. "Pray, ladies, let us stretch our legs. Don your mantles and meet in the garden. We have been sitting too long."

"Is that permitted?" Alice asked.

"We will not venture outside the garden," Mary answered. "I cannot see why that would be objectionable. We shall remain in full view of the guards."

Isabel walked down the passage to her chamber with Frances. "You were absent a long time this morning, dear Isabel," she said, smiling.

"Aye. I took a long walk. It was quite invigorating."

"By yourself? Gavin was not with you?"

Isabel could not hold back a laugh. Their interest in each other was becoming apparent, so what harm would it do to tell her the truth? Although she wasn't sure she should trust Frances since she'd seen her with Lesley the night Gavin was nearly killed.

"Aye, he was. Teaching me to play tennis."

Frances gave her a wry look. "Is that what it is called now?"

Isabel's face grew hot. "He instructed me until I was able to achieve some skill. Then we bandied the ball back and forth for a short time. I'm not very good at it yet."

Frances exploded with laughter. In fact, she laughed so hard, they had to stop at one of the window embrasures so she could recover herself. "Oh, Bel, you are such an innocent."

Isabel did not understand what was so funny. "Let's go, Frances. The queen will be waiting."

Wiping tears from her cheeks, Frances accompanied Isabel to their chamber, where they gathered mantles, gloves, and hats, then followed the others down the stairs. The guards did not question their departure from the lodging.

Once outside, Mary motioned to Isabel, who hurried over to see what she wanted. The little dog, Bisou, raced back and forth, releasing his pent-up energy. He looked exceedingly funny, with his little legs pumping so hard. Delighted, Isabel laughed. The queen linked arms with her and said, "Walk with me, *ma chere*. Where were you earlier? I thought perhaps you had left us."

"My apologies, Your Majesty. I should have asked your permission. It won't happen again."

She waved a hand through the air. "You did not answer my question."

Trapped, Isabel could not lie. Nor did she know why her first impulse was to do so. "I was with Gavin. After the mishap at the tennis court, he promised to teach me to play. We had not had the opportunity until today."

"All that time you were swatting tennis balls at each other?"

"Aye, madam." *For most of it, anyway.*

At least she did not dissolve into laughter, as Frances had done. "He cares for you, Bel. Do you return his regard?"

Did she? She certainly had not set out for Tutbury with the least expectation of finding a man. She left her home to escape a marriage. Of her ardor for Gavin, there could be no doubt. He was simply the most beautiful, virile man she'd ever encountered. Despite his occasional tendency to ignore her, he'd shown her the utmost kindness and consideration. More than any person who had ever graced her life. She was a sexual neophyte, but he had treated her with great tenderness, and she found him irresistible. If his kisses and embraces were any indicator, she suspected he felt the same.

By God's light, I am falling in love with the man.

Stammering a bit, she said, "I-I do, Your Majesty."

Chuckling, the queen patted her hand. "Have you been in love before, Bel?"

"No, ma'am. Nor did I ever expect to be."

Suddenly, Mary steered her off the path and over to a fountain, the base of which was surrounded by a ledge broad enough to sit upon. "May I confide in you, Bel?" the queen asked after they'd sat down. "You must not tell a single soul what I am about to say." Bisou jumped up and Isabel set him on her lap.

"I would never divulge your confidences, Your Majesty." The fountain was turned off, in anticipation of cold weather, and the surrounding foliage had withered and gone dormant.

"*C'est bon.* Of all my ladies, I trust you the most." Then, she lowered her voice to a whisper, so that Isabel had to lean toward her to hear what she was saying. "I am to wed the Duke of Norfolk."

Shocked, Isabel made a spontaneous decision to hide her initial reaction. "May I offer my most sincere wishes for your happiness, Your Majesty."

"*Merci,* Bel." Mary's smile was tentative at best.

What to say?

Since Isabel and Gavin's liaison at the tennis court, the weather had changed. Now, a stiff breeze ruffled her hair and burrowed beneath her mantle. Shivering, she said, "How did this come about, Your Majesty? I was under the impression your cousin would not condone a union between you and the duke."

"She has had a change of heart." Mary looked everywhere but at Isabel. "That is not quite the truth. She has not yet been informed, but I am confident she will give us her blessing when she knows we wish to marry. It will be in her best interest to do so."

Isabel would call it "permission" rather than "blessing." Mary and Norfolk could not simply announce their intention to marry and expect Queen Elizabeth to acquiesce. Recalling Gavin's warning to be wary and cautious with Mary, Isabel reined in her curiosity and merely said, "I understand." Even though she did not.

They were silent for a time, and the laughing voices of the others drifted on the wind toward them. Bisou suddenly jumped down, dropped on his haunches, and growled. It made Bel uneasy. Was someone listening? Mary, distracted, did not seem to notice. "We have plans, you see. Even though at present our marriage does not seem a possibility, in the coming months, there will, perhaps, be a re-ordering of things."

Horrified, Isabel clamped her mouth shut. What could she say to that? The implications of this were treasonous, and Bel would be required to inform Shrewsbury if Mary was determined to proceed with this…"re-ordering." Mary's own life would be forfeit.

The queen needed no encouragement from Isabel to proceed. "Many changes are in the wind, Bel. More than that I cannot say at present. Soon, you will understand."

Heart pounding, Isabel debated with herself. Should she warn Mary that whatever she and the duke were planning was treason and would put them both at risk? Surely, she must be aware of that. But Bel would not rest easy unless she advised caution. She kept her voice low, in case Bisou had picked up someone's scent. "Your Majesty, is this wise? I do not know what it is you refer to, but the danger to you would be great.

Are you certain you wish to be involved in such a…plot?"

Mary scowled, and Isabel regretted her comment. Rising, the queen paced away from Bel, who stood up when Mary did. Suddenly, she spun around. "Do you think this life is easy for me? That I enjoy being a prisoner? I am a queen, Bel! A sovereign! Many believe the throne of England is mine by right. In my position, would you not reach out and seize any chance to gain your freedom? To live the life you deserve? The life you were born to?"

Stunned, Bel said nothing. Mary had covered her face with her hands and was weeping.

God's mercy, what have I done?

She took a tentative step toward Mary. "Your Majesty, I beg your forgiveness. It was not my intention to upset you. This is no kind of life for you. I know that. We all know that, including the Shrewsburys."

Mary said nothing. Her heartbreaking sobs persisted, and Isabel fervently wished she could assuage the woman's torment.

Stretching out her hands to the queen, she said, "Your constant disappointments and vexations must be unbearable. But I implore you not to do anything rash. Anything that will have consequences severe enough to make your situation worse." *Much worse.*

Mary rose abruptly, her lips pressed into a flat line. "Enough, now. Let's find the others." She glanced ruefully at Isabel. "I will never be free, I fear." As they wandered down the paths, Bisou at their heels, Mary clung to her as though she were drowning and Isabel was her only means of staying afloat.

• • •

Gavin was conversing with the Shrewsburys, Blake, and

Dorothy Vere when Isabel entered the outer chamber. Before Mary could claim her, he excused himself and hastened to meet her while she was still standing in the doorway. Her eyes alight, an ecstatic smile broke across her face. God's mercy, but she looked like the Helen of Troy of his imagination. The-face-that-launched-a-thousand-ships kind of beauty. Then his heart dropped, for what he was about to say to her would most likely erase that smile.

"Good even, Gavin." A pause. "Is something amiss? You look quite somber." A servant offered Bel a glass of wine, after which Gavin grasped her elbow and escorted her to a nook near a tall window, where they might have some privacy.

Setting her wine on the window ledge, she turned to him and said, "I believe 'tis time you revealed to me your true occupation here at the castle. I have been mulling it over, you see. You say you are equerry to the earl, but you seem to spend most of your time on either the queen's safety...or on unraveling conspiracies." She sobered and leaned in. "You were nearly killed, Gavin! Why?"

Confounded, Gavin simply stared at her. Why, of all times, had she chosen this one to quiz him about his work? It had been inevitable, eventually, since he'd been sharing so much with her, but the very night he wished to speak of... other matters? "Isabel," he began, wanting to put her off, "we cannot have this conversation here, amid these people. Is that not obvious?"

Then he saw by her expression, her question had been only half serious. She was flirting with him, teasing him. He probably could have laughed and hedged, but since he'd misinterpreted, it was too late for that. Perhaps he should simply be honest. Telling her of his true purpose here should not affect the other conversation they must have. Her gaze remained steady, but her smile was slipping. He nodded, studying her. "You guessed my not-very-well-kept secret."

Glancing around the room, she lowered her voice. "Tell me more. Everything."

"I will, but not here, Bel. There are too many eyes and ears in this room. We cannot risk it."

She nodded. "Of course not. I beg your pardon."

"I do need to speak to you of something else, though." Just then, Mary announced dinner, and to Gavin's frustration, their talk would need to be postponed. Nothing was going according to plan. Had he imagined he could seduce her until she was drunk with pleasure, then mere hours later, in the middle of a pre-dinner gathering, tell her he was not seeking a wife and they must never indulge in such behavior again? *Jesu*, he was an idiot.

Shrewsbury sat on one side of Mary, and Gavin on the other. He did not know why he'd been accorded this honor, since the queen did not often bestow it upon him. On his other side was Cecily Blake, bedecked with pearls sewn onto her gown and artfully arranged in her hair. She was a temptress, no denying that. If only her manner was more inviting. Not toward him; he had no interest in her. Not for the first time, Gavin wondered why she was so unpleasant. He'd never truly made an effort to know her better; mayhap this would be a good time to do so, since Mary was deep into conversation with the earl.

"Mistress Cecily, are you looking forward to the move to Sheffield?"

Amusement lit her eyes. "That depends. It is another stone fortress, aye? No doubt it also stinks and is equally as cold as Tutbury. And what a deal of work to transport us there! So, no, I cannot say I am looking forward to it." She paused a moment. "But it was kind of you to ask."

Gavin laughed. Perhaps she was honest to a fault, and that was what made her seem so disagreeable. "Surely a change of scene will be welcome," he said. He glanced up, and his eyes settled on Bess Shrewsbury. With thinly veiled anger, that lady was gazing upon her husband. The earl of late spent a great deal of time in conversation with Mary, who was an inveterate flirt. She charmed every man who entered her orbit. Granted, she was lovely, and he'd witnessed her working her wiles on willing victims. But he had never felt himself in any danger from her.

"As I said, that depends," Cecily said. Then, noticing the focus of Gavin's attention, she added in a whisper, "The earl's lady is jealous. Did you not know? He's fallen under Mary's spell, as all men do eventually."

Shocked, Gavin did not have a chance to respond, because the queen herself was demanding his attention. "Master Cade, does it fall to you to organize our move to Sheffield?"

He laughed. So preoccupied had he been with other matters, he hadn't given it more than a moment's thought. "I suppose that task is within my purview, Your Majesty. Pray, do not ask how I do, because I've yet to accomplish anything. But it will be my first priority, beginning tomorrow."

"Ah, *oui*, I believe you have other priorities," she said knowingly, her eyes roaming toward the other end of the table, where Isabel was seated between Lesley and Blake.

Gavin made no answer, although Mary kept her intense gaze riveted on him. "I am very fond of her, Master Cade," she said softly. "I would not take it kindly were she to have her heart broken."

It was incumbent upon him to respond, but he could think of nothing to say that would not sound defensive. Or weak. He'd no idea Mary and Isabel had become so close. "I, too, am exceedingly fond of her, Your Majesty." That much was true. His intention of ending his flirtation with Bel was not the queen's business, and he did not believe Isabel's heart would be broken.

Mary nodded her head once, curtly, as if the business was done. He fervently hoped it was. He glanced at Bel, who was laughing at something Blake was saying. Christ, but he was a handsome devil. A living, breathing woman would have to be blind not to see his attractions. The memory of what he'd said to Gavin earlier came back to haunt him: "If you don't intend to bed Isabel, I may pursue her." The whoreson. He was no more interested in a wife than Gavin was. Less so. Blake did not intend to woo her. To him, "pursue" meant only one thing, and Gavin knew too well what that was.

• • •

After dinner, the queen retired to her privy chamber. Some members of the group paired off, and a few more joined together for cards. Isabel heard Gavin beg off. She waited for him, and he found her directly. "Come," he said. "I would like to finish the conversation we began earlier."

Little quivers of excitement shooting through her, Bel nodded. She was not thinking at all about their conversation, but was remembering something else entirely. He led her down the passage and into one of the unused chambers, the one with furniture. A settle was pushed against one wall, and he gestured to her to sit.

"Let me make certain we are alone," Gavin said. He'd brought tinder and a candle in a holder. When it was lit, he moved about the room, checking under chairs and opening cabinets.

Isabel could not suppress a giggle. "Those are hardly large enough to conceal a person, Gavin."

"I am carried away," he said, chuckling. He set the candle down on a small table near the settle and looked at her. His eyes, his manner, were serious. "You asked about my work here, but I would like to talk of something else first. Will you hear me out?"

"Say on, sir. I am all ears." She was trying to lighten the mood, but her efforts did not seem to be working, as his expression did not change.

He reached for her hand and clutched it tightly. "I am a widower. Did you know that?"

Did she? She thought not. "Nay, neither you nor anybody else has ever mentioned it. I am sorry to hear it."

"My wife died giving birth to another man's son. The babe died, too. I discovered the truth after her death and have been trying to come to terms with it ever since." He paused and turned his head to one side, as though working out what else he wished to say to her. Finally, looking at her straight on, he said, "I do not want your sympathy, Bel. I am telling you this because it's vital you know that what happened with Anna has caused me to be mistrustful of most women."

She stared at him, not knowing how to respond. Was he including or excluding her from that group? She waited.

"I have grown passing fond of you, Isabel. You have touched me in a way I hadn't thought possible since Anna died. But I am not ready to wed again, and you are not the kind of lady one dallies with. Things between us have gone far enough, and they must go no further."

Isabel's head was spinning. He liked her, but he did not want to marry her. Or anybody. They must not…kiss? Touch each other? Talk? All of that, she guessed. Couldn't he have told her this before she'd allowed him access to her body? Shame, spineless and insidious shame, planted itself in her belly like a serpent, and worked its way up. To a point just underneath her ribs. Then, to her heart. Her poor, ill-used heart. Shame could rip a heart out, and she had denied it a place in her life since her stepfather had done the awful things that had shamed her, years ago, now. She had let Gavin penetrate the wall she'd built around herself without even thinking twice about it, and now she once again would have to suffer the agonies of humiliation and the loss of her dignity.

How could she have been so reckless? She had vowed to protect herself, because her mother had not, her brothers could not, and look at the result. The first time she left her home, she'd forgotten everything she'd ever known. She wanted to hang her head and cry. But that would make matters worse.

"Bel?"

She yanked her hand from his grasp. "I perfectly understand," she said. "You need not explain further." She rose and walked toward the door. "I believe I shall retire."

He was beside her before she could exit. "Pray don't go. Please, Bel, tell me what you're feeling."

Her hurt turned swiftly to anger. He wanted to discuss her feelings. Perfect. She stepped back. "You believe all women are the same, and perhaps you are correct. At this moment, in my view, you are a braying donkey's arse. Given the opportunity, I would push you into the latrine pit." He gaped at her, as if he could not believe her words. "I should have known. I should have known better." Her throat was thick, and her words sounded strained. "You no longer believe in love, and I have long considered most men to be oppressors. And pathetic and weak into the bargain. I thought you were different. More fool, I."

"Listen to me, Bel—"

"Stay away from me, Gavin, and I shall do likewise for you."

Before he could speak another word, she hurled herself out the door and strode to her chamber. Thank the Lord and all the saints, she was alone. Isabel had told Ann she would not require her assistance tonight, hoping foolishly she would be with Gavin. Frances, as usual, was not there. Isabel scrunched up her nose at the idea her friend was in bed with

John Lesley. There was a man who could not be trusted. But she would judge for herself from now on. Was Gavin even telling her the truth about Lesley? About anything?

Isabel sank down onto the bed, and only then did she allow herself to weep. At length, she drifted off to sleep. In the middle of the night, she jerked awake in the full darkness. She rose and, after considerable effort, disrobed down to her smock. If Ann and Frances saw that she had not undressed, they would guess something was wrong, and the last thing she wanted to do was answer their probing questions. And word would spread in no time. She climbed back into bed and endured a troubled sleep the rest of the night, visions of her meeting with Gavin replaying in her head over and over.

· · ·

After Isabel parted from him so abruptly, Gavin extinguished the candle and hastened to his residence, still in shock over what had transpired. Her extreme reaction had stunned him. He climbed the stairs, remembering the way her face had crumpled and her eyes had glistened with unshed tears. How could he have been so mistaken? Isabel was right, he was an arse. A braying donkey's arse, to be precise.

The fact that he hadn't spoken up sooner, that he had taken advantage of her, burned in his gut. He hadn't wanted to acknowledge what he was doing was wrong. All he'd been able to think about was satisfying his raging lust for her. Thank God he hadn't…they hadn't done more. Entering his suite, he yanked off his mantle and tossed it on a chair. And began pacing.

He felt much more for Isabel than lust. No mistake, he felt that, too. But he didn't know what to do with his emotions, so he'd convinced himself to let her go. Why hadn't he simply told her about Anna and then asked if she would wait for him? Until he was ready to marry again? She might have refused, but at least he would have made his feelings clear. And would not have wounded hers. God's heart, if she had similar feelings and sensations toward him, no wonder she was hurt and angry. He paused, mid-stride. On the morrow, he would seek her out and apologize. More than apologize. Beg her to forgive him.

She'd said something that puzzled him. That she had long considered men to be oppressors. What had occurred in her past to sow such a degree of hatred toward his sex? He knew little about Isabel, come to think on it. Of her family, her life before Tutbury. Which showed exactly what a self-absorbed bastard he was. He recalled telling her he was a good listener, but he'd been so preoccupied of late he'd proved the opposite.

His eyes strayed to his desk and the packet of documents resting there. He'd never be able to sleep, so he might as well look them over one more time, to make certain there was indeed nothing there of concern. In the morning, he'd have to send Simon off with them. He lit more candles, sat down, and began perusing the documents.

Chapter Fourteen

Gavin read each document carefully, convinced in the end that his original assessment had been correct. He rubbed his eyes and strode about the small chamber for several moments, then poured himself a glass of wine and settled in for one more look. There was something off about the letters, yet he could not pinpoint it.

Fifty-two yards of lace from the Netherlands seemed excessive, even for the queen. As did fifteen tapestries and fourteen Turkish carpets. His vision was blurring; his brain, crying out for rest, but he was now almost certain this was a cipher. Stubbornly, he began playing with the numbers, using a simple grid that had originated with the Greeks:

	1	2	3	4	5
1	A	B	C	D	E
2	F	G	H	I	K
3	L	M	N	O	P
4	Q	R	S	T	U
5	V	W	X	Y	Z

Reading the matrix down and then across, 52 signified *W*,

15 was *E*, and 14, *D*. Wed! Mary and Norfolk?

Quitting now was not an option. He must keep on. The next set of numbers was tricky, and Gavin almost gave up. Exhaustion weighed heavily on him. It was a longer word, that was all. He simply must persist. Finally, he reaped his reward. The numbers stood for Harwich. A port town in Essex, on the east coast. The closest English port to the Netherlands.

What did it all mean? He racked his brain, trying to make sense of it. At long last, he thought he had something. Mary and the Duke of Norfolk were planning to wed, which Gavin already knew. The confirmation in the cipher strengthened their case. Troops from the Netherlands would land at Harwich. Pairing this information with what he had overheard that night at the receiver's lodging, he could draw some conclusions. The troops—Spanish, because they ruled the Dutch at present—would support the seizing of the throne by Mary and Norfolk. Gavin assumed, although with his meager skills he could not confirm it, that the duke would be rallying English Catholics to support their takeover attempt, and all forces would combine.

Who was financing this?

The next set of numbers, 35, 34, 35, 15 spelled Pope, and he had his answer. And the details the duke was about to expound upon when Gavin had been knocked unconscious. The code breakers who worked for Cecil would crack this and obtain much more information than he was able to do. But this was incontrovertible evidence that Queen Mary and John Lesley were implicated up to their ears. He did not doubt that Cecil's people would find references to Norfolk where Gavin could not.

It was nearing dawn, but he must inform Shrewsbury without delay. As much as Gavin longed for his bed, there would be no slumber for him this night. In his personal chamber, he splashed water on his face, donned a clean shirt, and brushed his hair. Then, with the packet holding the documents clutched to his chest, he hurried to the earl's residence.

He hadn't thought of Isabel once in the last few hours.

In the morning, Gavin strode back to his residence. Shrewsbury had roused his secretary to copy the documents while Gavin and the earl discussed what was to be done.

"Do we put an end to the plotting now?" Shrewsbury asked. "Or let it move forward? That would enable us to gather further evidence against all parties."

"There is risk either way. But allowing the plot to carry on could potentially lead to unmasking others who may be involved. Men we do not even know about at present. Plus, further proof."

"And what about Ridolfi, if in fact it was he who gave the lad his orders?"

Staring at the documents resting on his lap, Gavin rubbed the back of his neck. His eyes felt gritty, as though somebody had tossed sand in his face. "I could follow him, see where he goes. He may not be here on his own."

The earl raised a tankard to his lips and took a long swallow. "Chances are, he will head for the coast posthaste."

"I'm concerned for the lad's safety," Gavin said. It was not the first time that thought had occurred to him. It had been hovering at the back of his mind since he'd decided to keep Simon overnight.

"I imagine he'll hand the papers over and that will be the end of it. He doesn't read, does he?"

"It's not that. Ridolfi would not expect Simon to understand the missives even if he could read. It's the delay. He'll be wondering what kept the lad."

"You need only help the boy concoct a credible story." Shrewsbury had risen, indicating an end to the meeting. "Follow Ridolfi far enough to establish his direction, then return to Tutbury and report to me."

Gavin nodded. "The move to Sheffield. It requires organization."

"Do you think I have never managed a progress before? I will order the packing of the carts to begin, and you can take over when you return."

Entering his lodging, Gavin wondered if he could snatch a few hours' sleep before rousing Simon and setting off for Derby. No. He'd put this off long enough. They must be on their way as soon as they'd had a meal. Barnaby greeted him at the door, and Gavin asked him to pack a clean shirt, shift, and hose for the trip. When the man turned to leave, Gavin said, "Oh, and we need food, Barnaby. Something hearty." Then he went to Simon and woke him up.

• • •

The next few weeks passed in a haze for Isabel. She spent her days helping to prepare for the move to Sheffield, which was a monumental task. Assigned the job of packing the queen's personal belongings, including her wardrobe, she was often isolated from the others. When she was unsure of whether Mary would need a certain gown or bodice, she erred on the side of caution and included the item. Isabel gained a new awareness of the extent of Mary's extravagance.

The queen's other ladies had completed their work quickly, as it had involved nothing more than packing Mary's favorite *objets d'art* and her embroidery supplies. They were free to sit on their stools and sew, gossip, and laugh. While Isabel resented them for it, she was largely glad to be removed from their presence. She did not believe she could be sanguine with them at present, and she was afraid they would ask her about Gavin.

He had disappeared after that horrible evening. The evening he'd told her they must end their love affair, if indeed what they'd been to each other could be called that. She could not say where he was, but she assumed it was some business for Shrewsbury. More than anything, she wished to ask Lady Shrewsbury where he'd gone, but she seemed to have fallen into despair for some reason.

One day, after she'd carefully folded and laid at least a dozen bodices in a container, she abruptly sat. When she recalled what she'd said to Gavin that night…oh, her humiliation was complete. A flush came over her, blossoming on her cheeks, and she set her hands on them. Why hadn't she pretended he meant nothing to her? Instead she'd called him awful names and come close to weeping. Clearly, she was not important to him at all. He'd looked shocked at her reaction, and she had behaved like the classic spurned female.

And now he was gone. Had he asked Shrewsbury to assign him a mission that would remove him from this awkward situation with her? Aye, she would not be surprised if he had. What man wishes to be reminded daily that a lady desires his attentions if he does not feel the same?

They were due to leave two days hence, whether Gavin had returned or not, Isabel assumed. She may never see him again. Perhaps that was for the best. Her injured heart would heal faster that way.

Get a hold of yourself, Isabel. Self-pity is unbecoming and tiresome.

She had returned to her task, this time folding smocks and kirtles, when she felt a presence. The queen had entered the room. Smiling at Isabel, she said, "So this is where you've been hiding."

Isabel leaped to her feet and curtsied. Annoyed, she had

to work to conceal it. "Most of your apparel is stored in these chambers, Your Majesty."

"*Oui*. Even I forget how much there is. I am sorry this has fallen to you, *ma chere*. I cannot spare Aimee." She riffled through the clothing, which had been neatly folded and set into the containers, setting Isabel's teeth on edge. "Too many bodices—I have no need for all these." Yanking some from the stack, she said, "I detest this one. I have never cared for velvet. Would you like to have it, Bel?"

Isabel wanted to decline, but the queen would take it as an affront. "Thank you, madam." At least the color was her favorite, a deep aubergine. To her relief, Mary moved away from the clothing and sat on a chair. "Are you looking forward to the move, Your Majesty?"

Mary shrugged. "A change of scene is always beneficial. Provided Sheffield will be warm and clean, I have no objection. The journey will be enjoyable. Shrewsbury is allowing me to ride the entire distance."

Isabel smiled. Mary loved riding, and she had not been granted that privilege in a long while. It would be more work for her guards, but of course the queen did not consider that. "I am glad you will be able to enjoy one of your favorite pastimes. I don't relish the journey. I'll be riding in one of the carriages, and I suffer from motion sickness."

Mary made a sympathetic face and got to her feet. Isabel rose, too. "The journey will not be long. Compared to others I've undertaken in Scotland, it will be nothing. Unless, of course, the weather turns." She walked to the door and whirled around abruptly. "Where is Gavin these many days, Bel? We have not seen him in nearly a fortnight."

If only I knew.

"He said nothing to me about leaving. His departure was a surprise. I assume Shrewsbury knows where he is."

"You are probably correct in that assumption, but I

will not ask him. Nor his foolish wife. Bess has decided that Shrewsbury has *le beguin pour moi*. He is attracted to me. I cannot help it if that is so. Men seem to like me, and there is nothing I can do about it. Regarding the earl, I certainly do not return the sentiment."

"No, Your Majesty." At this point, Isabel was merely mouthing words, saying what she thought Mary wanted to hear.

She paused, then said, "You did not speak to Gavin of what I discussed with you, Bel?"

That was unanticipated. And it rankled, after Isabel had given the queen her assurances more than once. "No, Your Majesty. I swore to you I would never betray your confidences. Do you not trust me?"

Mary, her eyes hard, studied Isabel, and at length said, "I trust you. Forgive me."

And then she went on her way. It had been a strange conversation. Isabel had the feeling the queen wanted something from her, but she couldn't fathom what that was. She had hoped Mary would offer help in the form of Frances, or one of her other ladies, but for whatever reason, she had not. Isabel felt as if she were being punished, but what she had done to deserve it was a mystery.

That evening, Gavin mysteriously reappeared. He strolled into the queen's presence chamber as though he'd been gone several hours rather than days. Isabel was playing with Bisou, which gave her a good reason to ignore him. Philip slapped him on the back and said, "Well met, coz," and the others greeted him just as effusively, as though he were the prodigal son. Perhaps they would eat the fatted calf tonight to celebrate his return. *Ugh.*

They did not speak, but she stole glances at him whenever the opportunity arose. He was as wickedly handsome as ever, but his face was wracked with fatigue. And worry. His broad forehead displayed lines she swore hadn't been there before, and she had a crazed urge to take him into her arms and smooth his brow. At one point, he caught her looking. Instead of that roguish grin he'd given her the last time he'd caught her staring, he frowned and then looked away. And did not look back.

Isabel wangled a seat next to Philip at dinner and flirted shamelessly. "If you require a dancing partner tonight, Master Blake, do think of me."

"Truly? I thought you would be saving all your dances for Gavin."

"He seems careworn and distracted, does he not? I do not believe he is fit for dancing." She had tried to convey her disinterest, and apparently succeeded. A light sparked in Philip's eyes, and Isabel worried about what she'd set in motion. When the dancing began, he grasped her elbow and led her out. As they performed the honor, Isabel felt Gavin's gaze on them, sharp and pointed as a dagger. She was beginning to feel guilty, but he had hurt her, hadn't he? It was time to let him know she no longer cared.

Gavin did not dance, even though both Alice and Dorothy urged him to partner them. Rather, he hovered on the edge of the rectangle cleared for dancing, arms folded across his chest, and watched. He was present, and yet he wasn't. Obviously, his thoughts were a thousand miles away from Tutbury. Isabel wished she knew what preoccupied him. But she was not meant to care. That was what she kept telling herself as she performed dance steps with Blake, who eyed her with an eagerness that made her heart lurch uneasily.

• • •

After a few dances, Gavin had seen enough of Isabel's flirting with Blake. If he stayed much longer, he might drag his friend out by his ruff and beat him senseless, and that would serve no useful purpose. He exited quietly, not bidding anybody a good evening.

The last few weeks had been an exercise in futility and frustration. Add apprehension into the mix, and that accurately summed up Gavin's fortnight. After the meeting with Shrewsbury, Simon had climbed up behind Gavin for the ride to Derby and revealed a bit about his family. At eighteen years old, he was the eldest of eight siblings and responsible for keeping them all from starvation's door. His father, from the sound of it, came around only long enough to get another child on his wife and steal what little money they had to satisfy his craving for drink.

"Does your horse have a name, sir?" Simon asked.

Gavin patted the animal's neck. "He does. It's Brutus."

"I'd like to have a horse like him one day. A good-looking hack like him must be worth a lot," he said. Gavin could hear the longing in his voice and wished he could make that happen for the boy.

When they had reached the outskirts of town, Simon climbed down to walk the rest of the way. Gavin handed him a parcel of victuals he'd had the kitchen prepare. If he'd known Simon's circumstances, he would have asked for a great deal more. As it was, the meat pies, loaf of bread, cheese, and strawberry tarts would not go far. Before the lad resumed the journey on foot, he and Gavin shook hands.

"If the foreign man asks why you were delayed, say that Lesley kept you overnight while he completed work on the documents. And get word to me at the castle if you feel threatened by him," Gavin said. "I don't want you risking your life."

"He'll probably have more messages for me to deliver to the bishop." He'd hesitated a moment, then said, "Say, Master Cade, would you be wantin' to read 'em before I delivers 'em?"

Gavin pondered this. Since they suspected Ridolfi would immediately ride for the coast, there most likely would be no further messages. But if there were, learning exactly what the Italian was communicating to Lesley would fill in part of the puzzle. "Aye. But wait until dark. Then come to my residence. Understood?" When the lad nodded, Gavin handed him a shilling and said, "Now, go."

Simon's eyes widened, then he threw himself at Gavin and embraced him awkwardly. When he started to walk away, Gavin called out to him. "Wait!" The lad stopped and spun around. "Give the man the packet and be on your way," Gavin said. "Don't tarry, for any reason."

"But I got to wait for my coin," the lad protested.

"I gave you a shilling, lad! Hand over the packet and get as far away from him as you can." Unease pricked at Gavin. He wished there was another way to get the documents to Ridolfi, but he couldn't think of one that would not raise suspicion. "Off you go, now."

He hadn't told Simon about his plans to follow Ridolfi, judging it best the boy knew as little as possible. Gavin let his horse graze and waited. He didn't want to follow too closely on Simon's heels. He sat on a fallen log and drank from a wineskin he'd brought along. Having given all the food to Simon, it would be some time before he'd have the luxury of eating.

Gavin had been avoiding thoughts of Isabel, but now they flooded his mind. Remorse over the way he'd treated her hung heavy on him. The memory of his arrogance made him cringe, and he hadn't had time to apologize before leaving Tutbury. Now that he'd separated from Isabel, he found that what he truly desired was to know her better. To learn the workings of her heart. He knew her brain well enough. She could not hide her intelligence. But it was now clear she'd never revealed anything personal, about her home, her family, or herself. Probably because he hadn't asked.

With a sigh, he got to his feet, mounted, and rode into Derby, and that was when things began to go awry. He stabled Brutus at an inn and walked toward the square, which was where Simon said he was meant to meet Ridolfi. It was a market day, and throngs of people were milling about the stalls, the women looking at the mercer's and haberdasher's offerings, the men lining up at the stalls selling ale. Children ran to and fro, chasing each other and bumping into people. Ordinarily, Gavin would have enjoyed the hustle and bustle, but now he was worried he wouldn't be able to spot Simon. Then he spied a set of stairs leading up to a church off one end of the square. If you were short and needed to be seen by someone, it would make sense to wait there. Edging closer, but not close enough for Simon to catch sight of him, Gavin kept his eyes trained on the steps. Sure enough, before much longer, the boy came into view, wiping his hands on his doublet. Gavin chuckled. He'd probably been devouring some of the victuals.

Simon was glancing around, looking wary, and Gavin's level of concern grew apace. So unobtrusively he nearly missed it, the man Simon had described—dark, curling hair, tipped cap, elaborate coat—emerged from the crowd like an evil spirit and grabbed the lad by the scruff of the neck. Simon tried to wriggle out of his grasp, but the Italian was too strong.

Gavin wanted to intervene, but if he did, everything they'd planned would be for naught. Continuing to watch them, he followed at a discreet distance. As they walked, the man spoke heatedly to Simon, whose face had turned red. The boy looked frightened. Eventually, Ridolfi led him to a lodging off the square, and they disappeared inside.

Jesu, Gavin hated this. A young, naive lad should not be

dealing with a rogue like Ridolfi. But at least he knew their location. It would be wise to prepare himself for a long wait. He found a stall selling meat pies and purchased a few. After obtaining a tankard of ale, he rested on a ledge while he ate and drank, never taking his eyes off the lodging. It was a half-timbered dwelling, listing a bit toward the square.

He waited in vain, for Simon never came back through that door. Gavin finished eating, got to his feet, and mingled in the throng of people, all the while keeping one eye on the house. But he never saw the boy, nor anybody else, emerge. When it began to grow dark, he found a room for the night, intending to resume his watch in the morning. Frustrated and worried, he drifted to sleep imagining the worst and powerless to do anything about it.

For three endless days, Gavin returned to his vigil, varying his location in case Ridolfi had underlings who might be keeping their own watch. He paid a small boy to investigate and inform Gavin if there were any means of exiting from the rear of the house. On the fourth day, a man he recognized as Ridolfi finally emerged from the house. Gavin, by this time, had begun to think the entire endeavor would need to be scrapped. When he glimpsed the Italian, he leaped to his feet and followed him. The man headed to the same livery where Gavin had left Brutus. After Ridolfi led his horse out, Gavin saddled Brutus himself and followed.

He trailed the man most of the day, a safe distance behind him. When the Italian stopped for a meal, Gavin did likewise, carrying his trencher outside so Ridolfi would not notice him. Both changed horses once. Gavin disliked leaving Brutus, but he would rescue his beloved mount on the return trip. By day's end, they'd gone far enough for Gavin to determine the other man was riding to Hull, where he could board a ship to Europe. His final destination was Rome, most likely, but Spain was also a possibility. In truth, it made little difference.

He would be carrying the documents either to the Pope or to King Philip.

Gavin spent the night in an alehouse with a clean room. A buxom tavern wench, after treating him to a tempting display of her bosom, tried to entice him to her bed, but Gavin politely declined. He provided a generous tip instead, and the next morning he was off at dawn. He had a day's ride just to make it back to Derby. Once there, he intended to find out where Simon lived and make sure he'd returned to the fold.

When he arrived, it was too late to do anything about finding the lad. He was forced to spend another night at an inn. After breaking his fast on cheese, bread and butter, and ale, he walked out into the square. The good citizens of Derby were not lingering, but were hustling toward their day's work. Gavin figured the best people to ask about Simon were his peers. The other lads hanging about looking for work. In fact, he was soon approached by one.

"Sir, you got a job for me?" the lad asked.

"I don't, but I'll give you a twopenny in exchange for some information."

The morning was wintry, the threat of snow in the air. The boy's nose was running, and his near threadbare garments were not sufficient to protect him from the cold. He glanced suspiciously at Gavin. "What you want to know, then?"

"I am looking for a friend's house. He helped me with something and I want to reward him, but I don't know where he lives. His name is Simon. Do you know him? He's about your age."

"I know him, but not where he lives. George might know." He walked quickly toward another boy and Gavin trailed behind him. "Ho, Georgie, this man wants to find Simon's house. You know where it is?"

"What you want him for?"

Gavin went through his explanation a second time.

"He hasn't been round here lately. Maybe his mum needs him. They live about two or three miles that way, outside of town. You got to cross the river, then keep following the road."

Gavin nodded. "In a house? A cottage? What kind of dwelling? How will I recognize it?"

The two lads looked at each other and laughed. "You'll come to a village. Well, it ain't really a village, just a few houses, if you can call 'em that. Simon's is the worst of the lot."

Gavin thanked the boys and flipped both a twopenny coin. Returning to the livery, he asked the stable boy to saddle Brutus, then headed toward Simon's house. He crossed the Derwent River on the stone bridge and followed the road out of town. Eventually, trees near the river gave way to low scrub. Fields and meadows were withered. Last year's brutal winter had been hard on the land, and Gavin prayed, along with everybody else, for an easier time this year.

It did not take long to find the village, a settlement of four or five broken-down hovels. Children ran about, mongrels on their heels. No adults were to be seen. It was difficult to determine which of the dwellings belonged to Simon's family. Gavin chose the likeliest one, based on the description he'd been given. A heavily pregnant woman answered his knock, several young ones clutching at her skirts, and he thought he must have chosen correctly. "Sir?"

Gavin removed his hat and bowed. "Pray, mistress, are you Simon's mother, by chance?"

"Aye. The boy isn't here. He's not been home in a sennight or more."

"May I speak to you? It's important," Gavin said.

"You'd best come in, then." The woman seemed predisposed for bad news. Fear had crept into her eyes, and her shoulders slumped. She gestured to a chair, the only one in sight.

"Pray madam, be seated. I'll stand." She shrugged and did as he said.

The youngest of the children climbed into her lap, and Simon's mother summoned one of her older children. "Peg, take the little ones and play with them for a while."

"Is Peg your eldest, next to Simon?" Gavin asked.

"Aye, and she's a good girl. But we need Simon. He's the only one who earns money. Do you know where he is, master?"

"I was hoping to find him here with you. I'm from Tutbury. I was on my way to Derby and gave him a ride. After I left him, he went off with a man he'd said he was working for."

The child in her lap was now suckling at her breast. "What do you want with him?"

"Nothing other than to make sure he returned safely home."

"Well, as you can see, he hasn't. And I don't know what we'll do without him. How we'll live."

Gavin glanced around. Some effort had been expended in keeping the place clean, although it was dingy and sparsely furnished. "I'll help you," he said. And he spent another week doing just that. Chopping wood and repairing holes in the roof kept his mind off Isabel. At week's end Simon still had not appeared. *Where was the lad?*

Before leaving, Gavin gave Simon's mother enough coin to see the family through the winter, at least. But he continued to feel uneasy about the boy's whereabouts and whether he was safe.

Earlier, when Gavin arrived back at Tutbury, he'd reported to Shrewsbury. The earl had heard from Cecil, who ordered them to take no further action until they received word from him. He and his staff were going to decrypt the cipher and possibly interview the Duke of Norfolk.

Gavin was frustrated with the inaction. He didn't like what he'd seen in Derby. He didn't like the fact that Simon was missing. And now Isabel was provoking him with her blatant flirting with Blake. What had he expected? That she would be pining for him, waiting for his apology? It seemed too late for that now. He'd told her matters between them could progress no further, or some such nonsense, and she'd accepted it and was bestowing her favors elsewhere.

All was over between them.

Chapter Fifteen

At last, the move was upon them. The queen and her entourage would be progressing to Sheffield Castle in the morning. Since Gavin's return, Isabel had kept busy with last minute details, conferring with Mary and Bess Shrewsbury, who seemed to have composed lists of everything. Upwards of thirty carts were laden with the queen's wardrobe, wigs, shoes, curatives. Her embroidery supplies filled one cart alone, and her personal belongings, several more. Then there were the carpets, hangings, plate and cutlery—it was boundless. Other carts held wine and barrels of ale, foodstuffs, and table linens, and Isabel was grateful she bore no responsibility for these goods.

Isabel and Gavin had not spoken. Indeed, he'd barely spoken to anybody but the earl. His demeanor had altered. Whereas before he'd always had a smile and a good word for everybody, now he seemed defeated and depressed. Mary's ladies gossiped about him, but Isabel did not join in, even when asked directly. Alice prodded her for information while they were packing the queen's remaining items.

"Bel, what is wrong with Gavin? He is sullen. And he has certainly cooled toward you."

Isabel, who had believed she was growing indifferent to Gavin, felt a jolt to her heart at that comment. Burdened with an armload of smocks, petticoats, and kirtles, she said only, "You must ask him yourself, Alice. I've not spoken to him since his return." Walking away with her load, she heard the other woman mutter something under her breath and the resulting snickers of her friends.

Mary clapped her hands, silencing them. "Make yourselves useful, ladies. There is much to be done."

Isabel hurried outside and looked for the cart which held similar items. Shrewsbury and Bess were studying their lists and directing the work of the many servants loading the carts. The earl's secretary stood by, and even Philip had been pressed into service. John Lesley huddled with an aide, no doubt planning malice of some sort. She didn't trust him. Not after what Gavin had told her. When she had divested herself of the garments, Isabel glanced up to see Gavin striding toward them, a servant trailing behind him. Gavin was carrying something, and at first, she could not identify what it was. Then, as he drew closer, she saw clearly what he held so gently in his arms. A person. A lad whose form appeared lifeless.

By now, others had taken notice and stopped what they were doing to gape. Suddenly, the atmosphere grew charged, everybody waiting to find out what this was about. Chatter ceased. All eyes were on Gavin. Bearing his sad burden, he headed directly toward Lesley, the only one among them who had not noticed him and who continued talking with his aide. Shrewsbury broke away from his wife and stepped forth, then hesitated, waiting to see what Gavin intended.

Many of those gathered, including Isabel, emitted gasps of horror, shock, or sadness when they finally got a clear view of the dead boy, whose body bore the unmistakable marks of a cruel end. By the time Gavin stopped, directly before John

Lesley, that man had finally ceased his conversation and was looking uneasily at Gavin, who said nothing, waiting until he had the bishop's full attention. The silence grew fraught.

"Well, what is it, Cade?" Lesley said. "Why are you bringing that ghastly corpse to me?" It was bravado. Isabel could see the fear in his eyes.

"You did this," Gavin said, so softly she had to strain to hear him.

Lesley laughed nervously. "You are not in your right mind. Perhaps you should see a physician. Your humors are unbalanced." He chortled, but even his aide did not join in the laughter.

Gavin had turned, seeking something. Shrewsbury stepped up behind him and began to speak.

"Is this wise, Cade?" He had whispered, but Isabel was standing close enough to hear. The frown he directed at Gavin held a warning. Gavin passed the body to his servant, who, to his credit, did not flinch. "Take him back to my residence, Barnaby."

In a moment, it was over. Gavin punched Lesley in the face, then in the belly. His fists flew so fast that Isabel lost count of how many of his punches hit their mark. Lesley clumsily threw a few of his own, to no avail. In the end, Philip and a couple of Mary's guards restrained Gavin. Even with three of them, it had been difficult. Blood streamed from Lesley's nose and the huge cuts that had opened around his eyes and on his jaw. Gavin had not a mark on him.

"You'll pay for this, Cade," Lesley screamed. "You, too, Shrewsbury. You stood by and allowed this man to beat me."

"Calm yourself, John," the earl said. "You'd better have those wounds seen to." Isabel detected a note of humor in the earl's words and thought he was suppressing a smile.

"I can have you removed from your post," Lesley said to Shrewsbury. "I have influence with Elizabeth." Spittle flew from Lesley's mouth, and the earl extracted a handkerchief from his pocket to dab at it.

"Do use your influence to that end, for I will be a happy man when that day comes," Shrewsbury said. Then he spun around and shouted, "Everyone, back to work. We leave at dawn tomorrow, and if we're not ready, there'll be hell to pay." Then he strode off after Gavin, who was walking back toward his residence.

Isabel remained, watching Gavin, wondering who the lad was and, of greater significance, who he was to Gavin. The death of this boy had to be related in some way to Gavin's two-week absence. Otherwise, she would know. He would have told her. Had he anticipated this killing? Feared it? Was that why he had seemed so careworn, so beaten down, since he'd been back at Tutbury? There was only one way to find out. Ignoring the shouts of Lady Shrewsbury, she turned and ran after the two men. Her anger and bitterness toward Gavin fell away with every step she took.

Shrewsbury had one hand on Gavin's shoulder and was issuing orders. That was obvious from his demeanor. Gavin nodded and jerked out of his grasp. Isabel reached him just as Shrewsbury was striding away.

"Gavin! Wait."

He seemed to barely register her presence, only continued walking, staring straight ahead. Out of breath, she hurried to keep pace with him. "Won't you tell me who the lad is? I can see his death is a great sorrow to you."

At last, Gavin turned to Isabel. He grasped her hand and led her to the fortification where they'd sat together on the steps and talked. Without preamble, he drew her into his embrace. He brushed his hands over her body— down her sides, up her back, and into her hair. Not in a sensual way, but as though he wished to draw comfort from touching her. She allowed it for as long as he wanted. At some point, the fact that he was quietly weeping crept into her awareness. Hearing his soft sobs caused tears to course down her face, and she dashed them away with one hand. She did not know what was wrong. Nor did she know the dead boy, or even the poor soul's identity. Nonetheless, she shushed him with quiet, gentle words.

"Hush, now, Gavin. Won't you tell me what happened? Is the lad kin to you?"

He shook his head. At length, his weeping tapered off. He pulled a handkerchief from his pocket and wiped his eyes and face. The torrent of emotion subsiding, he pulled her down to sit next to him on the crumbling steps. Gavin related Simon's story to Isabel, clutching her hand the whole time. "He was a good son, who looked after his mother and siblings. Uneducated, poor, but the salt of the earth. If the boy my wife gave birth to had lived, I would have been proud if he'd become a lad as worthy as Simon."

That shocked Isabel. When he'd told her about his wife and her betrayal, he'd spoken rather coldly of the child she'd birthed. That must have been a way to mask, or perhaps simply not acknowledge, any feelings he may have had for the babe. It had been some time before he'd discovered his wife's infidelity, and in the interim, he would have mourned the boy's death. And surely, if the child had lived, Gavin would have raised him as his own, even after he'd learned the truth.

"That snake Lesley and his cohort, Ridolfi, had the boy murdered. When he was late returning to Derby, his death warrant was sealed. I should have realized. I could have protected him. Instead, I used him so we could find out what Ridolfi was up to."

Denying this would do no good, because it was the truth. Partly, anyway. But Gavin had neither planned nor carried out the murder. "Perhaps. But you tried to help Simon. You didn't kill him."

Suddenly, his arms were around her again and he was whispering in her ear. "You are the only good and true person in my life, and I pushed you away. Can you forgive me, Isabel? You are very dear to me, and I am heartily ashamed of what I said to you. I was an arse, and no mistake." His ravaged face held a world of pain, but she did not doubt his sincerity.

Could she forgive him so easily? When she did not speak, he said, "I want to know you, Bel. Everything about you. Your past life, of which you have spoken very little, because I have not inquired. How you were hurt. Why you cannot believe there are any good men. All of it. Will you tell me?"

"I-I need time, Gavin. I want to, but…"

"When you are ready," he said, smiling ruefully.

She nodded. It was the best she could do. Too many times he had encouraged her, then pushed her away.

He got to his feet. "I'm obliged to speak to Shrewsbury before I deliver Simon's body to his family, which must be done soon." He let her go and raked a hand through his hair. "And I am sorely in need of a bath."

"And I must return to my duties before Lady Shrewsbury has an apoplectic fit. You will not return in time to leave for Sheffield with us."

"No. I'll join you there." He leaned down and kissed her gently. "Fare thee well, sweet Isabel. Safe journey." And then he walked away, his resolute strides leading him to the earl. Isabel watched, feeling an odd sensation. As if the chambers of her heart were overflowing, with an emotion she could only describe as love.

Beware, Isabel.

Abruptly, she spun and headed back to her labors. Deflecting the questions the others were sure to ask would not be easy. And she had questions of her own. In his telling of Simon's story, Gavin had left out some salient details. Why was he so certain of Lesley's guilt? What, exactly, was in the documents he had read? Something damning. Something threatening enough that a young lad had lost his life because of it. And Gavin had never referred to any man called Ridolfi before. Who was he? The name seemed vaguely familiar. With Gavin's emotions boiling over, it had not been a good time to ask him, but the next time they spoke, she would find out.

Most of all, Isabel wondered what it had to do with Mary. Gavin had been careful not to mention her, but Isabel had a feeling the queen may have been the principle subject of the documents.

• • •

Gavin stripped and bathed before his visit to Shrewsbury. He intended to leave for Derby immediately afterward. The earl would be furious with him for tipping his hand to Lesley, but Gavin was sick of the pretext and subterfuge. By God's light, Lesley had tried to kill him. He was encouraging Mary in her plotting against Elizabeth and using Norfolk to that end as well. Were they simply to stand by and pretend ignorance?

He had his answer soon enough.

The earl was pacing around his study, pausing every so often to scowl at Gavin. "God's teeth, Cade, what were you thinking? You were to keep this operation under wraps, so that we could gather as much information as possible. The final nail in the coffin. Thanks to you, we've lost that ability. It's likely they'll cease their plotting at once."

"If his plotting involves the murder of innocent young lads, perhaps that is a good thing. Do we not have enough to arrest them? Norfolk, Lesley, and Mary?"

"Recall, there is nothing in the documents implicating Norfolk."

"Nothing that *we* could find. Cecil's people may already

have discovered more."

"*May* have. And the rest is hearsay. A conversation you overheard before they knocked you on the head. None of it can be proved."

"It is in the documents!"

"It is not enough. Lesley can claim the wording in the documents means something else entirely." At last, Shrewsbury dropped into his chair, looking defeated.

Gavin's unwavering belief that they had sufficient evidence was broken. It had been wrong of him to confront Lesley. He'd allowed his emotions to cloud his judgment. Had he waited until their case was solid, Lesley would have gotten his just deserts in the end. He didn't know what more to say, so he said nothing. Shrewsbury was right, about everything.

"Go," the earl said, gesturing. "Carry out your sad duty and get to Sheffield posthaste."

Gavin nodded and took his leave, shocked that the earl hadn't dismissed him outright. He exited the Shrewsbury residence and immediately, to his chagrin, encountered John Lesley. Gavin had no intention of speaking to the man, but Lesley had other plans. He stepped directly in front of Gavin, blocking his way.

"I am on my way to speak to Shrewsbury about you, Cade. You should be removed from his service."

Gavin entreated himself to remain calm, taking a degree of satisfaction from the cuts, bruises, and swelling on the other man's face. Shoving him aside without responding, Gavin started on his way. Until he heard Lesley say, "Isabel Tait is a lovely young woman. I would hate to see any misfortune befall her. Or you, come to that."

At which point Gavin spun around, grabbed Lesley by his doublet, and hoisted him into the air. Ah. Now they were eye to eye. "If any harm should come to Isabel, you're a dead man, Bishop." Gavin lowered him to the ground, hoping he'd scurry off to the earl.

Lesley straightened his doublet and tugged at his hose. "Stay out of my—and the queen's—business, Cade."

Gavin, who'd been about to turn away, halted. "Or...?"

"You may find you've gone too far."

"And I might give you the same caution."

"I am innocent of any wrongdoing!" Lesley insisted, drawing himself up.

"Tell that to the rack master," Gavin said. He walked away, and when he glanced back over his shoulder, he took great pleasure in seeing Lesley abandon his plan to talk to the earl. Instead, he was hurrying to his own lodging.

Chapter Sixteen

The trip to Sheffield Castle was a necessary inconvenience. The weather had turned with a vengeance, pelting them with icy rain that soon became sleet. Even Mary, known for her love of riding, eventually surrendered to the elements and rode the remaining miles in her gilded carriage. Dorothy, Cecily, and Alice accompanied her, while Isabel, Frances, and Lady Shrewsbury rode in the conveyance belonging to the earl. Given what had happened upon her arrival at Tutbury, Isabel was afraid she would succumb to travel sickness once again, but apparently she wasn't prone to it after all. Although the air inside the coach was stagnant and the ride jarring, she did not become ill.

They arrived late and in full darkness. Torches flamed, lighting their way across the drawbridge. The retinue paused, awaiting the raising of the portcullis and the opening of the heavy oak and iron doors. This was a far cry from the situation at Tutbury, which offered very little in the way of protection other than a manned gatehouse. Perhaps Shrewsbury felt the remote location of Tutbury offered protection enough. Isabel wondered if the remoteness also served as a punishment for Mary. A reminder that she was a prisoner of the queen of

England.

Isabel, to her great relief, was not required to assist in the unpacking. Mary had assigned that task to Aimee, who organized and supervised the unloading and putting away of all Mary's clothing. Nonetheless, the queen took Bel aside and asked her to see to her personal memorabilia and *objets d'arts*, after she had dealt with her own belongings. The other ladies had been assigned the task of unpacking and sorting Mary's embroidery supplies, which would end up being a much greater task. Perhaps the queen was feeling guilty about placing such a great burden on Isabel's shoulders prior to the move. Isabel laughed at her own ridiculous idea—royalty never felt guilt about anything, did they?

On Christmas Eve, she kept one eye out for Gavin. She did not know how long a journey it would be from Derby to Sheffield, but surely it was doubtful he would arrive before Christmas Day. After inquiring of Bess Shrewsbury—whose knowing look irritated Isabel—how far it was between the two locations, she calculated it was possible he could arrive that evening. Not wishing to be disappointed, she tried not to dwell on it.

Sheffield employed a large cadre of servants, and Isabel had asked one of them to carry the containers of Mary's personal items up to her chambers. Trailing behind, Bel inhaled the enticing aroma of cinnamon, cloves, and nutmeg wafting up from the kitchens and into the living area. The cook and her staff were baking mince pies, and Isabel's mouth watered in anticipation. The servant placed the containers on a table, and Bel began opening them and setting the various objects in locations she judged would be pleasing to Mary. A jeweled penner given to her by Henri II. A rectangular bronze box etched with a salamander, from her first husband, Francois. Voices drifted from Mary's bedchamber, screened off from the outer room. After a moment, Isabel realized it was not one of the other ladies with the queen, but John Lesley. Without consciously debating the right or wrong of it, Isabel moved close enough to hear what they were saying.

"...should have been in on the decision-making. At the very least, you should have informed me before the plans were set. I do not even know when this takeover is to occur."

"Now, now, Your Majesty, you know I do not like to pester you with insignificant details given your ill health. No firm dates have been set, as we are still waiting on word from the Pope and King Philip."

"You refer to seizing the throne from the queen of England as an 'insignificant detail'? You are a fool sometimes, John." Isabel heard the disdain in Mary's voice.

"I may be, but always in service to you, my queen."

Lesley's obsequious tone was nauseating. Surely Mary could see through it.

"Your Majesty, this is your chance for freedom! You want to see little James again, do you not? You and Norfolk will rule both Scotland and England."

It was quiet for a moment, and Isabel backed away in case Lesley was leaving. Then Mary began speaking again. "This plan seems more to the duke's benefit than to mine. He informed me Scotland was not currently in play because of the warring factions there."

Lesley tutted. "You must leave this to us, madam. We know the wisest course of action. Everything has been set in motion, and at this juncture, you've really no choice but to see it through, have you?" His tone had hardened. It grew quiet, Lesley perhaps waiting for a response. When nothing was forthcoming, he went on. "And I would advise you to show caution in what confidences you share with Isabel Tait. She and Cade are close. Too close."

"He no longer seems to care for her, so I am not concerned."

Isabel's heart plunged.

"I hope you are right, but that is not what he said during my last conversation with him."

Mary made no answer, but Isabel imagined her glowering at the man. "Leave me, John. I am exhausted from yesterday's journey."

Isabel flew to the door, and as Lesley exited Mary's chamber, she pretended to be entering. "Bishop." He acknowledged her with a nod and brushed past without speaking. Isabel completed her task quickly, hoping Mary would not emerge from behind the screen. Once back in her own chamber, Bel curled up in the cushioned window seat and mulled over what she'd heard. Lesley seemed to be threatening the queen, who was unhappy at the advancement of this scheme. Were they coercing her to go along with it? Judging from Mary's questions and responses to Lesley, they were. Considering all she'd heard, Isabel believed it was the men, Lesley and Norfolk, who were making the decisions, forcing the queen to become their unwilling partner.

Odd, when Isabel thought about it, because when Mary had revealed the plan to her, she'd seemed in favor of it. What had changed? Perhaps she'd simply had more time to consider the arguments for and against.

After a light midday meal, Philip announced the men were venturing into the forest to find a Yule log. If they wished, the ladies could join them. The sun had reappeared, and although it was frosty outside, Isabel thought it would do her good to get out. She stopped by the queen's chamber to ask if she wished to accompany them. Aimee sat at her mending and nodded toward the screened area. Isabel rapped lightly to get Mary's attention and asked her question.

"*Non, merci,* Bel. I am not feeling well enough. But will you take Bisou? He needs the exercise." The little dog scurried around the screen and plopped down at Bel's feet, waiting.

"Are you sure, Your Majesty? The out of doors may do you good."

"I am sure." And that was the end of it.

"Come, little friend," Isabel said. "You, at least, will have the benefit of the sun and fresh air."

The size of their party had increased, and Isabel assumed the newly arrived men and ladies were guests of the Earl of Shrewsbury and his wife. They were all acquainted with one another and with Mary's ladies. Isabel was the only one who did not know the newcomers. In time, she supposed she would be introduced to them. Frances hung back from the group and walked with Isabel. "What do you think of our new residence, Bel?" she asked.

Isabel smiled. "I like it very much. It is warmer, there are no foul odors—yet—and we each have our own chamber. Compared to Tutbury, it seems a virtual paradise."

Frances laughed. "Aye. 'Tis more comfortable, indeed."

"Who are the guests? I have not been introduced."

"Oh. I assumed you knew. Dorothy's husband, Walter Vere, and his sister, Jane. Also Alice's husband, Henry Alymer, and their friend Anne Ramsay."

Isabel could not hide her astonishment. Two of the women bouncing from bed to bed with various men were married? Never had she considered this. At her shocked expression, Frances laughed. "Taking lovers is very common, Bel. It is an accepted practice among ladies of the higher classes. Why should they not do so when their husbands bed other women?"

Did John Lesley have a wife?

"Another reason not to wed," Isabel said, causing Frances to laugh even harder. "Truly, what is the point?"

"To bear children, of course," was the answer.

"But how can they know who the father is?"

Frances smirked. "Sometimes they do not. Usually the husband raises whatever child is born to his wife as his own. Speaking of husbands, where is Gavin? Why is he not here?"

"Gavin is not my husband!"

"But perhaps he will be one day," Frances said slyly.

"Nay, you are much mistaken. He—he had an errand near Derby, after which he intended to ride to Sheffield. That is the extent of my knowledge." Handing over a dead youth to his mother should hardly be termed an errand, but Isabel preferred not to discuss any of what Gavin had told her with Frances. Bisou chose that moment to bound after a hare, and Isabel excused herself to hurry after him. It wouldn't do to lose the queen's beloved pet. And she was glad to escape Frances's questions.

"Bisou!" When she did not immediately see him, she lifted her skirts and picked up her pace. On the little dog's trail, she was reversing back toward the outer wall of the castle. "Bisou! *Ici!*" Off in the distance, she heard laughs and shouts of the party searching for the perfect Yule log. But within her, everything had stilled. Gavin was riding over the drawbridge and through the entrance, quite alone, his slumped posture revealing the level of his exhaustion.

• • •

After carrying out his sad duty and making sure Simon's family had the necessary resources to get through the winter, Gavin wasted no time in riding to Sheffield. He wanted, needed, to see Isabel and make sure she was all right. He took Lesley's comment as a tangible threat—he would be a fool not to, given everything that had happened.

Riding over the drawbridge, he felt a great sense of relief, and at the same time, an encroaching exhaustion he could no longer fight. And then he thought he heard Isabel's voice.

She was calling for Mary's dog. He twisted in the saddle and glimpsed her just outside the outer curtain wall. She waved to him while the little dog scampered about her feet. Smiling, he held up a hand in greeting, and a feeling that he'd come home enveloped him. Wherever Isabel was, was home.

That was a shocking thought. And yet it had become a fundamental truth. But before he could seek her out, he needed to bathe and sleep. He hadn't rested for more than a few hours since he'd been away. He could not present himself to Isabel looking and feeling like a beggar from the streets of London. Fortunately, he'd no cause to report to Shrewsbury, because his absence had nothing to do with their chief concerns.

After his few hours with Simon's family, Gavin had ridden back to Derby and found a jeweler. He explained what he wanted and waited while the man made a few changes to the piece Gavin had chosen. Now, he patted his pocket to make sure it was there, wrapped in its small velvet bag. Sometime during Christmastide, he would give it to Isabel.

Gavin bathed, and Barnaby trimmed his hair and beard. After asking the servant to wake him by six, he fell into a troubled sleep. When he entered the hall near seven o'clock, it was a scene of great merriment, with many more people milling about than he expected. Had the earl invited the whole damn neighborhood? Gavin didn't like it. There was no way of determining who was friend or foe. A Yule log was burning on the expansive hearth, putting out plenty of smoke. Everyone's eyes and lungs would be burning before long. Looking around, he spied Isabel with a few of the ladies. They were weaving wreaths and kissing boughs, from the looks of it. She did not glance up.

Somebody tapped him on the shoulder and he turned. "Cade, well met," Shrewsbury said. Gavin could tell from his eyes he was far into his cups.

"My lord. This is quite a party." Gavin made a sweeping gesture. "Who are all these…guests?"

"Ha! Husbands, in-laws, friends. Don't know them all. Zounds, does it matter, man?"

It does, you idiot.

Gavin wanted to argue the matter, but what would be the point? Shrewsbury was drunk to the point of slurred words and unsteady legs. He turned his gaze toward Isabel, and this time she looked up at him. Her eyes were cold, their icy daggers directed squarely at him. But when he tried to excuse himself, the earl held him back.

"M'wife thinks I'm sleeping with the queen, Cade. What do you make of that?"

The man was drunk, so Gavin didn't bother guarding his tongue. "Are you?"

Shrewsbury sputtered. "I vow I'm not! We are thrown together a great deal, and the woman flirts. No denying she's a beauty. But I love Bess." He looked so sorrowful, Gavin regretted his question. "She's banned me from her bed, devil take it."

"I'm sorry for it, my lord. Give her time, and she'll get over it. And stay away from Mary as much as possible." Shrewsbury looked as though he might keel over, so Gavin helped him to a chair. "Perhaps you should retire, sir."

The earl waved him away. "Go. I know it's the Tait lass you wish to talk to, not me."

True enough. Gavin made his way toward Isabel. Cecily whispered something to her, but instead of glancing up, she steadily worked on. By the time he reached her, both Cecily and Alice had retreated, leaving the object of all his thoughts alone.

"Isabel," he said, somewhat breathlessly.

At last she dropped the wreath to the table and looked up at him. "Gavin. You are back."

He smiled. "Aye. I saw you as I came over the bridge earlier."

She started to smile, then checked herself. What in hell was she angry about?

"May we speak in private, Bel? Somewhere away from this crowd. And the smoke."

She seemed to be weighing his request, but at length she rose. Without exchanging a word with him, she led Gavin from the hall and outside into another building. After climbing a spiral stairway leading to the living area, they entered a chamber, a small but cozy one, with its own fireplace, window, and a tester bed with its curtains tied back. She had brought him to her private chamber. Should he read anything into that?

"I have my own stairs," Isabel said. "What do you think of that?"

"Very impressive. What did you do to deserve such an honor?"

She laughed, relieving some of the tension between them. "Nothing. I was assigned the smallest chamber, and the stairs happened to be here, along the outside wall. I believe they were meant for servants at one time."

They'd barely crossed the threshold when Gavin said, "Isabel, why are you angry with me?"

A faint blush bloomed on her cheeks. He'd flustered her. "I-I'm not."

"Aye, you are. Your eyes are full of it. What have I done?" When she didn't answer, he took her arm and led her to the settle before the fireplace. A log was still burning, warming them and casting flickering light into the chamber.

"Pray, don't be afraid to tell me what is upsetting you."

She hesitated, then seemed to reach a decision. "Very well. I simply wondered why you did not come to me right away, after your return. Why you waited until tonight."

Ah, she'd missed him then. He could not prevent a slow smile from breaking over his face.

"Do not look so smug, Master Cade," she said. "You are treading on thin ice."

At that, he laughed out loud, and after a moment, she joined him. "If you had seen me face-to-face, dear Isabel, you would have been quite happy to delay our reunion. I was covered in filth from my days on the road, and exhausted into the bargain. I required a bath, a shave, and most of all, sleep."

She looked thoughtful, and he waited for her to speak. "It is only that I never know with you, Gavin. How things stand between us. One day you proclaim how dear I am to you, and the next you push me away, in word or deed. Sometimes both. Sometimes even at the same time. You cannot seem to make up your mind about me."

She was not far off the mark. He had changed his mind more than once about Isabel. Not because he didn't like her; on the contrary, he admired her keen intellect and gloried in her loveliness. A combination he found irresistibly alluring. No, it all had to do with Anna. He'd given her his love and trust, and she had betrayed him. To commit to another woman—well, it simply seemed too soon. And yet…he could no longer imagine life without Isabel. Without knowing he would see her. Be near her. Hold her.

He took her hand, caressed it, and said, "What if I told you I missed you every minute I was away? That I could not keep my mind on what I was doing, because you filled every nook and cranny of it. And of my heart. What if I told you I recalled everything we'd ever talked about, and it brought me a great deal of comfort during a dark time?"

Her eyes gleamed in the firelight, and she did not speak immediately. "I would be surprised. But happy." She glanced shyly up at him, and he could bear it no longer. He wrapped his arms around her and drew her against him. "Bel, my darling, Bel. Kiss me, sweetheart." He covered her mouth with his and she melted against him. Her lips were velvet and tasted of spiced wine. With an eagerness born of anticipation, he stroked her long, glossy hair while he gave himself over to kissing her more deeply, offering his tongue, taking hers into his mouth. Her skin was the epitome of soft. He ran his hand over her face, the alabaster column of her neck, her bosom, until finally, reason called him back from the brink.

"Isabel, we must stop. Not because I don't want this. I need to talk to you about something, and we should not be absent for much longer."

"But I—"

"Later, sweetheart. I'd like nothing better than to make love to you tonight. I've been dreaming of it for days. But what I have to say cannot wait."

Eyes a bit glazed, she nodded. "Go ahead, then. Tell me."

Before speaking, Gavin rose, opened the door, and checked the passage to make certain they were alone. When he was satisfied, he returned to her but remained standing. Earlier, he'd made up his mind to get straight to the point and convey the sense of urgency he felt without hedging. "We must leave Sheffield. You and I. As soon as an opportunity arises."

Isabel shook her head. "But why?"

Realizing he may sound irrational to her, nevertheless, he had no choice but to plunge ahead. "I believe an attack on one or both of us is imminent. The safest course of action is to remove ourselves from danger." He waited, studying her.

She simply stared at him for a moment without uttering a word. When she finally spoke, her words were measured. "Not long ago, I asked you what your true position was in service to Shrewsbury. You never answered me. Not directly. Will you tell me now?"

He crossed his arms over his chest. "Is it not obvious? I

am working for men who serve the queen. Queen Elizabeth."

"And what is your purpose?"

He should have known she wouldn't let it go at that. This was Isabel, after all. "More than that I cannot say. I've told you too much as it is."

"You have given me bits and pieces. It is difficult to put it all together." When he did not speak, she sighed and said, "What has led you to draw this conclusion, Gavin? That we are in danger?"

He rubbed the back of his neck, trying to ease the tension. "Everything. Beginning with the attack at the river. Ending with Simon's murder. And many other matters you do not know of." He would rather not reveal Lesley's direct threat to Isabel. It would frighten her. He'd prefer to simply keep a close watch on her.

"You believe Lesley was responsible for Simon's death. But do you have proof?"

How much to tell her? He felt as if every jagged piece of the puzzle he shared with her endangered her further. Best to be vague. "I do."

Was that vague enough?

"But you will not tell me what that is? Was it within those documents you mentioned to me?"

Frustrated, he got to his feet and began pacing. "The more you know, the greater the risk to you." He paused mid-step and studied her. "They are on the offensive, Isabel. Lesley and his minions have shown they are not afraid to do what is necessary to have things their way."

"I'm afraid if you cannot be more specific, then my answer is no. I won't leave Sheffield. If I were to flee from this place, it would not be because of some vague threat which cannot even be explained to me." She grasped his arm. "Do not forget, I am here at the invitation of Lady Shrewsbury, to act as one of the queen's ladies. To simply run away from that duty, without even understanding why, is out of the question. I could be sent home, and I couldn't bear that."

"Returning to your home is so abhorrent to you? 'Tis better to risk your life?"

She shrugged. "I-I cannot explain. Not now."

He had not expected her to make this so difficult. Perhaps she merely needed time to think it through. He could grant her that, and in the meantime, prepare to leave. Devise a plan. He would force her to leave with him, if it came to that. Although the idea of an abduction was repugnant, if the danger became too great, he would do it. For now, backing off and allowing her to believe he was reconsidering seemed like the safest course.

He misliked it, but without further explanation, she would not agree. "Very well, Isabel. We shall carry on as usual. I will simply need to be vigilant. And so should you."

A flicker of emotion lit her eyes, but he wasn't sure what she was feeling. Disappointment that he had given in so easily? Or that he wouldn't confide in her? He could not speculate, nor did he wish to. "We must return to the hall. We'll be missed."

Chapter Seventeen

Christmastide 1570

Christmas morning dawned fair, but with a deep chill across the land. Mary's entourage, including Isabel, gathered in the hall and walked a short distance to the town for services.

Afterward, Isabel and the other ladies completed the wreaths and kissing boughs, adding holly, ivy, and berries. When they'd finished, they hung their handiwork around the queen's living area. "We all know who Isabel wants to kiss under the bough," Cecily said.

"Oh, you discovered my secret," Isabel replied, deciding to give as good as she got. "That tall, well-built fellow who stands guard outside the queen's door. What is his name? Alfred?"

It was common knowledge the man was one of Alice's lovers, one whom she was particularly partial to. The women dissolved in laughter, all except Alice. Even Mary chortled.

It had been a difficult morning for Isabel. Even at services, she could think of little else but what had transpired between her and Gavin the previous night. She did not know what to make of his announcement that they should leave Sheffield. It irked her that he wouldn't be more forthcoming about why he believed they should take such a drastic step. It was plain that

Gavin didn't trust her with the facts he'd uncovered. Perhaps she was being too hard on him, for she had no doubt that he cared about her and wished to keep her from harm. His revelation that thoughts of her had sustained him—and that he'd dreamed of making love to her—made her heart jump and her skin heat.

He must have unassailable reasons for believing they may be in danger, but whatever those were, he was keeping them private.

The annoying reminder that she also had facts at her disposal which she hadn't mentioned to Gavin hovered at the back of her mind. Mary had revealed things to her in confidence, and she could not breach that trust. Could she? Gavin would, in the blink of an eye, if it meant pursuing his agenda for the crown. To be fair, protecting the Scots queen seemed also to be a high priority for him.

Perhaps Isabel should speak to Mary about her concerns again. She would need to confess she'd overheard her conversation with Lesley, and Bel could not predict how the queen would react to that. But if Mary was being coerced into something she really did not wish to do...shouldn't Bel urge her against it? When Bel had advised caution previously, however, it had not been well received by the queen. She'd become defensive, self-pitying, and ended up crying.

It was a conundrum not easily solved. Isabel would simply need to wait and see what the following days would bring. She could not credit that anything nefarious was in the works during Christmastide, however.

That evening after a meal featuring an elaborate Christmas pie—turkey stuffed with a goose stuffed with a chicken stuffed with a partridge stuffed with a pigeon—they gathered in the great hall and the cooks brought out the mince pies. Besides the usual members of Mary's circle and their guests, neighbors had been invited to share the pies and the Wassail bowl. This merrymaking was a tradition Isabel's family had never observed, and the number of people milling about was making her head spin. She glanced around for Gavin, but didn't see him. He'd sat between the two female guests at dinner, Anne Ramsey and Jane Vere. Mistress Ramsey was somewhat silly, and Bel had heard her giggles pierce the undertone of conversation more than once. Jane Vere, on the contrary, was a quiet girl, not more than fourteen or fifteen. Isabel, to her dismay, was wedged between John Lesley and Alice's husband, Henry. She marked him immediately as a rake. He looked at her with hungry, lust-filled eyes, and at one point, she'd had to remove his hand from her thigh. The only conversation he'd managed during the meal was, as he gestured toward a platter of roast capon, "Those thighs and breasts are quite plump, eh?" Said with a waggle of his bushy brows. Perhaps Alice's liaisons were a bit more understandable now.

John Lesley, after a curt, "Mistress Tait," said nothing else, but had spoken, in a voice too low to hear, only to Mary.

As Isabel wandered about the hall, she heard laughter break out whenever somebody was caught beneath one of the kissing boughs. Not paying attention, she was startled when a strong hand tugged on her arm and forcefully dragged her forward. At first she didn't recognize the man. Reminded of her talk with Gavin, fear stabbed at her. But when Alice, Cecily, Dorothy, and Frances all popped up beside her, hooting with laughter, she guessed what was about to happen. Bel tried to free herself from the man's grasp, but it was futile. Underneath a nearby kissing bough, Alfred, the guard she'd described earlier to her friends, kissed her soundly, in a much more familiar way than she could countenance. She tried to break free, pushing her hands into his brawny chest, but it was no use.

"Unhand her!" The hall suddenly hushed. She recognized

that commanding voice. The burly guard, accustomed to following orders, complied immediately, and Gavin pulled her to his side. He was looking at the poor fellow with murder in his eyes, while off to the side, the ladies who'd orchestrated the whole thing tittered.

"It were just a prank, Master Cade," he protested.

"Not a very funny one," Gavin growled.

"Gavin, why don't *you* kiss Isabel?" It was Cecily, of course. Cries of, "Kiss her, kiss her!" went up. Isabel had never seen him look so rattled. Instead of satisfying the playful goading of the merrymakers, Gavin grabbed her hand and led her away from the crowd.

"Not up to the challenge, eh, Cade?" That taunt came from Blake, but Gavin steadfastly ignored it, as well as others just like it.

"Where are we going?" Isabel asked as he resolutely pulled her along.

"Just away. Away from all these drunken louts."

. . .

After a moment, they reached the passage, lit at intervals with rush lights. It was empty save for a few guards. Starved for fresh air, he sucked in deep breaths and hurried Isabel along toward his small private chamber.

She protested. "Gavin, no. We can't be in here alone."

"We can. We were alone when we left the hall. No doubt they're all convinced we're going someplace to kiss in private, since we refused to do so in public."

"But still…"

He was losing patience. "Isabel, we were alone in your chamber last night, and you didn't make a fuss about that. How is this different?"

"That was less conspicuous. Few took note of our leaving.

Tonight, everybody did."

Raking an impatient hand through his hair, he said, "If you are so concerned about the opinion of those people, most of whom aren't worthy of your consideration, we shall leave the door open. Will that help?"

"Very well. I suppose nobody can impugn my virtue that way."

"Pray, sit down." He poured them each a glass of wine and joined her on the settle. Trying to marshal his thoughts, he sat silent for a moment. He had wanted to ask Isabel about her past. Find out what had caused her to believe men were nothing but weak-willed aggressors, and this was his opportunity. "When we first became acquainted, I told you I was a good listener. Will you do me the honor of telling me about your home and your family, Bel?"

Silence enveloped them while she considered his request. Her reluctance was unmistakable, yet he did not believe she would refuse. "My father died before I was born. I would give anything to have known him."

Gavin squeezed her hand. "I am sorry you never had the chance."

She shrugged, as though it hadn't mattered. "It is not uncommon. Many people suffer the same loss. In my case, it was made worse by my mother's second marriage to a despicable man."

Isabel glanced over at him, as though waiting to see if she should continue. He nodded and said, "Go on."

"My mother bore two sons with him, Thomas and Andrew. Although austere, my life was not that different from that of any other child of my class until my half brothers were old enough to have a tutor. I was six or seven by then, and they were a few years younger."

An age-old story. A cruel tutor who did not hesitate to use the whip. "The man was cruel to you and your brothers."

"No. Only to me."

"And your mother and stepfather did not intervene?"

"The tutor *was* my stepfather, Nathaniel Hammond."

"Oh, Isabel." He tried to draw her into his arms, but she wouldn't permit it.

Her voice trembling, she said, "Let me finish. It is not a pretty story, and 'tis best gotten over with quickly."

She did allow him to hold her hand, clutching his as though he were her salvation. "When I first began my lessons, it was bearable, although if I erred with my letters or numbers, he punished me. But in those early days, it was standing in the corner, or making me sit facing the wall. I'd had the foolish notion I might help him with the boys, but when I suggested it—that was when he administered my first beating."

Jaw clenched, Gavin said, "How old were you?"

"I can't be certain. Those years have blurred together, but seven or eight, I think." When he tried to ask another question, she protested. "No, don't say anything, Gavin. I may not have the strength to continue if you interrupt."

Feeling dread pool in his gut, he nodded.

"The real trouble began when he added Latin to our lessons." She hesitated, looking bashfully up at him. "I was a quick study. I am not saying so to be prideful, but that is the truth of it. The boys were slower. They were both bright, especially Andrew, but I was older and adept at learning. Latin particularly appealed to me. I loved the order of the language. The cases and declensions. My stepfather detested me for it, for catching on faster than his own sons. If one of the boys missed an answer, he would turn to me, and if I answered correctly, inevitably a punishment would follow. I caught on and began feigning wrong answers. But then he punished me for that, too."

Isabel had been on the mark when she said this was not a pretty story. Hearing it was making him want to hit something. Someone. "What were the punishments?"

"He forced me to lift my skirts and whipped me about my ankles with a willow switch. Gradually, as I grew older, he made me lift my skirts higher and higher. I-I began to believe he took some perverted pleasure from it. From seeing my bare ankles and calves and causing me pain. I tried not to cry, because the lashing went on longer and harder if I did. I learned to hold it in. He made the boys watch. Once, when Andrew defended me and refused to watch, he received a sound beating. He did not protest again." She laughed bitterly. "Thomas, by the look on his face, enjoyed the whippings as much as his father did. I have never liked him because of it."

Gavin did not believe Isabel was aware of it, but tears were streaming down her cheeks and dripping onto her bodice. He fished for a handkerchief and handed it to her. "Your mother. Did you tell your mother?"

Isabel wiped away her tears and dabbed at her nose. "I was a little girl. Of course I did. I begged her to help me, to put a stop to it, but she always refused. She said I was a disobedient child and must learn to show proper respect to my stepfather and to God. To this day, she argues that my recalcitrance and defiance made her marriage difficult. That if her husband did not like me, I was to blame."

"Come here, sweetheart." Gavin hoped she would allow him to hold her. He wished he could take away the hurt she had suffered. She would carry the scars forever. Surprising him, Isabel hurled herself into his embrace and sobbed on his shoulder.

"I am sorry he's dead. I would love to kill him," he said, stroking her hair.

Between sobs she choked out, "After my stepfather died, my mother couldn't wait to get rid of me. Within days of his death, she announced her plans to marry another man, my stepfather's lawyer. And she instructed Thomas to find me a husband. That was why I was so happy to accept Lady Shrewsbury's offer and why I cannot bear the thought of going back."

Gavin patted her, shushed her, until gradually she quieted. He desperately wished to make the horrible memories fade, but felt powerless to do so. Isabel drew away from him, and reluctantly, he let her go.

"Are you close with your family?"

He chuckled. "Aye. I am my mother's favorite. All my kinsmen, even Mother herself, say it's true. We all work in the family business, which is provisioning military garrisons. There are plenty of those along the border."

"What about your father?"

"He was away a fair amount, making deliveries or picking up supplies. He only knew what my mother chose to tell him. If he'd learned of the mischief my brothers and I got up to, there would have been hell to pay."

She canted her head to one side. "You are obviously well educated, Gavin. You could not have spent all your time getting into trouble."

"We had tutors. My father insisted."

"How did you end up here, assisting Shrewsbury?"

"It is a long story, but suffice it to say, this is not work I intend to continue doing."

The melodious sounds of musical instruments and singing rang down the passage. "We should return to the hall," Isabel said.

Gavin stood and raised her up beside him. "My mother would love you, Isabel," he said. "She would treasure you, as you deserve. What you experienced is not...the usual way children are treated by their parents."

She nodded, tears shimmering in her eyes. "Thank you for saying that. A mother's love—that would be a new experience for me." Holding hands, they found their way back to the holiday celebration, singing carols and dancing into the wee hours.

• • •

Isabel had been avoiding breaking her fast with Queen Mary because she had not decided if she should speak to her about what she'd overheard. The morning after Christmas, though, Mary was dining alone in the small chamber adjacent to the living area. When Isabel entered, the queen motioned to her. "*Bonjour*, Bel. I am glad to see you." Isabel curtsied and sat down, while Mary signaled to one of her attendants to bring an extra plate of food and a tankard of ale.

They ate in silence for a time. There was the usual fare of bread, cheese, and figs, and to Bel's delight, a special offering of mince pie. All the while, her conscience carped at her.

Don't be such a coward, Isabel Tait. Now or never.

"Your Majesty, may I speak to you about something?"

"Oh, do not say it is about Gavin! *Alors*, I am not somebody who should advise about matters of the heart."

Isabel laughed. "No, it is not about Gavin." She lowered her voice because George Douglass was hovering about, as well as other retainers. "A few days past, I was in your chamber unpacking some of your personal items, when I overheard a conversation between you and John Lesley."

Mary took a swallow of ale. Her eyes were guarded, but at least she hadn't lost her temper and shouted at Isabel. Yet. "And did you not feel it incumbent upon yourself to remove from the room, so that you would not be party to a private discussion?"

Isabel cleared her throat. How to answer that? All things considered, it would behoove her to be honest. "I did not care for the tone of his voice. Nor his words. It sounded as though he was threatening you, and at the time, I thought you should not be alone with the man." Not exactly a lie, but not the truth, either.

"You believed you could protect me?" Mary leaned forward and lowered her voice. "How...quaint. Don't be such a little fool, my dear. Lesley is my most trusted ally, and has been so for many years. You should not insert yourself into matters which do not concern you."

So Isabel was not to be forgiven so easily. "I apologize, madam. Clearly, I misinterpreted the situation. Pray forgive me."

Although Mary smiled, her eyes were hard and her expression distant. "Have you ever noticed that piece of embroidery?" she asked, gesturing toward the wall. It was one Isabel had seen many times and pondered over. The inscription was in French rather than in Latin. *En ma fin est mon commencement.* In my end is my beginning. Did it mean that Mary, despite years of adversity, would be freed and live to rule another day? Or did the "beginning" refer to her son? That after both she and Elizabeth died, he would inherit the throne?

"I begin to believe that my little James is the future. I gave him life, and he will carry on after I am dead. After my cousin is dead. That is truly the only thing that matters." She bowed her head briefly. "You see, Bel, I have little hope for my own future. That I will ever be free."

Perhaps it was not too late to ask her to be wary. But before Isabel could gather her courage enough to speak, Mary had risen and left the table. Bel thought she had never seen the queen look so sad, and her heart broke for this woman, so full of contradictions. She had been robbed of the life to which she was born. And of so much else.

Was Mary saying she was willing to risk everything, even her life, because her son was the only thing that truly mattered?

Chapter Eighteen

After the queen left, Bel made a half-hearted attempt to finish her meal, but she'd lost her appetite and no longer felt like eating. In fact, the only activity that sounded appealing to her was a walk. The weather continued to be bitterly cold, but if she dressed in her warmest garb, she would manage. Stopping by the queen's chamber, she asked Dorothy if she could take Bisou with her. Holding the little dog in her arms, she went to her own chamber to prepare for the out of doors. Bisou jumped up on her bed while she donned a woolen cloak, a thick scarf, leather gloves, and heavy boots.

When Isabel was ready, she called to Bisou, but he seemed loath to follow her. Perhaps he did not like the cold. To her surprise, he growled when she tried to pick him up. A low, barely audible rumble. Despite his reluctance to leave his perch on the bed, she lifted him into her arms and said, "Come, little stubborn one. You cannot avoid going outside." Isabel wished the queen would make her a gift of the pup, but there was absolutely no reason why she should. Especially now, when Bel had poked into her private business and received a reprimand for it.

After exiting her chamber, Isabel traversed the short

distance to the door. She would use her "private stairs." Much more convenient than walking all the way back through the passage and down the main stairs, only to be stopped by the guards. Unconsciously, her thoughts turned to a blue-eyed, strapping man with chestnut hair. Gavin had been so kind to her last night. She was torn about denying his request to depart Sheffield. Perhaps she should reconsider. Isabel opened the door, and a blast of cold air hit her, stealing her breath. Bisou started to whimper. "What is it, scamp?"

Isabel stood in the doorway, and a feeling of unease gripped her. She sensed a presence behind her. Was that why the dog had been whining and growling? She spun around, but glimpsed only inky darkness. Eager to get away, she placed a foot on the top step. From behind her, a steady, firm hand settled on her back and shoved. Immediately, Isabel lost her footing and went down, tumbling in a jumble of arms and legs all the way to the bottom.

· · ·

"Isabel! Isabel, wake up." Gavin patted her cheeks and sprinkled water on her face. After several minutes, during which he could barely breathe, she began to come around. Her amber eyes opened, but quickly closed again. He thought perhaps the light was bothering her. "Close the drapes." Someone, probably Blake, did so.

About fifteen minutes after the bell for nones had chimed, Blake had burst into his office shouting that Isabel had fallen down the stairs and was unconscious. Gavin had not even taken the time to throw on his cloak, but simply dashed toward Bel's chamber, where someone had carried her.

There hadn't been time to ask any questions, so he posed them now. "Where did this happen?"

Blake gestured toward the stairs outside Isabel's chamber. "Just there. Those treacherous steps that run along the outside wall. They must have been covered with ice, invisible to the eye."

Like hell it was ice. Rather, it was something a great deal more insidious, and Gavin harbored no doubts about who was responsible.

Isabel's eyes flickered open again. "Gavin? Is Bisou...?" Her voice was weak, but she was awake and asking questions, a good sign.

Gavin glanced at Blake. "The pup was with her?"

"I don't know. He wasn't there when I arrived on the scene."

"Gather everyone together. The men who found Isabel after her fall. Mary and her ladies. Anyone who may have witnessed what happened. I'll meet you in the queen's chamber shortly."

"I'll do what I can," Blake said.

Isabel's eyes were closed again. After Blake left, Gavin spoke softly to her. "Isabel, we need to determine if you have broken a bone or sustained other injuries. May I examine you?"

She opened her eyes and nodded. "My head hurts like the blacksmith has taken his hammer to it. And breathing is painful."

Gavin opened the door and found some of the women waiting for news. Cecily stepped forward. "How is she?"

"That is what I am trying to ascertain. Her head is causing her much pain. Can you find somebody who knows about these things and can prepare a decoction of some kind?"

"Aye. The queen's maid, Aimee, will know. Or Dorothy." She ran off to do his bidding.

Gavin resumed his place next to her on the bed. Isabel seemed to be fading in and out of consciousness. Taking her head gently in his hands, he ran his fingertips over her scalp, not finding any wounds. "Can you sit up if I hold you, love?" When she nodded, he placed an arm under her shoulders and lifted her, enough to examine the back of her head. He was horrified to see blood on her pillow, and when he felt the back of her head, he found an abrasion atop a swelling the size of a goose egg.

Isabel sucked in a breath and moaned.

"Forgive me for hurting you." Laying her down gently, he said, "I'm going to check your body for other injuries now."

Pulling the coverlet down, Gavin began his perusal, lifting and moving her limbs, making sure nothing was dislocated and that she bore no other open wounds. This would be more easily done if she were undressed, but he would leave that to the ladies. When he pressed on her ribs, she let out a howl of pain.

"Ah. I believe you have some broken ribs." Miraculously, he did not find any other injuries, although he was certain her body would bloom with bruises by day's end. He wanted to climb onto the bed and hold her, but it would only cause her additional pain. It was time for him to leave and allow the women to undress, bathe, and bandage her. But before he exited, he had a few questions.

"Isabel, can you remember what happened? What caused you to fall?"

She opened her eyes and gazed at him. "I'm not sure. When I opened the door, I was holding Bisou. He was whimpering—he even growled—as though afraid of something. I had the oddest feeling that somebody was standing behind me. I glanced around but saw nothing."

"And then what happened?"

"That is the fuzzy part. I remember feeling suddenly terrified and wanting to get away, so I started down the steps." Her brow furrowed and she hesitated, trying to collect her thoughts. "That is all I can remember. Afterward, only darkness."

Damnation. "Perhaps it will come clear later. I am going to leave for a short time, sweetheart. The ladies will attend you while I ask some questions, and then I'll be back."

"Gavin, what about Bisou? I'm so afraid he was hurt."

"We'll find him and bring him to you." He shouldn't make rash promises. The poor animal could be dead for all he knew, but he could not say that to Isabel.

"You won't be far?"

She was frightened, and it pained him to see her this way. "I will be questioning the guards who found you, and others, but I'll be nearby, probably in Mary's chamber. Your friends will be in to attend you." He kissed her forehead and then walked out into the passage. Dorothy was waiting with a cup in her hands, and Aimee stood nearby, holding a container of salve and fresh cloths.

"She has broken ribs and a huge bump on the back of her head. It's raw and bleeding. And she'll need—"

"We know what she needs, Gavin," Dorothy said, looking amused. "She must drink the tea first—it will help with the pain. We will take good care of her."

"Of course. I thank you. I'll be close by if you need me."

Before heading for Mary's chamber, Gavin wished to inspect the steps. He must do so now, before the sun melted any ice that may have covered them. He banged open the door and a gust of wind hit him. It was colder than a gravedigger's shovel out there. Visualizing what Isabel had described to him, Gavin attempted to imitate her movements. He folded his arms against his chest, the best substitute for holding a dog he could devise, and glanced behind him. It was dark and it would have been difficult to make out a form. He set his booted foot onto the first step and swept it back and forth. It was clear of ice. Or snow, gravel, or anything else that may conceivably have caused Isabel to slip. Then he descended the stairs, all the way to the ground, examining each step as he went. No ice. Not a single patch. At the bottom lay a grassy area which was slightly disturbed. He hunkered down and took a closer look. The ground was covered with blood, from Isabel's head wound, no doubt. Rising, he easily made out the footsteps of the men who had come to Isabel's rescue and the path they'd taken from the inner courtyard.

Troubled, Gavin climbed back up the stairs and strode toward Mary's chamber. He must use caution. He didn't want to convey his worst fears. Not yet, anyway. If this was no accident, and the perpetrators found out he was on their heels, they would run to ground, and he'd have no chance to catch them. He heard excited voices emanating from the chamber before he reached it. When he walked in, everybody quieted.

He bowed to Queen Mary, and she spoke first. "How is dear Bel, Gavin?"

"She has some significant injuries, but none critical. Dorothy and Aimee have given her a potion for pain and will bathe her." Murmurs broke out among them, and he interrupted, raising his voice slightly. "Did anybody see Isabel as she walked down the passage and out the door to the stairs?"

They all shook their heads, as he'd known they would. "I'd like to know the whereabouts of everybody when this happened. Your Majesty, let's begin with you."

Everyone gaped at him. It was highly irregular for anybody to question a monarch this way. Especially a man without rank. Gavin didn't care. Mary could refuse, and he would be powerless to do anything about it. But if she were willing to talk, everyone else would follow suit.

Her expression was severe, but she answered. "Bel and I ate breakfast together. I finished first and returned to my chamber, where I took up my work until I heard the commotion in the passage. It was soon made known to me what had befallen Isabel."

"Who informed you?" Gavin asked.

"I believe it was Cecily. Was it not?" She turned toward the other woman.

Cecily nodded. "I was on the lower level, intending to walk over to the hall to find my brother. We had talked about riding today, and I wanted to see if he was ready. The guards burst through the door with Isabel just as I was leaving. I sent one of them for Philip, who then ran to find you, Gavin."

One by one, the others explained where they were. Alice and Henry Alymer were still abed, as was their friend, Anne Ramsey. Dorothy Vere and her sister-in-law, Jane, had been here with her, Mary said. "Aimee as well, attending to her duties."

"Sir, Mistress Isabel stopped by and asked if she could take the little dog outside with her," Jane said.

"Any idea of the time?"

"Half eleven had just rung, I believe."

"And Dorothy's husband?"

Again, it was the lass who answered. "He went out riding with the earl. They are still not returned."

Which reminded Gavin that Bess Shrewsbury was also not present. As if anticipating the question, Cecily said, "Bess was in her chamber. She does not spend much time with us of late."

Because she believes her husband is swiving Mary.

Gavin would check to make sure about Lady Shrewsbury's whereabouts, although he could not conceive of any reason why she would wish to harm Isabel. "What about Frances?"

A few people snickered. "We have not seen her this morning," Alice said, covering her mouth to quell a laugh.

"She is with Lesley?" Gavin asked.

"It is most likely," Mary said, giving Alice a stern glance.

Gavin nodded. Everyone was accounted for, although he would check with Bess, Alice, Frances, and Lesley for confirmation.

"Gavin, was this not an accident? Surely you do not believe someone wished to hurt Bel."

"I am simply trying to gather information, Your Majesty. Given the attack at the river, as well as the murder of young Simon, I want to make sure I have all the facts." He paused and glanced at the assembled folk. "I would like to enlist some volunteers to look for the little dog. Who's willing?"

Mary froze. "Bisou is missing? I-I did not know! Why didn't anyone tell me?"

Shouldn't it have been obvious? "Isabel was carrying the dog in her arms when she fell, and as far as I know nobody has seen him since."

"*Mon dieu*," Mary said with a deep sigh, and Cecily helped her to a chair.

. . .

When Isabel awoke the following morning, Gavin was sleeping on the settle, his feet hanging off one end of it. He had dragged it over next to her bed, having brought his down coverlet with him. He looked vastly uncomfortable. Although it was growing dark, she studied him. It was rare to have such an opportunity, for the man was always rushing about from place to place. His wavy chestnut hair, usually brushed back from his high forehead, was mussed, and it made him appear younger, somehow. Fleetingly, Isabel wondered how old he was. She'd never asked. He had a small scar on his chin, just below his full lower lip. She reached out and traced it lightly with her finger. Unable to resist, she ran her hand over his cheeks, darkly shadowed with stubble.

"*Bonjour, Isabel*," he said, startling her. "*Comment allez-vous?*"

She jerked her hand away. "I-I apologize for the intrusion. I was just, that is, I—"

He opened his eyes, and the full force of their ice blue hit her. "No need for explanations, *ma cherie*. I loved what you were doing."

Why was he spouting endearments in French? Isabel didn't know, but she liked it.

She fell back to her pillows, waiting for him to say more. "You didn't answer me, Isabel. Tell me how you are feeling."

"Sore. Help me up and I'll know more. I need to visit the garderobe."

Gavin stood and stretched, affording Isabel a fine view of his chest. His lawn shirt pulled tight across the bands of muscle, and she couldn't resist staring. Getting to his feet, he said, "I am going to lift you and try not to jostle you. Ready?"

When she nodded, he flung back the covers. "Oh," she gasped. "I forgot I'm wearing nothing but a chemise!" Which was rucked up around her thighs. Embarrassed, she glanced up and caught him staring. Isabel couldn't fault him, since she'd been indulging in the same behavior only a moment ago. "Would you find my cloak, Gavin?"

He draped it over her shoulders, then lifted her off the bed and set her down.

"It hurts. Moving, turning, simply standing up straight hurts," she said, dismayed.

"Broken ribs are quite painful. Is the pain only on one side, or both?"

"On the right. I believe the other side is uninjured."

"Does it hurt when you take a breath?"

Isabel thought about it. "A little. It was most painful when I coughed during the night."

He crooked his elbow. "Hold on to me."

"Gavin, I can do this alone. You don't need to escort me."

"Oh, no. I'm not letting you out of my sight. Come along."

When they reached the garderobe, Isabel said, "You are not coming in with me."

"I'll wait out here, but I'm going to make sure nobody is inside first."

Isabel rolled her eyes. He was being overly cautious, yet he made her feel safe and protected. He quickly reappeared. "All clear. I'll be waiting."

Once inside the small chamber, Isabel was grateful Gavin had preceded her. The interior was all murky shadow. There was no window, nor any candle burning. She relieved herself and rose, tugging her chemise down and putting the cloak back on. A basin of water rested on a small oak table, and she washed her hands. As she moved toward the door, dizziness engulfed her. That same odd feeling she'd had just before falling gripped her. There was no real danger, but she panicked nevertheless. To stem the tide of hysteria, she tried to take deep breaths, but her injuries were too painful. Was she mistaken? *Was* someone there, lying in wait for her, as they'd been yesterday?

Feeling helpless and weak, she cried out. "Gavin! Help me!"

He came running, banging the door open. "What is it? What's wrong?"

"Someone is in here. Just like before."

Gavin picked her up and carried her back to her chamber, seated himself, and lowered Isabel to his lap. "There, now. Lean against me. You are safe."

"Was there...did you see anybody?"

"You were alone, Bel. There was nobody else. I checked before you went in, and I stood there the entire time you were inside."

"I was so sure." She ducked her head. "You must think me

deranged. But Gavin…I remembered more about yesterday. Right before I fell, I felt a hand on my back. For a fraction of a second, I knew someone was going to push me."

"God's wounds, Isabel! Now do you believe we must flee this place? I cannot be with you every minute, not in the long term. And I trust very few of these people."

Isabel was not surprised that he'd brought this up, for once he'd formed an idea, he was tenacious. "What will we do? We cannot simply ride away from here in broad daylight."

Gavin was stroking her hair. His body heat warmed her. She never wanted to leave the cocoon of his arms, let alone Sheffield. "You're right. We must sneak away like thieves in the night. I'll need to inform the earl, but nobody else must know. Agreed?"

"Of course. What should we say about my fall? Should I pretend not to remember?"

"Aye. That is the safest course. I questioned the group about where they were when you had your so-called accident. They all made a reasonable accounting of themselves. At least one of them must be lying."

Reluctantly, Isabel slid off Gavin's lap. "One or more of the women will be here to check on me soon, and I don't want them to find us like this."

He helped her back to her bed, plumped her pillows, and arranged her covers. "I'll stay until they arrive. Ask them if you might rest in the queen's chamber. Say you are bored and want company. I don't want you here alone, Isabel."

Nor did she wish to be. It was beyond belief that a member of Mary's circle wanted her dead, yet she was positive someone had pushed her down those steps. "I forgot to ask—has Bisou been found?"

"Several of the group volunteered to look for him, but no luck yet." She must have looked distraught, because he squeezed her hand and said, "'Tis a good sign that he's gone.

That means he had the use of his legs. Most likely he was scared and is hiding somewhere. If they don't find him, he'll come back when he's hungry enough."

"Of course, you are right. He is not trained to hunt, but he's a smart little creature and knows where his meals come from." Looking steadily at him, she said, "What will we do, Gavin? How will we manage this?"

"I cannot answer that—yet. I have a few ideas, but I need to determine which one of them is most likely to succeed." He rose and said, "I shall see where your friends are and inform them you are awake."

She nodded. Gavin paused on the threshold and turned back to her. "Be ready to leave at a moment's notice, Bel. Who knows when an opportunity may arise?"

Very soon after Gavin left, Dorothy and Aimee entered. Aimee carried a tray, which Isabel assumed was her meal. Now that she smelled food, she was hungry. "What have you brought me?"

"Nothing exciting, I'm afraid," Dorothy said. "Beef broth, bread, and a little wine."

Aimee helped Isabel sit up and rested the tray across her legs. Isabel lifted the bowl of soup to her mouth and sipped. It was surprisingly delicious, with tiny pieces of beef floating in the rich broth. Dorothy perched on the settle, while Aimee moved about the chamber, straightening, gathering up soiled clothing, and collecting the used cups and tankards.

"Has Bisou come home?" Isabel asked between sips.

Dorothy laughed. "No, and the queen is beside herself. I understand you were holding him when you fell."

"I was, but I cannot remember what became of him. Gavin says it's a good sign that he ran off, because his legs must not have been injured."

Dorothy looked thoughtful. "Perhaps, but he may have crept away to die beneath a bush."

Aimee muttered an impolite French expression, barely loud enough to be heard. "What exactly happened, Bel?" Dorothy asked.

Isabel broke off a piece of manchet. "I don't remember anything except a cold wind buffeting me when I opened the door. And then nothing, until I woke up in my bed. I must have thrown my arms out to arrest the fall, which is how I lost poor Bisou. Is the queen very angry with me?"

"No. Only sad her little dog is gone."

Bel finished her meal while Dorothy prattled on. Most of it was gossip, requiring little attention and very limited responses. Which allowed Isabel to focus on Gavin and what they had discussed. Because of her "accident," his fears had ratcheted up, and she could no longer deny that removing themselves from Sheffield was of the utmost importance.

When she saw an opening, she interrupted Dorothy's never-ending litany of gossip. "I am bored and restless in here by myself," she said. They gathered up a few of her things and helped her down the hall to the queen's chambers.

Chapter Nineteen

That evening Gavin deflected questions about Isabel, and by the next day, interest in the incident had waned. He visited her several times during the day, and on one of those visits, she announced her intention of attending dinner that night.

They were taking a pass about the room. Isabel was champing at the bit after two days of confinement. "I'm not sure that's wise," he said. "Are you feeling well enough?"

"Much improved. I don't deny my ribs are still sore, but my head has quit aching. Besides, isn't it best if I act as if I've not been completely traumatized?"

"There will be questions."

She cut him off before he could go on. "I'll repeat exactly what I told Dorothy. That I remember nothing until I woke up. 'Tis not far from the truth." She'd curled her hand into the crook of his elbow, and now she gazed up at him.

At that moment, his world shifted.

When had she become so important to him? God's heart, spending so much time with her seemed like the normal way of things. If he didn't see her several times during the day, couldn't confide in her, couldn't touch her, couldn't *breathe* her, he would be immeasurably…less.

He loved the lass. And his body responded.

"If you are well enough to dress and come to the evening meal, perhaps you are well enough for other...activities," he said, looking deeply into her eyes. Her gaze did not waver.

Framing her face with his hands, he set his lips on hers. She smelled of roses, fresh and inviting. He licked the seam of her mouth, but she needed no urging to open to him. To his delight, she offered him her tongue, blatantly stoking his desire for her. Groaning low in his throat, he said, "What are you doing to me, Isabel?" It came out rough, and anguished. He steered her toward the bed, and they dropped onto it still clinging to each other.

He kissed her, sliding his hands down her bodice until he reached her breasts. There was something infinitely sensual about teasing a woman's nipples through a fine, soft fabric. And Isabel liked it, lifting her chest so that her breasts fit fully into his hands.

Just before the door opened, they heard voices in the passage. God's mercy, what was he thinking? Losing his head with Isabel in her chamber, when women paraded in and out throughout the day. He leaped to his feet and put some distance between himself and the bed—from Isabel—and folded his hands loosely before his fully aroused cock.

Dorothy and Ann, the lady's maid, entered. Before either could speak, Isabel said, "I would like to bathe, dress, and come to dinner tonight. Ann, perhaps you can help me? Dorothy, could you choose my apparel? I don't feel up to it."

"You must be on the mend, in that case," Dorothy said. "Of course, we will assist you however we can."

"Until later, then, ladies," Gavin said, making for the door. Ann and Dorothy had set about their work. He caught Isabel's eye and winked, and her smile lit up her lovely face.

If only persons unknown weren't trying to murder them, Gavin would be a happy man. He felt ready now. Ready to ask

Isabel to be his wife. An idea that would have set him back on his heels a mere few weeks past. He exited the building and strolled toward the great hall, noticing a wagon in the inner courtyard and several men removing the canvas cover. Who in hell were they? He swore under his breath. Shrewsbury apparently had issued a blanket invitation to anyone who sought access to the castle. Didn't he realize how dangerous it was?

After they'd dispensed with the cover, the men surrounding the wagon began removing some unusual garb. A chain mail shirt, a fool's cap and bells. Women's apparel. This could only mean one thing. Mummers.

Gavin stopped in his tracks. So they were to entertain tonight? He eyed the conveyance. Was it large enough to conceal both himself and Isabel? It would be an ideal way to sneak out without anyone being the wiser. He walked over to have a word with them.

A few minutes later, Gavin was standing in front of Shrewsbury. He'd not yet had an opportunity to tell the earl of his suspicions regarding Isabel's fall. The man had conspicuously absented himself from the company of Mary and her ladies since his wife had accused him of having an affair with the Scots queen.

"What is it, man? I need to finish here and dress for dinner." Then, looking somewhat guilty, Shrewsbury said, "How fares Mistress Tait? I understand she suffered an accident."

"It was no accident, my lord," Gavin said. And then he told the earl everything he knew about what had happened, beginning with Lesley's threat against Isabel. Sometime during the recitation, the earl had motioned to the chair and Gavin sat down.

Shrewsbury steepled his fingers, gazing over them at Gavin. "You cannot be certain, though, can you? It sounds as if her memory is foggy."

Why was the man's first inclination always to refute every bit of information Gavin presented to him? It was frustrating. Worse, it was counterproductive. Gavin liked the man, but he was too indecisive, and it made him ineffectual. With that realization, he determined his course of action.

"Add everything up, and we have an escalation of their scheme, whatever it is. To seize the throne? Or perhaps it is simply to spirit Mary away to Scotland. Whatever it is, they're not afraid to do what is necessary to accomplish their goals." Shrewsbury continued to stare at Gavin, but he did not respond.

"I'm taking Isabel to safety, because the situation has become too dangerous for her. I cannot spend every waking hour protecting her. Once I've removed her from Sheffield, I'll await orders from Nicholas Ryder. If he wants me back here, I'll return. I thwarted one attempt to kill me, and I can do so again if I must. But I will not risk Isabel's life."

"Well," Shrewsbury said, leaning forward and dropping his hands to his desk. "I cannot stop you. But have you considered other alternatives? We could assign guards to her. She would never be alone, night or day."

"To do so would mean tipping our hand to Lesley. He's aware of our suspicions, but he can only guess the extent of our knowledge. We may as well come out and accuse him of attempting to murder Isabel, and who knows what would happen then? They are growing bolder, sir. The killing of poor Simon and the attempt on Isabel's life prove it."

Shrewsbury, an arm propped on the desk, laid his head against his palm and sighed deeply. "What would Lesley hope to accomplish by killing Isabel?"

"He knows Mary confides in her, and he can't be sure of what those indiscretions may have been. Killing Isabel would eliminate that threat."

Merciful God, saying that out loud made his gut churn. "I'm going to offer the mummers coin to smuggle us out in their wagon. If I pay well enough, they'll do it."

The earl nodded, and Gavin was thankful he would not stand in the way. "How shall I explain it to Mary and company? Won't both of you disappearing be suspicious?"

"I've thought about that. Say that Isabel sickened during the night, and we thought it best to take her home. To her mother's."

Shrewsbury gave him a sly look. "And is that in fact your destination?"

"No. But if anybody is inclined to follow us, it will be good to let them believe it is." Gavin rubbed his forehead. "I hope nobody will associate our leaving with the mummers' departure."

"What is your route?"

"The mummers are heading to Huddersfield, then on to Skipton. Carlisle will be our final destination, near where Ryder lives. We'll get there on our own."

Shrewsbury's brow furrowed. "You have a long journey ahead of you. I can do one thing to help. I'll send a messenger to Skipton Castle, to Lady Anne Clifford. She is the widow of the Earl of Cumberland and a relation of mine. At least for a night or two you will have fine accommodations."

"Thank you, my lord. Could you send the messenger on my horse, Brutus?"

The earl barked a laugh. "Of course." Sobering, he said, "You'll be missed, Cade. I've grown to depend on you. I mislike the idea of dealing with all this subterfuge by myself."

"Have you received any word from Cecil? Are there any new developments concerning Ridolfi and the other players?"

The earl shook his head. "I assume they are watching and waiting and gathering evidence where they can."

Gavin got to his feet. "We must ready ourselves for dinner.

Isabel is going to be there, and I'll speak to her afterward about our...escape." He exited Shrewsbury's office quickly, leaving the man looking pensive and subdued.

• • •

"Ah! *Vous etes belle!*"

When Mary glimpsed Isabel, she gathered her up in a hug and welcomed her back to the festivities. "You are well, *ma chere* Bel?"

The queen's heavy perfume aside, she was. "*Oui*, Your Majesty. I am sore, still, but what could I expect, tumbling down the stairs as I did?" Isabel hoped she sounded as if she blamed her own clumsiness for the fall.

"She's covered in bruises," Dorothy said. Isabel's cheeks flamed and she was grateful that only the ladies were close enough to hear the comment. Should she mention Bisou? Gavin had told her he had not come home. But the mood was festive, and it did not seem like the right time. She would wait for a private moment with the queen.

"Gavin was certainly worried about you," Alice said. "He questioned us as though he believed one of us had shoved you down those stairs. Even Her Majesty was not exempt."

There was an awkward silence, and Isabel tried to come up with an appropriate response. The idea he'd worried about her touched her heart, but at the same time, made the current situation more fraught. "He is a man who looks for explanations," she said. "I suppose he didn't wish to believe the most logical one—that I simply lost my footing and fell. As you are all aware, I'm not known for my poise and grace."

That drew laughs, for once good-natured rather than mean-spirited. Some of the guests, both men and ladies, approached to wish Isabel well. Oddly, Frances kept her distance, standing away from the others and sipping wine. She had not helped to nurse Isabel, nor had she visited. Distracted by a prickling at the nape of her neck, Isabel thought no more about it after Gavin entered the room and stood beside her.

"Isabel. How do you fare?"

Only a little more than an hour ago, they had been clinging to each other in a sensuous dance, the mere memory of which made her skin tingle. He well knew how she did. Gazing at him, she perceived he was quite serious, and she concluded she'd better play along. "I am well, sir, I thank you."

"You gave us a scare, mistress," Philip said. "Have you remembered anything more about how it happened?"

Isabel had not expected the question to arise so soon. If she made light of the accident, it would sound too cavalier. Yet she needed to bolster the impression she had been at fault. "I recall stepping outside and a gust of wind nearly knocking me over. And wishing there was a railing to hold on to. I must have started down, but I cannot remember."

"The wind may have disturbed your balance," Mary said.

"Aye. My feet tangled together and that was that. And then I woke up in my bed, battered but whole." Her heart thumping, Isabel put on an earnest expression. "I offer my sincere thanks to everybody who came to my aid, and to all of you who have been nursing me these past few days."

"We are grateful you've returned to us," Mary said. "Enough of misfortunes and adversities! Let us proceed to our meal."

The talk at dinner centered around the mummers and their performance. "It has been a long time since we've been entertained," Alice said. "Thank you, Lord Shrewsbury."

"It was not my doing, but my wife's. You must thank her." Everybody turned their attention to Lady Shrewsbury. The poor woman seemed so glum of late, but now she smiled softly. She did not look at the gathering around the table, but directly at her husband. An understanding seemed to pass between them, and Isabel was glad to see it.

For once, she had been seated next to Gavin. During the meal, he leaned over and said quietly, "I must speak with you. During the entertainment, I will stand at the back of the hall. When I slip out, wait a few minutes and do likewise. I'll be waiting for you in the passage."

She had time only to nod in acknowledgment. Blake, on her other side, asked her about Bisou and told her he believed the dog had been frightened so badly, he was hiding somewhere.

Isabel wished he'd not mentioned Bisou. Whenever she thought of the little creature, tears pricked her eyes. "I fear he cannot survive too much longer in the cold, and without food," she said.

"Perhaps he's more of a hunter than we imagined."

John Lesley was in his usual spot next to Mary. But something was different. The queen virtually ignored him throughout the meal and spoke instead to Dorothy's husband. This confirmed Isabel's opinion that the queen was either angry with Lesley or felt threatened by him. Had she decided not to take part in Lesley and Norfolk's schemes?

The tempting array of food on offer made Isabel's mouth water. She consumed her share of veal pasty, haunch of venison, artichoke pie, and assorted sweetmeats and pear tarts. Because of the entertainment, they did not linger at the table as they usually did. Servants cleared away the food and moved the tables aside. Some of the men, including Gavin, pitched in to help create a makeshift stage for the performance. More citizens of Sheffield arrived and the hall grew stifling, for the Yule log was still burning in the massive hearth.

One of the players introduced the evening's entertainment, and before he'd even finished, the fool appeared and frolicked around him, his belled cap ting-a-linging. Flute and drum played an accompaniment to his prancing. In a moment, the play began. It was much the same as others Isabel had attended. A heathen knight slays a virtuous Christian hero, and a doctor soon appears and revives him. Isabel did not need to pay close attention to laugh in the right places.

She was seated toward the rear of the hall, surrounded by the other ladies. Surreptitiously, she glanced about the room and found Gavin standing against the wall, a bit farther back. When the mummers were about halfway through the performance, she noticed he had slipped out. After waiting a reasonable length of time, she did likewise. "I am going to get a breath of air," she whispered to Cecily.

"I'll accompany you," she said.

"No, stay and enjoy the performance. I'll only be a few minutes." Cecily nodded, and Isabel took her leave.

Gavin was waiting in the shadowed passage, and reached out a hand when he glimpsed her. He led her to his chamber, and once he'd confirmed nobody was lurking about, closed the door.

Grasping her upper arms, he said, "It is time, Isabel. We will leave with the mummers tomorrow."

Of course, she'd known this was coming. Now that it was upon them, she was reluctant. But it was time to summon her courage. Somebody had tried to kill both her and Gavin. They had survived, Gavin with his wits and she by dumb luck. How much longer would luck prevail? "What should I bring?"

He looked surprised, as though he'd expected an argument. Letting go of her, he said, "Your warmest clothing, sturdy boots, gloves, and a cloak. There will be very little room for any extras in the wagon." Gavin rubbed the back of his neck. "I've informed the earl."

"You trust him?"

"Completely. Shrewsbury will say you sickened in the

night and wished to go home to Derby."

"They'll wonder why we did not travel in the carriage."

He shrugged. "Perhaps, but that is the least of my concerns. Meet me outside by the mummers' wagon before dawn. They will be expecting us."

When Gavin stopped speaking, they could hear raucous laughter coming from the hall. "We should get back before the performance ends." He turned toward the door, but she stopped him. "Gavin."

Searching her face, he said, "What is it?"

"We should ask Mary to join us. To escape with us. That way we can save her from becoming embroiled in a plot not of her making."

"No."

Isabel rolled her eyes. "Just 'no.' Is that the best you can do? I am asking a serious question."

Gavin paused, hands loosely on his hips. "Bel, I understand your desire to help Mary. But we don't know the extent of her involvement in this. Not to mention, it may look as though we abducted her." When Isabel did not respond, he elaborated further. "Mary travels with an entourage. How do you think she would fare in a wagon with only you and me for companions? And she is wedded to a life of luxury. Why, she couldn't get along without her plate and tapestries and silver goblets—not to mention her extensive wardrobe."

Isabel sighed. "You have a point." If only she had told Gavin about the conversation she'd overheard between Mary and Lesley, if she'd shared everything Mary had confided to her, maybe he would agree. But she'd promised not to, and now it was too late.

Standing at the door, Gavin pulled her close for a quick kiss. "Have I said what a brave lass you are?"

She rewarded him with a smile, albeit a lukewarm one.

"You go first," he said. "I'll follow in a few minutes."

Chapter Twenty

Never had Isabel been more grateful for her private chamber. In the small hours, after a sleepless night, she dressed and then collected a clean smock, extra bodice, and a fresh pair of stockings. She crammed everything into a small traveling bag, along with her copy of Christine de Pizan's writing and a miniature of her father. When she was a young girl, her mother had gifted her with it. As far as she could recall, the miniature was the only gift her mother had ever given her.

Now, the challenge. In order not to wake anyone, Isabel must take the outer stairs. The very ones she'd tumbled down— been pushed down. Hesitating at the door, but knowing it was the only way to avoid alerting the guards, she eventually opened it. Gavin had told her he'd found no ice on the steps, but her inner self urged caution nonetheless. Leaning into the wall, she descended cautiously. It seemed to take forever, but finally she stepped on solid ground and heaved a sigh of relief. Out in the courtyard, near the gatehouse, Isabel glimpsed the wagon and several figures moving about it. She hoped Gavin was one of them.

"Good morrow, Isabel," he said as she approached. "This is William, the chief mummer."

In the dark, she could barely make out the man's face. "Madam," he said, offering a bow. Then he and another man lifted the canvas cover.

Gavin said, "We'll remain under the cover until we are well away from the castle and the town. Then William will remove the canvas and we'll be more comfortable."

Handing Gavin her bag, Isabel looked at the wagon in dismay. With the mummers' costumes and gear, there was precious little room for them. William must have sensed her distress, because he said, "You can lie on top of our costumes. They'll be soft, at least, and protect you from the worst of the jolting."

Gavin, thank God, had thought to bring a coverlet. He spread it over the costumes, then held out his hand to her. "Come, Isabel. We must leave before the sun is up." He grasped her hand and bent his knee. She stepped on his thigh, and he boosted her up into the wagon. In one fluid motion, he was beside her. Stretching out, he pulled her down next to him. Even though she dreaded having the canvas laid over her, closing her in, she rather liked this part—lying so close to him she could feel his heart beating. The driver clucked to the horse, and they began their slow journey north.

"Are you all right?" Gavin asked.

"I don't like the dark, or the confined space. But otherwise, yes."

He tucked her head under his chin. "*Hmm*," he said. "Perhaps we should take advantage of this...opportunity." Just then, the wagon hit a pothole and dipped precariously, finally righting itself. They both laughed, and that relieved her anxiety. She could do this.

"It will be slow going, because not all of the mummers have mounts," Gavin said. "Why don't we try to get some sleep? I don't know about you, but I was awake most of the night."

If she could sleep, the time would pass more quickly. "Excellent idea." She snuggled closer to him, and as she did so, she felt something wiggling beneath her. "Gavin! Do you feel that?"

"What?" Then, "Ah, we have company. Don't panic. It's likely a badger or a hedgehog burrowed in for warmth. I'm sure he doesn't appreciate our lying on top of him. Move over."

After she had shifted position, Gavin very awkwardly began lifting layers—coverlet, costumes, apparel—out of the way. When he shoved his hand under the remaining items, Isabel cautioned him. "Be careful! If it's a wild thing, it may bite."

In a moment, they heard a whimper. A very familiar one. Gavin and Isabel looked at each other, both recognizing the culprit at the same time. "Bisou!" Isabel said, delighted. Gavin fished the little dog out from under the layers and passed him to her.

She crushed him against her bodice. "Devil! How long have you been hiding out in here?" He licked her face, sniffed her, and then cuddled against her bosom.

"Remove yourself, varmint," Gavin said. "You've stolen my woman." But Bisou had found his spot and would not be persuaded to move.

The three cuddled up together and slept until the wagon juddered to a stop a few hours later.

• • •

Gavin gently squeezed Isabel's shoulder. "We've stopped, Bel," he said. She blinked, looked at him with unfocused eyes, and came fully awake. In a moment, William and another man had lifted the canvas covering. After stretching, Gavin jumped down, gripped Isabel around the waist, and set her on the ground. While she was smoothing her skirts, he reached for Bisou and handed him to her.

Looking up at William, Isabel said, "Have you seen this dog before, sir? He was burrowed beneath the costumes."

William chuckled, and Gavin thought it a strange sound coming from him. He was a sober sort, tall and thin with protuberant ears. "We found him last night hovering about the wagon while we were packing up. One of the men said he'd fed him a few morsels. It was cold, so I let him sleep inside. Forgot all about him. Does he belong to you, madam?"

"Not exactly," Bel said, at the same time Gavin pronounced an unequivocal "yes."

Gavin reached out and scratched Bisou's ears. "You look pretty good, scamp." The dog was scruffy and smelled of mud and rotting things, but that would be easily remedied with a bath. "He's been missing for a few days. You have my thanks for taking care of him."

Isabel set Bisou on the ground. "I need to find the necessary."

They'd stopped at an inn yard, but Gavin had no idea where. When Isabel walked off, he turned to William and asked.

"Stocksbridge. We'll stay only long enough to refresh ourselves and then be off. How was the ride?"

"Overall, not bad. After we found the dog, we fell asleep. How was the road?"

"The surface is hard packed. Mostly frozen. Highwaymen, thieves, beggars—they're a bigger worry."

Gavin had noticed the mummers were armed with rapiers and daggers, as he himself was. "Perhaps we'll be safe because of Christmastide. Most citizens are home celebrating with family and friends."

"I pray you are right about that," William said before striding away. When Isabel returned, Gavin left to see to his own needs. Afterward, he hastened inside and bought two meat pies and a tankard of ale. He and Bel leaned against the wagon, eating and drinking and tossing bites to Bisou. It was one of the best meals Gavin had ever eaten, the first he'd consumed in days without anxiety knotting in his gut. They finished just before William said it was time to leave.

The day was a gift. Though the air was chilly, the sun's rays were strong. "How far is it to Huddersfield?" Isabel asked once they were underway.

"We should be there just before nightfall," Gavin said. Isabel groaned.

They had managed to fold some of the costumes to cushion their ride. Though far from comfortable, at least it was bearable. Isabel insisted that Gavin tell her about his family's business, how he'd met Anna, and what he'd been doing since her death. He was voluble on work and family, but hesitated when it came to his wife. What was there to say? "I loved her, and believed she loved me. I was mistaken."

"I am sorry, Gavin. Had you no inkling prior to…to her infidelity?"

"My brothers and father always called her a shameless flirt, but I thought it was a jest. I was, in fact, proud that other men found her beautiful. They competed for her attention." And then a memory flashed through his mind. He and his father watching from a distance while Anna stood among a group of admirers. Supposedly, they were helping her with the apple picking. In truth, they were sneaking looks at her pretty ankles and her breasts when she leaned down to toss more apples into the basket. His father had leaned close to him and said, "Have a care, son. Have a care with that one."

He must have looked stricken, because Isabel said, "Let us talk of other matters. I am heartily sorry I brought up something so painful." Her hand had snaked over and grasped his.

"I had a sudden memory, a time when my father told me to have a care with her. I'd forgotten it. Suppressed it, I suppose." He chuckled. "No doubt there were many of those instances, and I was too blinded by love to see the truth."

Just then, a teeth-rattling jolt knocked Isabel off her perch atop a band box. "Whoa," Gavin said, righting her. He pulled her closer and kept hold of her arm. The highway, partially frozen, had made for decent traveling, but potholes surprised them here and there.

Isabel did not comment, so he went on. "The night on the riverbank, when I almost drowned, I tried to prepare myself by seeking forgiveness for my many sins. I acknowledged my gravest sin was in not forgiving Anna and vowed to do so. And yet something inside me still asks why. What did I do that caused her to seek out the favors of another man?"

Isabel looked sheepish. "I am afraid I have little knowledge or understanding of these matters, Gavin. Perhaps there is no real answer. Mayhap it was in her nature and had nothing at all to do with you."

He squeezed her hand. If the other men hadn't been nearby, he would have kissed her. It was good of her to try to help him come to terms with his wife's betrayal, but it was not so simple as Isabel suggested.

It was growing dark when they arrived in Huddersfield. William steered the wagon to an inn yard. When they asked about accommodations, however, they were disappointed. Because it was market day, there was only one small room available, which would go to the lady, of course. The men were welcome to sleep in the main room, in chairs or on the floor.

"The lady will have a bath after supper, sir. Will you see to it?"

Isabel had looked on in surprise. "Thank you, Gavin. I wouldn't have thought to ask."

He laughed. "I have a selfish motive. I want to bathe when you are done. And then we can scrub that little varmint, Bisou. He reeks."

They joined the mummers for supper in the main room. The innkeeper's wife and a serving wench brought out platters of roast beef with vegetables and loaves of bread. Gavin requested wine for him and Isabel. The atmosphere was raucous. It was drawing close to the New Year celebration, and joviality prevailed. When the citizens discovered a troupe of mummers was among them, they demanded to be entertained. Reluctant at first, the men finally agreed. Their protests were perfunctory, for they would pass round the hat both before and after.

"We'll leave you to it, gentlemen," Gavin said, "since we have already seen the show."

Gavin signaled to the innkeeper. It was time to bring the hot water upstairs for Isabel's bath.

. . .

"I am sorry you do not have a chamber," Isabel said as they climbed the stairs.

"No matter. It won't be the first time I've slept in a taproom."

Gavin unlocked the door and they went in. The chamber was small but clean, with one window overlooking the inn yard. The bathtub rested before the hearth, which Gavin lit. To Isabel's distress, a degree of awkwardness had sprung up between them. They were a couple, but not man and wife. Yet here was Gavin, seeing to her needs. It felt like a wedding night. After lighting candles from the spills on the mantel, she lifted Bisou into her arms and petted him, to keep herself occupied while servants carried in the steaming hot water.

They finished at last, and Gavin said, "Your bath awaits,

madam." He made a sweeping gesture with his arm.

"Yes, well, I'd better prepare."

"Do you require help?"

Merciful God, what should she say? "Yes. No. That is…"

Gavin chuckled. "Put that malodorous dog down, and I'll unlace your bodice."

That would be all right. She set Bisou on the floor, and he promptly curled up by the fire. Isabel had underestimated the danger she was putting herself in by allowing Gavin to unlace her. To get anywhere near her. The feel of his hands at her back, the nearness of him—was he deliberately standing so close to her? So close she could feel his powerful thighs pressing against her. His breath tickled her neck, whispered in her ear. Her own thighs were quivering, and the private place at their juncture throbbed and hummed.

Just when Isabel thought she might turn and throw herself into his arms, he said, "Done. I'll take Bisou outside while you bathe." He left the room without a second look. She didn't know if she was relieved or grievously disappointed. The latter, if she were honest. She very nearly called him back.

Quickly, Isabel undressed and sank down into the hot water. After the long day of travel, it was not only cleansing, but provided consolation and balm for her weary and confused self. Not wanting to linger too long, she began scrubbing herself, using the bar of soap left for her. In the end, she washed her hair as well.

After she'd dried off, she donned her clean chemise, took up her comb, and sat before the fire to dry her hair. In a few moments, she heard Gavin and Bisou in the hall. Her heart leaped. At length, he tapped on the door. "Isabel? Have you finished your bath?"

"Aye. You may enter." Her chemise was of fine lawn, nearly translucent. Gavin would see her body clearly, almost as if she were naked. That was what she wanted. While she'd bathed, she'd reached a decision. If Gavin wanted to bed her, she was his.

The door opened, and Bisou trotted in, settling near her. Then Gavin stepped over the threshold and came to an abrupt halt. He looked. He hesitated. His expression warmed, eyes gleaming with desire. He simply stood there for a moment, drinking her in. "Isabel. I-I can't be in here with you, like that. It's simply not possible."

"What if I want you to be? Would you reconsider?" She was part trembling need, part consuming fear. Of rejection. Of...taking an irrevocable step. Gavin hadn't said he loved her. He had not asked for her hand. She could be committing herself to an act she may regret the rest of her life. But she wanted him anyway.

He strode toward her, grabbed her comb and hurled it across the room, then pulled her into his arms. His kiss was tender and needful, yet rampant with desire. He raised his head long enough to say, "Are you jesting? Would I reconsider? I've been wanting you for so long, I may embarrass myself."

Isabel wasn't certain what that meant, but she got the gist.

"I can't make love to you like this," Gavin said. "I'm dirty and smell as bad as Bisou. Let me wash first." He discarded his doublet, then pulled his shirt over his head, baring a chest sculpted with muscle. "Avert your eyes if you do not care to see me completely naked," he said, but she could tell he was teasing her. She would not avert her eyes if God himself commanded it. Then Gavin removed his hose, and his aroused male part sprang free. Watching her, he climbed into the tub. He took his time about it, and Isabel thought perhaps he was preening for her. Her excitement surged. She couldn't wait for him to be inside her. Fleetingly, she thought of the other ladies and how jealous they would be that it was she who would make love with Gavin. A grin must have broken over her face, because he said, "What is so amusing, Bel?"

"Remember when I told you about the ladies speculating on your…your organ? I was recalling that conversation and it made me smile."

"Come here," he said, suddenly serious.

She approached warily. "What?"

Holding out the soap, he said, "Pray, wash me. Everywhere."

"My chemise will get wet," she protested feebly.

"Perhaps you should remove it."

Her shyness won out and she carefully rolled her sleeves up as far as she could. The servants had left ewers of water, and after ordering him to tip his head back, she lifted one and poured it over his hair. Then she soaped and massaged his scalp with the tips of her fingers. Another pitcher of water to rinse.

"Lean forward so I can wash your back." She ran the soap over that long, sleek expanse. When she was done, he dipped into the water and rinsed off. She washed his arms and his chest and midriff, leaving off when she neared his groin. "Legs." Her mouth was dry, and that was all she could manage to say. It was difficult to ignore that part of him, jutting out of the water.

He raised one leg and balanced it on the edge of the tub. She started with his foot and worked her way up to his divinely muscled thigh, again stopping when she neared his erection. She couldn't ignore it, so she gazed at it until the soap dropped from her hand and onto his other thigh. Blushing, she retrieved it and moved on to his other leg, working quickly. This was torture. When she made to rise, Gavin said, "I think you forgot one part of me."

"I-I wasn't sure if you wanted me to touch you there."

Gavin wrested the soap from her hand and lathered his rampant erection. Then he took her hand and placed it around his member. "Move your hand up and down, like this, sweetheart." His flesh was soft and hard all at once. It burgeoned with her touch. Gavin had leaned back, resting his head against the tub, but he was watching her. After a minute, he said, "Enough. I can't take any more." With lightning speed, he climbed out, dried off, and lifted her into his arms. He carried her to the bed and laid her down gently.

"Tell me what you want, Isabel."

• • •

Gavin held his breath, waiting for her answer.

"I do not know how to describe it. All I know is this. I want you to touch me, wherever it pleases you."

Thanks be to a merciful God. He hadn't been certain if she wanted him as much as he did her. His body may have been an experiment to her, something to discover and scrutinize.

"That would be everywhere," he said wryly. He lifted her chemise over her head, first asking, "May I?" Then she was completely naked and lying next to him. He adored her with his hands, cherished her with his mouth. Kissing his way down her body, he palmed one breast while suckling at the other. Her breaths grew shallow.

"You are so beautiful, Bel," he said. "From head to toe. Your hair flows in waves about your shoulders and feels like silk. Your skin is soft and smooth as a rose petal. Your lips are velvet."

When he reached her core and the folds that hid her sex, he hesitated. But only for a moment. "Gavin?" she said. And then he knew she wanted everything. He stroked her there until she gasped with need. He could not hold back much longer. Rising up on his knees, he gently coaxed her legs apart and placed himself at her entrance.

God's breath, he did not know if she was a virgin. He

couldn't inquire now, not when they were in the throes of passion, but he would need to be gentle. "Tell me if it hurts, sweet Bel, and if you wish me to stop."

He entered her slowly, pausing, waiting for a signal from her. He got one when she said, "Gavin. Pray do not stop again." She grabbed his buttocks and squeezed, lifting her hips, begging him. He eased the rest of the way into her passage. It fit him like a fine kid glove. "Are you all right?"

"Aye. Yes, I believe so."

He waited a moment before he began thrusting. Dear God, she felt like heaven. He was on the verge, but determined to wait for her. When she was close, he wedged his finger between them, into her folds, and caressed. She came with stunning alacrity. One final, powerful thrust, and he withdrew from her body, spilling his seed onto the drying cloth. A guttural cry emerged from deep within him, manifesting an intensity of feeling he'd never experienced before. He lowered his body so that he covered hers, wanting to hold her close before they separated. Isabel encircled him with her arms and held him tightly.

In a moment, he rolled off and said, "Are you all right, sweeting?"

"Oh, yes. Very much so." Smiling, she ducked her head, her shyness suddenly returning. "Gavin? Why did you...do that? At the end?"

Chuckling, he tucked her against his side. "We are not married, sweetheart. I do not wish to get you with my child."

Not yet.

They fell into a languorous sleep, but at length, Gavin rose and began to dress. Sleepily, Isabel said, "What are you doing?"

"I'll sleep with the men downstairs. No troublesome questions to deal with that way. But first, I'm going to bathe the little varmint. Do you wish to help?"

"Oh, I wouldn't miss it for the world."

Chapter Twenty-One

It was onward to Skipton the next morning. Isabel was giddy and not the least inclined to curb her elation. She remained in a feverish delirium of love. Sitting by Gavin in the wagon was torture because she couldn't keep her hands off him. When they could be confident no one was looking, they stole frenzied kisses and clung to each other. Then Bisou would jump in their laps and lick their faces, making them laugh. But she thought they might laugh at anything, given the blissful mood they were in.

"How long is our journey today?" she asked Gavin.

"Another lengthy day, I'm afraid. We'll probably arrive just before nightfall."

At midday, they stopped at an alehouse. Men, horses, and dogs lingered outside. "Come, let's go in and find something to eat," Gavin said. "You must be as hungry as I am." Isabel followed him to the taproom. They sat at an ancient-looking table and the alewife walked over and asked what they wanted. "Pottage, bread, and two tankards, if you please."

It was then that Isabel noticed a man staring at them. Though she'd never seen one before, she recognized him for a beggar. His smock and jerkin were in tatters, and his long, lank hair hung in strings down to his shoulders. The alewife stopped to speak to him.

"Off you go, Rennie. I don't want the likes of you bothering our customers."

"It's one of them I need to speak to. Only take a minute." He had a roughly hewn crutch under one arm, and he pointed it toward them.

"Gavin, look. That man wants to speak to us."

Gavin motioned him over. "We may as well see what he wants."

When the fellow reached them, Gavin pointed to a chair. "Pray, be seated, sir."

He glanced about, as though he thought maybe Gavin was addressing somebody else. Finally, the man sat. His eyes were rheumy, and from the odor wafting toward them, he hadn't washed in weeks. Perhaps longer.

"What may I do for you? Would you like food? Ale?"

The man waved a dirty hand. "Nay. I've some information you might be interested in." His voice was surprisingly high pitched.

"You don't say," Gavin said, skeptically. "How many folks hear the same from you?"

He leaped to his feet so quickly, Isabel started. Never would she have guessed he could move so fast. "Hold," Gavin said, drawing a shilling from his purse.

When he glimpsed the coin, Rennie dropped back into his seat. "Don't like having me honesty questioned, that's all." He reached for the money, but Gavin jerked his hand away.

"First, let's hear what you have to say."

Scratching his chest, Rennie began to speak. "There was some men askin' about you earlier. I heard 'em."

"Did they identify themselves? Were they wearing livery?"

The other man shook his head. "Nay. Never said who they were. No livery."

"How can you be sure they were asking about us?"

He chortled. "They said as 'ow you'd be with them mummers. And you fit their description. Big, tall fellow, and a pretty lady with dark, shiny hair."

Isabel froze. Unidentified men were trying to track them down. How had they known she and Gavin would be traveling with William and his troupe of mummers?

"What else?" Gavin was trying not to show it, but he was worried. She could tell by the way his eyes had gone cold and his words were clipped and concise.

When Rennie only shrugged, Gavin asked another question. "What direction did they take when they left?"

"I'd like that coin now, if you please. Then I'll tell you." Gavin flipped it to him. He caught it and held it tightly in his fisted hand. "Skipton. They headed toward Skipton." He rose just as the alewife brought their meal.

"You have my thanks," Gavin said. Rennie beat a hasty path to the door.

In a low voice, Bel asked, "What does this mean, Gavin? Who do you think is following us?"

"Lesley's men, most likely. Along with some of Norfolk's people."

"How could they have known where to find us?"

"It was always a possibility. Either someone saw us, or they put two and two together when our departure coincided with that of the mummers. I'll speak to William about leaving."

A cacophony erupted in the inn yard, and at the same time, Isabel saw Rennie, who was still hovering near the door, turn back and look at them, smirking. Peering out the window, she gasped and grabbed Gavin's arm. "They're here," she said.

. . .

Gavin quickly assessed the situation. "Come with me." He and Isabel rushed to the table where William and his troupe were seated. The mummer, sensing trouble, looked up. "We have company," Gavin said. "Armed men who mean us harm. You'd best leave now if you don't wish to be caught up in the fray."

William cut him a look that said, "What do you take us for?", causing Gavin to smile despite the dire situation. In seconds, more than ten men burst through the door and drew their swords. Gavin unsheathed his rapier and said to Isabel, "Hide in the kitchen. It's you they're after."

"But I want to help you."

The last thing he needed was an argument. "You don't have a weapon. Pray, do as I ask. Now, before they see you!" He could see she was frustrated, but in the end, she turned and ran. Most of the customers had departed, but a few stood their ground, including the mummers. Gavin had no idea how they'd fare in a fight, but he appreciated their support.

The leader of the armed men swaggered over to Gavin and said, "Where's the lady? We have orders to take her."

"Orders from whom?" Gavin was a good head taller than the fellow, but he was muscular and looked strong enough to best most men in a fight.

"No concern of yours."

"She's not here," Gavin said, stalling for time.

"I'd prefer to do this the easy way. Turn her over. Now."

With that statement, any hope of settling this amicably dissolved. Gavin lunged, so did the other man, and their blades met, hilts locking. Chaos broke out as the mummers also engaged, along with other men left in the tavern—the sort who loved a good fight.

Gavin and his opponent both jumped back, circling one

another. Then it was lunge, jab, dodge, until at last Gavin backed the other man into the wall. The fellow cursed, having no room in which to wield his weapon. With one blow, Gavin knocked his attacker's sword to the floor and ran him through with the point of his rapier. One down.

He spun around, noticing that William was in trouble. He was fighting off two men, one of whom was poised to stab him. Charging over, Gavin slammed the side of his rapier against the man's shoulders, leaving William free to go after the other assailant. Out of the corner of one eye, Gavin noticed a couple of the attackers walking toward the kitchen, and his blood went cold. In the split second his attention had been diverted, his opponent managed to slice into his side. Ducking further blows, Gavin planted his feet solidly and kicked the man in the stomach. He dropped to the floor.

The mummers were holding their own while the fighting escalated and ebbed. Several of the attackers were down. Gavin bent, twisted, dodged, all the while stabbing and slicing with his blade, desperately wanting to finish off the remainder of them so he could find Isabel. He was barely aware of the pain from his wound, nor the blood trickling down his side. The room was clearing out. Some had fled, others would not live to do so again.

Parrying blows from the last attacker, Gavin lunged. Their rapiers clashed in a vicious dance of sliver blades. In the end, he caught his opponent in a weak moment, swung his blade, and knocked the man's weapon to the floor. He turned tail and ran.

William and his troupe stood by, mopping sweat from their brows and sheathing their weapons. "Thanks to all of you," Gavin said, "they're either dead, wounded, or gone. Are any of you injured?"

"A few cuts and bruises, but otherwise I think we'll live," William said. "Eh, fellows?"

Gavin smiled. "These were not the first men you've had to fight."

William looked as if he were trying to suppress a grin. "Nay. When you travel as we do, you encounter quite a few bands of thieves and murderers. Never any like these, though."

Gavin knew what he meant. Well-outfitted and well-armed men, who claimed the authority to remove Isabel. One of the mummers piped up. "You're injured, sir. You should have that wound seen to."

"I will, but first I must find Isabel. William, would you tell the alewife I'll pay for the damages?" Striding toward the kitchen, it occurred to him that the two men who'd headed for that direction had never re-emerged. At least, he didn't think they had. With the chaos, he may not have noticed. God's blood, if there was a backdoor, they may have abducted Isabel and made off with her.

A shock awaited him. When Gavin entered the room, the first thing he saw was Isabel and one of the tavern wenches. They were sitting on kegs playing hazard, as if they hadn't a care in the world. The cook and another servant were standing at a long oak work table chopping carrots, onions, and leeks. And the two attackers who'd gone in search of Isabel? They were on the floor, hands and feet securely tied. On closer inspection, they both seemed to be unconscious.

He shook his head in wonderment. When Isabel noticed him, she sprang to her feet. "Gavin! Are you all right?"

"Little you care, madam, in here gambling."

"Humphrey, the pot boy, brought us reports of the fighting. So, you see I knew you had vanquished the enemy. We were dicing to pass the time."

"And how came you to unman these two and tie them up?"

The cook spoke up. "I clonked one of 'em with a pot. The

lady tripped the other, and 'e lost 'is footing and dropped like a stone. An awful blow to 'is 'ead, it was."

Humphrey stepped forth and said, "I tied 'em up."

Gavin started to laugh, then clutched his side. Now that he was assured of Isabel's safety, his own pain reared its ugly head. Isabel noticed. "You're hurt. Come, sit down, and let me have a look."

In truth, Gavin was feeling rather woozy. Some of the mummers helped him upstairs to a chamber, where Isabel, assisted by the alewife, stitched his wound, applied salve, and forced him to drink a nasty-tasting potion. He slept throughout the remaining miles to Skipton.

. . .

Isabel shook Gavin awake as they crossed the drawbridge and waited for the guards to raise the portcullis. The mummers were expected, so there was no trouble with their admittance. They drove through the outer courtyard, the wagon wheels clanging on the cobbles, and halted once again, this time pausing until the huge oak doors swung open.

Gavin sat up and groaned. "You are in pain," Isabel said.

"It could be worse." He looked about, as though expecting someone to greet them. "Shrewsbury was sending a messenger, who should have reached Skipton before us, to inform them we were on our way."

But Isabel did not see anybody other than a few stable boys who were helping unhitch the horses. Gavin lifted their bags down and insisted on carrying them, even though Isabel assured him she was perfectly capable of managing her own. Bisou ran about sniffing, and after a moment, she swung him into her arms. Torches were flaming at the top of a set of curved stairs. A good sign. Perhaps they were expected after all. Gavin moved slowly, and she guessed every step pained him. Just as they reached the top, the oak door opened and a servant beckoned to them.

Inside they passed under an arch and climbed a set of stairs. At the top, in a well-lighted gallery, a woman awaited. Stepping forth, she said, "I am Lady Anne Clifford. Welcome to Skipton Castle."

Gavin bowed and Isabel curtsied, studying their hostess. She was a handsome woman, somewhere in her forties, with a long, narrow face. A fine linen bib covered her bosom. Her burgundy gown was slashed to reveal white skirts, and a French hood sat upon her head like a crown. How disheveled they must appear to her after their days on the road! And Gavin having just been in a fight.

But Lady Anne proved most kind. "Follow me. I will take you to your chambers. You'll wish to bathe before dinner." She could have asked a servant to do this, but undertook the duty herself. She set a brisk pace, and Isabel had to hurry to keep up. After showing her to a small chamber, where a bath was being readied, Lady Anne said, "I'll return in a moment, Mistress Tait." She walked on down the passage with Gavin trailing after her.

True to her word, she very soon reappeared on the threshold with a young female servant in tow. "This is Dorcas, who will be your lady's maid while you stay with us. Dinner will be served in an hour. Dorcas, pray show Mistress Tait to the hall when she's ready." After smiling kindly at Isabel, she left.

"Would you like to bathe first and then have a rest before dinner?" Dorcas asked.

"Aye, thank you." After helping Isabel undress and climb into the copper tub, the maid left her alone to enjoy her bath.

Inevitably, Isabel's first thought was of bathing Gavin. She sank down into the hot water and envisioned it. How she had slid the washing cloth over his chest and legs. She had touched every part of him. Isabel had no regrets and hoped Gavin didn't, either. Had she been wrong to surrender her virginity to him? It felt quite the opposite. Like the truest, finest thing she had ever done. And the most exciting. Merciful heaven, she was becoming aroused. It would behoove her to turn her thoughts to something less…titillating.

Isabel wished she had more time to linger in the bath, but the water was already cooling and she wanted to rest before Dorcas returned. She dried off, donned a robe which had thoughtfully been provided, and climbed onto the bed. Without intending to, she fell asleep and didn't wake up until the young maid entered and said she must dress for dinner.

When they entered the passage, Gavin was waiting, and Dorcas escorted them both to the banqueting hall. "How are you feeling?" Isabel asked.

"My wound is throbbing and painful, but nothing a few glasses of wine won't cure." He smiled good-naturedly, but she could tell he was uncomfortable. Dorcas motioned them to go ahead of her, and they entered the hall, where Lady Anne was sitting on the dais. It was a magnificent space, with a hammer beam ceiling, tall mullioned windows, and an enormous hearth. A Yule log was still burning, hissing and crackling and warming the hall. Their hostess rose to greet them.

"It was our custom to entertain friends, neighbors, and other guests on New Year's Eve, but my husband died last year. We are still in mourning."

"It was kind of you to receive us on such short notice," Gavin said. "How did you come to invite the mummers?"

"The performance is for the town. The good people of Skipton should not be deprived because of our loss. Pray, be seated." Servants filled their wine goblets, and with the first sip, Isabel felt some of the day's worries fall away.

"My son George is staying with the Earl of Bedford,

his guardian, for Christmastide," Lady Anne said. "He is barely thirteen, and I did not want him to sacrifice holiday celebrations. He suffered enough loss this year."

"That was kind of you, my lady," Isabel murmured.

Lady Anne smiled. "George is a high-spirited youth. When he comes of age, I doubt he will be satisfied with playing lord of the manor. Adventure is what he craves."

"'Tis a wise mother who has such an understanding of her son," Gavin said, grinning.

"How were your travels?" Lady Anne asked, her face a perfect blank.

Isabel kept her silence. She had no idea what the lady knew of their situation. When neither she nor Gavin spoke up immediately, Lady Anne said, "The earl told me a little of your troubles. Not the particulars, mind you."

Gavin drank from his goblet. "Most of our journey was without incident. However, when we stopped a few hours outside Skipton, a band of men attacked us. God be thanked, we bested them. With the help of the mummers, I should add."

"The entertainers will be well taken care of, with hearty food and drink. I assigned them to the guest lodgings." She paused to drink from her goblet.

"You have guards in the watchtower, my lady?" Gavin asked.

"Always. Are you expecting further trouble?"

"I doubt they would attack again so soon, but we should be prepared."

"Since the rebellion in the north, we have a small garrison of men here. I'll have the steward inform them."

Gavin nodded in acknowledgment.

"Gavin was injured, my lady," Isabel said. "I tended the wound, but we may need your assistance with bandages and salves."

"A knife wound?"

"Nay, sword. I stitched it."

"You must keep a close watch on it, as those cuts can fester and send poisons throughout the body. I can supply whatever you need." After a brief pause, she said, "I have missives addressed to you, Master Cade, from both Shrewsbury and one Nicholas Ryder. I'll give them to you after our meal."

Isabel stole a look at Gavin, but he simply thanked Lady Anne and turned his attention to the food, which was plentiful. Servants were setting out large platters of salads, beef roast, capons, salmon, and buttered peas. The scents wafting toward her made her mouth water with anticipation. Isabel had to check herself so as not to appear gluttonous. Neither she nor Gavin had eaten all day, and she was ravenous.

It was so quiet here, compared to what she'd been accustomed to. For a time, there was no need of conversation, because the three of them were partaking of the various dishes with gusto. Lady Anne ate as heartily as she and Gavin. By the time the minced pies and custards were served, Isabel felt too sated to eat another bite. Oddly, though, she did. How could one resist a minced pie?

At length, Lady Anne rose. "If you'll follow me, pray." Once in the drawing room, she handed Gavin a packet. "I shall retire to my chambers, but do stay here and enjoy a glass of sack while you read your missives."

They thanked her for her hospitality, and she left them alone. Isabel poured them each a measure of sack, and, seated on a cushioned settle, they settled in to read.

Chapter Twenty-Two

Gavin opened Shrewsbury's missive first and read it out loud to Isabel. It was brief, consisting of a few hastily scrawled lines. "*Do not continue on your journey to Carlisle. Remain at Skipton and await Nicholas Ryder's arrival. He has important news to impart. Have made no progress investigating the other matter.* And his signature. That's the entire message."

Gavin dropped the hand holding the letter to his lap and locked eyes with Bel. "Very cryptic. Is he referring to my fall?" When Gavin nodded, she said, "Open Ryder's letter. Perhaps it will tell us more."

After handing the earl's letter to Isabel, he unsealed the second one, from Ryder. "Merciful God," Gavin said, after scanning it:

29 December 1570

Brampton

Cade,

I will soon be en route to Skipton. Wait for me at the castle, where I will join you late on the New Year. We have arrested John Lesley and the Duke of Norfolk.

As I write this, both are being held in the Tower. They are undergoing interrogation. The information you provided was instrumental in capturing them, although our case was bolstered by a packet of ciphered letters addressed to the bishop and seized at Dover.

Pray, do nothing until we speak. Your safety, and that of Mistress Tait, may be at risk.

Regards,
N. Ryder

"What does this mean, Gavin? Is it over? Why are we still in danger?"

Gavin knew full well what it meant. It was Isabel whose life they wanted to snuff out in pursuit of their goals; he had no doubt that Lesley's underlings would continue to pursue that end. She was the one in whom Queen Mary had confided. He was at risk only as her protector. But he had no intention of revealing the truth to her at this juncture. He didn't wish to frighten her, and he would be here to watch over her. "We must wait and see what Ryder has to say. Perhaps he needs to record our testimony regarding the attempts to kill us. Not to mention the attackers on the road to Skipton. Of course, he does not yet know about that piece of devilry."

Yawning, Isabel rested her head against the back of the settle. Dark smudges under her eyes gave away her exhaustion. Gavin folded both letters and tucked them into a pocket in his doublet. "Come, Bel. It is time to retire. Shall I carry you to your bed?"

She laughed. "Given your injury, I don't think that's a good idea." At her door, he drew her into his arms and gently kissed her lips. "God keep you, sweet Bel."

"Good night, Gavin. Sleep well." Just inside the chamber, she suddenly stopped. "Your wound. I should check it before we retire."

"Nay. I'll examine it. I promise to summon you if it needs your ministrations."

"Swear?"

"I swear. Now, to bed with you, because the thought of you touching my body in any way is causing me discomfort in my nether regions." Gently, he pushed her over the threshold.

• • •

New Year 1571

Isabel was awake the next morning when a servant quietly entered to light the fire. Bisou was nestled next to her. When the fire caught, the flames lit the room, their shadows dancing on the walls. An uneasy feeling had been lurking at the back of her mind since her fall down the stairs at Sheffield. Yesterday, as the attackers were nearly upon them, Gavin had stated explicitly it was she the assailants were after, which had significantly increased her unease.

Why? What did they want with her?

She already had the answer, though it pained her to acknowledge it. They knew Mary had confided in her. She could give evidence against the Scots queen, and they needed to eliminate her. Isabel did not know who "they" were. Secret Catholics? Norfolk's men? Associates of Lesley from Scotland? Whoever they were, it was no game they were playing. After two attempts to kill her, she could not doubt the seriousness of their intent.

Isabel would never betray Mary. In her view, the queen had been forced into this conspiracy by Lesley and Norfolk. Would she provide evidence that might send Mary to the block? *No. Never.* She would be loyal to the queen no matter what. As her own mother had never been to her.

When this man Gavin worked for, Nicholas Ryder, arrived,

what would he require of her? Gavin had never demanded Mary's secrets, just as she, Isabel, had never demanded he reveal all he knew regarding the machinations swirling about Mary, Lesley, and Norfolk. She hadn't wanted him to. He was protecting her, and she in turn was protecting Mary.

Where would this all end? If Ryder's purpose was simply to inform Gavin of where things stood at present, perhaps Isabel would not be required to divulge anything.

A larger question loomed. What would happen between her and Gavin?

Beyond a doubt, she loved him and wanted to spend her life with him. But did he want the same? He had not said so, even after they'd made love. Certainly, his words implied love and commitment, but he had not asked for her hand. If he did not offer marriage, what would become of her? Returning to her home in Derbyshire would be her only choice, and it was possible her mother would refuse to take her in unless she could be married off immediately. Isabel dreaded the prospect of a loveless marriage, even more so since Gavin had made her aware of what it meant to love someone with her whole heart.

There was a knock on her door, and Dorcas glided in. "Are you ready to dress, Mistress Tait?"

"I hate the thought of rising from this warm bed, but I suppose I must." Dorcas dressed her in front of the fire and then departed, promising to return with breakfast. She left the door ajar, and Gavin peeked in.

"May I come in?"

"Good morrow." She felt a sudden urge to throw herself into his arms. Kicking the door closed, she did just that, burrowing into his chest. The soft wool of his tightly fitting jerkin brushed against her cheek.

"What's all this?" he asked. "I'm not complaining, mind you, but is something amiss?"

Everything. And nothing.

She raised her head, fixing her gaze on his mouth. His compellingly sensual mouth. She pulled him down for a kiss, and he came willingly. "Isabel," he said on a groan.

Pliable lips and sweet tongue. She could go on kissing him forever. Not simply a kiss, but a secret language between them. Gavin drew back, they looked at each other, and she imagined her eyes were glazed, like his. He pulled her back to him, molding his body to hers. And then they heard Dorcas coming and reluctantly separated.

"Mistress Tait and I would like to dine together, Dorcas," Gavin said. "I'll bring my meal over here."

"Nay, sir, you and Mistress Tait be seated at the table." She gestured to the oak table and chairs in the window embrasure. "I'll fetch your food."

They did as she asked, stealing guilty glances at one another and smiling like besotted fools.

Later, they sought out Lady Anne in the withdrawing room, where Dorcas said they would find her. She sat near the tall windows with her embroidery. Looking up at their approach, she said, "Good day to you both."

"And to you, my lady," Gavin responded. Isabel curtsied.

"Be seated, pray. I trust you both broke your fast?"

"Aye," Isabel said. "I have never before eaten an orange. I should be content eating one every day for the rest of my life." It was the juiciest, most luscious fruit she'd ever tasted.

Lady Anne laughed. "They come from Sicily. Aren't they delicious?" Setting her work aside, she said, "Tell me, if you please, are you expecting a visitor today?"

"Aye," Gavin said. "Nicholas Ryder should be here by the evening meal. I hope that will not inconvenience you, my lady."

"Not at all. The earl informed me we may have an extra

guest for a few days. After the mummers' performance, there will be food aplenty, and the Wassail bowl. I thought about canceling the festivities this year, but our mourning period is nearly past. For many of the local citizens, it is their only celebration during the twelve days of Christmas.

"As it appears to be a fine day, perhaps you both would enjoy exploring the grounds. Do look at the Conduit Court, the center of the castle. It's a lovely space, although perhaps not so much in the winter. Visit the towers, the kitchens—even the dungeon, if you'd like." At Isabel's visible shudder, she smiled. "We haven't had any...guests there for quite a while."

After thanking Lady Anne, they bid her good day and left her to her sewing. Once in the passage, Isabel said, "Let's explore indoors, then we can dress in cloaks and hats and go outside."

"Excellent plan." Gavin grasped her hand, and for an hour or more, beginning on the first floor, they roamed about the castle. First, the kitchens, warm and filled with tempting aromas. They passed the great hall, in which they'd dined the night before, the withdrawing room, and the lord's dayroom, which boasted richly colored tapestries on the walls and a fire blazing in its enormous hearth.

Before venturing downstairs, Gavin steered Isabel toward the watchtower, which displayed a commanding view across the countryside. Excusing himself, he spoke to one of the guards for a few minutes. Isabel caught snatches of the conversation. Gavin was describing yesterday's attack. "The men were not identifiable by livery. I believe they are no longer following us, but I would not rule out the possibility."

"We will be vigilant, sir," the guard proclaimed. "You can depend on that."

From there, they made their way downstairs to the ground floor, where they visited the wine and beer cellars and the curing room, the strong scent of both brine and smoke tickling their noses.

Stopping by their own chambers, they dressed for the out of doors in cloaks, gloves, hats, and warm boots and collected Bisou. While they tramped over the frozen ground, Isabel's thoughts returned to Gavin and his feelings toward her. He had such presence, and walking alongside him, she was acutely conscious of his virility. With every touch, whether to help her over a stile or tuck a stray lock of hair under her hat, a jolt of awareness shot through her. Isabel wished she had access to his mind, so she might know what he was thinking. Apparently, not about her, for he said, "I wonder if Lesley and Norfolk are being tortured."

Involuntarily, she flinched. "I hope not. No man deserves such treatment."

"Even the one who ordered our murder?"

"Are you so sure it was one of them?"

"Lesley himself came close to admitting it to me." Gavin stopped and looked at her, his eyes soft. "Isabel. It is the New Year, a time of joy and celebration. Let's not think of these matters today. Time to go inside—it's devilishly cold out here." The sun was already lowering, the daylight waning. In silence, they tramped past the gardens, withered and brown in the winter season, and made their way to the castle. Bisou pranced after them.

• • •

At the door to her chamber, Gavin said, "I'll return in a few moments. I have a surprise for you." He had decided not to press Isabel further, at least not today. There were so many questions he wanted—needed—answers to, but he was treading a fine line with her and didn't wish to drive a wedge between them. By God's light, he loved the lass. He wanted to wed her. Thinking back over everything that had transpired since Isabel's arrival at Tutbury, he saw an endless number of half-truths and omissions regarding Queen Mary in his dealings with Isabel. If he hadn't been forthcoming with her, how could he expect her to be open with him?

Inside his wardrobe, Gavin found the small pouch holding the necklace he'd gotten Isabel. Rubbing his fingers over the velvet, he imagined the soft skin of Isabel's neck and smiled. For a moment, he felt an unbridled sense of joy. Before it slipped away, he crossed to her chamber and rapped lightly. Hearing nothing, he slowly pushed the door open. "Isabel? Are you there?"

"Come in, Gavin." She was standing before the fire, Bisou curled up on the floor beside her. Natural light shone through the glazed window directly onto her, and the full force of her beauty nearly knocked him senseless. The raven hair and deep-set, dark eyes. The porcelain skin. The feminine curves hiding beneath her bodice and skirts. But her astonishing physical beauty wasn't the reason he gasped. For the first time, he was struck by what she was within. Her sharp mind, a repository of a true depth of knowledge. Her unflagging sense of humor, even when she'd just been dunked in freezing river water. Her compassion for Mary, and for him when he'd sobbed over Simon's death. How had it happened, when she'd been dealt nothing but unkindness, even cruelty, her whole life? How had she become such a remarkable woman?

He was quite overcome. Rather than going to her, he stood still, simply drinking her in.

"Gavin?" Her voice finally penetrated his disjointed thoughts.

"Isabel. You look so lovely standing there, with the light shining on you. It's rather daunting, I'm afraid."

She blushed and tried to suppress a smile. But she could not. Walking toward her, he said, "Come. Sit with me." They lowered themselves to the small settle before the fire. "This is for you, Bel. Because you are the best of my world. The dearest person in my life."

He held out the small velvet bag.

• • •

Gavin had a gift for her. Coupled with the way he'd been watching her, his eyes liquid with emotion, Isabel was overwhelmed and could only say stupidly, "For me?"

He laughed a little. "Aye. Open it."

With trembling fingers, she pulled the drawstring and the bag fell open. Reaching inside, she drew out a necklace, a pendant on a delicate gold chain. It was exquisite, a small ruby set in a circle of gold etched with vines. Glancing up at him, she smiled. "I've never owned anything so beautiful."

"Let me fasten it for you," he said. Near tears, Isabel passed him the necklace. His hands brushed the sensitive skin at her nape, shooting little tremors through her body. Gavin pulled her to her feet, saying, "Come near the window so I can see it better." He studied her for a time, then said, "It suits you, Isabel. Dark, vibrant colors complement your beauty."

"Thank you, Gavin. A gift for me is rare indeed, and this one is perfect. You chose it with such care." Her voice was shaking, and the tears she'd been relentlessly holding back began to trail down her cheeks.

And with love. She could not put words in his mouth, though. He hadn't said anything about loving her. "Don't cry, sweetheart. I hoped this would make you happy."

"Oh, be assured, it does. I shall treasure it always."

No matter what happens.

Gavin framed her face with his hands. "I love you, Isabel. God help me, but I do."

Not precisely the declaration of love she craved. It sounded as though he loved her against his will. Against his smarter self, standing to one side, telling him he should not.

Was it enough?

Lowering his hands, Gavin crushed her against him and kissed her lips, her cheeks, her ears, his hot breath fanning over her. Desire pooling in her belly, Isabel's knees buckled, and he tightened his hold. He trailed kisses down her neck, and then she felt his hands at her back, unlacing her bodice. No fool, she knew where this was leading. Should she allow it? She wanted it as much as he did. An aching need for him lodged against Isabel's heart. But should she make love with him again, when he'd said nothing about marrying her? Did she want to end up his mistress? Because Gavin didn't seem to want her as his wife.

The decision was taken from her when a light knock sounded at the door. Guiltily, they pulled apart. "Enter," Isabel called out.

Dorcas stepped in and bobbed a curtsy. "A Master Nicholas Ryder is here to see you, Master Cade. He is waiting in the lord's dayroom."

Gavin turned to Bel. "I didn't expect him so early. How long has he been here, Dorcas?"

"He arrived while you were out walking. Said not to send anybody after you, seeing as he wanted to wash and rest."

"Pray tell him I'll join him shortly."

After Dorcas left, Gavin re-laced Isabel's bodice and then gently spun her around. "Bel, you know he will wish to speak to you as well."

She wanted to say, "Why? I've nothing to tell him," but the last thing she wanted was to argue with Gavin about Mary. She simply nodded. He left to report to Ryder, and Isabel sat by the fire, first lifting Bisou into her lap. "What am I to do, *mon petit chien*? What am I to do?"

Chapter Twenty-Three

Gavin had been with Ryder above an hour when the man asked to question Isabel. Throughout, Gavin had debated whether to inform him that Isabel would tell him nothing he did not already know regarding Queen Mary. In the end, he decided not to. Both Isabel and Ryder were astute, keen observers, good at assessing others. Gavin would merely witness—unless Ryder threatened Isabel. Then he would step in.

Ryder sent a footman to summon her. When she entered the room, she held her head high and exuded confidence. Yet because he knew her so well, he also sensed trepidation. A slight hesitation on the threshold. A stutter as she greeted Ryder. God's wounds, how he wished she did not have to suffer this.

"Mistress Tait, good even," Ryder said.

And it *was* evening now. When Isabel opened the door, Gavin had heard voices and laughter, and the clatter and general disruption of the mummers' preparations. The tantalizing odor of the dishes being laid out for the banquet drifted in, making him wish to God that was all they need think about on this night. Revelry, silly mumming plays, and excellent food.

Ryder's voice intruded, and Gavin was drawn back to the reality of their situation.

"Mistress, Gavin has explained what has transpired in a general sense, and from his point of view. I need your perspective on all of it." He waved a hand through the air, as though that explained what he meant by "all of it."

"Where shall I begin?" Isabel asked.

Ryder handled her prudently. Rather than beginning with a demand to reveal everything Mary had spoken to her about, he asked her to tell him everything she could recall about her fall down the steps at Sheffield. Ryder dipped his quill into an ink jar and made notes while she spoke. Her description of the event was exactly as before.

Ryder laid down his quill. "You have been attacked several times, mistress. Why is it thus?"

Isabel paused, gathering her thoughts. "The perpetrators—whoever they are—believe I have information which, if generally known, would harm the queen."

"And is it so?"

"I suppose it is, yes."

"Were you not frightened by all this? The attempts on your life?"

At that, she glanced at Gavin, and a tiny smile curved her lips. "Of course. But directly after the incident at Sheffield, Gavin arranged our escape. He has always been there to protect me."

Gavin cringed at that. It had been a near thing, both by the river and yesterday, at the tavern. And he'd not been there to prevent someone shoving her down the stairs.

She went on. "And I feel safe here at the castle. The men in the watchtower, the garrison—I am well guarded. The people who want me dead could not get past them."

Ryder leaned back in his chair and studied Isabel. "You

are very matter of fact about it, mistress."

"I am not given to hysterics, sir," Isabel said.

Ryder glanced at Gavin, eyebrows lifted. Both men chuckled. "I warned you," Gavin said.

Suddenly, Ryder's posture straightened and his expression sobered. Now he would get to the heart of it. "Gavin has told me you were much in Mary's favor. I ask you now to tell me what she confided in you."

Isabel shot a wary glance at Gavin, then looked back at Ryder. "The first evening I met her, she told me she believed Queen Elizabeth loved her and cared about her well-being. She also said how very much she missed her son. And always, I heard much of her ailments and physical complaints."

"And going forward, as you spent time with her and came to know her better?"

Isabel began to relate what Mary had told her about her husbands, beginning with the young Francois and ending with the Earl of Bothwell. At one point, Ryder interrupted. "And did you believe she was being completely honest with you?"

"To be sure, I wondered at times. There were lies of omission, perhaps. She was—is—very unhappy about her imprisonment. Her abdication was forced upon her—those are her words—and she believes she would be in Scotland with her son if only Elizabeth would free her."

Ryder had folded his arms across his chest. "For a prisoner, she lives in the lap of luxury, does she not?"

"I cannot gainsay that," Isabel admitted.

Ryder's next question surprised Gavin. "What do you know about the plot conceived by Mary, John Lesley, and Norfolk to free Mary and seize the throne?"

Isabel appeared to be shocked by the question. "Why, nothing, sir."

"Nothing? In your frequent, private conversations with

the queen, she never mentioned this?"

Isabel hesitated. "Not in so many words. Perhaps obliquely. I-I warned her against doing anything rash."

"Ah," Ryder said, placing his hands on the desk and leaning toward Isabel. Gavin stepped forward, ready to intervene if necessary. "What prompted you to warn her?"

"I cannot say, Master Ryder. I swore to the queen I would not reveal any of her confidences."

"Would you be shocked if I told you John Lesley had been threatened with the rack? And in pleading with his jailers, proclaimed Mary to be a 'serial adulterer?'"

Isabel flinched, but she remained composed. "I don't care for the man, but I am sorry to hear he was threatened with torture. I have had very little contact with him, although I am aware Gavin believes he is the enemy. Perhaps, fearing the worst, Lesley spoke rashly."

Ryder got to his feet, a typical power ploy. "Mistress Tait, William Cecil is convinced by an abundance of evidence that Mary herself was a key player in a plot to overthrow Elizabeth. I would ask you to consider carefully the consequences of your refusal to reveal what the Scots queen told you."

Gavin wanted to throttle the man for the threat, but Isabel either didn't recognize Ryder's statement as such, or she was not intimidated by it. "Sir, it sounds as though you have sufficient evidence. I doubt I could tell you anything you do not already know."

"That, madam, is for us to decide." Ryder circled round the desk and looked at Gavin and Isabel. "I will leave you now, with the suggestion that you enjoy the evening's festivities. But I implore you, mistress, to judiciously consider my request. We will speak again tomorrow."

With that, Ryder left the room. And Isabel, who had maintained her equanimity throughout her interview with him, said, voice sounding accusatory, "You believe I should betray Mary and tell him, don't you, Gavin? Or who knows what might befall me."

What a lackwit he was. Of course she'd recognized the threat. She was too smart to have missed it. Should he have told Ryder to draw back? Not yet. But it may come to that.

. . .

Slowly, Isabel got to her feet and moved to stand before the blazing fire. The interview with Ryder had left her cold, in body and spirit. Suggesting they enjoy the festivities was laughable after he'd threatened her. And Gavin had said nothing in her defense. Nor had he yet responded to her question. After pouring them each a glass of sack, he said, "Come, Isabel. Sit beside me."

Reluctantly, she joined him on the upholstered settle. "You showed remarkable composure, Bel. And yes, I do think you must tell Ryder everything you know about Mary's involvement in Ridolfi's plot. It is your duty to do so, as an English citizen."

Isabel sipped her wine. She needed time to contain her anger. Finally, when she thought she could keep her temper in check, she said, "My first duty is to Mary. It is she for whom I work, and therefore, she deserves my loyalty."

Gavin looked baffled by her response. "Can you not throw him a bone? Give him some bit of information you had from Mary, if only to appease him?"

Ignoring that question, she went on as though he hadn't spoken. "You realize, do you not, that you have never explained anything to me regarding this Ridolfi person. After Simon's death, you mentioned him as a cohort of Lesley's. But never again did you speak of him."

Gavin gave her a sheepish look. "Suffice it to say, he was one of the prime movers in this conspiracy. You need know nothing else about him."

Angrily, Isabel set her glass down, so hard, some of the sack spilled out. Quickly, she mopped it up with her handkerchief. "Because I am a female? I thought you were a different kind of man, one who respected my intelligence." She couldn't keep the rancor from her voice.

Gavin got to his feet and moved away from her. "I have the greatest admiration and respect for your intelligence. You know that. I wanted only to protect you. The more you knew, the greater the danger to you."

"And yet, here I am, in greater peril than ever, this time from the other side."

Gavin's mouth hardened. "If you believe I would stand by and allow any harm to befall you, you underestimate me."

"You cannot protect me all the time, Gavin. Events you can neither control nor prevent have happened, and will again." She sighed deeply, shaking her head. "We have been friends, and more, for a long time now, without you ever being honest with me. You have hinted that the queen lied, that she cared only for herself, that I should be wary of her. But you never truly justified why I should not trust her. You never once looked me in the eye and said, 'Let me give you the truth about Mary, Isabel.'" She blurted out, "The way matters stand now, I trust Mary more than you."

Eyes wide with shock, Gavin began to pace about the room. Every so often he halted, spun about, and stared at her, hands on his hips. As if he wished to say something, but could not quite make up his mind to do so. Isabel waited, hands folded in her lap, for him to sort out his thoughts.

When Gavin returned to her, he didn't sit beside her. Rather, he stood before her, his expression dark. "You judge me harshly if you trust that woman above me."

Isabel's heart plunged at that, and she wished her rash words unsaid.

"Did it occur to you that my work was clandestine? That as an agent for the queen, I was sworn to secrecy?" He laughed bitterly, shaking his head. "Indeed, I told you far more than I ever should have."

The sting of tears burned at the back of her eyes. Everything was going so wrong, and she couldn't seem to change the tone of the conversation. "Aye, it did occur to me. But after I'd become so fully involved, after we'd become so close, wouldn't it have been more prudent to make certain I was well informed about all matters pertaining to the queen?"

"Our feelings for each other were separate. Private."

"Perhaps we wanted them to be, but in the end, what we meant to each other...it was mixed up together with this whole business. Can you not see that?"

Gavin lowered himself beside her and grasped her shoulders. "I wanted to keep you out of the maneuverings as far as possible. Only a few hours ago, I confessed my love for you. Can you not trust me enough to tell me of your dealings with Mary? I could then determine, with your assistance, what to tell Ryder. While I would do anything in my power to assure your continued safety, I don't know Ryder well. I don't know what he will do if you refuse to answer his questions."

When she did not answer, he leaped to his feet and said, "God's wounds, Isabel!"

Softly, she spoke up. "When you said you loved me, it sounded as if it was against your better judgment. You said, 'God help me,' as though loving me was an anathema to you."

"For God's sake, Isabel. How could you think such a thing?"

"Admit the truth, Gavin. You cannot yet commit to another woman."

"I said I loved you. What more do you want?"

Sobbing, she cried out, "I am not Anna!"

After that, a heavy silence hung in the air. Isabel wept

quietly, hoping Gavin wouldn't notice. Having turned his back on her, he was gazing into the fire. What he was thinking, she couldn't know and didn't care to guess. She felt as if she'd been punched in the stomach with an iron fist. She fought to control herself, dabbing at her eyes with her handkerchief.

At length he turned, raked a hand through his hair, and said, "Pray, pardon me for offending you. I think it best we do not see each other the remainder of the day. I'll retire to my chamber so that you may pass your evening in company."

Isabel wanted to speak, to say something to break this awful impasse, but couldn't find the words. So she said nothing, the moment passed, and Gavin strode to the door. He paused, his hand on the latch. "Ridolfi murdered Simon. Is that enough truth to satisfy you?" The door banged behind him.

Isabel covered her face with her hands and wept at Gavin's cruel revelation. Shivering, she sat before the fire a long time, fearing she would never be warm again. It was growing late, and she should return to her chamber and dress for the evening's revels. She felt numb inside. Hollowed out. She had hoped Gavin would reiterate his love for her in no uncertain terms. But instead, he'd given a cold, curt apology. By God's light, why could he not realize that not every woman was like Anna Cade? That Isabel was not the same at all?

Nothing he'd said, even regarding Simon's murder, had persuaded her to break her vow to Mary. God's mercy, Norfolk and Lesley were being tortured! What if the same fate awaited Mary because of information Isabel provided? She refused to bolster their case against the queen, and she'd no idea what the personal cost of that would be.

• • •

Gavin awoke the next morning, eyes gritty due to his wakeful night. Merciful God, what a hellish sleep he'd had. Isabel's anguished cry, "I am not Anna!" had affected him deeply, echoing through his mind in the darkness. How many times had he drawn Isabel close and then backed away, all because he dreaded a recurrence of what had happened with Anna? And Bel was right about his declaration of love for her. Half-hearted as it had been, he could well imagine how it must have sounded, and it made him cringe.

But he also burned with anger and yes, hurt. Isabel had said she trusted Mary more than him. If she only knew all the lies Mary had presented as truth, all the falsehoods with which she had portrayed herself to Bel. But she did not know, because Gavin had never told her.

God's teeth, she was right about that, too. Long ago, he should have sat her down and told her all he knew. Given that she'd become Mary's primary confidant, she deserved to have the truth, even if she refused to believe it. Instead, he'd decided it was more important to tease information from her about Mary. In his defense, he'd quickly gotten over that. The closer he'd gotten to Isabel, the less he cared about what secrets of Mary she held. It was Bel he'd come to care about, far more than his work for Ryder.

Speaking of whom...he'd been truthful when he told Isabel he did not know what to expect from Nicholas Ryder if she refused to inform on the queen. He seemed like a reasonable man, but Gavin had seen reasonable men throw caution to the winds to achieve their goals. It was within Ryder's power to arrest Isabel on the spot and throw her into the dungeon right here at Skipton. But his instincts told him Ryder was not that kind of man, that he would, despite his threat, be patient with her.

A servant had been in earlier and stoked the fire in his hearth. Gavin was quick about his morning ablutions, and as soon as they were completed, dressed with haste. A man servant tapped on the door and carried in a tray of pottage, bread and butter, and ale.

He ate, not truly tasting his food, pondering the day ahead of him and what would happen. How would he save Isabel if Ryder attempted to arrest her? Gavin didn't relish another escape and the hardships that would impose on them in the cold January weather. But if it came to that, so be it. Pushing away the remainder of his meal, for which he had no appetite, he exited his chamber and made for the lord's dayroom, where he suspected Ryder would be waiting.

On the way, it occurred to him that perhaps Isabel would not want rescuing—at least, not by him.

Chapter Twenty-Four

Isabel entered the lord's dayroom, where Nicholas Ryder was situated. She curtsied, and he said, "Good morrow, mistress." No sooner had she sat than Gavin walked in.

"Cade," Ryder said. "I was on the verge of summoning you."

Gavin glanced at her. With dark smudges beneath his eyes, he appeared as haggard as she felt. He too must have passed a restless night. "Isabel," he said, his voice flat.

"Gavin." She could be equally as cold.

Ryder looked pointedly at Gavin and said, "I think perhaps 'tis time we told Mistress Tait everything. The whole truth about Mary. Shall I do so, or would you prefer to?"

"I'll cede the task to you."

Isabel had no desire to hear it from either of them. What was the point? But Ryder had begun to speak, and she'd better attend, if only to show respect. The tale was more absorbing than she'd anticipated, especially when it came to Mary's husbands. It was a long story of murder, treachery, and duplicity. In the end, Ryder asserted, it was clear that Mary and her lover, the Earl of Bothwell, were complicit in the death of her second husband, Lord Darnley.

Isabel held up a hand. "Stop, pray. How do I know this is all true? I have no proof of any of it. Nor corroboration. 'Tis only your word."

Once again, it was Ryder who spoke. "We have sworn testimony from numerous sources, some of whom served the queen. And written proof as well."

"Now do you see that she has lied to you, Isabel?" Gavin asked.

Isabel did not answer immediately. "What you have told me does not differ appreciably from what Mary herself said."

Gavin huffed a laugh. "Truly? Didn't she act the innocent in all these doings?"

Isabel had to admit Mary had. "It is true, she omitted certain aspects of this in her relating of it to me." Isabel's fingers strayed to her pendant, brushing her thumb over the stone. Last night, she'd vowed never to wear it again. But already it felt a part of her. Refusing to wear it would represent a permanent end to her relationship with Gavin. "Tell me the rest."

Finally, Gavin took up the story. "The night I nearly drowned, I overheard a conversation between Mary and the Duke of Norfolk. They planned to wed, seize the throne from Elizabeth, and rule England. The plot was instigated by an Italian banker named Roberto Ridolfi, who had connections to both Philip of Spain and the Pope. Norfolk said Ridolfi had visited him twice in London. Unfortunately, I was rendered unconscious before I learned the important details. The how, where, and when, if you will."

"So Ridolfi was the instigator?"

Gavin nodded and carried on. "Later, I learned some of those details from the missives I seized from the poor lad who died, Simon. He was the unfortunate boy Ridolfi paid to deliver ciphered messages to Lesley."

"You told me of the messages, but not what they

contained," Isabel said. "Why the need to kill Simon? How did that help them?"

"They could no longer trust him as a messenger. Sending the lad's body to me served as a warning to back down. Murdering Simon was a particularly nasty gambit."

Ryder broke in. "Meanwhile, we have had men watching the ports, and we seized a packet of damning letters from Ridolfi to Lesley. It gave us enough to arrest both Lesley and Norfolk. But now we need to know how deeply Mary was involved in this."

What they wanted was condemning evidence against the queen. Strictly speaking, the conversation Isabel had overheard between Mary and Lesley was not a confidence shared, and it would prove Mary's reluctance to take part in any plot against Elizabeth. Isabel would need to tread carefully, however, and not divulge the specifics. Mary had expressed her reluctance to participate in the conspiracy; nonetheless, the conversation revealed she'd been fully aware of all but the minutest details.

"There is one thing," Isabel said. Gavin blew out a breath, as if that statement lifted a weight from him. "But it is not much. After the move to Sheffield, I was setting out some of Mary's personal items when I heard voices from behind the screen. It was the queen and John Lesley. He was speaking in a most demeaning way to her. I-I cannot tell you all of what was said, but Mary expressed a great reluctance to be involved in his scheme."

"That is the extent of what you heard?" Gavin asked, his tone laced with skepticism.

"Lesley warned Mary against confiding in me, because I am 'too close to Cade.' That is how he put it."

"It seems he had nothing to worry about there," Gavin said, "since you guard her confidences as though they were the crown jewels."

"Nothing more, then?" Ryder asked.

"That is all I can tell you. It sounded very much as if she were being forced to do something against her will."

Ryder's brow furrowed. "This is of very little use to us, mistress."

Isabel rubbed her hands together, trying to warm them. "I fear it is the best I can do."

Gavin threw his hands up, signaling his ire and frustration. "Mary is a traitor, her cohorts are traitors and murderers, and yet you will protect her. Why? Has she promised you something?"

That shocked Isabel to her core. "How can you accuse me thus? And what could Mary possibly have promised me?"

"To keep you in her retinue. You are loath to return to your home and family. It would be quite a boon if you could continue serving her. Or perhaps she offered coin."

The thought of remaining with Mary had occurred to Isabel, if Gavin did not offer her marriage. A possibility which now seemed like a cruel joke. But Mary had made her no promises—they'd never discussed such a thing. At present, Isabel wanted nothing more than to be away from all this. Even going home would be preferable.

She shook her head in disbelief. "You think Mary promised me some sort of favor, or even money, in return for my silence. You think I can be bought?"

Thus far, Ryder had sat silent, observing. Now he rose and said, "I shall return shortly." Saying nothing more, he exited, closing the door quietly.

"God's breath, Isabel, I no longer know what to believe." Gavin plunked down on Ryder's empty chair, leaned back, and fixed his gaze on her. "Your loyalty to the queen is unfathomable to me. I'm grasping at straws to find an explanation."

"You'll find none other than what I've already said. May

I return to my chamber now, pray?" Isabel felt all hope, all prospects, shriveling up inside her. Including the love she bore Gavin. Obviously, he'd never truly felt any for her.

"Oh, I do not think you will escape so easily. Ryder will have more to say to you. As for myself, I am through with you, Isabel. With us."

Shaking inside, Isabel said, "Since you have never made any commitment to me, it is no more than what I expected from you."

Angrily, he leaped from his chair and drew close to her. Then, hunkering down before her, he said, "Make no mistake, we are better off apart. In matters pertaining to the queen, we cannot agree. Your stubbornness regarding this, your intractability, tells me there would be many other problems that would drive us apart."

Isabel's ire rose at his curt dismissal of what they had meant to each other. "I am an uncomplicated woman who got caught up in matters beyond my imagining. Beyond my control. I made a promise. A vow. Perhaps it was naive of me. That I did so with an agenda, with favors from Mary in mind, is the furthest thing from the truth."

At that moment, a thought struck her, so onerous she could scarce say it out loud. "Now I would seek the truth from you, Gavin. Did you lead me on, indeed, make love to me, so that I would reveal Mary's confidences to you?"

They were at eye level. Something flickered for the briefest moment in his eyes, and he rose. "I, that is…it is not what you imagine."

Isabel had struggled to hold back the tears, but now she allowed them free rein. "You have used me in the basest way imaginable, and yet you accuse *me* of treachery. You are right—there is no future for us." He was blocking her way. She pushed against him, and he yielded. Just then, the door opened and Ryder stood on the threshold.

"Will you pardon us a moment, Mistress Tait?" he asked, motioning to Gavin.

Isabel remained where she was, wondering how her world had collapsed about her so completely and thoroughly.

• • •

Ryder led the way toward an unoccupied chamber and pointed to a settle. When both men were seated, to Gavin's surprise, he said, "I think we must leave it for now. Mistress Isabel may change her mind, and we should give her time to do so. She deserves a few days to mull over all we told her about Mary."

When Gavin did not respond, Ryder continued. "I do not know what lies between you and Isabel Tait, but I sense there is much more going on here than meets the eye. My eye, in any case."

Gavin looked away. He was torn up inside at the mess he'd made of things with Isabel. "Give me something to do. Send me on a mission, anywhere away from here. From Isabel. I'll go mad if I remain."

A servant passed, and Ryder summoned him, requesting hot spiced wine. "And inform Mistress Tait she may retire to her chamber. Wine for her as well, pray."

While they waited for the wine, another servant came in and lit a fire. Warmed by both comforts, Gavin began to feel human again. Finally, he asked Ryder the question that had been plaguing him. "You said you would give Isabel time to think things over. In the hope, I assume, she'll change her mind. But what if she does not? Something which would not surprise me in the least. When she believes she is in the right, she's as stubborn a lass as I've ever known. What will become of her?"

"Are you asking if I'll arrest her? Or worse?" Ryder

place a hand over his mouth, ostensibly to clean off a dab of wine, but Gavin thought the true purpose was to hide a smile. "Nothing will happen to her. She's a good woman, caught up in a plot she had no knowledge of. As she pointed out, she knew nothing about most of it. I'm beginning to believe that she has no information that will be of much help to us."

"That may be. But the fact that what Isabel does know came directly from Mary could work against her."

"True enough. But Elizabeth has shown great reluctance to deal harshly with the Scots queen, and I for one do not believe that will change soon." He paused to swallow a draft from his goblet. "You implied that Isabel does not wish to return to her family. Has she anyplace else to go?"

"No. I could speak to Shrewsbury about putting her into Bess's employ. But Isabel would not be welcomed back by the others, I fear. Will Queen Mary remain where she is?"

"At Sheffield? I think not. Cecil will want her returned to Tutbury as punishment for her sins." Ryder leveled his green gaze on Gavin. "Why don't you marry Isabel Tait? You are a widower whose mourning period is past, and you love the lass. Where there is love, things can always be worked out."

"I imagine your path to true love with your wife wasn't strewn with brambles, as ours seems to be."

Ryder laughed, and Gavin looked at him in surprise. "What?"

"Let me sum it up briefly for you, Cade. My wife—Maddy is her name—was arrested for participating in a raid against the queen. I offered to save her from hanging if she agreed to spy for our side. I then placed her in a house full of traitors." He paused, collecting his thoughts and now looking quite sober. "One of them nearly killed her. I used her, lied to her, yet I was falling in love with her the whole time. In the end, she forgave me. We are happy beyond reason."

Gavin stared at the other man. "I see." Could it be, that

after such turmoil, a couple could forgive each other?

Ryder set down his cup, and both men rose. Slapping Gavin lightly on the back, Ryder said, "Don't give up, Cade, if you love her. If you must get away, go to London, to Cecil. I'll have a report you can deliver, and you can answer his questions. Do not mention Mistress Isabel. If he should ask about the source I thought might provide proof against Mary, say I was mistaken in that belief."

Gavin gave a curt nod. "What will you do?"

"Lady Anne said I may stay as long as I like. I've much work to do, and will wait here for your return. I'll send some men with you—it's not safe for you to travel alone." Ryder turned and walked toward the door. Just before exiting, he said, "Perhaps the trip will allow you time to clarify your thoughts regarding Isabel."

• • •

In her chamber, Isabel prowled about, restless and impatient. She had sat before the hearth and drunk the hot wine someone had ordered for her. Was she a prisoner? Could she leave? She wanted nothing more than to be outside, tramping about the grounds and breathing the fresh, crisp air. Perhaps that would revive her, body and mind.

Gavin believed she'd been bought, or bribed, by Mary. That he could believe such a thing was the final straw. According to him, Isabel would do anything to avoid returning to her childhood home, including covering up Mary's perceived crimes and accepting bribes from her.

She was half rage, half anguish—one equally as fierce as the other.

A light rap sounded on her door. Still in motion, she paused long enough to say, "Enter."

Gavin walked in. She hadn't expected to see him, couldn't

fathom what else there was to say, for either of them. Gazing at him coldly, she waited for him to speak. If he dared take one step farther, she would stop him.

"I am leaving for London shortly. I'm aware you probably would wish me to hell, but I wanted you to know where I was *actually* going."

Did he believe she would laugh at that feeble attempt at a jest? "Safe journey," she said, and even that seemed false.

"I go to report to Cecil, on Ryder's behalf."

That was odd. "Why isn't Ryder going himself?"

Gavin shrugged. "He has much reading to do, a great deal of evidence to sort through. Lady Anne said he might remain here if he needed to, and he decided to do so."

"He and his wife have a new infant. He told me while we were waiting for you earlier. I find it surprising he would not wish to be at home with his family."

Another shrug. "Ryder informed me that nothing…that there would be no consequences for your refusal to divulge Mary's confidences. Thus, you need have no fears about that."

Isabel smiled weakly at the irony. Ryder, who barely knew her, would accept her decision, but not Gavin, the man whom she had believed loved her. The man she had loved with all her heart. And her body. She walked over to the bedside table and picked up the velvet pouch.

Holding it out toward Gavin, she said, "This rightfully belongs to you. Perhaps you will wish to bestow it upon some other lady in the future."

Instinctively, he accepted what she offered, before he even realized what it was. Then, "Nay, Isabel, I want you to keep this."

She stepped back. "I no longer want it."

He looked crestfallen. "But the jewel is yours. I had it made for you." When she didn't answer, he shoved the pouch into his pocket and said, "Will you be here when I return?"

She answered truthfully. "I don't know where I will be."

When he took a step toward her, she held up a restraining hand. "No, Gavin."

He nodded. "God keep you, Isabel."

And then he was gone.

• • •

Several days passed in a blur for Isabel. She kept busy helping Lady Anne put away Christmastide decorations, and when that task was completed, she assisted in the stillroom, working under the other woman's supervision. At odd moments, she wondered where Mary and her entourage were at present. Sheffield? Or had they returned to Tutbury?

Ryder made himself scarce, though he joined them for dinner each evening.

One day while Isabel was reading in the lady's withdrawing room, a servant told her Ryder wished to speak to her. She found him in the lord's dayroom, where he sat at a large table, with numerous documents spread out before him.

"Pray, be seated, Mistress Isabel."

When she was comfortable, he said, "How would you like to return to Tutbury and help with the questioning of Mary? I do not expect her to make any great revelations. If you were the one taking her testimony, it may go easier for her."

Before refusing outright, Isabel needed to know more. "Indeed, sir, given my feelings on the matter, this seems like an odd request."

"Perhaps. But the political landscape has changed. Norfolk and Lesley are both imprisoned. Now it is simply a matter of wrapping things up. As I said, I do not expect Mary to confess her part in the plot. Nonetheless, we must have an official accounting from her about the conspiracy."

Two thoughts occurred to Isabel. What if by undertaking

this task, she could somehow prove Mary's innocence? And the second: what else was there for her? She could not remain at Skipton indefinitely, imposing on Lady Anne's hospitality. And at present, she had nowhere else to go. At least, nowhere she would be welcome. "I'll do it," she blurted out.

Ryder smiled. "Excellent. We'll leave on the morrow. Lady Anne has offered to give me the use of her carriage."

Isabel cocked her head at him. "You were that sure I would agree?"

Smiling enigmatically, he said nothing.

Back in her chamber, Isabel wondered what Ryder's ends really were. It felt as though he was manipulating her. Even so, she was galvanized by the opportunity to have some purpose once again. She summoned Dorcas, and together they packed Isabel's travel bag.

In the morning, she thanked Lady Anne for her warm welcome and generosity and bade her farewell. Isabel had grown quite fond of the older woman, who had treated her with care, respect, and kindness. Then Ryder helped her into the carriage and they set off for Staffordshire.

Chapter Twenty-Five

A lower echelon official led Gavin through the dark recesses of Whitehall to William Cecil's office. A good thing—he'd never have found the way on his own. Ushered into a spacious office, Gavin took the opportunity to study the great statesman before he glanced up from the document he was examining. A peaked cap covered part of his high forehead, his beard overlapping a starched ruff. Cecil's doublet looked to be of the finest velvet, a deep burgundy in color. With an abrupt wave of the hand, Cecil directed Gavin to a chair. He sat, and the other man finally raised his head.

"Forgive me. I did not wish to lose my concentration." He smiled wryly before going on. "You are Cade?"

Gavin nodded. "Aye. Lately arrived from Skipton. I bring you missives from Nicholas Ryder."

Cecil reached out, and Gavin handed them over. After perusing the documents, Cecil sighed and looked at Gavin. "The young lady could not help us learn more about Mary's involvement in the affair."

"No." Gavin remained impassive, not wishing to encourage any questions regarding Isabel.

Cecil went on. "So Ryder is taking Mistress Tait back to

Tutbury with him to interrogate Mary? He thinks perhaps the queen will be more cooperative with someone she trusts. Do you agree?"

Gavin's jaw dropped. *What?*

He must have misunderstood. Rather than answering, he stared at the older man.

"Well?" Cecil finally said.

Feeling like a fool, Gavin pondered how to respond to something he'd had no prior knowledge of. He thought it best to be truthful. "Ryder told me nothing of this. He may be right. Mary is to be returned to Tutbury?"

"Aye. They should be there by now. The whole lot of them. Mary, Shrewsbury and his wife, and the queen's attendants. I must remind Ryder to be on the alert. Someone from within Mary's circle was working closely with Lesley and may still pose a threat. But I'll warrant you already knew that."

Gavin felt as if he'd been hit with a cast-iron cannon ball. Of course he knew it, but the events of the past several weeks had taken center stage. The attempt on his life. Simon's murder. Isabel's fall, and their escape. He'd been so consumed with Lesley as the chief villain, he'd given no more thought to who was aiding him. If given a choice, however, Gavin would prefer not to appear the fool before Cecil.

"After the attack by the river, I assumed as much. Somebody had to have given the word on where we would be that day. Shrewsbury and I believe the entire event was staged as a cover for Norfolk's visit. We questioned every member of Mary's circle, with no success." He paused, considering. "Has Lesley revealed the identity of the informant?"

"Indeed. One of the ladies, Frances Barber."

"You've not yet arrested her?"

"Nay. We are keeping a close watch on her to see if she might incriminate herself. She must be on edge, given the turn of events."

On edge—and desperate. Icy fingers of fear crawled up Gavin's neck. Frances had shared Isabel's chamber, had been the first of Mary's ladies to show her any kindness. Despite Isabel knowing Lesley was bedding Frances, she had continued to like and trust the woman.

When Gavin had questioned the group the morning Isabel fell down the stairs, several people had said they'd not seen Frances yet. They'd snickered, and Gavin said, "She's with Lesley." The others had confirmed this was most likely the case. He had meant to follow up, but never had, his primary goal at that point being to get Isabel out of harm's way.

His mind quickly jumped to a conclusion he should have reached by now. Frances had been the one who'd pushed Isabel down those steps. She and Lesley had planned it together, each serving as the other's alibi. It would not be unusual for Frances to be found lurking near Isabel's chamber; thus, she'd been the one to do the deed.

Vile, traitorous woman.

And now Ryder was taking Isabel back into the heart of the danger. Isabel, sweet, trusting Isabel, would be glad to see Frances. She wouldn't be afraid of her; she would welcome her continued friendship. And Frances? She would be enraged when she found out Isabel had returned to question Mary. She would do whatever it took to put a stop to it.

Gavin looked up at Cecil. "Pray, sir, send me. I'll go immediately."

If Cecil was shocked by Gavin's authoritative manner, he didn't show it. "Very well. Wait outside while I pen a reply to Ryder. I'll summon you when I've finished it."

Gavin nodded, exiting the room. He paced in the corridor until Cecil opened the door and handed him a document pouch. The older man seemed to realize Gavin had some personal stake in the matter. "Leave London through the

Derby gate. Faster that way," he said.

On horseback, making his way out of the city, Gavin hoped never to return. The narrow streets, with their tall structures listing inward, made for dark and dismal surroundings. Dung heaps everywhere, beggars trying pitifully to survive, packs of dogs roaming the streets. And the stench. He couldn't wait to breathe free once again, in the northern climes. In the clean and lovely borderlands he'd called home all his life.

Pray God he would be in time to save Isabel, for he had no doubt Frances would try to do her harm.

• • •

Once they had arrived at Tutbury, Ryder installed Isabel in the receiver's lodging near the main gate. He didn't want her residing with the queen and her ladies. She had a new role and purpose. Isabel dreaded encountering the others—they would view her as a traitor to the queen. Oddly, she dreaded isolation as well. It would be lonely and force her to look inward. What could she have done differently to salvage her relationship with Gavin? To put the broken shards back together? Things were so muddled she preferred not to think about it.

While unpacking the few belongings she'd brought, she wondered about Gavin's meeting with Cecil. What had he learned? More details about the plot? Or was his purpose simply to inform the man of what they'd discovered? Which, thanks to her, was very little. In the middle of her musings, a knock sounded at her door. She hoped it wasn't Ryder—she was not at all prepared to begin her sessions with Mary.

"Enter," she said, albeit reluctantly. Frances came through and remained standing near the door, a forced smile on her face.

"Good even, Isabel. We were all surprised to hear you

were returning. And as an agent of Queen Elizabeth."

If Frances, her only true friend among Mary's ladies, felt this way, Isabel imagined the others did, too. "I am not an agent of Elizabeth." Isabel certainly did not view herself as such, even if Ryder did. "I'm merely here to record Mary's testimony regarding…certain events. I'm not an interrogator."

"Hmm. 'Tis a fine line, is it not?" In a moment, Frances walked farther into the chamber, without an invitation from Isabel. She wandered about, looking at the worn painted cloths, the faded paintings, the threadbare tapestries. "These living quarters are not precisely what you are accustomed to, are they?"

"I never lived in any kind of luxury until I came to Tutbury. It seems normal to me." This was not quite true—her own home, while not sumptuous, had been well-furnished and decorated. Her mother had seen to that. Frances's prowling about put Isabel on her guard. "Come, sit down. Tell me the news." Isabel lowered herself to the bed.

The other woman plunked down on the settle. "The only news is about the queen. She is officially a prisoner, being punished for something she was not involved in. And Lesley would not do anything to place Mary in danger. It was all Norfolk's doing, and an Italian banker called Ridolfi."

Isabel longed to say she agreed with that—except for the part about Lesley—but Ryder had strictly cautioned her not to comment on anything relating to the conspiracy. Her own common sense told her it would be a mistake. She changed the subject. "How are things between Bess and the earl?"

Frances laughed. "Oh, I believe they've made up. For now. Shrewsbury is much occupied with matters concerning Her Majesty and rarely makes an appearance. Bess and Mary are no longer permitted their friendship. And we are not allowed any singing, dancing, or guests. And no outings. We ladies eat with Mary, sit with her, and sew, and that is the extent of our activities. Mary is not well; she keeps to her chamber a great deal of the time."

When Isabel gave no answer, Frances said, "How is Gavin? You disappeared together. Why did you leave?"

This was tricky, and Bel avoided a direct answer. "Gavin, the last time I saw him, was well. He was summoned to London and departed in a hurry."

"Rumor has it that you arrived here accompanied by a handsome man. Nobody has actually seen him, though."

Isabel couldn't help smiling at that. "He is handsome, I suppose." In her eyes, Gavin was the better looking. At times, all she'd wanted to do was gaze upon him. She gave her head a shake and said, "Perhaps you will meet him. I don't know."

Frances rose, as did Isabel. "I must go. I was told not to approach you, but I wanted to see for myself you were here and what you were about. But I can see you will not be forthcoming with me."

Isabel started to speak, but Frances cut her off. "I love him, you know."

Confused, Isabel said nothing.

"Lesley. I love John Lesley. There is little I would not do to protect him, and Mary, too."

Before Isabel could comment on this astounding declaration, Frances was gone. Had that rash statement been a threat? Possibly, but it seemed an empty one. Frances was in no position to cause harm. According to Ryder, Mary would be brought to the drawing room downstairs for her meetings with Isabel. That was for the best. After this reunion with Frances, she did not care to see the others.

Later, she and Ryder sat down together for dinner. After a servant had presented the first course, Isabel asked how her sessions with Mary would proceed. He smiled. "You might begin with her dog."

She had struggled mightily with Ryder's suggestion of

returning Bisou to the queen. Isabel was the only one who truly cared about the little dog, who played with him and made sure he had a walk or two each day. But she agreed that returning Bisou would get her off on the right foot with Mary, so she'd reluctantly consented.

She sliced pieces of bread for each of them, then helped herself to salad and roast venison. "Then what?" she asked.

After Ryder finished chewing a bite of roast, he answered. "Initially, you may need to take your cues from Mary. She may treat this as a cozy little chat, although the presence of the scrivener should disabuse her of that notion fairly quickly." He stabbed at another piece of venison. "Don't wait too long to begin discussing the plot. You have the list of questions I gave you?"

"Of course." He had also given her a list of permissible topics and another of those she was to steer clear of.

"Mary, as you know, is very skilled at manipulating people. At showing her sweet and gentle side, and do not doubt she will do so with you. Be patient, but don't let her evade. Insist she answer. Emphasize this is for her benefit."

It will *be for her benefit if I have anything to do with it.*

Ryder dropped his knife and leaned forward. "Above all, do not allow her to take control. She'll ask why you and Gavin left, although she may already know the answer. She'll want to know where you've been and what you've been doing. Guide her back to the subject at hand. Always."

They went over more of what Isabel should and should not say, until her brain was spinning with it. The following morning, Mary would be brought to her and they would begin.

Chapter Twenty-Six

Isabel, stomach churning, was waiting for Mary in the drawing room. A servant had brought wine, marchpane, sugar cakes, figs, and dried apples, now laid out on a sideboard. Earlier, she had taken Bisou for a walk and glimpsed Mary's ladies clustered together, talking excitedly about something. When they saw her, all of them pointedly looked away. The queen wasn't with them. Isabel supposed she should be grateful they hadn't jeered or thrown stones at her.

The outer door opened, and Mary preceded Ryder into the room. Isabel couldn't see them, but she knew there were at least two guards posted out front. Cradling Bisou in her arms, she rose and dropped into a deep curtsy. "Your Majesty."

Ryder unobtrusively exited.

"Isabel," Mary said coldly, "is that my dog you are holding?"

"It is. I guessed you would be happy to see him again." Isabel placed the animal in Mary's waiting arms. The queen rubbed noses with him, cooed and clucked, then looked up at Bel and smiled.

"I have missed him so much," she said.

Ryder had been right; Bisou was a perfect way to break the ice. "How did you find him?"

"May I pour you some wine, Your Majesty?" The queen assented, and Isabel poured them each a glass. While filling a plate of the sweets and fruit, she said, "When Gavin and I left Sheffield, he followed us. He must have been hiding under some bushes. It's astonishing he hadn't frozen to death by then."

"And I suppose you will tell me nothing of why you left, sneaking out like thieves in the night. Shrewsbury spouted some nonsense about your injuries, and Gavin taking you home. Is that where you've been?"

"I apologize, Your Majesty, but I cannot answer that." Isabel gestured to an upholstered chair. "Pray, be seated." She set the wine and plate of food on the table.

Mary set Bisou on the floor. Instead of eating or drinking, she folded her hands and glared at Isabel. "All the time you were with me, were you spying on me? When I welcomed you into my circle, encouraged the others to be kind to you, shared meals—and confidences—with you—all that time were you spying on me?"

Isabel began to see why Ryder had cautioned her. Mary was attempting to take control of the interview, and she must put a stop to it. "I was not. I have never shared your secrets with anybody, then or now."

"So you say."

"Shall we begin? I would like to start by asking how you came to be involved in Ridolfi's plot."

"I am not involved in any plot!"

"Your Majesty, you forget I overheard your conversation with John Lesley. Your comments indicated you knew what was afoot."

She shrugged. "Very little. It was so ill planned as to be laughable. And as I told Lesley, far more to the duke's benefit than to my own."

"You were angry not to be in on the decision-making. They had moved ahead without you." She hoped the scrivener was getting all this down. It could be to Mary's advantage.

"This is true. They planned; I acceded. Or not. It has always been thus for me."

Isabel did not want to get into a catalog of Mary's troubles. She sipped her wine and thought about her next question. She'd memorized Ryder's list. "You've been champing at the bit because of your lack of freedom to do as you like. Didn't a plot to wed Norfolk, seize the throne, and rule England appeal? You would have been reunited with your son, among other things."

Mary's face flushed. "Of course, it appealed. I had tried to seek help from France, to no avail. And I continued to correspond with my cousin, Elizabeth. I had faith in her, that she would visit me, that we could talk together of our mutual interests and concerns." She stopped speaking abruptly and took a long swallow of wine. "But now I stand accused of this heinous crime."

"You were overheard talking with the Duke of Norfolk about the plot. You agreed to marry him and rule England together."

Mary slammed her hand down on the table. "They were manipulating me. I was too trusting, do you not see, desperate for my freedom and a chance to make a life with my son. Do you think I truly wished to marry Norfolk? A man I had met exactly once?" Her bosom heaved, her nostrils flared in anger. But Isabel plunged ahead.

"There is some evidence that you agreed to Ridolfi's scheme. That it was you who sent him on his way to Europe, to put this before both the Pope and King Philip."

Mary's mouth tightened. "If there is any such evidence, it is false. I knew nothing of this until Lesley informed me of it."

"And why did you not immediately inform Shrewsbury? That would have proved you were opposed to these maneuverings. You yourself told me you intended to wed Norfolk, that Elizabeth would give her blessing, and there would be a 're-ordering' of things."

She ceased speaking and drew in a long breath. Merciful God, Mary's protestations sounded insincere. Dishonest, weak, and invented on the spot. Isabel did not believe the queen to be naive. God knew, she herself had been the very definition of naive when she'd arrived at Tutbury. But Mary? *Never.*

Flustered, Isabel rose and walked over to the window, where she gazed out at the forbidding winter landscape, all the vitality sucked from it. That was, she realized, how she felt. The truth hit her like a bolt of lightning.

Mary was lying. Or telling only partial truths, which she'd always done. Relying on Isabel's innate empathy, she'd expected the younger woman to believe whatever she said. The scrivener's quill quit its ceaseless scratching. The only sound was from the queen, her labored breathing filling the silence.

"I am not well," Mary said. "May I return to my chambers?"

Isabel spun around. She doubted it was a physical ailment plaguing Mary. Opening the door, she called for Ryder, who appeared almost immediately. "The queen is not feeling well."

He gave her a questioning look, but said, "I'll escort her to her chambers."

They left, and Isabel moved to stand by the windows. With both hands, she rubbed her face, hard, hoping this might bring clarity. What had changed? Essentially, she'd learned nothing new from Mary. So what was causing Isabel to doubt her?

It was the undeniable fact that Mary was lying. Lying about matters she herself had confided to Isabel. Isabel's final question to her had remained unanswered. Why had she not informed Shrewsbury? That was perhaps the crux of it. If she'd been opposed to the scheme, if she had truly not wished to be involved, she should have reported it to the earl without delay.

But she had not.

Isabel felt something brush against her legs, heard whimpering. It was Bisou. Leaning down, she lifted him up and he snuggled against her chest. Mary had left him. After waxing eloquent about how happy she was to have him back, she'd not given him another thought.

Gavin had been right after all.

After the evening meal, which Isabel ate by herself, Ryder tapped on her door and entered. "I beg your pardon for leaving you to dine alone," he said. "Shrewsbury demanded a meeting with me."

At her raised eyebrows, he shrugged. "Wishing to have this matter over with, the earl is impatient. His wife is unhappy with the situation." Ryder looked as if he were suppressing a smile. Isabel gestured to the table, and after seating himself, he said, "I told him you'd only just begun with Mary and had not even reported to me yet. What can you tell me?"

Isabel's spirits had been low since her meeting with the queen. For nearly four months, she'd served as Mary's confidant. She had trusted her, believed in her, and sympathized with her dire situation. At some point after her session with Mary, Isabel had to acknowledge the woman had been using her. Mary had needed somebody new to bolster her spirits, listen to her stories, and, yes, occasionally probe for information. The other ladies had heard about her childhood, marriages, children, forced abdication, and troubles with Elizabeth many times over. But then, here came

Isabel, fresh and unworldly, open to anything Mary needed to confide. She had unburdened herself to her heart's content, and Isabel had willingly and sympathetically listened.

Had the queen been complicit in the attempt to kill Gavin? To kill *her*? Isabel could not rule it out.

A rap on the outside door pulled her out of her musings. Ryder got up to see who it was. She heard him speaking to one of the guards, then he returned carrying a tray with two goblets on it. "Somebody has an eye out for our comfort," he said. "Hot spiced wine."

Choking a bit when she caught a whiff of the spicy draft, Isabel steeled herself with a long swallow before speaking. Then she told Ryder everything he needed to know. He dipped his quill into the ink jar repeatedly and wrote rapidly, recording her every word, pausing occasionally to drink. When she was done, he leaned back, drained his goblet, and stared at Isabel.

"Well," he said.

She smiled. "I was gullible. Innocent. Call it what you will. I believe Mary knew I would never betray her secrets, and if she stood accused, I would defend her. She was shocked today when she realized she could no longer rely on my steadfast belief in her. I'd become a different woman from the pliable, easily led girl who had first shown up at Tutbury."

"You did well, Isabel," Ryder said, and then he yawned, long and deep.

Suddenly, Isabel felt exhausted, battered by the day's events. "I need to retire."

Yawning again, Ryder said, "Pray, pardon me, but I am unaccountably sleepy. Too much wine. I drank with Shrewsbury as well." He moved toward the door. His chamber was down the hall from her own. A good thing, since he seemed unsteady on his feet. "Thank you, Isabel. We now have a solid case against Mary. Whether it will come to anything, I don't know. But we have done our part." He bade her good night and left.

Isabel summoned the servant she'd been assigned. She had thought she wouldn't require assistance, but now she was glad of it. Her limbs felt heavy, cumbersome. She couldn't wait to climb into bed, which she did as soon as her maid left. She was asleep as soon as she blew out her candle.

• • •

Having ridden for two days straight, Gavin was saddle sore, hungry, and on edge. The sun was low in the sky. He had only a few hours of daylight left, and hoped to arrive at Tutbury shortly after nightfall. Instinct told him Isabel was in danger, and his instincts were seldom wrong.

During his endless ride, he'd done a fair amount of thinking. Nicholas Ryder had tricked him. It had been his plan all along to convince Isabel to return to Tutbury with him and question Mary. He had to admire the man's cunning, for he agreed there was no better person for the job. But he was furious with Ryder for putting Isabel at risk.

Gavin cringed when he remembered the accusations he'd hurled at Isabel. That she had accepted favors, or indeed, money, from Mary. Then he'd told her he was through with her, as if he could use her and cast her aside without a second thought. No wonder she'd concluded he had exploited her to gain information about Mary.

He had insisted they were better off apart. She had rejoined by saying he'd never made any commitment to her, so this was no more than she expected from him. She was right. He'd behaved like a scoundrel in all his dealings with her, especially in his belief that she would be no better than his dead wife, Anna. And he'd made love to Isabel with no pledge of marriage.

Bloody hell. What an arse he'd been.

It may be too late to regain her love, but he would try. With everything in him, he would try. What struck him then was how much Isabel had changed from the reticent, shy young lady, cowed by Mary's ladies. Dominated her entire life by her mother and brothers, and chiefly by her stepfather, she now possessed the confidence to disobey directives from Ryder and urgent pleas from himself. To do only what she believed was right. Even though he was furious with her, he admired her courage. Loved her for it, and for so much more.

As he drew near Tutbury, the sky took on an orange glow. Christ Almighty. *Isabel.*

Chapter Twenty-Seven

Something woke Isabel. A noise in the passage? The snick of the outer door? She ignored it, burrowed into her mattress, and fell back to sleep. Later, the acrid smell of smoke roused her. This time, sensing danger, she climbed out of bed, fumbled for her robe and shoes, and cautiously opened the door to her chamber.

Merciful God, the lodging was on fire.

Thick smoke clogged her nostrils and burned her lungs. Flames shot out of the drawing room, lighting that end of the passage. Through the haze, Isabel glimpsed the figure of a woman. Her skirts twirled as she turned for the stairs. Isabel ran back into her chamber, found a handkerchief, and tied it around her face.

She rushed back into the passage in pursuit. Whoever was hurrying upstairs had to be stopped. It was likely she'd started the fire and was on her way to set the second story ablaze. Pausing only to alert Ryder, Isabel flung his door open. She glimpsed the outline of his sleeping form. "Nicholas! Wake up!" He didn't move, so she hurried to his side, placed her hands on him, and shook him awake. Finally, he sat up. "What?" he said groggily.

"Fire! Get out of the building." Before Isabel left him, he was up and fumbling at the desk for his document pouch. Typical that those blasted papers would be the first thing he thought of.

The flames were shooting from the drawing room, and Isabel knew what was said of fires. Eager for more fuel, they love a staircase. Knowing she had very little time, she rushed up the stairs. The smoke swirled about her, obscuring her view. The upstairs appeared to be one large room, possibly traversing the entire length of the lodging. Close by, near the windows, she glimpsed the woman holding a lit candle toward the drapes. It was Frances.

Isabel screamed. "No!" But it was too late. The heavy draperies, perfect fodder for a blaze, ignited. She approached warily. Now was not the time for questions. Isabel pulled the handkerchief down, held out her hand, and said, "Come with me, Frances. If we hurry, we can get back down the stairs and out the door. There is no time to waste."

Frances laughed. A high-pitched, crazed sound. Instead of moving toward Isabel, she headed farther into the room. Isabel followed. Frances had grasped a heavy oak chair and was pushing it toward the windows. "You seem to be indestructible, Isabel," she said, breath heaving as she pushed the chair. "You were supposed to die in this fire. With any luck, you will."

Fear spiked in Isabel's breast. She should turn and run back downstairs, before Frances's wish came true. But something rooted her there. She had to try to save the other woman, who was acting deranged.

Frances had reached the windows, and with more strength than Isabel would have thought possible, she lifted the chair and slammed it into the panes. They shattered with alarming ease, shards and splinters of glass shooting into the room. The air blowing in fed the fire, flames leaped, and Isabel stepped back. "Frances. I beg you, come with me. There's still time to escape."

Frances laughed again, in that weirdly maniacal way. "I don't wish to escape. Do you think I will be forgiven all my sins? No. I'll be thrown in the Tower, tortured, and then executed. Better to die here."

"No one need know about any of your deeds." Of course, that was a lie, but Isabel would have said almost anything to convince Frances to save herself. She couldn't leave the woman here to suffocate, or even more horrifying, to burn.

Just then, she heard a voice calling to her. It couldn't be, yet it was.

Gavin.

• • •

When he'd drawn close enough to see flames licking the sky, Gavin spurred his horse into a full gallop. The main gate loomed high, silhouetted against the night sky. It appeared that the burning building was the receiver's lodging. The very place where Isabel would most likely be housed. He dismounted among a small number of men trying to organize a human chain to pass buckets of water. He recognized a few guards, the stable boy, and Blake. Grabbing his friend, he said, "Isabel. Is she in there?"

The other man seemed barely awake. He shook Gavin off and said, "What?"

"Is Isabel staying there?" he roared.

"Aye. But I've not seen her."

"I'm going in," Gavin said. Blake tugged his shirt off over his head, dunked it into a bucket of water, and handed it to Gavin.

"You'll need this. Are you sure you want to play the hero? It looks hopeless."

Gavin shoved him away. "This isn't some game, Blake. Get out of my way." The other man lurched aside, as though Gavin were a lunatic. Bracing himself for the smoke and heat, he dashed through the door. And ran smack into Ryder. "Have you seen Isabel?"

"She's not outside? She woke me up a few minutes ago. I assumed she left the lodging directly afterward."

"Merciful God, she's still inside." He shoved Ryder. "Go. I'll find her."

"Her chamber is on the left," Ryder said. "If you can still tell left from right."

The walls were beginning to catch. There wasn't much left of the chambers. Tapestries, wall hangings, carpets, bedding—all was burning. Gavin shouted Isabel's name over and over, but he didn't see her. He remembered the staircase at the end of the hall. She must have gone upstairs, although he couldn't fathom why. Without considering the wisdom in doing so, he zigzagged up the steps, dodging flames licking at his feet, singeing his hair as he ran. "Isabel!"

The great chamber at the top was aflame, fire licking up the heavy drapes, hot enough that the walls and floor would soon catch. He couldn't see through the thick smoke and crashed into Isabel. Thank God. Fresh air was blowing in, and it cleared away some of the smoke. She reached out a hand to him, and it was only then he realized she was speaking to somebody.

He grasped her hand and said, "Sweeting, we must leave. Even now it may be too late."

"It's Frances. I'm trying to persuade her to leave with me." Only then did he see the other woman.

"Come to save your lover, Gavin? I fear you are too late."

"I believe it is she who wishes to save *you*, although I cannot understand why. But no time to argue the point now. We must get back downstairs before our way is blocked."

And then he heard it, an ominous cracking and low rumbling. Spinning around, he saw the staircase giving way to the flames.

Jesu. Now he would have to find another way out. When he turned back around, Frances had climbed onto the window ledge. In one horrifying instant, he realized what she intended. Gavin stepped forward, hoping he'd be in time to stop her, conscious of Isabel's screams, but in mere seconds she was gone. They could hear her screams as she fell to the boulders below.

"Oh, no," Isabel said. "Gavin—"

He coaxed her handkerchief up over her nose. "Don't lose courage now, my love."

Eyes wide, she said, "What do we do?"

He breathed a sigh of relief, grateful she was not hysterical, as Mary's other ladies would have been. Gavin guided her to the opposite end of the room. Drawing his rapier, he used it to break the glass in the windows. Several men were gathered below, and he shouted at them. "We need help getting down! Is there a ladder?"

Tobias, the stable boy, ran off to get one. Gavin could feel the heat through his boots. Flames from below were shooting upward, beginning to burn through the wood floor. On the other end of the chamber, the fire had progressed toward them, devouring tapestries and wall hangings in its frenzied journey for more fuel.

Weakened, the floor could collapse at any moment. Gavin drew Isabel close, murmuring words of encouragement. "We'll be out of here soon, my lovely, brave girl."

She managed a chuckle. "Promise?"

Finally, Tobias reappeared with the ladder. The men below propped it against the building. Turning to Isabel, Gavin said, "You can do this. It will be nothing to you, and there are plenty of men to catch you if you fall. Ready?"

She bit her lip and nodded. "Let's go." As he helped her onto the top rung, she spoke again. "You'll follow right after me?"

He smiled with relief. She wanted him safe. It was something.

In moments, they were both back on solid ground.

• • •

A few days after the fire, Isabel found herself in a coach traveling north toward Buxton, somewhere in the Peak District. Gavin said it was famous for its curative waters. She had never heard of it and wasn't quite sure how this had come about.

In the immediate aftermath of the fire, Gavin had carried Isabel to Shrewsbury's private lodgings and Bess had ministered to her wounds. She'd sustained superficial burns to her forehead, neck, hands, and ankles, and had a sizable gash on her arm, thanks to a flying shard of glass. Bess had stitched up the gash and applied salve to the burns. Isabel had been in considerable pain, and Bess had given her an herbal remedy. Isabel had slept for a few days and now, slowly, she was healing.

Before departing Tutbury, Isabel, Gavin, and Ryder had met with Shrewsbury. She'd rested on a cushioned settle in his office, the reassuring presence of Gavin bolstering her courage. While they'd spoken, it had become obvious both Gavin and Ryder had met previously with the earl and filled him in on what had happened.

"Mistress Tait," the earl began, "I've been informed of what transpired the night of the fire. You, Ryder, and Cade have been absolved of any wrongdoing. Can you remember anything these two men may not have heard or witnessed? Anything you believe may be important for me to know?"

Isabel realized she'd never told Ryder about Frances's visit to her. She'd been in such dread of meeting with Mary, she'd forgotten to mention it. "Frances came to see me at the lodging. I forgot to tell you, Nicholas.

"She was on edge, prowling about, accusing me of treachery. Before she left, she said she loved Lesley and there was little she would not do to protect him and the queen."

"You should have told me this, Isabel," Ryder said.

"I know. I simply forgot, preoccupied as I was about interviewing Mary. In any case, Frances didn't seem deranged, as she did the night of the fire. Only agitated. Not like a woman who would set fires and then leap out the window to her death."

Gavin spoke quietly. "Isabel, we have concluded it was Frances who pushed you down the stairs."

"I gathered that, from what she said the night of the fire. Before you got there."

All three men stared at her. "What did she say?" Shrewsbury asked.

"That I seemed to be indestructible, but with any luck, I would die in the fire. You probably already knew this, or guessed it, but I believe she put a sleeping draft in the wine Nicholas and I drank that night. Both of us were unusually sleepy. I barely made it to my bed and had trouble waking up, even when I first sensed danger."

"I agree," Nicholas said. "Had you not awakened me, I would have slept through it and suffered a horrible death. I'm indebted to you, Isabel."

"Did you know what Frances intended? That she wanted to die?" Shrewsbury asked.

Feeling the sting of tears, Isabel nodded. "She told me she would be arrested for her sins, tortured, then executed, and she would rather die there, at Tutbury. I-I wasn't sure what she was referring to, but I tried to convince her she could be forgiven and should leave with me, before it was too late." She paused and glanced at Gavin. "That was when you found us."

Later that day, Gavin had told her he was taking her north to recover. That Shrewsbury had offered one of his properties to them, where they could rest and recuperate from their injuries. Isabel assented to the plan, largely because she didn't know what else to do. If she'd asked, she probably could have remained at Tutbury with the Shrewsburys, but after the tragedy with Frances, Mary and her ladies would despise her. Life would be lonely indeed with only the countess and earl for company. They would both be otherwise occupied most of the time. And returning to her mother was out of the question. She would see Isabel married off in the blink of an eye.

The coach hit a bump. The young maid looked frightened. Recalling her own fears the first time she'd traveled in this same vehicle, Isabel patted the girl's hand and said, "It's all right. We are bound to encounter ruts and rough spots on the road." Then she opened a volume of the *Iliad* and tried to read, but it was no use. She ended up staring out the window and thinking of Gavin.

Why did he wish to make this journey with her? He'd made his feelings infinitely clear when they'd quarreled at Skipton. He thought she'd used poor judgment in refusing to reveal all she knew of Mary, and worse yet, he believed she'd accepted favors from Mary in return for her loyalty. He'd said he was through with her, that they were better off apart. And somewhere in all of this lay his closely held belief that she would betray him, just as Anna had.

After a time, she rested her head against the window and dozed. The next thing she knew, they were stopping, and the maid was shaking her awake. Just in time, too, for the door opened and Gavin stood there.

"What?" she said irritably.

He laughed. "Sleeping, were you? Good. That's what you need." Then he spoke quietly to Jane, who exited the coach with Bisou. From what Isabel could see, they were in the middle of nowhere, in a valley surrounded by peaks. The sun streamed in; for January, the day was warm. Gavin climbed into the coach, plunking down in Jane's place, directly across from Isabel. Not saying a word, he simply watched her.

"What?" she repeated, feeling stupid, but also annoyed by his scrutiny.

His slow smile sent tingles along her spine. Her face felt hot. Would the arrogant man never speak?

"I simply wished to check on you. You must be comfortable, or you would not have fallen asleep. Are you in any pain?"

She leaned back. So he'd only wanted to see she was all right. "I'm fine. The burns are healing. What about you?"

"Same."

"How long is the journey?"

"We should arrive by late afternoon, provided we don't fall into a rut and break an axle. I know next to nothing about these vehicles." He leaned forward, took her gloved hands in his. "Isabel, I—"

The door swung open. "Master Cade, I'm cold." It was Jane.

"One moment, Jane." He heaved an audible sigh. "According to Shrewsbury, there's an inn up ahead. We'll refresh ourselves there and not stop again until our arrival at Buxton." That said, he removed himself from the coach, and Jane climbed back in, handing the pup to Isabel.

Chapter Twenty-Eight

They arrived at Shrewsbury's property in Buxton, called the New Hall, around five o'clock. The earl had promised to send a messenger ahead of them to prepare for their stay, and he'd been true to his word. Servants greeted them and escorted them to their adjoining chambers. He did not know what they had been told about their guests, and in truth didn't care. Gavin only wished for peace and privacy. Time alone with Isabel, so he could tell her how much he loved her, beg her forgiveness, and ask her to be his wife.

Gavin would take his cues from Isabel. He didn't want to rush or overwhelm her. At the same time, he ached for her. Not only for her body, but for the easy way they'd been with each other, almost from the beginning. The shared stories, jests, walks—even the tennis lessons. Undeniably, he wanted her back in his arms, in his bed. But if she wanted wooing, he could woo. If she needed more time, he would go slowly. It might kill him, but he could do it.

Gavin ordered a bath for them both. As he slipped into the hot water, inevitably he remembered when Isabel had bathed him and what had happened afterward. His cock stirred. She was probably relaxing into her own bath at this very moment.

Enough. He would see her at dinner, and perhaps afterward they could speak privately.

Coincidentally, they exited their chambers at the same time. Isabel had donned a burgundy gown he'd never seen before. When he asked her about it, she said, "It was laid out on my bed. Jane said one of the servants left it for me, but had offered no explanation." She laughed. "I was thrilled to have something clean and comely, even if it had been worn before by some other lady."

Gavin offered his arm. "It's lovely on you. The color goes beautifully with your hair." She smiled up at him, making his heart leap. *Isn't that a good sign?*

They made their way through unfamiliar passageways to the dining chamber. Sitting close together, they sampled each dish on offer, but neither of them ate much. They talked, and it seemed almost as if they'd never quarreled. That he'd never hurt her with his sharp, cutting words.

Avoiding talk about the fire, they focused instead on good memories. They laughed about her arrival at Tutbury. Isabel confessed how humiliated she'd been. And to his delight, she said, "You were very kind to me. Carrying me up the stairs. Encouraging me when you saw the others laughing behind their hands. Teaching me to dance that first night."

She was letting him back in, if only a little. He smiled broadly. Gavin itched to take her hand, but not yet. It was too soon to make any assumptions about her feelings. "That was the night it all began." Isabel looked puzzled, so he elaborated. "Mary. Lesley. Everything. I kissed you outside Mary's chambers. Remember?"

She eyed him askance. "So the guards would not know what you were really up to."

He grinned sheepishly. "You haven't told me how your questioning of Mary went. Ryder hadn't informed me of it, you know. Of what he had planned for you."

"I don't believe he thought of the idea until after you left."

"You're wrong about that. It was in the letter I delivered to Cecil from Ryder. Cecil read it out loud to me. He also told me Frances had been identified by Lesley as the insider who was working with him."

Isabel looked down, cleared her throat, then fixed her liquid eyes on Gavin. "Is that why you came back?"

"Of course. After meeting with Cecil, I understood it had to have been Frances who'd pushed you down the stairs. I should have figured that out long before, but so many other things happened. My attention was diverted."

"You asked about my meeting with Mary. She was accusatory, and evaded answering my questions directly. When she did respond, she contradicted statements she'd made to me in the past. For the first time, I realized she was lying—about so many things."

"What was the critical point?"

"I asked her why she had not informed Shrewsbury when Lesley told her of the plot. She couldn't, or wouldn't answer. And that was that. I told Ryder everything."

"I knew you would see the light if given a chance."

Her eyes darkened, and he realized he'd made a mistake. His comment sounded smug and self-serving. *Damnation.*

"Make no mistake, Gavin. I still have sympathy for Mary. Although I believe she was invested in the conspiracy, her claim of being manipulated by Norfolk and Lesley rings true. She had a long history of powerful men ruling her, from the Duke of Guise to the Earl of Bothwell, and many others in between."

So Isabel would defend Mary to the end. Her face had taken on that feisty, stubborn look. She threw down her napkin. "I too have been manipulated by men for much of my life. Or perhaps 'controlled' is a better word. God knows, that includes both you and Ryder."

With that, she stood and ran from the room.

• • •

Isabel slammed her door shut and latched it. She sat on her bed and lowered her head into her hands. She was being defensive and overly sensitive, but couldn't seem to stop herself from overreacting with Gavin. Would they never make peace? Were they doomed to misunderstand each other forever?

A rap sounded at her door. "Isabel? May I speak to you?"

"Go away," she said, feeling certain more talking would only lead to further misunderstandings.

"Give me a chance. At least hear what I have to say."

Isabel's head came up, yet still she wavered. Would it do any harm to hear him out? She walked over and lifted the latch. He was standing there, a look of desperation on his face.

"Thank you. May I come in?"

Opening the door, she motioned him toward the settle. He did not sit, but simply stood before the hearth, gazing at her. A fire blazed behind him, and she noticed he was wearing a purple velvet doublet and fine hose and canions. He looked very handsome indeed. How had she missed that at dinner? Because she'd been thinking only of herself. Because she was full of anxiety.

"Can you forgive me, Isabel, for my foolish accusations? None of which I truly believed. The idea that you could be bribed by Mary—I knew it was absurd, but I was looking for something, anything, to explain your unflagging loyalty to her. It was cruel and unjust, and I am heartily sorry for saying it."

Isabel did not yet trust herself to speak. She feared she

might ruin the moment. When she said nothing, he carried on. "You have been my partner in all of this. You listened patiently to my confidences, you offered sympathy when Simon died, you tried to understand, even when I withheld crucial information. I trusted you completely, and I still do."

Well. Now they were getting somewhere. She felt an almost irresistible desire to throw herself into his arms.

Her voice shook. "I didn't mean what I said, either. About you using me to get information—"

"For the sake of complete honesty between us, I did do that at first. Oh, I liked you, I was attracted to you, but in my mind, where was the harm in also finding out what Mary had told you? But that ended rather quickly. It wasn't long before you were all I thought of. Night and day. After the raid at the river, I knew I loved you."

"But you kept pushing me away."

"Because of my fears about marriage. I was a fool." He gestured with his hands to emphasize the point.

She waited.

"The world—this world we've been residing in—is a dangerous place, my love. Loyalties change at a moment's notice. That was why I said what we meant to each other was private and must be kept separate from the roles we were playing. But, as you so wisely pointed out, it all got mixed up together. That is why I brought you here. To physically separate us. Here we can see each other clearly. Here, I know beyond a doubt that you are all I care about. All I treasure and love."

Isabel, tears streaming, gave up trying to control her urge. She flung herself into Gavin's arms. "Oh, Gavin. I am sorry for being so wrongheaded and stubborn about Mary."

He held her tightly. "Don't apologize. In many ways, you were right about her. One can be fully aware of her trickery and still find much to sympathize with. But let's not talk of

Mary."

Gavin set his lips on Isabel's, kissing her with an urgency she'd not felt from him before, with a tenderness that bespoke a hunger he'd been aggressively suppressing. He raised his head long enough to say, "I'm sorry for saying I was through with you. I'll never have enough of you."

He kissed her again, and she opened to him, feeling as if they were discovering each other anew. Something inside her yielded, offering up emotions she'd been guarding. No more holding back. After a moment, he lifted her into his arms and carried her to the bedside. "You're wearing far too many layers, Isabel." He spun her around to unfasten her gown and corset, then unhooked her petticoats, and they dropped to the floor with her other garments. All the while her chest was tightening, her core was burning, and her knees had simply deserted her. She fell against him, and he lifted her onto the bed. Then he began to undress.

Isabel watched unashamedly. Off came his doublet and smock, canions and hose, ultimately revealing a body shaped by years of labor. She would wager most men of nobility would pale in comparison. In seconds, he was beside her in the bed.

Gavin drew her against him, so their bodies joined snugly together and their limbs entangled. For a moment, they remained that way, and Isabel marveled at how well they fit. Her head against his shoulder, her breasts against his chest. His organ pushed into her belly, and she never wanted to let him go.

He began to kiss her again. First her mouth, and when he'd tasted his fill, he trailed kisses down her neck and chest, until he found her nipples and suckled one, then the other. Her pleasure building, Isabel smoothed her hands over Gavin's chest and up and down his spine. She wanted to learn every inch of him, to explore the span of him. Where he began and where he ended. Surely this act, this coupling, signified the ultimate knowledge of each other.

Gavin worshipped her with his hands, stroking lightly over her arms, breasts, buttocks. Until finally he spread her legs and found the folds concealing her most intimate place. Isabel was ready for his touch. He caressed her with one finger, spreading her liquid heat. Gasping, bucking, she raised her hips to increase her pleasure. That seemed to please Gavin, who growled low in his throat. When she was at the breaking point, he withdrew his hand and rose above her.

"Now, Isabel. Now, sweeting." He positioned himself at her entrance and slowly pushed inside her. Then he began the slow, intimate dance of thrusting and withdrawing. She said his name, over and over, "*Gavin. Gavin.*" And, "*Don't stop. Pray do not stop.*"

In another moment, she came apart with unspeakable elation so intense she wept. It was more than physical pleasure. It was a melding of their souls. He covered her body with his own and held her until her sighs and gasps lessened. And then he found his own completion, throwing his head back and crying out. Gazing down at her, he said, "I cherish you, my sweet Isabel. Don't ever leave me."

She framed his face with her hands. "And I love you. With all my heart."

He drew her against him, and they fell into a doze. Isabel did not know how long they slept, but eventually Gavin stirred. She loved the feel of his breathing, his chest pressing into her with every inhalation. "Awake?" he asked.

"Aye."

"Have you a robe? I want to talk to you, and we can't be naked. Far too distracting."

Isabel chuckled. "I believe there is one hanging on the pegs."

Gavin climbed out of bed and quickly pulled his shift

over his head. He retrieved the robe and helped her into it. "Let's sit here," he said, gesturing to the settle. He stirred the fire to life, then added a log before joining her.

Gavin took her hands in his. "Will you be my wife, Isabel?" She started to answer, because she had no qualms and knew her heart. But he stopped her. "Wait, hear me out before you say anything."

She nodded and he continued. "I know I've compared you to Anna in the past. It was wrong of me. You've made me feel whole again. You've made me want to live again. Before you, I wasn't sure I would ever regain my confidence, my zest for life, even my passion." He paused for a moment, looking unsure of himself. "What do you think?"

She laughed. "What do I think? Nothing would make me happier, Gavin. I can't imagine my life without you."

Smiling, he held out the necklace, the one he'd given her which she had returned. "Will you wear this, as a symbol of our betrothal? And of our love?"

Isabel turned so he could fasten it for her. "I hated giving it back. Make no mistake, it's mine now. I won't be returning it again."

"I would never let you, my dearest Isabel." He drew her into his arms and soon they found their way back to the bed.

Isabel's heart was so full, she thought it might burst. She had longed to escape the ties binding her to her old life. Never had she expected to find a man like Gavin. Never had she expected to find love.

"I'd like to see you wearing nothing but the necklace, sweeting," Gavin whispered.

Isabel laughed and shrugged off her robe.

Epilogue

Isabel and Gavin had decided to travel to his home in Scotland for their marriage. His family, he persuaded her, would be ecstatic and would welcome her unconditionally. Isabel hadn't needed much persuading. After Gavin had told her about his family, and how his mother would love her as a daughter, she'd longed for that connection.

Before they left Buxton, they enjoyed soaking in the thermal baths, dining opulently, and walking about the town and countryside. They spent hours talking, each one finding the other endlessly fascinating. "Do you hope for children, Isabel?" Gavin asked her one day.

"I never thought I would be married, so I haven't seriously considered it."

He looked a bit distraught. "I would love some bairns," he confessed.

"Then my answer is yes. But you'll have to help me. I've never had the example of loving parents."

At last, they were ready to go. Gavin had already written to his mother. Isabel had been putting off writing to her own mother, but could avoid it no longer.

11 January 1571

New Hall, Buxton

Dear Mother,

I am writing to inform you of my pending nuptials. I met a wonderful man, Gavin Cade, during my time at Tutbury. He has proposed to me, and we are traveling to Scotland for our wedding. His mother is Scottish, his father, English.

I trust you are now wed to Peter Fleming, although I have heard nothing from you since my leave-taking.

Please inform my brothers of my marriage.

Yours sincerely,
Isabel

Isabel left the missive lying on the desk while she packed, and Gavin read it. "Are things so bad between you? This letter is so cold."

"Truly, Gavin? I considered writing one line: 'I am traveling to Scotland to be married.' My mother's only reaction will be gratitude I've been taken off her hands. She believed I would return to Derby after my stint at Tutbury, and she'd be forced to find me a husband. This should make her quite happy."

He set the letter down and grasped her arms. "Let's invite your family to the wedding."

She wrenched out of his grasp. "No! My mother would find a way to spoil the day." She gave a brittle laugh. "She would not come, Gavin. I know it seems unfathomable to you, but she dislikes me intensely."

"So you have said, and I am sorry you have such a mother.

Nevertheless, I think we should invite them. You're probably right that she will not come, but what about your brothers?"

Isabel thought it over and grudgingly admitted she would like Andrew to be there.

"Do you have his direction?"

"I do."

"Excellent. Once in Scotland, I shall write to him—to all of them—myself."

After an exhausting but uneventful journey, they arrived in Melrose, Gavin's home. His mother seemed beside herself with joy, opening her arms to enfold Isabel. She was a tall, sturdy woman with chestnut hair the color of her son's, although hers was now streaked with gray. Gavin had gotten his blue eyes from his father, however, who also greeted her warmly, if not quite as effusively. Over the next week, Isabel met the entire family. Gavin's brothers, Paul and Mark, and their wives and children. And an assortment of aunts, uncles, and cousins.

The banns were called, the wedding date set. Gavin's mother and sisters-in-law were making her gown. They sat her down one day and announced her hair needed a good trimming. Isabel sat very still while Judith, Paul's wife, plied the scissors. Bisou jumped about her feet, as though protecting her. Isabel could not remember the last time anyone had cut her hair. Afterward, she loved the way it looked. So did Gavin. Whenever they had a private moment, he buried his face in her hair, lifted handfuls of it to his lips, and told her how beautiful it was. "Could we steal away to the hay loft?" he asked her one day.

"Gavin! We'd be caught, and besides, it's freezing."

"I'm teasing you, Bel. But God, I miss you." He cocked his head at her. "You seem relaxed and happy, more so than I've ever seen you."

He was right. "Because I am," she said. "I keep thinking

I'm going to wake up, and it will all have been a beautiful, fleeting dream."

At last, her wedding day arrived. Isabel had steadfastly refused to reveal anything about her gown to Gavin. The warm appreciation in his eyes told her it had been worth it. The dress was aubergine velvet, slashed in front to show fine white petticoats. The sleeves attached separately, and the bodice, although modest, exposed an expanse of white skin.

To Isabel's delight, Gavin was wearing a kilt, the plaid of his mother's clan, with belt, long socks, and a sporran at his waist. She was nearly overcome by how handsome he looked. It was customary in the Cade family that the bride and groom walk to the church together. Isabel stepped forth and took Gavin's arm.

"You are so beautiful, Isabel. Thank you for marrying me."

Isabel, tears in her eyes, said, "Thank you for asking me."

As they approached the church, or kirk, as they called it, Isabel spotted a familiar face. "Gavin! Andrew is here."

"I know, love. I wanted to surprise you. It wouldn't have seemed right if no family of yours came." They paused so Isabel could greet her brother.

"Isabel!" Andrew hugged her, cautiously. "I don't want to spoil your gown. You look lovely, sister." He turned. "And this big brute must be Gavin." He held out his hand, but Gavin ignored it and wrapped her brother in a hug.

"You're a lucky man, Gavin Cade."

"I know it well."

And then they entered the kirk and spoke the vows that would unite them for life.

Author's Note

Gavin Cade and Isabel Tait, as well as Mary Queen of Scots' ladies and other minor characters, are products of my imagination, but most of the others are actual historical figures. This includes Queen Mary; the Earl of Shrewsbury and his wife, Bess; John Lesley, the Bishop of Ross; the Duke of Norfolk; Roberto Ridolfi; William Cecil; and Lady Anne Clifford, among others.

The main settings in *Game of Spies* are actual places, and Mary stayed at, or visited, all of them. She was moved often, and for the sake of a consistent narrative, I chose the various locations and times of her visits to suit my story.

While the Ridolfi Plot was a real conspiracy, I altered the timeline and the order of events. Mary continued to involve herself in conspiracies for the remainder of her life, which eventually led to her execution by Elizabeth I in February of 1587.

Acknowledgments

Thanks once again to the members of the Entangled Publishing team who work so hard to make each book perfect, from cover design to the final page. And special thanks to my editor, Erin Molta, for her keen eye and discerning judgment. I'm grateful to Julia Knapman for her thorough copy editing. Thank you to Holly Bryant-Simpson and Riki Cleveland for working so hard to make sure my books are welcomed to the world.

A huge thank-you to my friend Gladys Matthews who helped ensure correct French usage.

Jill Marsal, my agent, is always available to offer much appreciated support and guidance.

And, as always, I'm deeply grateful to my husband, Jim, for his help with every aspect of my writing.

About the Author

Pamela Mingle found her third career as a writer after many years as a teacher and reference librarian. Her love of historical romance was nurtured by Jane Austen, and her novels have all been set either in the Regency or Tudor periods. Many long walks in England, Scotland, and Wales have given her a strong sense of place around which to build her stories. She is the author of *Kissing Shakespeare*, *The Pursuit of Mary Bennet*, *A False Proposal*, *A Lady's Deception*, and *Mistress Spy*.

Learn more about Pam and sign up for her newsletter at www.PamMingle.com. She enjoys hearing from readers and would love to connect with you on social media.

Also by Pamela Mingle...

A FALSE PROPOSAL

A LADY'S DECEPTION

MISTRESS SPY

Discover more Amara titles...

HOW TO BEST A MARQUESS
a *Raven Club* novel by Tina Gabrielle

Lady Ellie learned at an early age that men were more trouble than they're worth. Now she's all grown up, with secret ambitions to run her brother's infamous gambling establishment—the Raven Club. Everything's progressing as planned until the man who broke her heart, the Marquess of Deveril, wants to take over the club. Dark, dominant, and strikingly handsome, Hugh's reputation for sin precedes him, and suddenly, her dreams—and her heart—are in jeopardy.

THE MADNESS OF MISS GREY
a novel by Julia Bennet

All of society believes former actress Helen Grey to be mad, but after a decade imprisoned in a crumbling Yorkshire asylum, she's managed to cling to sanity. When a new doctor arrives, Dr. William Carter, she finally sees an opportunity for freedom. Helen and Will need to work together if she's ever going to be free. It won't be easy, not when her mysterious benefactor is determined to keep her locked up and hidden from society forever. When Helen is entangled in her own trap and begins to fall for Will too, she must fight not only for her liberty but for her right to love.

HOW TO TRAIN YOUR BARON
a *What Happens in the Ballroom* novel by Diana Lloyd

When Elsinore Cosgrove escapes a ballroom in search of adventure, she has no idea it will lead to a hasty marriage. Now she's engaged to an infuriating, handsome Scottish baron who doesn't even know her *name*! But Elsinore is determined to mold her baron into the husband she wants. Quin Graham is a man with many secrets. If another scandal can be avoided with a sham marriage, so be it. Only his fiancée isn't at all what he's expecting. For reasons he's unwilling to explain, the last thing Quin needs is to fall for his wife.

SCANDAL IN SPADES
a *Lords of Chance* novel by Wendy LaCapra

The Marquess of Bromton loses a card game and must court the unmarriageable Lady Katherine. She vows to do everything she can to discourage the imperious marquess...despite his knee-weakening kisses. Scandal has hardened Katherine and she doesn't trust the Society she's left behind, especially the marquess. Except, the more their connection deepens, the more Bromton surprises the self-avowed spinster. But the truth about their courtship could destroy everything...